MW01125474

From His

Rib

BOOK 3 OF THE UNDERWORLD

Nako

To Nako's Reading Group on Facebook, I love each one of you beautiful women in different ways. The strength that I see, the growth that I am observing. There is no way we have only been into digital contact for a few months, no way!

The support is at an all-time high and yall are the reason I WRITE.

On any given day, I can come into the group and instantly my spirits will be lifted.

A few of you, I have texted, spoken to over the phone and even got the chance to have lunch with while in Atlanta.

Books written by me brought us together but the bond was created all on its own.

I pray that for every book you buy, every encouraging post, every like/comment, every motivational thing that's written not only to me when I'm in my feelings but to each other, I'm praying that each and every one of your cups run over.

To my official/unofficial admins, Lena, Maria and Enique, I think Quita and Prettii Ladii made themselves admins too LOL! Thanks for the keeping the group moving forward when I'm ducked off trying to finish a book.

Powerhouse 2016, yall rock. xoxoNAKO!

*As an author who prides herself on only producing their best work, which include full-length books that master the art of storytelling. I ask in advance that you bare with the story, **reviews** have showed that novels written by me take quite some time to "pick up and get good" These stories have been **created** and hand-crafted to connect with you beyond the pages of your Kindle. As you turn the page, I want you to get something from each **character** and chapter. There are themes **present** that you should personally relate to while reading this story, The importance of friendship, Betrayal, **Faith** and Dreams coming true are a few.*

*If you have not **read, Please Catch My Soul (Book 1) and The Pointe of No Return (Book 2)** check those out before reading **From His Rib**.*

*From His Rib is a **standalone** so I hope that you enjoy.*

*Please leave a **review** once you are finished.*

God Bless You

From my heart to yours,

From His Rib

NAKO

Then the LORD God made a woman from the rib he had taken out of the man, and he brought her to the man – Genesis 2:22

Introduction

Miko waved at her co-workers as she walked down the hallway and out of the office. She was so happy that it was Friday, it seemed like it had taken the weekend forever to come around. Miko was looking forward to her two-day weekend since she had a date with her television and a pepperoni pizza.

She smiled at the security guard, "See you Monday morning," she said cheerfully.

"Alright Miko be safe na" the guard told her.

Miko had been working at The White House for three years now and every day she considered her job a real blessing from God. Fresh out of college and looking for a job just to keep the lights on over her and her mother's head, she had even thought about waitressing at the local strip club.

After slaving in school and with student debt up to her knees, Miko knew her hard work hadn't been in vain. After five interviews and an extensive background check, she was hired at The White House putting her Finance degree to work.

Miko went from working in the file room to working with The Cabinet to a direct position with the Vice-President, to now being the head of the President's travel arrangements along with a few other amazing people. She had access to anything travel related for the President and his family. She loved her job and thanked God every day for a successful career. The places and people that she encountered were considered a big deal to a girl who came from nothing.

She unlocked the doors to her Lexus, got in and made her way home, downtown DC was always a mess before and after five p.m. However, she enjoyed her ride home every day. She would listen to the radio and scroll through her social media pages at every red light.

She ordered her dinner for the night so when she made it home, she wouldn't have to wait too long for her food. Stopping to grab a cheap bottle of wine, she was now headed towards her condominium and didn't plan to leave until it was time to go to work Monday.

Once she made it to the parking garage and took the elevator up to the floor she lived on. She began humming and getting giddy just thinking about sliding her stockings off, unclasping the very uncomfortable bra she wore today and putting on one of her Howard University t-shirts and a pair of fuzzy socks.

Miko walked into her home and tossed her keys on a small table in the foyer, not even bothering to turn any of the lights on to guide her towards her bedroom because she knew her way around her own crib.

"Why don't you have an alarm?" a voice startled her.

Miko screamed and dropped her cell phone and workbag on the floor. Backing up towards the wall, not really knowing what else to do besides pray that whoever the hell was in her house, didn't try to kill her.

"YOU CAN HAVE WHATEVER YOU WANT" she told the intruder.

The man laughed, "You don't have anything I want trust me, come sit Miko I'm not here to hurt you"

Miko wondered if this was a dream and she was still at work dozing off.

She closed her eyes and clicked her heels.

But when she heard the man coming closer, she knew that this was not a dream.

"Come have a seat I'll be gone in five minutes I promise," he told her

Miko asked, "And you're not here to kill me?"

He told her, "I have no reason too; you live a pretty good life besides that little affair you got going on that you don't think nobody knows about but I'm not here for that"

Miko finally opened her eyes and squinted trying to see his face, it wasn't much light in her condo, which is how he managed to sit on her couch and she didn't notice his presence.

He reached over and flipped the light on so he could look at her up close. Finally…

"Do you know who I am?" he asked.

Miko sighed and nodded her head, "Yes"

"Good, let's take a seat. I got shit to do," he commanded.

Chapter 1

"Let me get this right, you're my intern? I don't need an intern"
Miko's supervisor asked to be sure.

"Well no maam, I'm not an intern. I actually received the job to work in the Cabinet," she said happily.

"Hmmm I guess, that's your desk right there, don't talk unless I ask you too" the woman told her.

Miko wouldn't allow the woman to ruin her good day, she was so thankful that she finally received a job.

There was once a time when she never thought she would even have a job. She had begun to regret even going to college; it was beginning to look like a big waste of her time. Miko couldn't catch a break…until that call came from The White House telling her she had an interview. She clapped for joy and claimed it as hers. It was if God said, "Okay Miko, it's yours"

Well, that was three years ago and now Miko walked past that same rude woman's desk every morning and she still flashed her a smile and on a few occasions she stopped to have a conversation with her. She would never tell the woman how thankful she was for her blatant disrespect and almost prejudice behavior, she was the reason that Miko worked her ass off to move up in The White House. She went from that tight and congested cubicle to the top of the food chain at The White House and she now had her own office with an assistant and a secretary. She went from being just Miko the Intern to Ms. Sanderson, Director of Travel for the President of The United States of America.

She sat her coffee mug and purse on the desk, getting to her office every morning was such a tedious task. Miko's palms were sweaty and her underarms were starting to perspire, she was so nervous.

This past weekend, her long-lost brother who was rumored to be a drug-lord or Kingpin of some sort broke into her home and threatened her to use a flash drive and get him the President's schedule, mainly to scope out his International travel.

She wasn't allowed to ask any questions even though she constantly expressed concern about going to jail or being exiled. Miko loved her job and she worked her ass off to make it to where she is now.

Her *brother*, she hated that word especially since there was nothing "family" about them. It was obvious that he was well off and established. There were no blemishes on his nice skin whereas she had several from growing up Korean in the projects, she had no one growing up and was forced to defend herself in the majority of the situations she found herself in.

She belonged to a mother who barely spoke English and was raised in a very strict Korean household.

She shook the thoughts out of her head, took the flash drive, and stuck it into the side of the computer. It was apparent that her brother did his research on her. He knew the job wouldn't be complicated for Miko considering that she was the Head of the President's travel. Still, The White House ran a very tight ship, Miko was searched every morning and afternoon when she came and left from work. She had to go through security clearance daily and was drug tested on the regular.

The White House did not play when it came to their employees and she was just praying there was no secret radar on her computer that alarmed the people in IT of an unknown device being attached to the computer.

It only took two minutes for the itinerary to be transferred to the flash drive and after it was completed, she tossed it into her purse and began her workday.

After the morning rush of dealing with her interns and two meetings with the Secret Service, Miko was now ready for lunch.

She changed out of her pumps and into the New Balance tennis shoes that she kept in a drawer under her desk for when she chose to walk to one of the local spots near the White House.

The option to eat at her normal lunch hour didn't come too often, normally The White House was in an uproar but today the office was quiet and she was relieved.

Miko stayed cooped up in the house all weekend, drinking wine and replaying the conversation her and her "brother" had, it was so awkward and now that she knew she was being watched, she was very hesitant.

On most mornings when Miko woke before her alarm clock she would masturbate to get her day started but suddenly she felt disgusted with herself, she tossed the clit stimulator under her nightstand, and went to take a cold shower.

Miko waved to a few of her co-workers, the ones she actually cared for.

She made it to the elevator and pressed L for lobby. Miko went to the back of the elevator knowing that it would stop a few more times before taking her where she needed to be and soon the elevator would be full of people.

But when he stepped on, Miko knew that no one would be on the elevator with her today.

"Hello" she spoke to him.

He smiled, "How was your weekend?" he asked.

Miko answered, "Pleasant" which was a far cry from how she really felt.

He stared at her in admiration, if he didn't recite those vows twenty something odd years ago or didn't have three children to consider…oh and the fact that he was the President of The United States of America he would have married Miko Sanderson.

As he lay in bed some nights by his boring wife, his mind went to Miko and he wondered why she was single? Peering into her slanted tight eyes he wished he knew more about her besides what her file said. She wasn't an open book; she wasn't big on discussing her life, personal feelings or even emotions. What they had was physical but he knew it was more, he wanted more from her. Miko never crossed the line, only when he was stroking her and kissing her neck did she submit to his will and way, but once her pantyhose were pulled up over her bottom and his shirt was tucked into his pants, the butterflies flew away.

Miko was tall, charming, sophisticated and quaint. Her long arms and legs did nothing for her slender frame and small yet pleasant breasts. He knew that she hated clothes and often walked around her home naked. He also knew that a fun night for her was reading and doing research on politics in other countries.

Miko was quiet, her Vanilla bean complexion was compliments of her mother there weren't many visible traces of her African-American father who she never met nor had a conversation with.

Miko's teeth were covered by her plump and very juicy lips, the only thing she probably did get from him. She had chiseled cheekbones that models would pay for and a structured jaw line along with furry eyebrows that she had threaded every two weeks.

Her long, dark and thick hair was normally in a bun depending on the mood she in. every now and then, she would wear it in its natural state.

She wore cat-framed designer glasses by Miu Miu on the daily because she was too cheap to pay for Lasik surgery.

In her spare time, she enjoyed playing the piano and chess with random people in the park.

Although, she didn't have many friends and not much family, she was an avid lover of life and liberty and of course, she was on the pursuit of happiness.

The man that she currently sexed on the nights where she wanted to feel love was also her boss but she was just *"living in the moment"*

Miko didn't brag about bagging the President, she didn't consider it her dirty little secret or any of that shit. There was a physical attraction and in her defense, a political one as well.

For goodness sake, the man was a genius; she loved to see him in action. The way he would defend his viewpoints on several controversial topics and argue back and forth with activities over different subjects and a few touchy ones that he hated to even have to offer his opinion on.

Jonathan went to bat with numerous peace leaders in the world but the one thing he didn't tolerate was disrespect. He stood firmly by his values and that's what she loved...liked, about him.

John eyed her boobs in the shirt she wore, he liked it.

"New shirt?" he asked.

Miko smiled modestly, he noticed everything concerning her and it was sometimes overwhelming but with the weekend she had, she was welcoming it right about now. He seemed to always know how to find her, like today as she was headed out on her lunch break and here the President was on the elevator sizing her up.

"Yes it is," she told him.

"Where were you headed?" he asked.

"Lunch" she said.

"How hungry are you?" he asked, with a smirk on his face. She looked away, his aggressive nature didn't turn her off but sometimes she wondered how his secret agents felt knowing about their affair. Sometimes she appeared shy but it was her fear of being exposed that made her reclusive.

"Very" she lied.

"I'll make it up to you, I can have the chef prepare you something and bring it to your office," he told her.

She shook her head, "No special favors"

She refused to be one of those Monica Lewinsky cases; she worked hard as hell and didn't suck or fuck her way into The White House. She and John's relationship had nothing to do with her business and how well she performed.

There were days when he was in his feelings about cheating on the first lady and wouldn't so much as bat an eyelash in Miko's direction. She didn't drop her head, fret, worry, or cry...*nope*, none of that. She would never let anything jeopardize her job...not even her weird brother who popped up out of nowhere.

"Meet you in twenty" he told her and got off the elevator.

Miko sighed, she wasn't expecting to be fucked on a Monday at noon but hey, when he called she often ran and here she was going back upstairs to get her heels.

"Change of plans?" Natalie, her assistant asked.

"Yes, I'll be back before two" she said quickly and dashed out of her office.

She made it to the parking garage and drove to the Ritz-
Carlton, the hotel they often frequented when the White
House was too crowded for them to get it on.

Miko checked into the hotel first as she always did,
making sure to keep her shades on until the key card slid
into the door and it was closed.

As soon as she got there, she undressed knowing that time
was of the essence but she made sure to put her heels back
on.

 She applied a fresh coat of the Mac red lipstick she wore
for some reason; John loved to see traces of her lipstick on
his penis.

The door clicked and in walked her Mr.

Miko turned around, covering her frame with her two
small hands.

"What are you covering up for?" he asked.

She didn't answer as she made her way to him and began
to unbuckle his belt as he removed his suit jacket and tie.

"I've missed you so much," he admitted.

"I was just with you Friday morning," she told him,
shaking her head.

She was unsure if he was telling the truth when he told
her how much he liked her, missed her, admired her and
all kinds of other romantic things that most women loved
but she rather avoid.

If they could stick to the script, she would be great.

It was when John sent roses to her home on Valentine's Day or approved her holiday bonus before anyone else's did she begin to feel just a little bit special. She was confused as to what they had going on and the depth of their relationship.

Once he was just as naked as she was, Miko wrapped her arms around his waist as he pulled her in for a tender kiss. "Hmm" she moaned, as he used his tongue to wake her body up. She tilted her head as he graced her neck with sweet and wet kisses.

Oh yeah this would be worth my lunch, she thought to herself as Jonathan kneeled before her, inhaling her essence. Miko closed her eyes and held on to his shoulders as he pushed his head further into her love and stuck his tongue as far into her as he could. She bit down on her bottom lip, careful not to react to loud knowing that his secret agents were inches away from the hotel door.

She couldn't scream his name or even scratch his back, nor could she kiss his neck in fear that the First Lady may notice. So, like a child who was scared to get a beating from her mother, Miko stayed quiet and kept her hands to herself as Jonathan did all of the work.

Once he was full off her juices, he brought her to the bed and laid her body down as he crawled on top of her, kissing her in the mouth, giving her a taste of herself. She kissed him hungrily, wishing that the moment didn't have to end but she knew that what was next wouldn't last for too long.

It wasn't likely for the President to be away from The White House without reason, so Jonathan was always in and out, promising Miko that it wouldn't be this way forever.

She sometimes felt like she allowed him to degrade her but she wasn't in a position to request anything from him, so she prepared herself for the brutal beating he would put on her pussy.

Jonathan rolled her over in one swift motion, sticking his penis into her from the back and digging her guts out in a rough motion

"Aaahh fuck me!" he roared, spit flew out of his mouth and onto Miko's back.

She bit down on the pillow as she allowed him to get his the best way he knew how too and for some reason that was fucking her doggy style.

Jonathan raked her thighs with his fingernails and held on to her waist as he pumped into her for as long as he could before pulling out and climaxing all over her ass.

She struggled to catch her breath as *she too came* down from her own orgasmic high.

The sex was amazing but sometimes she wanted the *lovey dovey* feeling that she saw on movies, she wanted to be held after their naughty activity but Jonathan peeled himself from in between her legs and washed up quickly.

"I'll see you back at the office," he told her.

Miko slowly redressed.

"Chef Salad" she mumbled.

"What?" he asked.

"Chef Salad, my lunch." she told him.

Jonathan smiled and came closer to her, kissing her forehead.

"It will be on your desk when you return," he promised.

She smiled and turned her back, not wanting to see him go.

Jonathan Wilburn, twenty-two years her junior, Caucasian man with the most daring eyes anyone had probably ever seen.

It was rumored that those dreamy eyes were what captured the people's votes, and not the way he delivered his speeches and made promises to the citizens of the United States of America.

Before becoming president, Jonathan Wilburn had done a great job as a congressional representative in Colorado. He and his wife, Laura Ann were most known for their charitable hearts. Both were proud graduates of Stanford

University, and just recently, he was chosen as the guest speaker at graduation.

With his wife, Laura Ann by his side, Jonathan considered it an honor to speak at his alma mater. Laura Ann was the perfect accessory for the president. She had the smile and rosy cheeks and the personality to be First Lady. It didn't hurt that her father had served two terms as president in the early fifties. Laura was damn near deemed first lady, walking in her mother's shoes, of course.

Miko sat in a chair in the corner of the hotel room, staring out into the downtown view of D.C., now that the euphoric feeling of sex had come and gone, she was feeling stupid all over again. As she often felt whenever she was alone after sex. She was torn between questioning her actions and then convincing herself to not give two fucks. Miko sided with who gives two fucks. She enjoyed her time with him for the most part.

A knock at the door surprised her; she looked around the room wondering did John forget something.

But when she looked into the peephole and saw her brother, she opened the door and before she could ask him what the fuck did he want. He walked in without being asked.

"Excuse you?" she said.

Malachi sniffed the air and turned his nose up.

"You can do so much better than him sis," he told her.

Miko turned her head, "What do you want?" she asked, not making eye contact with him.

"Where is the flash drive?" he asked.

"Did you follow me here?"

Malachi smiled, "Trust me I wasn't the only one"

Miko knew he was bullshitting, her and John were very discreet and she was one hundred percent no one knew what was going on, or so she thought.

"I'll get it to you," Miko told him, assuming he was there to inquire about the flash drive.

Malachi stared at his sister, hating that they didn't grow up together. He was a very family-oriented person he had always been that way. Malachi believed that family was the core foundation of any person and he knew without a doubt that if he were in his sister's life she wouldn't be sleeping with a married man.

"Do you wanna meet your other sister?" he asked.

Miko frowned; she had no interest in him, her father or sister. She was just fine how she was.

"Nope" she said quickly.

Malachi didn't buy her answer though, "Well I want yall to meet, what you doing this weekend? Let's do dinner at my place"

She shook her head, "Look, I'm going to give you the flash drive and then that's it. You can go on with your life and I'll go back to mine. Okay? Now I have to get back to work" she told him and headed towards the door with her car keys in hand.

"How did it feel when you were at your graduation and no one came, not even your mother because she had to work?" Malachi asked.

She turned around with tears in her eyes.

Miko didn't cry nor did she get emotional that wasn't her thing but damn why did his words just touch her soul like that. She wasn't expecting Malachi to target her heart but damn he did, no one knew how that felt but apparently he did.

"Don't do that," she warned.

"No, it's a serious question" he told her.

"You do not fucking know me!" she yelled, warning him to tread lightly.

He softened his tone and told her from the heart "But I'm trying too"

"Why? Cus you need my help. Where have you been this whole time? Do you know how old I am? Where the hell you been" she asked, wiping tears from her face

"We aren't too much apart in age for one and my friend found you, Pops didn't even wanna tell me about you but fuck that. We family now and that's all that matters" he told her.

Miko knew it was much more to the story and she planned to get the whole thing but until then she wouldn't deny that his words weren't comforting to her very cold and bitter soul.

"And you sure you aren't using me?" she asked again.

Malachi smiled, "Of course I am but you'll be compensated and on top of that I want you to come around, we're family sis," he told her.

Miko rolled her eyes, "Whatever" she said.

He came and draped his arm around her shoulder as if they known each other forever.

"Don't trip big bro got you" he said.

Miko followed him out of the hotel and down the hallway.

"So I'm going to text you my address this week, come to New York its only a four hour train ride and bring the flash drive" he told her, as he pressed the elevator for her while he decided to take the steps.

Miko nodded her head and stepped on the elevator.

She didn't know what her brother had in store for her *but* what she did know was that it was most likely illegal. For the first time in her life, she believed the words that came out of another person's mouth other than her own and when he told her that he had her, she instantly trusted him.

Miko could only pray that she didn't end up in a fucked up situation or worse jail.

The week passed her up and she stayed clear of John as much as she could. Although she couldn't ignore his lusty stares as he walked past her office and into his, own every day,

Instead of lingering around the office as she normally did in hopes of squeezing in a quickie, when the clock struck five she was well on her way out the door.

Friday afternoon came and she had her overnight bag in the trunk of her Lexus as she headed to the train station. Her brother checked on her throughout the week and often wished her a good day and night. It was a bit overwhelming considering her phone rarely rung if it wasn't work-related or a chime from any of the numerous applications she had on her cell phone but she was growing more comfortable with him, he didn't stop so she really didn't have a choice.

Once she made it to New York, she smiled at the big city. She had only been there a few times and was somewhat happy she was there now. She would definitely take advantage of the two days she would be in the city.

Her brother called and asked her what side she came out on because he was illegally parked in the front.

Miko said, "I didn't know you were coming to get me"

"Hell yeah why would I not?" he asked.

She smiled as she walked towards him and hung the phone up.

Her brother picked up her bag, tossed it over his shoulder, and gave her a half hug with his other arm.

"How was the ride?" he asked.

She told him, "I slept the whole way"

Malachi ushered her into his car and she was very impressed with how nice and sleek the exterior was and how clean it was on the inside.

"So you're from Brooklyn?" she asked.

"Long Island but I live in Manhattan, well I live in California too," he told her.

"How does that work, the bi-coastal life?" she asked.

"My wife is an artist"

"You're married?" she was very surprised to hear that.

The wide smile that spread across his face told her that he was a happily married man. She then wondered was John a happily married man as well, but she quickly shook thoughts of him from her mind.

"Yeah I got three kids, two girls and a boy," he said happily.

"Oh wow, I've went from being an only child to being a sister and an auntie" she laughed.

She couldn't wait to meet them, she had never really been around kids before but she was looking forward to trying a few new things over the weekend.

Miko asked, "So how old are you?"

"Thirty two" he told her.

"I'm twenty four," she said.

Malachi told her that he already knew that.

"How old is your sister?"

"She's the same age as you," he said.

"Wow" Miko replied.

"Yeah, pops had a lot going on," he laughed.

"Are yall close?' Miko asked.

"Don't really know how to answer that right now," he told her.

She took that as him not really wanting to talk about it so she let the conversation die and she enjoyed the scenery as they made it to Malachi's residence.

She followed him from the parking garage and into the building where he and his family lived. It definitely put her little condominium to shame especially when she saw Malachi press the PH button on the elevator panel.

"Penthouse level huh?" she asked.

Malachi told her, "After you hand me that flash drive you can go upgrade"

She raised an eyebrow, she wasn't even expecting any money considering he somewhat threatened her to get the files, *or else*...but now that money was involved she made plans on paying off her student loans and paying a few of her mother's bills.

Miko didn't want to look thirsty; she made decent money at her job and didn't want her brother to think she needed anything extra from him. She wasn't into illegal shit and didn't plan to start now that they were possibly working on a relationship.

The elevator opened right into their kitchen, the woman she assumed was his wife turned around and went to greet her man.

She stood by a tall vase with her purse in hand.

Malachi said, "Babe this is my sister Miko, Jade, Miko."

"Jade Morgan?" Miko eyes bugged.

Jade smiled and said, "Nice to meet you come on in"

Miko asked again, "The artist Jade Morgan?"

Malachi said, "You're familiar with her work?"

Miko said, "Of course, I have one of your paintings behind my bed"

Jade was happy to hear that they had something in common, she was wondering what would she possibly have to talk about with a Korean but once her eyes laid on her she knew that was way more than how her husband described her to be.

Miko was skinny as hell for sure, but she had a lil booty on her.

Jade welcomed her into the living room and brought her a glass of wine.

Malachi went to change for dinner and told her to make herself at home.

Jade came and sat on the opposite couch.

"So how is the White house?" she asked

Miko said, "Nothing like television"

Jade laughed, "I'm sure it isn't"

Miko eyed the house, taking it all in, the open floor plan and the view was breath taking from what she could see from where she sat even at night the skyline was magnificent.

If the check was as pleasant as her brother assured her it would be, she would definitely have to upgrade her place.

A young boy came her way and introduced himself as MJ.

Miko smiled and was surprised when he reached in for a hug, laying his head on her bosom.

Jade laughed, "MJ get up!"

She told Miko, "Just like his daddy girl"

Miko laughed as well, "I can tell" he was a spitting image of Malachi.

Soon after, she met Malachi's daughter from a previous relationship and his other daughter, Mikayla and they all sat down for dinner.

Miko wasn't big on soul food being that she was mainly raised on rice and vegetables. However, she still enjoyed the plate of fried chicken, greens and mashed potatoes.

"Where is your sister?" Miko asked, after dinner.

"Our sister" he teased.

She remained quiet; he was taking her just a little too fast.

"She'll meet us out tonight for drinks," he said.

"Drinks?" she asked

"Yeah a lil turn up tonight nothing major. Did you have plans while you were here?" he asked her seeing the look of uneasiness on her face.

Miko wasn't sure if she would be comfortable drinking with complete strangers, she had already turned down the invitation to stay at his home for the weekend.

She liked her space.

"Oh no, I was just scanning my bag to see if I brought nightlife attire" she told him.

Malachi would have to get used to the way she talked, she was definitely her mother's child.

"You speak Korean too?" he asked randomly.

She stared at him, they didn't look alike at all but she was sure he was her brother. Her mother didn't speak about her father often but she had always known she had a brother; the other sister was what came as a surprise.

"Yes I do," she said.

"That's wasup" Malachi told her and began to text on his phone.

Miko stood there awkwardly, she asked Jade if she needed help with the kitchen but Jade told her, "No you're guest but the next time I'll be sure to save a few for you."

Miko said, "Well okay then, is there somewhere I can freshen up before we go?"

Malachi pointed to a bedroom that had a bathroom connected to it.

Miko took her bag with her and changed into denim jeans and a thin razorback t-shirt, she wasn't too big on bras since she barely had titties so she took the bra she had on all day off and tossed it into her bag.

She removed her tennis shoes, slid her feet into wedge heels, and added a bracelet and necklace.

She pulled her big hair out of the ponytail it was in and fluffed it a little before dabbing some perfume behind her ears and on her wrist.

When she came back into the living room, Jade said, "I love your shoes"

Miko noticed she was now changed into a pajama set, robe included.

"You're not going?" she asked.

Jade shook her head, "Girl no, I'm teaching a class in the morning. I need my rest"

She was disappointed to hear she would be alone with her newly found siblings by herself. It was something about Jade that made her feel comfortable. She had that motherly feel that relaxed Miko.

"See you tomorrow" Jade told her after she kissed her husband on the lips before retreating to their master bedroom.

Malachi said, "You ready to ride?"

She nodded her head.

She silently said a prayer that the night wouldn't be as awkward as she expected it to be and to her surprise, everything went well. Her sister was happy to have met her and made plans to come to DC soon.

Malachi told her, "So tomorrow we will handle business"

She had a pretty decent buzz, she was bobbing along to the radio as they headed back to his house.

Miko asked, "What business?"

Malachi hesitated before speaking.

………..."Underworld business" he told her.

Chapter 2

One Year Later

Miko stood in the mirror staring at her appearance, the white, Dolce and Gabbana pantsuit that she chose to wear in honor of her 25th birthday didn't look so hot now that it was actually time for her to head to dinner.

"Ugh" she said loudly, tearing the jacket off and turning back into her closet to find something else more appealing to her slim figure.

She tossed clothes to and fro until finally remembering that during her recent trip to the city to visit her nieces and nephew, her and Jade went to Barney's to do some shopping and she picked up a very expensive dress that Jade encouraged her to get.

Although, her life seemed to be a fairytale these days she still was very cost-efficient. The checks she received from her "day-job" were used to pay the few bills she had but other than that, Miko stacked her checks. The only big purchase she made during the past year since being employed by The Underworld was a new home. She rarely drove considering she didn't go anywhere but work and home, aside from the few trips she took to New York but they were via train and Miko did her grocery shopping one block from where she lived so for the most part a new car wasn't needed.

She didn't consider herself important in relations to her brother's illegal dealings, all she did was insert a flash drive into her hard drive once a month and give it to him. For this simple procedure, she was paid five hundred thousand dollars a month, it was safe to say, she was a millionaire at this point.

She never asked any questions about what they did with the information, her brother ensured her on a few different occasions that everything was good. There were times where she would panic in the middle of the night, thinking the police would be coming to get her at any moment, Malachi was only a phone call away.

Miko wouldn't deny that life hadn't did a one-eighty, not only did her bank account quadruple but she was welcomed into a family so loving that she was actually happy her brother broke into her apartment that day and damn near threatened her life.

She adored her sister and had begun to spoil her just as much as Malachi did.

Jade would act a little distant, Miko didn't know how to react the first time it happened but Malachi told her not to worry, Jade had a rough start and not to take it personal.

Miko loved her nieces and nephew as if she birthed them herself. She knew that Malachi trusted her when he asked her to watch them for the weekend while he whisked Jade away for their anniversary.

What did take some getting used too was The Underworld, even to this day, she still hadn't been able to wrap her head around everything they were involved in but she did know they handled their business well.

Everything was under the table and communication was rare amongst the group.

A lot of information she had to figure out on her own since Malachi wasn't too big on talking about it.

The Underworld consisted of five men including her brother; she had met all of them on a few occasions.

Along with Miko, there were three other women that worked for The Underworld; she didn't see them around much just as she didn't see the other men too often.

Mary Jane, Lo and Sasha, all lived in New York while she resided in D.C. because of her job and her mother.

The one thing that kept a smile on her face was the relationship she had with her big brother, Malachi had pressed her to meet their father and his mother too but she told him now wasn't the best time.

However, she loved her brother very much and she spoke to him every single day. In the one year that they had been in contact, there wasn't a day she didn't talk to him. Miko shared everything with him and Malachi had become her voice of reason. The only thing he was openly disgusted about was her relationship with the President and in return, it was the one topic that was off-limits. Somehow, Jade convinced Miko to let Lo, one of the girls who worked for The Underworld to put her a dinner together.

This was her first birthday party ever, growing up, birthdays weren't really celebrated. Her mother could barely afford to pay the bills, let alone Miko ask for a cake or worse…a gift. She wasn't big on gifts or celebrating accomplishments, which is why she was currently freaking out about this birthday dinner. Miko wasn't hard to please and even though she rarely received gifts from her mother growing up, their relationship didn't suffer over wants because her mother made sure all of her needs were taken care of. She looked up to her mom, although she wasn't the ideal role model, she loved Miko more than anything.

That morning when she made it to work, her office was decorated by her staff and they even had lunch catered and a small cake with her name scrambled in hot pink icing. It felt good to see that her hard work didn't go unnoticed and they came together to celebrate her born day.

John had sent roses to her new home that morning but she tossed them to the side. In previous years, the roses would have made her day but she wanted more for herself now that she had recently entered a new phase of life.

She left work right after the luncheon telling her staff she would see them Tuesday instead of Monday. Miko never took off work so she didn't feel bad at all when she requested the day off, giving her a three-day weekend.

A knock at the hotel door shook her from her thoughts as she pulled the dress down over her waist.

"Hold on" she said loudly.

She slid her feet into the patent leather nude pumps by Christian Louboutin, an early birthday gift from Jade, her sister in law.

Jotting to the door to see Jade, "Oh wow you look amazing" she said shockingly.

She looked down at her outfit, "Why do you sound so surprised?" She asked.

Jade laughed, "I never seen you with your hair pressed or makeup on"

She shrugged her shoulders nonchalantly, "And it will probably be your last time, I'm about ready, let me spray some perfume" she said and went towards the back of the suite she was staying in.

"Everyone is already there," Jade said loudly.

"Who is everyone?" Miko asked.

She didn't give Lo a guest list when she asked for one because she had no one to invite, Miko was surprised when Jade told her that Lo said everyone confirmed his or her attendance.

Miko wasn't expecting people to show up to celebrate her birthday, in her eyes they were associates of Malachi's not hers.

Jade said, "Just come on you'll see"

They left the hotel and hopped into a cab driving to Gio's Steakhouse, which had quickly became one of Miko's favorite places to dine at when she was in the city.

She assumed that they had reserved a few tables or so. But, when the host escorted them through the entire restaurant and down a hallway where two tall double doors were Miko's first thought was *What the hell?*

She looked over at her sister in law for an explanation but Jade just smiled and opened one of the doors so Miko could enter.

When she walked in, the lights turned on, and people yelled, "Surprise"

Miko was in complete shock.

The room was filled with the most beautiful flower arrangements and balloons; in the corner was one of her favorite pianists.

Her eyes laid on her mother, grandmother and cousins; she was very surprised to see her family.

Miko ran over to them, "What are you doing here?" she asked in Korean.

Bending down to hug and kiss all of her family members since Miko was the tallest due to her inheriting her dad's genes.

They were so happy to see her and she was happy to see them too.

She went to punch her brother in the chest, "Oh my God Malachi, I'm speechless, thank you so much," she told him, happily.

"This was all Jade and Lo, I just paid for it," he told her, not wanting to take any credit.

Miko somewhat understood Jade doing this but why Lo? She had literally only said two words to the girl before.

Miko made a mental note to tell her thank you before the night was over.

She went to sit with her family as dinner was served. Miko noticed that the menu had her name on it and she thought that was adorable, since she had never seen it before. The menu included shrimp tempura as an appetizer along with crab rangoon, sirloin steak served with grilled asparagus was the main course and for dessert in lieu of a cake, there was an array of desserts to choose from. Miko sipped some of the finest wines the entire night and mingled with the few guests that attended. Although it was only about twenty people there, she was happy and knew that it wasn't always about quantity but quality.

As the night winded down her grandmother complained about having too much wine so they all departed.

Malachi made sure they were in the truck safely as his driver promised he would get them back to the hotel safely.

Miko's mother was happy that Miko, Malachi and Melissa were all-together but didn't really say much on the situation.

Miko came back into the restaurant and took a seat at the round table where only The Underworld members remained.

"Thank you everyone seriously, I wasn't expecting this," she told them, modestly.

Sean smiled at her, "Thank you for everything do" he said.

Miko wanted to ask what exactly did she do but she felt like the less she knew the better.

Demi, Papa's wife told her, "I love your dress"

Miko smiled and said, "I kept the tag on it taking it back tomorrow"

Julia, Rod's wife laughed," I know that's right"

Miko eyed Lo in the back of the room talking to one of the bartenders, she excused herself from the table and went towards her.

"Hey Lo, I just want to tell you thank you so much for this beautiful dinner" she told her.

Lo smiled at Miko, she liked her and didn't mind being her friend, she was actually looking for more girlfriends. Lo was tired of hanging by herself and she wasn't afraid to admit it. Unlike Sasha and Mary Jane, Miko didn't seem weird or gritty as they did.

Lauren better known as Lo, Howard was just two years older than Miko she remembered her 25th birthday and to her the year of twenty-five should be celebrated the right way.

Lauren enjoyed her career as a party planner she loved being in charge of making someone's day special whether it was a birthday, wedding or a baby shower. Lauren loved events and she missed her job every day.

Even though The Underworld consisted of multiple drug rings and all kinds of other illegal shit, each of the men understood the struggle.

They all came from humble beginnings and a few of them were products of broken homes.

It was Lo's job to plant good seeds all across the United States, she spent her days donating funds to non-profit organizations, cutting the ribbon at small businesses, opening daycares in poverty stricken neighborhoods and even placing play grounds in the projects.

Lo was like the Mother Teresa of The Underworld and she loved her job, *she really did* but when she was asked to put Miko's 25th birthday dinner together she almost had a heart attack she was so excited.

She placed her all into planning the perfect night because she would want the same done for her.

According to the men of The Underworld, their income tripled when Miko's position was secured. Lo didn't really know what she did, but what she did know was that she worked at The White House and although she and Malachi looked nothing alike, she was his sister.

"You are so welcome," she told her happily.

Miko noticed that she was always happy, vibrant and full of life, she was such a somber spirit she wanted to be more lively but she had always been quiet and to herself.

"What are you doing tonight?" she asked.

Lo told her nothing at all, which was rare that she had no plans

"It's my birthday let's go out" she suggested.

Lo smiled, "Okay I'm with it, give me a minute to cut the check," she said.

Miko went to tell the others they were going out tonight.

Jade told them, "Yall have fun"

"Aww you don't wanna go out it's my birthday!" she said.

Jade yawned, "Next time"

Miko knew that Jade was a homebody, just as she was, but tonight was her birthday she wanted to celebrate.

Demi looked at Papa before telling Miko, "'I'll go with yall"

Miko clapped her hands.

Julia said she would take a rain check and Miko understood that they had kids to get home too, well Demi did too but Papa told her to enjoy herself.

Once Lo came back with a checkbook, she asked Miko was she ready to go and Demi followed.

Papa called after them, "Demi don't get nobody killed tonight baby"

She turned around and blew a kiss to her husband.

"We got her," Lo said.

She eyed Nasir before turning back around and following the other two women out of the restaurant and into a cab.

"Where are we going?" Miko asked.

Demi looked at Lo, "Where we going party girl"

Lo said, "well it's still early we can hit a few bars, the clubs aren't popping yet"

They all agreed that was a cool move for now, after the third bar Demi was too drunk to do anything else and Papa came and got her from the curb.

"Happy burf-day Miko!" her words slurred as Papa put her in the car.

Miko and Lo laughed as they waved her goodbye.

They were drunk as well but not enough to go home

"What's next?" she asked.

Lo said, "To the club bitch!"

She through her head back and laughed, "Let's go"

It didn't take long for her to find out that Lo was some sort of socialite, they didn't stand in line nor did they pay for anything at any of the venues they visited. Everyone flocked to her, calling her name and pulling her in multiple directions. She watched her take pictures with so many different people everywhere they went.

Once they made it to a new popular club that hadn't been open too long, Lo held her hand as they made it to the front of the line bypassing everyone standing outside waiting on their access to be granted.

"My favorite preacher's daughter, what it do Lo-Lo" a big tall and greasy bouncer said to Lo.

Lauren rolled her eyes and said, "Oh cut it out, it's just me and my girl" she handed him a hundred dollar bill and didn't wait on a response and as she pulled Miko into the club behind her.

She eyed the bright lights and coughed because the smoke in the air was so thick, Miko could count on one hand how many times she had visited a club.

But tonight was her 25th birthday so what the hell.

Lo yelled in her ear over the loud music, "Let's go get drinks first then go find a section to crash"

She nodded her head not hearing anything that Lo had just said.

They went to the bar, ordered drinks, and were back into the crowd, Miko fought to make it through the confined area but Lo held her hand tight and pulled her through.

She felt like they had crossed the Red Sea once they finally made it to VIP.

"Lauren what you doing out?" some dude asked Lo.

She smiled and kissed his cheek, "This is my friend Miko, it's her birthday" she said ignoring his question.

"Heyyy, happy birthday princess, come come, what yall drinking?" he questioned.

Miko held his hand as he helped both of them walk up the steps leading to the section, she was relieved that the air was flowing and there was somewhere to sit because her feet were killing her.

She grabbed a bottle of water out of the ice bucket and damn near drunk it all. She refused to wake up with a hangover the next morning fooling around with Lo.

When Lo handed her a champagne bottle after she had took a swig of it, she didn't protest and turned the bottle right up.

"I heard you're out of the party business is that true?" the dude asked Lo.

"If you need me just let me know," she told him.

She noticed how smooth she was; Lo never really came out and answered a question but would turn around and put it on you.

"Guess who's performing tonight?" he teased.

Lo smiled and waited on him to tell her, she was drunk and wasn't in the mood to play the guessing game.

"India Rose" he said.

Lo screamed in Miko's ears and clapped her hands happily, "Oh my God I didn't see that on the flyer," she shouted.

He laughed and tossed his head back, "She's a special surprise sweetie, and she's going to be so happy to see you"

Miko asked, "Who is India Rose?"

Lo said, "Girl the hottest Indy singer out right now she's a fucking beast"

She wasn't familiar with the term, Indy.

"Indy?" she asked.

Lo said, "You know solo, like she's on her own but she's deep girl wait till she come out I love her music"

Miko preferred classical music and maybe a few throwbacks from J-Lo or Biggie every now and then, but she would give the girl a try.

She was enjoying the DJ along with the shots that her and Lo kept taking, she tried to take it slow but the more shots Lo passed her the easier it became for her to forget her plan of waking up sober.

She worked a lot and that's all she did for the most part so she wouldn't beat herself up for enjoying her night.

The DJ stopped the music and the lights changed in the club from neon and electric too one big spotlight on the stage.

She stood on the cushions of the red velvet couch to get a better look towards the stage.

Once the DJ announced who was there tonight, a few people left not knowing who the chick was while others flocked closer to the stage.

There was a live band on the stage that consisted of two guitar players, a drummer, a piano player and the singer.

She was a cute girl and *boy* could she blow.

Her voice belonged in a pulpit it was so powerful.

Miko watched Lo sway to the beat and snap her fingers, she knew every song.

After her two-song performance, she bowed and left the stage.

Minutes later the same girl that had just sung her heart out was now in their section.

She and Lo hugged for a long time and Lo introduced her to Miko, "Nice to meet you" the chick said.

Miko told her likewise and went back to watching the younger girls gyrate on the floor.

She was so into the scene that she didn't notice someone staring at her but that's just how Miko was, always in her own little world.

Nash stared at Miko; he had never seen what he assumed what a Japanese girl in the club was before. She was fine as hell and he knew that she had to be mixed with something. Even though she was a little skinnier than what he normally went for he wasn't tripping.

Lo caught him looking at Miko and she winked her eye, Nash blushed and put his head down. He wasn't one of those guys who commanded a lot of attention, which is why even though he was multi-talented he played the background by just sticking to the drums.

Nash could do it all, play the piano, sing, rap, drums, guitar, violin, but to keep money his pocket and food on the table he hustled. He was secretly searching for the courage to one day become the World's greatest rapper, which is what he truly desired to be.

When he laid down at night he saw himself on stage in front of millions of people, shutting it down, breaking records and creating classics.

His cell phone vibrated in his pocket, once he pulled it out and saw the name on the screen, he knew it was time for him to dip so he could make a play.

The little money that he made from playing the drums for India wasn't enough to keep him off the streets.

He dapped everyone up and got a good look at Miko's sexy ass once more before he left, he would never forget her face or her smile.

The club faded out and Miko staggered out on the sidewalk behind Lo.

"I gotta get to my hotel," her words slurred.

"I know honey you keep telling me," Lo said, patting her on the back.

She hauled them a cab and hightailed it to Manhattan. Before she knew it, she had passed out in the backseat of the cab with her head on Lo's lap.

The next morning, she woke up with a throbbing headache.

"Might want to lay back down love," Lo told her, she got out of the bed placing her laptop on the side of her and left the room.

She laid back down and kept her eyes closed, the light peering in the room was giving her the worst headache, or so that's what she decided to blame it on.

Lo reentered the room and sat a mug on her glass nightstand.

Miko sat up, this time a little slower, "What's that?" she questioned.

"Drink it you'll feel better" she told her.

Miko picked it up and sniffed the concoction before taking a sip; the hot liquid was refreshing for her very parched throat.

Lo got back into bed and went right back to typing on her computer.

"What time is it?" she asked.

Lo told her it was three thirty in the afternoon.

"Was I snoring?" Miko asked.

Lo giggled, "No do you normally snore?"

She shrugged her shoulders, maybe she was still drunk.

"I'm starving," she complained.

"Let's go to lunch," she suggested.

Miko asked, "Can we order in?" holding her aching stomach.

Lo got up and went to grab all of the take-out menus she had collected over the years.

They settled on pizza, Miko went to shower while they waited on the food to get there.

Lo left her a t-shirt and a pair of sweat pants on the counter for her and she was appreciative.

"I feel like I'm in college again," she told Lo once she found her in the living room.

"Tell me about it," Lo said.

"You went to Howard too right?" she asked.

"For a semester but I graduated from NYU" Lo told her.

"This smells so good," Miko, said grabbing a slice of pizza.

Lo had already had two slices she had a figure to keep up so she wouldn't over indulge.

Miko eyed the small apartment, although it wasn't as big as hers she was pretty sure Lo was probably paying twice the amount she was. The cost of living in New York was very expensive.

Lo had bright colors in her home and stark furniture, there was a lot of glass and the color white, only accents in teal and hot pink filled the home. She had black and white over sized photos of herself; it was obvious the girl thought highly of herself. Miko noticed the Holy Bible on the coffee table.

"You read the Bible?" Miko asked.

Lo smiled" I'm a PK," she said.

She didn't know what the hell a "PK" was.

Lo said, "My parents are preachers" noticing that Miko was lost.

Miko nodded her head now understanding what she was saying.

Lo didn't act like a preacher's kid, she really didn't know how a preacher's child was supposed to act but she was sure that they wouldn't work for an illegal organization or stand on couches in the club drinking out a champagne bottle.

After she finished eating, she wanted to lie back down but didn't want to impose not knowing what Lo had going on today and she didn't want to be in her hair any longer. She had already slobbed all over the girl's very comfortable pillows and sheets.

"I'm going to call a cab so I can get some sleep" Miko spoke up.

Lo said, "No don't leave, why are you leaving?"

"I thought you wanted your home to yourself I know how I am on the weekends" she told her.

"I come from a very big family, don't leave. You're not bothering me," she said.

"Are you sure?" Miko asked to be sure.

"Girl yes let's rest up because tonight we're going to do it all over again," Lo told her happily.

Miko said, "Oh God, let me go take a nap then"

Her and Lo were complete opposites but for the time being, she seemed cool.

Lo watched her leave the living room and turn into the only bedroom in the apartment.

She smiled and thought to herself, *She's cool.*

When her phone rung and she saw that, it was *him* she sent the call to ignore.

He didn't have one word to say to her last night and now on today, Lauren didn't have one for his ass either.

Chapter 3

Miko kissed her mother when she walked into her home, the house she grew up in and the one that her mother refused to leave.

"How are you Miko?" she asked.

"Good mama, it smells good are you cooking?" she questioned.

Her mother nodded and pushed her into the kitchen. She sat while her mother made her a cup of green tea.

"Thank you I needed this" she said.

Miko inhaled the tea and allowed the smell to consume her, she loved tea and it had been quite a while since she had tea with her mom. She had questions about her father but her mom would always cringe at the mentioning of him so she stopped bringing him up. Malachi and Melissa had been on her ass about going to visit him but she didn't understand why now? She had no desire for a daddy. In her eyes, she had made it this far without a daddy and was doing well.

She didn't smoke and rarely indulged in alcohol other than wine; she went to church and said her prayers. Miko was a college graduate, her credit was sustainable and she had a good job. In her opinion, her mother did a good job all on her own, without any help or assistance.

Miko's mother asked her; "You work in the morning?" her English was very broken.

She nodded her head.

"Work too hard, never take no time to sleep. Skinny girl" she complained.

Miko didn't say anything, all her life she had been told she was so skinny; she was comfortable in her size four pants and B cupped breasts.

She enjoyed her time with her mother, which was mainly spent in silence. Her mother was never one to have a lot to say. When Miko would run home with good news from school, her mother would nod her head and smile. Miko learned a long time ago to celebrate herself. It wasn't that her mother wasn't proud her mama was very proud of her she wasn't much of a talker.

She stayed with her mother for another hour before catching the train back to her side of town.

Downtown DC was an amazing scene to be on, Miko stopped at one of her favorite coffee shops because on Sundays they had live jazz, she was a big fan of jazz music. She took a seat near the back and ordered a coffee with a splash of hazelnut. She got comfortable in her seat and pulled out her planner, making a few changes to her schedule. She smiled when she saw that there were plans to visit Lo in the city this weekend. Once the set began,

Miko placed her planner back into the satchel that she brought along with her and directed her attention towards the stage. Her fingers played an imaginary piano and she secretly wished she were up there with them.

Her infatuation with the piano wasn't discussed. Her family knew that she played well and her grandmother was who taught her. But, no one knew that she missed playing and once had a dream to become a classical pianist as a child.

She closed her eyes and enjoyed the female singer who remixed some of Miko's favorite songs. She grew up Korean and didn't know much about the African-American side of her, but one thing that was for sure she loved all of their music.

Miko enjoyed the sultry voices of Lauryn Hill, Ledisi and even Janelle Monae. In her musical opinion, good music was good music, no matter who was behind the track. Feeling very good about life, she stood up and swayed her tiny hips just a little, one of her favorite songs was *Golden* by Jill Scott and the sister on stage was killing it.

She loved this song and it was so fitting, especially since she had been living life like it was golden these past few months.

After the set was finished, Miko decided that it was time for her to go home. She still had to walk a few blocks and didn't want to be walking too late at night by herself. She had a very long workweek ahead of her so she planned on showering and going straight to bed.

Unbeknownst to her, Nash, the drummer from the night of her birthday had his eyes on her while he was on stage. Once the set ended, he wasn't able to focus on breaking his equipment down because he was too focused on the beauty who sat in the back of the lounge. From her demeanor alone he knew that she was unaware of her beauty. His eyes stayed with her until she checked the time and departed from his sight.

Nash knew that he was high from smoking two blunts before hitting the stage but it was something about Miko and whether he was intoxicated or not, she still captured his attention like no woman had ever been able to do before.

Once Miko made it home, she turned the alarm on and went to shower. Not too long after drying her body and hair, was she climbing in bed and falling fast asleep.

The next morning came before she knew it, without needing a clock to wake up, Miko rose before the sun did, and went to make a fresh pot of coffee. She stretched and did one hour of yoga before bathing and dressing for work.

The Diane Von Furstenberg wrap dress she wore along with Sam Edelman pumps complimented her tall frame. Miko pulled her hair into a tight bun at the nape of her neck, she took off the diamond earrings her brother purchased for her birthday and put on a pair of pearls to match the necklace and bracelet she had on. She swore that she looked dead without mascara and eyeliner so she never left the house without applying the two.

After ensuring that she looked decent for work, Miko headed to her safe haven with a big smile on her face. She was looking forward to a productive week at The White House.

"So Miko you'll be going to Belgium at the end of the week" the President's publicist told her.

Not hearing anything that she said because she was too busy staring at the chipped nail polish on her index finger, as soon as she left work today she would be heading back to the nail shop. Chipped nails were disturbing, she found herself staring at the nail wishing she had polish in her desk drawer.

Miko shot her head up and for the first time in the briefing meeting, she was now all ears.

"Huh?" she asked.

The publicist ignored her it wasn't a secret that she hated repeating herself but today Miko didn't care because she needed to know what had just been said.

"What did you just say?" Miko questioned.

Everyone looked at her in shock, but she was unconcerned with their thoughts.

"You will be traveling with the President to Belgium this week, his assistant requested the days off months ago"

"And I'm the next person in line?" she asked.

The publicist pressed her lips together, Miko was really getting on her nerves.

"See me after the meeting" she dismissed any other questions she had and continued with the meeting.

After the brief was over, Miko received her itinerary and she wasn't looking forward to traveling this weekend at all. She had plans to go to New York and hang out with Lo.

Ever since her birthday, they both traveled back and forth having girl's nights on the weekends and each one was better than the last. The two had been making tons of memories over the past few weeks.

Miko had even convinced Lo to try sushi and now she was in love.

In return, Lo had introduced Miko to all kinds of new things and so far, the friendship was working out to be beneficial on both ends. Miko was never anti-friends; in fact, college was the best four years of her life, but the people she hung with during her undergraduate years, well the majority of her college girlfriends were now married and on their second baby.

The difference between Miko and the few gals she called "friends" was that she went to school to obtain a degree and pave a better way for her and her mother. The others went to school in hopes to find their college sweetheart, and for the most part, they were all successful in doing so. Miko went to the President's office something she rarely did.

"He's in a meeting," the secretary told her but she didn't give a fuck.

He knew what he was doing and Miko wasn't having it at all.

"I'm not going to Belgium," she said once she barged into his office.

He was alone, playing a game of some sort on a tablet.

Once he laid eyes on Miko they sparkled and she caught it too although she wished she hadn't.

The effect that he was beginning to have on her was growing and it got on her nerves, she because didn't want to like him.

She wanted more out of life, whenever she went to go visit her brother and his family, her little heart would fill with envy.

Miko loved Malachi and she prayed that one day she met a man who looked at her the same way he looked at Jade.

Jade worshipped the ground Malachi walked on and he did the same for her. Miko didn't want to continue to settle for just half of a man, especially when she knew she deserved so much more.

Miko wanted love, she wanted someone to lay her down at night and wake her up in the morning. The sneaking in and out of hotel rooms were growing old, especially when she had a house that he refused to come too.

"Ms. Sanderson what I do owe this surprise visit?" John asked pleasantly.

Miko knew not to cut a fool; the ears and eyes in The White House were always open even when you thought they weren't.

She whispered, "I know what you're doing and it's not going to work"

John smiled, "Not sure if I'm following you, my assistant can't make it her niece is having surgery. So you have to with me"

Miko hissed, "Bullshit John and you know it"

He was surprised to hear her curse; Miko didn't talk like that at least not in his presence.

"See you Friday, Miko I have a meeting" he told her and went back to playing his game.

He wasn't comfortable with her in his office with the door closed; John hated rumors and didn't want to get one started today.

Miko pursed her lips together and left the room before she stepped out of character.

She was so fucking mad; a lick of work wasn't done for the remainder of the day.

When she made it to the parking garage, Miko didn't smile or wave to the security guards like she normally did. She was pissed off.

John texted her, something he didn't do often.

"You looked beautiful today"

She rolled her eyes at the message and didn't even bother to respond, she had nothing to say to him.

Before she knew it, the end of the week had come and she was boarding the flight to Belgium. She didn't bother speaking or even smiling for the press as she walked across the airway to the private plane.

The secret service agents checked her for the third time before allowing her to go up the steps and get a seat on the plane.

Miko looked out the window at John and his children hugging and saying their goodbyes. His wife, the first lady dabbed tears from her eyes. They would only be gone for five days so Miko wondered would she really miss her husband or was she doing that because the press was present.

John held her close and continuously planted kisses on her face. They were one affectionate couple.

Before their fiasco began, she used to see the pictures in the newspapers of the couple kissing at baseball and basketball games.

Once they began to talk and eventually it became physical and Miko received the same amount of affection. The President was big on kissing, hugging and spanking too. She rolled her eyes, laid her head back on the headrest, and got comfortable. For the trip, she packed snacks, a few books, magazines, and a blanket that she had started knitting in hopes that it would be ready for Christmas. Once John was on the plane, he patted Miko's shoulder along with the rest of his staff and went to take his seat. Miko stared at him as he buckled his seat belt.

She asked herself all of the time what did she like about him but she knew it was the sense of security.

Although John was married, in her head he was hers too.

Miko hated how bipolar she was when it came to him. He motioned for her to join him in the restroom (she assumed) but the conversation that she overheard from earlier in one of the press rooms amongst the interns turned her stomach and she refused to stoop low and have sex with him while so many of her co-workers were sleeping on the plane. Miko wouldn't risk her job or her reputation for a few minutes in heaven, it just wasn't worth it. Her career meant everything to her and it was her gateway to the huge check she received every month from The Underworld.

She shook the thoughts out of her head and tried to fall asleep.

Hours later, she woke up and ate lunch on the plane with the rest of the President's staff and went back to sleep. She didn't know how tired she was but apparently her body needed the rest and when they landed in Belgium, she was refreshed and well rested.

They checked into the hotel they were staying in and after she showered and changed, with a book in hand Miko went and had a glass of wine at the bar.

She couldn't believe she was in Belgium, the next day she planned on being a tourist and seeing as much as she could while they were there.

The seat next to her became occupied and without her turning to the right, she already knew who it was.

"You're going to get us caught," she told him.

John asked sarcastically, "What am I doing wrong?"

"Everything" she said and scooted down one bar stool to give them some space, much needed space at that. John smelled like fresh cucumbers with a hint of cologne, the smell was turning on her on.

"Why do you always look amazing?" he asked her.

Miko took a sip of her wine, "I don't try," she told him honestly

Since her bank account had done a one eighty and money was no longer a worry, Miko began to shop more and more, and more.

She loved clothes, jewelry, shoes and purses too.

"What are you doing tomorrow after the conference?" he asked.

Miko shrugged her shoulders, she planned to be a tourist since it was on the White House dime but she didn't tell him that.

"I was thinking dinner and wine, maybe a dance or two," he suggested, leaning in and grazing her thigh with his fingers.

She blushed, the idea of being at diner with him with candles did sound good, and especially when all they did was, have sex in random hotel rooms.

She asked, "Where did you have in mind? I heard the lamb in Belgium is exquisite"

John gave her a disappointed look, "I was thinking room service honey," he told her.

The smile dropped from Miko's face and after she tossed the remainder of the wine back, she sat the glass on the coaster and told the bartender, "Charge that to the room" and stood up.

When she stood, so did John and all six of his secret service agents formed a circle around him and her.

She shook her head, "Move" she told John.

"I didn't mean to get your hopes up" he apologized.

"Of course you didn't, goodnight" she said and walked off.

John couldn't call her name or run after her like most men did when they hurt the woman they loved or in their case, enjoyed fucking.

Therefore, all he could do was watch her walk away and decided to try again tomorrow. Hoping that she would have forgotten his mishap by then.

Miko lay in bed in the cold hotel room, naked as the day she was born. The room was dark besides a light that occasionally struck the room from an airplane or something high up in the sky.

She asked herself, "What am I doing?" but didn't have an answer.

She wanted more out of life but was unsure of how to grasp it. Until then, she had a job to do and tomorrow would be a busy day so Miko went to sleep, and instead of dreaming about random shit, real love was on her mind for the first time.

***

Miko and Lo walked into the meeting together, all eyes were on them, which led her to look down at her watch.

"I'm not late am I?" she asked aloud.

Malachi told her, "No"

Papa asked, "When yall started hanging together?"

She could have sworn she heard a little disgust in his voice but she wondered why.

Miko looked at her brother for answers but he shook his head.

Lo took the seat next to Sean and Miko sat beside her brother and next to Roderick.

"How are you?" she asked Roderick.

He smiled at her and told her he was fine, "You look nice" he flirted.

Miko told him thank you then turned to her brother, "I want to take the girls to see a musical if that's okay?"

Malachi nodded his head, "Of course it is, see if Jade wants to go, she loves stuff like that"

Miko made a mental note to call her sister in law before purchasing the tickets.

She pulled out the flash drive and handed it to her brother. The Underworld tried to meet as less as possible, although they lately they had been meeting monhly. It was always a different location and time, just in case someone was following them or keeping up with their moves.

Because business had been booming a little more than lately, it was starting to require more meetings of everyone together. The Underworld were taking on new clients and expanding into unfamiliar territory, so often a vote had to be done. It was very important that the men stayed on the same page.

Once everyone was present, Papa called the meeting to order.

"Yo, MJ what's the word?" he asked Mary Jane.

"Everything is good my way, I could use some help but I'm not complaining," she told the group.

"No help" Nasir spoke up.

Mary Jane sat back in her seat, she never understood why they always asked her questions or for her opinion if every time she did say something it was shot down immediately. She was just going to stop talking and play her position. Mary Jane felt like her voice didn't matter. Honestly, she didn't think any of their opinions did, except Nasir's and he barely spoke. Unless it was to say, "NO" which she had learned was his favorite word.

Lo said, "Well I have a few charity events lined up this week and next week oh and don't forget, I'll be taking up donations soon for the holidays"

Malachi cut her off, "So what's up with the paperwork in the south?"

He personally felt like Lo's position in The Underworld was stupid and a waste of fucking time, money, and resources.

Lo looked at him with a disgruntled face but she said nothing, neither did Miko, but she never did.

Sean asked, "What you mean what's up with it?"

"It's looking etchy to me," Malachi said.

Papa nodded his head agreeing with his brother.

"Well yall niggas come down there and handle it then" Sean said with an attitude.

"Nigga always in his feelings" Papa mumbled.

"Speak up down there," Sean said.

Roderick said, "I know I was behind last month but I added something extra to the pot for this month"

Nasir said, "We good on the extra homie just try to stay above water"

Miko stared at Nasir, he was so handsome to her but his demeanor made her question his intentions at times.

He didn't talk often nor did he smile, she wondered what made him happy or what his hobbies were.

Lo rolled her eyes, she looked impatient and ready to go.

Sasha never said anything in the meeting; she was too busy doing something on her phone.

"Sasha did you handle that for me?" Papa asked.

Sasha nodded her head.

"Miko do you know of any trips yall could possibly have to London?" Nasir asked.

She shook her head, "Not that I know of as of right now we're pretty much done with trips"

"Damn for real?" Papa questioned.

Miko nodded her head, "Yes I am for real"

Her proper dialect caused everyone to erupt in laughter; she looked around confused and wanting to be included in on the joke.

Malachi said, "Pay them no mind" he too was laughing

She caught Lo staring at Nasir and wondered what did they have going on?

The meeting didn't last too much longer and before she knew it, Nasir was skating out along with everyone else. Malachi asked her, "How long are you here?"

"Just for tonight, I'm catching an early flight and going straight to work," she told him

"Come on let's go get some beer and hot dogs"

"I'll pass on the beer but I am hungry," she laughed.

She looked around for Lo to tell her that she was riding with her brother but she had dipped too.

"I was looking for Lo…,"Miko told Malachi as her eyes scanned the parking lot.

"She probably dipped off" he told her.

"Dipped off? Where?" Miko questioned.

Malachi stared at his sister.

"You don't know do you?" he probed.

Miko was lost, "Know what?"

He shook his head, "Nothing that's not my place" he told her, pressed the start button on his car, and peeled out onto the street.

They found a booth in very crowded bar and ordered hot dogs and snacked on peanuts until their food arrived.

"Have you thought any more about going to see pops?" he asked.

Miko said, "Nope not at all"

Malachi didn't want to get on her nerves but their father really wanted to see how she turned out. The pictures that Malachi brought him weren't enough. He hadn't seen Miko in years, many years at that.

"Just let me know something so I can tell him"

"I have no desire Chi, I don't want to see him," she admitted.

Malachi knew that already but he thought that with him consistently asking her she would give in.

"He wants to be in your life now," he told her.

"From prison? I'll pass" Miko said.

Luckily, their food had arrived and he didn't have to refute what she said.

"So you still seeing the old man?" he asked.

Miko eyed him, "Not that it's any of your business, but I've been too busy"

"Good" he said.

"I do think I'm ready to date though" she went on and told her brother.

He smiled, "What's your type?"

Miko said, "Well I like white men but I wouldn't mind talking to a black man"

"Getting your Kimora Lee on, okay," he laughed.

She chuckled, "Now if he's as rich as Russell then that's definitely a plus"

"The right one will come trust me"

"Is that how you feel about Jade?" she asked.

Malachi nodded his head, "Yeah but I chased Jade, like I damn near kissed her ass for about three years before she gave in"

She smiled, she wished that someone showed that much interest in her, chasing her down and patiently waiting on her to be ready for love. If only she could meet a man who she didn't find boring and actually captured her attention. Little did she know, there was someone that was smitten about her and she had yet to notice him.

The next day, Miko traveled back to DC from New York and went straight to work. She didn't complain about her low energy because as soon as she made it home she would be going to bed. Her only prayer was that the workday flew by and it did. When the clock struck five, Miko was putting her heels back on and locking her computer.

A knock at her door caused her to roll her eyes; she prayed that no one needed anything from her. She was the head honcho over her department but she still had to answer to a boss. And her boss favorite saying was "The White House doesn't sleep" which meant even though they were only paid to be there for nine hours out of the day, Monday through Friday he still expected them to go above and beyond to ensure that everything is ran smoothly.

Miko believed in this principle but not today, she was experiencing jet lag and was ready to lie down.

She said, "Come in" in a very dry tone

When the President walked into her office, her heart stopped.

What is he doing here? She thought to herself.

John smiled at her but she didn't return the gesture, ever since he tried to play her in Belgium, she had been keeping her distance.

Miko knew that he wasn't in a position to give her more so she preferred to stay away. She was tired of settling for being his dirty little secret.

John asked, "You're leaving early today?"

She told him, "It's 5 pm" Miko was one of those employees that stayed long after every one clocked out but not today, she was tired as hell.

"Never see you leave at 5, you must have a date?" he asked.

She heard the jealousy in his voice, and thought it was cute.

"If you call me getting comfy with my bed a date, then yes I have a hot date" she joked.

Miko stood and re-tucked the mustard blouse she wore today, into her black dress pants.

John loved her style; she wore everything as if it was custom made to fit her body. Miko had so much grace and poise.

Grace, that Miko wasn't even aware that she possessed.

"Can I help you with something?" she asked him

John nodded his head, "Yes but I see you're in a rush so it can wait"

Miko didn't bother protesting, she wasn't in the mood for sex tonight, especially sex with *him*.

"*Se*nd me some pictures tonight," he told her.

She raised an eyebrow, "Pictures?"

The President said, "Yes for when I can't be near you"

She didn't tell him yes or no, instead, she said, "It's been three minutes you probably should go before someone thinks of something"

Jonathan grazed her hand but she stepped back and folded her arms, she knew how quickly she could give in to him. In addition, her office was not the place for her to be screaming his name, especially with the First Lady's office not too far from hers.

"You're right," he said.

She handed him a green folder just to make it look like they were discussing business in case someone was lurking around the hall.

After waiting a few minutes, she left her office and clocked out.

"I hope you're not doing what I think you're doing" one of the file clerks who worked on the same floor as she told her.

Miko said, "I don't know what you're referring too but have a good day" she told the old witch and got on the elevator.

She wished that people wouldn't speak on something they had no idea about; she knew that if she stated her case she would look guilty.

 So she went for the offended act and before the elevator closed the lady mouthed to her, "I'm sorry" but Miko looked down as if her feelings were so hurt when really she could care less and was curious to know what all did the clerk hear.

Gossip in The White House was worse than a barber or beauty shop, whenever she went to the cafeteria to grab lunch, she would receive an earful on whose fucking who and all kinds of other bullshit.

Miko would have to do better with being discreet, especially with the President's signature cologne lingering on her skin.

She got off the elevator and went through security clearance before making it to her car and going home.

She was tired and mentally exhausted; Miko spent the entire night talking to Jade and drinking wine.

Once Miko made it home, she kicked off her heels and removed the pins from her hair, allowing the tresses to hang freely.

She ran a bubble bath while she called her mother but got her voicemail.

Miko was so tired that dinner was the last thing on her mind but she knew she would end up waking up in the middle of the night starving. So she took a pack of chicken strips out for a salad later on.

After feeling the water with a few of her fingers, she slid her body down in the tub and laid back, relaxed.

Miko took a deep breath and inhaled the aromatherapy. She needed this bath, the combination of hot water and bath salts and her lights were dimmed, she felt like she was in heaven for the moment.

Miko stayed in the tub longer than she expected too, she threw a t-shirt over her head and pulled her hair up into a sloppy bun and tied it with a bow.

Miko climbed and got settle under the covers. Today had been long enough for her to not bother with watching television in an attempt to help her fall asleep.

Miko tossed and turn before realizing it was too many lights on in the house for her to sleep comfortably.

She went and turned the lights off near the front of the house, only leaving the light on under the microwave. Miko stopped and got a good look at the view, she smiled at how beautiful DC looked at night, it made the pretty penny she paid monthly all worth it.

Miko tiptoed on the cold hardwood floors as she made it back to the comfort of her King sized sleigh bed

She lay back down and took a deep breath, after she tossed and turned once more.

She got up yet again but this time she went to close the curtains in her bedroom. She didn't even notice the person across from her building with a camera, snapping it up. Her brother had told her on several occasions but she would have to learn on her own, how to be aware of her surroundings, *always.*

Chapter 4

"Relax girl" Lo told Miko, she came and stood behind her and moved the direction of the gun from the sky to the actual target, which was in front of them.

"Relax," she told Miko again.

Miko took a deep breath and said, "Okay I got it now" she pushed the goggles she wore back up and shot again.

The power of the gun took her back a few steps, Lo shook her head and went back to her again.

"Girl you need to relax your damn shoulders," Lo laughed.

Miko was getting frustrated. When her brother suggested that she hit up the gun range just in case something was to pop off, she thought it would be cute and fun but she soon realized wasn't nothing amusing about holding and shooting a gun.

Lo seemed to be regular at the gun range, they hugged her and everything when her and Miko walked in.

"How long have you been coming here?" Miko asked.

"It's my duck off spot," she told her nonchalantly

She told her, "Let's come back after lunch I can't concentrate because I'm hungry"

Lo smirked, "Okay, let's ride I want pizza"

She turned her gun in, Lo tucked hers in the back of her jeans, and they got into Lo's car and headed to a pizzeria she said was good.

"So where is your boyfriend?" Lo asked.

"Where is yours?" she returned the question.

Lo laughed, "Ooh bitter maybe?"

Miko laughed, "No not at all, I'm enjoying my singleness if that's what you want to call it"

She was unaware of the proper title when you were sleeping with a married man; she damn sure wouldn't come out and say she was a man's mistress.

"Are you in a complicated situation?" Lo probed for more information.

"No, it's an understood relationship" she said.

Lo nodded her head, she definitely understood how those, "it is what it is" relationships could be.

"Do you want kids one day?" Lo asked.

Miko sat her soda down on the table, "is there something you need to talk about?" she asked.

Lo eyed her, "No why you ask that?"

"Seems like it's something on your mind, I could be wrong"

"We've been hanging and I don't know much about you," Lo told her.

"Same goes for you," she said.

Lo shrugged her shoulders, "Girl I am an open book" she said.

"Well are you sleeping with Nasir?" Miko came on out and asked.

Lo kept a game face on as if that wasn't her first time being asked that question.

She looked dead at Miko, her new "best friend" and lied, "No, what made you ask that?"

"He stares at you like he loves you and you look at him the same way," she told her.

Lo smiled, "And how does one stare at you like they love you?"

Miko didn't have an accurate answer, but it looked like Malachi and Jade, Roderick and Julia…it looked like the love you see on television. Although it's not our reality, it still seems like it. She didn't know what love felt like, she cared for the President but it was in a weird political/nympho way. Being an avid lover of politics and the government since a kid, she loved him for what he stood for not so much for who he was.

Miko wanted to one-day fall in love with a man who loved her and only her. The president was something to do because there wasn't anything else to do. She wasn't sure that if he ever left his wife and became a single man that she would be interested in him.

It was the thrill and the suspense that fed her, the satisfaction of having something that technically didn't belong to her.

She loved her personal space, her Friday nights were all hers and she had the power to spend them how she wanted too.

On some weekends, she spent time with her mom, on other Saturdays she traveled to New York but she did that because she wanted too.

Miko assumed that once she was in a relationship it would have to automatically be about the man she was with and she wasn't mentally prepared to give all of herself to someone.

What would she get in return?

Relationships were amazing, that she could never deny. She believed in love, real love at that.

She wanted to experience love one day, whether it was her becoming a mother or becoming someone's wife, or better, both. True enough, she desired these things but at the same time, she wanted to love herself more before loving someone.

Miko wanted to be confident in the woman she was before she submitted to a man. She wanted to be free of all of her insecurities so that when her man was out of town or away for whatever reason she didn't worry about his whereabouts.

She was the "other" woman and it was all good when John was fucking her, but when his wife called he answered without a second thought

She would watch his eyes dance and his heart flutter at the sound of her voice, the first lady had his heart and Miko just had his dick and balls in her mouth whenever he craved her.

Miko desired a love so sweet that it consumed the both of them to the point where they became blind to others.

"What do you think love is?" she asked Lo.

Like a young teenager girl who had just received her first kiss, Lauren's cheek seemed to turn a rose color almost close to red and her eyes lit up before she closed them and pressed her arms close to her breast.

"It's complete; I believe that love completes you. Your degree can't do that, your job can't, your mama cant, your friends can't but that love…. Love holds and protects you. Love comforts you. Love is completion. It's a sacrifice because you're letting your guard down and giving yourself to someone in hopes that it lasts forever. Love brings me peace when I think about it. It's that joy that you're scared to talk about because no one wants to be the girl that's obsessed with their boyfriend but real love makes you not care what others think. Love allows me to be who I am and love him unconditionally no matter who's watching. I want that no matter what love, that without a doubt, when I'm broke and feeling miserable, his love is the energy I need to bounce back. That's what love is to me"

Miko watched the tears form in the corners of her eyes and that's when she knew that she loved him.

She didn't love John like that and probably never would, she couldn't relate or connect to anything that Lo just said but did she pray that one day that kind of love would find her and knock her over the head.

Miko reached over and grabbed Lo's hand, "You need to write a book"

Lo busted out laughing and wiped tears from her eyes with her other hand.

"Girl I need too all the shit I done been through" she said sadly.

Miko smiled at her, "I'm here for you, no more going through alone" meaning every single word she just said.

Lo took a sip of her water, she didn't respond but she received it.

She was too scared to get close to someone; although they were slowly becoming inseparable, she would still keep space between them.

Someone like her, Miko didn't need to be closed too. At least that's what she had brainwashed herself to think.

After lunch, Miko told Lo she had to go meet up with her brother which is what her plan was until a tinted Escalade truck pulled up to the curb and the window only rolled down far enough for her to see his eyes.

She turned around quickly but it was too late, someone as famous as the President...it didn't take a rocket scientist to guess whom that was rolling through Brooklyn, New York almost ten trucks deep.

She told her friend, "Work...I'll call you later"

Lo smiled, "I know how that it is"

Miko hopped in the back seat of the truck and Lo stood there before it peeled off. She would have never thought little Miss Miko was fucking Mr. President but hey, many people wouldn't have thought she was sleeping with her boss but she was.

Miko turned to the President "You can't summon me when you're ready this isn't how this works" she fussed

John chuckled, "I've missed you Miko"

She rolled her eyes, he never took her serious, always laughing at any and everything she said, she was unsure of why she even spoke at times.

"What do you want?" she asked snidely.

He brushed her thigh with his hand and lifted the denim dress she wore up just a little to get a better look at her long legs, his favorite pair of legs to look at.

Miko had legs for days, at many of the President's balls, dinners and galas he would request to see in her something with a slit. His fetish for her legs was outrageous, he preferred her in heels while they sexed simply so he could stare at her legs in pumps while he fucked her.

"I want you, you know that," he said huskily.

Lo's recent confession on what love meant to her was replaying in her head and she wasn't even the least bit concerned with John and what the fuck he wanted. The question was what she wanted and what she deserved.

"How much do you love your wife?" she blurted out.

John's eyes went cold and he slipped his hand from her thigh and turned his head to look out the window.

"I mean you just drove what four hours to come pick me up on the side of the street, so how much do you love your wife?" she pressed for an answer.

John asked in a very irritated tone, "What has gotten into you?"

"This is over" she told him, holding back tears. In that moment, she saw herself for what she really was in his eyes, a piece of ass.

Miko was a piece of ass.

She told the driver to let her out and John didn't protest this wasn't a six-month fiasco going down the drain. But two years of lust and late nights and finally she was saying goodbye.

Before linking up with Mr. President, her sex toy was the only dick she knew, and on occasion a one night stand would suffice but other than that John had been her everything.

He didn't tell her goodbye or nothing and neither did she. After hailing a cab to the nearest hotel, she checked in and crashed out. There weren't any emotions for someone who clearly had none for her. Miko would place the energy into her work and her family, hopefully love would find her one day but if not she wouldn't press it.

Once she woke up, she called Lo to get her so they could go out, "Catch a cab to my crib your clothes are here, I know you wasn't wearing what you wore to the gun range?" Lo asked.

"You're right okay I'm on the way" she told her and disconnected the call.

Miko caught a cab to Lo's house and the loud music blaring from outside the door told her that Lo was pre-gaming for tonight.

Lo opened the door with a terry towel around her thick body and half of her face done, "It's wine and shit in there" she told Miko and went back to the bathroom.

Miko fixed her a glass of wine and snatched a piece of cheese off the tray before going to fumble through her overnight bag to find something to wear. Before she made it to New York, Lo told her they were going out to see the same band they saw on her birthday, apparently, the girl was slowly blowing up and these were her last few local shows.

Miko stepped into the bathroom, naked as the day she was born, "Girl I don't want to see your white ass," Lo teased.

"Korean but whatever" she joked back and stepped into the shower stall and turned the water on.

"So girl you know I got a million and one questions" Lo told her.

Miko acted as if she couldn't hear her, as she bathed her body.

"How long you been fucking him? I always thought he was handsome. I voted for him too, girl did you know that his daughter-"

Miko cut her off, "Lauren please not tonight please" she asked.

Lo put the eye shadow brush on the bathroom counter, she heard that voice one too many times, and it matched hers perfectly.

"I'll let you shower in peace" she told Miko kindly, left the bathroom, and closed the door

Miko dropped to her knees and wept.

She hated crying and being emotional but now she was alone? There was no one to compliment her even when she was looking a hot mess.

She wouldn't be kissed or held even it was only for thirty minutes sometimes or sometimes less.

Why was it so hard for her to see that settling for not even half of what she deserved was beneath her.

She had reached a level of comfortably and had grown okay with what she was getting and that wasn't much of nothing.

She would rather settle for being a piece of pussy than keeping herself together for the man who rightfully deserved her.

Being alone did not mean you were lonely.

Many women failed to realize this that their singleness is a period in your life that they should openly embrace.

Don't shy away from being by yourself; learn yourself during this time, so when someone does finally come along it's not the highlight of your life. We as women hurriedly jump into relationships in fear of being alone on those rainy nights and holidays, and ignore the fact that we aren't even happy.

How do you fake happiness just so you don't have to sleep alone at night? What planet do we come from where this is deemed acceptable?

It's okay to date yourself, it's okay to spoil yourself, and it's even more okay to expect more for yourself. Raising your standards and reevaluating your morals doesn't mean your bourgeois it simply means that you are aware of who you are and what you expect from a man. Be you and make no apologies for it.

 The right man will come along one day and meet all your needs and more.

Once the water ran cold, Miko pulled it together and stepped out.

She wrapped a towel around her body and went into the kitchen to get her wine glass.

Lo was jamming to Anita Baker and painting her big toe,

"I was thinking," she said once she saw Miko

"Let's just stay here tonight and get drunk," she suggested

Miko loved the sound of that, Lo was the party girl whereas Miko would have a drink or two then go sit at the bar once her dogs started barking and she would watch Lo work the room the whole night, laughing and dancing the whole night

"What about the show, I thought your friend was performing?" Miko asked.

Lo told her, "It's all weekend show before she goes to London"

"Wow okay so we can go tomorrow," she said

Lo nodded her head, "Yep bring that bottle here girl"

Miko smiled, she appreciated her friend trying to cheer her up because she really needed it right now.

Hours later, every wine bottle was emptied and the little food she did have was now gone.

"You know I'm not perfect but I can tell you that I think you're amazing" Lo's voice slurred.

Miko laid on the floor, face up.

"Well why am I alone?" she asked.

"Cussssss you mean acting, like when we was at the club that fine ass nigga with the blonde dreads was staring at you and you didn't even notice him" she told her.

Miko sat up, "Who?"

Lo laughed and palmed her face, "You see what I mean?" she shook her head.

"You need to drop that zero and get with a hero," Lo told her.

Miko's drunk ass then asked, "Who is the hero?"

Lo busted out laughing, "Girl carry your ass to bed I don't know who the hero is but when you find him tell I need a man too"

Miko rolled over so she could get up, "You got a man"

Lo said, "No I don't"

Miko pointed her finger at Lo once she was on her feet, her hair was all over her face and her eyes were lower than they already were.

"It's not what you think it is" Lo told her seriously.

If she could be without him, she would. However, it was as if he was a drug that no rehab could get rid of.

Miko stumbled to bed but once she made it, she fell face forward and crashed.

The next morning, Miko was up and sitting at the bar on her laptop, making sure things were taken care of on behalf of the President. She found it amusing that he wanted to whisk his wife away for a romantic getaway considering he had his hand up her dress less than twelve hours ago. But when the email came through for her to book a presidential suite along with dinner and shit, she did it with a smile and even went as far as too schedule them a couple's massage.

Lo came out of the room, "'You working?" she asked with a yawn.

"Almost done," Miko told her.

Lo put a pot of coffee on and said, "Girl I was knocked out last night"

"Yes it's time for a two bedroom you sleep too wild," she laughed.

"Bitch I know you ain't talking" Lo shook her head.

"I made bacon and eggs," Miko told Lo.

She turned around and saw the plate of food, the eggs were runny and the bacon looked microwave.

Lo forgot that Miko was Korean sometimes but whenever she saw her attempt to cook food other than Korean food, she was quickly reminded.

"Coffee will do," she mumbled.

Miko was so into her work that she didn't even notice Lo.

"Let me know when you done I wanna go shopping for tonight" she said.

"What were you going to wear last night?" Miko's cheap ass asked.

"I'm not in the mood to wear that no more," she told her.

Miko shook her head Lo spent money like it was going out of style but what she needed to do was cop her a new crib, her condo was nice but it was small.

Lauren was a grown ass woman that loved to entertain; her house wasn't big enough for more than two people at a time.

Miko was starting to think that the party scene is where Lo felt alive and important, when they were out in other public places that didn't involve alcohol she didn't act that way.

Lauren was reserved, quiet and almost nervous acting. After she finished working, she went to get Lo; they both slipped on yoga pants and sneakers and headed to the mall.

"You're not getting anything?" Lo asked.

"I bought clothes with me," she told her.

Lo said, "Try this on"

Miko shook her head, "I have something to wear," she told her again.

Lo gave up on trying to get her to shop and she ended up buying more than one outfit for tonight.

Once she was done, fucking the mall up, they went back to her apartment to drop her bags off and decided to walk and grab lunch.

"Let's go in here I never even seen this place before" Lo pulled Miko into a small and quaint restaurant.

It ended up being a pleasant experience and the food was delectable.

"I'm sleepy now" Lo yawned

"Me and you both" she said.

They both agreed on sleeping the day away until it was time for them to get dressed to go the show tonight. Hours later, Miko stepped onto the scene in denim-distressed jeans and a white v-neck, she went for a simple yet plush look, and she wore a rose gold chain and a gold watch. The nude pumps she wore complimented the ensemble along with her wild hair that she teased to look even crazier.

As usual, she wore dark lipstick and mascara and eyeliner, she could care less for makeup.

On the other hand, Lo who had a natural beautiful look had a full face of makeup on and her hair pressed bone straight. She wore a mini plum colored dress with six-inch heels to match; those two together had shut the scene down without even trying.

It wasn't too often you saw a tall Korean girl and she was dressed nice? But, Miko was of rare breed. Lo escorted her into VIP before promising she would be right back with their drinks.

Miko crossed her leg and got comfortable, she was thankful for Lo knowing damn near all of the club owners, they never stood in line nor did they have to be in the overcrowded areas of the club.

VIP was spacious and airy.

Lo returned with a server in tow, she carried a bucket with a sparkler.

"Sit it right here thanks boo" she told the girl and tipped her a hundred dollar bill

Miko always saw Lo spending money like it was nothing, she wanted to ask her if The Underworld came crumbling down what was her back-up plan. Lauren was a college graduate but she wasn't really putting her degree to use. Miko would be holding on to her good ass job and its good ass benefits until the age of retirement approached or she was fired.

Being that she did a damn good job at holding her position down she doubted she would be fired any time soon but if it did come to that, she had so much money saved up, she would be okay for at least two years if needed be.

The DJ announced that India Rose would be coming to the stage in two minutes, Lo clapped her hands happily.

"I'm rooting for her, I've seen her grind it out for so long she deserves everything coming to her," Lo said.

Miko wondered if she would have taken playing the piano more seriously, could she have been famous or traveling the world by now?

She was too scared to step out on faith and be the Korean girl who played classical piano so she went for the safe job and was okay with that. It was only every now and then did she wonder the what-ifs.

Once India Rose came to the stage along with her band, Lo whispered into Miko's ear, "That's the dude I was telling you about, the one that was looking at you"

Miko got a good look at him; well as good as she could consider there was tons of smoke coming out of different machines to add special effects to her show.

"I can see that he has dreads though" she commented.

Lo said, "He fine as hell"

Miko shook her head she wouldn't be saying he was fine until she saw him up close and personal.

The show was amazing and Miko made a mental note to get her album this week. A person couldn't deny the girl's raw talent and her deep voice put you in the mind of Mahalia Jackson. But with a modern twist and Lo told her that she wrote all of her own songs, which was an added bonus. Miko loved originality and creativity, she had both and so did Lo.

An hour or so later, India Rose came to their section with her arms wide-open telling Lo thank you for everything. Miko didn't know what she was referring too.

India came and gave her a hug saying that she remembered her.

Lo's match-making ass spoke up and said, "What's your drummer's name?"

India eyed Lo, "Nash and he's single"

Lo laughed, she wouldn't put Miko out there like that but Lo wasn't interested, her heart already belonged to someone.

"Come on" Lo said, pulling Miko towards the ledge of the VIP area where Nash and someone else was standing.

"Nash you did so good out there tonight" Lo started the conversation.

He took a sip of whatever he was drinking and then said, "Sorry I'm feeling dehydrated, but thank you," he told her. Miko loved how raspy his throat was, you would have thought he was the one that had just finished performing but little did people know he wrote the majority of India's songs so when she sung on stage he liked to sing too even if he was just *"her drummer boy"*

Nash could sing just about any note and play every instrument on stage, he had taught himself to be good at everything in relations to music.

"I'm Nash, Miss Lady how are you?" he turned his attention to Miko. Lo was surprised that she didn't have to do the formal introductions.

Miko smiled, keeping it cordial, "I'm good, Miko" she told him since he didn't ask for her name.

"And I'm Lo" Lo butted in.

Nash held his hand out, "it's a pleasure to meet you Miko...and Lo," he laughed and so did they.

"Can I get you anything to drink?" he asked her.

"No we have plenty of bottles I should be asking you do you need anything" she teased.

"I really want some tea my throat is killing me" he admitted.

"I know how that can be," she told him.

The music was loud in the club so he came closer and asked her to repeat what she had just said.

"I couldn't hear you," he said.

Once she got a whiff of his cologne that was all that had to happen before she realized he was as sexy as Lo told her he was.

He was tall in stature; his shoulders were broad, from what she could see tattoos adorned every inch of skin on his body. He had the body of a running back, his dreads graced his shoulders, and the front of his dreads was honey blonde and jet-black. They reminded Miko of curly fries in the way he had them styled.

Miko loved how tight his eyes were they were similar to hers, he had diamond caps on the bottom row of his teeth.

The gages in his earlobes were something she wasn't familiar with but it was a turn-on in a skateboard, rock star way.

He wore skinny jeans and a long t-shirt and black combat boots.

"I said I know how that can be" she stood on her tippy toes in her heels. Although Miko was tall, she didn't come close to Nash's height. She spoke into his ear using, her tongue touched his ear but it wasn't on purpose, in reflex, it caused Nash to touch her waist.

He looked down at her and smiled, causing her to blush. Lo caught them looking at each other as if they were lost lovers, she let them have their moment and went back over to India and the others.

"I've had my eye on you" he bent down and confessed. Miko said, "So I've heard"

The two stole a few more lustful glances at each other before pulling away. Miko went to enjoy the rest of her night with Lo and her people.

Nash turned around and turnt up, he finally had the conversation with the girl of his dreams.

When the night ended, he came back towards the VIP section to get Miko's number but she was long gone.

He decided to not trip because when the time was right it would happen.

After making his way backstage to receive his cut for the night, he would be heading home.

He counted the money twice thinking that maybe a few hundred slipped through his hands, "Where is the rest of my money?" he asked India's manager.

"Talk to India" he told him nonchalantly.

"Man don't fuck with me tonight, rent is due in the morning," he yelled.

"Aye man I said talk to India" he yelled right back.

All eyes were on him so he decided to clear out before he acted an ass.

He dropped his drums off at the only person he trusted with his life and that was his mama.

After catching a cab and walking up a few blocks, Nash turned his head and made sure the coast was clear before he pulled the ski mask out and took his gun off safety. He was tired of robbing people but bills didn't stop coming and him playing the drums wasn't paying enough.

He picked the lock at the back door of a nice upscale town house where he hoped to find a few things to pick pocket. In hopes of reselling it tomorrow on the street or at the pawnshop.

Nash was in and out in less than twenty minutes with more than enough shit to profit of it.

This wouldn't be his life forever; he told himself that as he ran for his freedom once he heard a man coming down the sidewalk after him.

He had plans to be the next biggest rapper/singer and he knew that one day very soon he would have to step out on faith and stop playing the background of his selfish ass ex-girlfriend, India Rose.

Chapter 5

"I don't understand how yall been staying afloat this long, this is so unorganized! So you're telling me that whatever someone tells you they made for the month, you believe them?" Miko asked her brother.

He sat back in his chair and looked at her, she was visiting for the weekend. Something she seemed to do every weekend since they came into contact.

Miko was sitting on the floor with her pajamas on and a cup of coffee right next to her. Her hair was pulled up in a bun and the Tory Burch glasses she wore sat on the top of her nose.

"It's a loyalty thing sis," he told her.

Miko's face was scrunched up; she was still trying to understand this whole Underworld thing.

"So you're telling me if I say I made two hundred thousand dollars this month when I really made two hundred and eighty thousand dollars you're going to say okay cool?" she asked for clarification.

He shook his head, "It's not like that, Mary Jane tells us how much you copped and that's what we should get back at the end of the month. We get 40%," he told her.

Malachi knew he trusted his sister because this was something he didn't even discuss with his wife.

"But what if they steal then what?" she asked.

Malachi touched his temple, the shit wasn't rocket science. "What do you suggest Miko?" he questioned.

She hesitated and chewed on the tip of a pen before telling him; "This is what I use for the president" she told him and turned her laptop around as if she was just waiting on him to ask.

Malachi got down on the floor and put the laptop on his lap, "Explain this to me"

All he saw was a bunch of graphs and lines.

"I input the data mainly numbers and proposed dates and stuff and then at the month with receipts and such I add it here" she pointed around the computer.

"What's this red line?" he asked.

"Over the budget, like him taking his wife to Paris or to the mountains random shit like that," she explained.

"And how would this help us?" he didn't get it.

Miko laughed, "A whole lot"

"Well handle it I'll tell Nas to up your pay," he said nonchalantly.

Miko shook her head, "Oh no I'll teach someone else for you though"

"Why you can't do it?" he asked.

"Because I have a job and budgets and stuff are tedious, I'll never sleep" she refused to get her hands tied up with The Underworld

Miko liked her one little simple task that only occurred once a month, it was the easiest check she ever obtained.

"Just think about it no pressure," he said.

Miko told him okay but she knew it was nothing to ponder over; she wasn't doing it point blank period.

If she were to ever be caught with those files on her computer, her life would be completely over.

 She couldn't risk her freedom like that, bad enough she had the government mixed in with their bullshit.

"So you're not scared of getting caught?" she finally asked her older brother.

"I don't live in fear, that's how you get caught" he schooled her.

"But the thought never crosses your mind?" she pressed him to open up and keep it real.

"This isn't something we sat around the playground and put together, it was carefully thought out, trust me," he told her.

Before she could retort his response, the elevator had chimed and all of the kids were running towards their father with a tired Jade in tow.

Malachi stood to his feet and scooped his daughter in his arms, "Hey kiddos" he said happily.

Jade spoke to Miko and reached up to kiss Malachi on the cheek before going to their bedroom.

"I'll be back" he told Miko and followed jade.

Miko went back to work, she didn't plan to spend her entire Saturday afternoon sending emails back and forth to the team, her weekends were her weekends and in all truth, the things they were asking her could wait until Monday.

The President was golfing for the weekend so there wasn't anything that needed her instant attention. Miko phoned Lo to see if she wanted to do dinner tonight but she didn't answer.

When Malachi returned to the living room, she asked him had he spoken to her.

"You talk to Lo way more than any of us" he chuckled.

"I like Lo, she's like my best friend," Miko said happily.

"You're too old to be making friends," he said in a serious tone.

Miko wasn't stunting what her brother was saying so she changed the subject.

"What are you doing tonight?"

He turned the television on and told her, "What I'm doing now, absolutely nothing"

She smacked her lips; she should've stayed in DC for the weekend and caught up on some reading.

"But tomorrow I'm going to see my pops you should come with me" he suggested.

Miko quickly told him "No thank you, have fun"

"Just come it will be cool I promise" Malachi tried to pursue her but she wasn't fazed at all.

"No" she told him with finality on his voice.

"I hope you don't regret not having a relationship with your father," he added.

She looked at him not believing he pulled the regret card on her, "he should regret turning his back on my mother" Miko snapped and got up and went to the room that Jade basically turned into her room for when she visited.

She had been up since early that morning so it was definitely time for a nap. Miko didn't even allow her brother to upset her, before she knew it sleep had succumbed her.

The next morning Miko was up, dressed, and sitting at the bar, just thinking.

When Malachi came into the kitchen he was surprised to see his sister, she didn't come out the room at all yesterday even when the kids knocked on the door and asked her if she wanted dinner.

"I'm sure you're hungry" he joked.

"I don't have much of an appetite" she didn't join in on the laugh.

"Why you sitting here in the dark" he asked, turning on a few more lights.

"When you found out about me what did you say to your father?" she questioned.

Malachi sighed, "That's not really how it went," he told her.

"Well how did it go because I'm twenty five years old and I've never met this man but all of a sudden he wants a relationship with me?" she shouted.

Malachi silenced her, "My children and wife are sleeping lower your voice in my house"

Miko turned from him; she was getting emotional and didn't want too.

She didn't care that his kids were sleeping, there were plenty of nights that she couldn't sleep too worried about her where her mama was.

Malachi had no idea the life she lived and she really believed her mother's actions are the reason she behaved the way she did when it came to men.

"Let's just get this over with" she mumbled and slid off the bar stool.

Malachi was surprised, "you're going with me?" he asked.

"Yeah just this one time" she told him.

He nodded his head and snatched his keys up, "I'm driving today," he told her.

It was very rare that Malachi drove around the city since he preferred to be chauffeured.

Miko slept the entire way to the prison, which was cool with Malachi; he was hoping that she didn't have any more questions about their father. He wasn't comfortable taking the heat for his daddy; he was the one that should be in the hot seat not him.

Since finding out about Miko he had been nothing but nice and sweet to her, treating her just like he treated Melissa.

Once they made the long drive to the jail, her palms began to sweat and so did her underarms and forehead.

Miko had never been to a jail before and once they were cleared by security to enter the visitation room she told herself she never wanted to come back. The smell was horrendous, the area was tight and confined and the walls looked as if they had grime and shit plastered on them.

She would be taking a long hot shower as soon as she got back to the city.

Malachi asked if she wanted anything from the vending machine while they waited on their dad to come out and she told him, hell no

"Suit yourself sis" he told her, went to get powdered donuts, a bag of chips, and bottled water.

As soon as he made it back to the bench, their father arrived.

She looked at him for a few seconds, maybe two to three minutes or so. Staring. Contemplating. Wondering. She was perplexed and completely astonished.

"I look nothing like you," she finally blurted out.

Malachi and Maxwell busted out laughing.

"Well your mama genes were stronger than mines baby girl," he said, with a toothpick hanging out his mouth.

"Why don't I have your last name?" she asked him.

Maxwell cracked his neck, "I was a lil lying mother fucker back in the day, and gave your mama my homeboy's name, last name Sanderson" he told her.

Miko stared down at his hands; they were full of sores and bruises. She could tell he had a hard life, but that still wasn't an excuse to not stand up and be a man. The least he could've done was give her mother the right last name. She hated to have just been given some random ass last name, as if she was a nobody. But growing, up that's exactly how she felt.

"How are you? Your big brother treating you good?" he asked.

She nodded her head, "He's great"

Malachi smiled.

"How is your mama?" Maxwell questioned.

"She's good, works a lot," she added.

Maxwell raised an eyebrow, she quickly told him, "At a hotel"

Her mother had put her old life behind her once Miko got a little bit older and was able to work as well to handle bills and other things around the house.

"Oh okay that's good, she probably can't stand me but tell her I said hey" he told her.

Miko nodded her head, she wasn't telling her mother shit.

"So, no kids no husband?" Maxwell asked.

"My job is my child," she told him seriously.

"Yeah Chi told me you work for that cracker" he grunted.

She rolled her eyes, she hated racist terms such as nigga, and cracker, gringo, and rice cake...she didn't talk like that.

Miko was raised in the slums of DC, there were all kinds of people on her block, which is why she didn't have a preference on men, and cute was cute in her eyes.

"Pops I think Jade is pregnant again" Malachi changed the subject, knowing how quick Miko could flip the script.

Maxwell smiled, "You popping em' out ain't ya son? Yeah you got that from ya grand daddy"

Malachi laughed, "Man I want a house full"

She just sat there, staring at the man who was her father.

She used to dream about her daddy as a little girl, wondering did he think about her just as much as she thought of him but looking at him....years later...finally. Nothing magical happened.

Miko didn't have any emotion, no happiness, no joy, and no resentment.

She realized that she didn't give a fuck; she turned out just fine without him.

She sat in silence for the duration of the visit but she wasn't rude about it, whenever they included her, in the conversation she spoke up but other than that, she sat there, checking the clock on the low.

Finally, the visit came to an end. Her father reached over for a hug and Miko had to refrain from smacking his arms away.

Once they made it back to Malachi's condominium, she went to gather her things. She needed some space and a drink

"Where you going?" Malachi asked

Jade then said, "I'm making spaghetti for dinner"

"I'm going to head on back I found an earlier flight" she lied.

Malachi stood and told her, "I'll take you to the airport then"

She quickly told him "My cab is already downstairs"

Malachi asked, "Are you sure sis?"

She nodded her head and went to kiss Jade on the cheek and hugged Malachi, "I'll call you this week" she told him and left quickly with her overnight bag over her shoulder.

Miko hopped in the cab and gave them Lo's address, she didn't answer the phone last night but Miko had nowhere else to go until it was time for her flight.

Once she got off the elevator, she knocked on the door that belonged to and waited on her to come to the door.

Minutes later, she was about to just walk away until the door opened and she was face to face with Nasir.

He turned around and looked at Lo, she asked him "What you looking at me like that for?"

"Lauren I've been calling you" Miko spoke up.

Lo came in open view, "What are you doing here?" she asked.

"You didn't hear me knocking?" Miko questioned.

She looked at her body, "Do it look we could have heard you" she snapped.

Nasir told her, "I'll hit you later" he didn't even bother speaking too Miko and she thought that was rude.

She bypassed him and went into the house.

"Oh yes come on in girl, sorry it smells like hot sex in here" She said sarcastically.

Miko was steaming and Lo didn't even notice.

Lo locked the door and went to take a shower.

Miko took a seat on the couch and pulled a book out of her carry-on.

When Lo returned she was now dressed in yoga pants and a NYU collegiate t-shirt.

"Look we cool and all, I love you like a sister but don't ever come to my house without calling first" she told her straight up.

Miko slammed her book close, "I've been calling you all weekend, what happened to us going to the Tapas bar you found. You're the one that told me to come up this weekend then I get here and no call from you. The least you could have done was tell me you were busy I would have done that for you" she snapped.

"Okay first of all, you not my man or my mama I don't owe you no fucking explanation I'm a grown ass woman," she told her in defense.

"You're missing my whole point, it's the principle you left me hanging," Miko told her.

"We not in the tenth grade bitch if I'm getting some dick I'm getting some dick," she said...

Miko didn't like the tone Lo was taking her or the things she was saying, it was as if she was talking to a completely new person, not the cool and easygoing Lo she had been hanging with for the past few months.

"What is wrong with you?" Miko asked.

"What's wrong with you? You don't just come to somebody's house. You don't know who I had over here," Lo told her, with her hands on her hips.

"I asked you about him and you looked me in my eyes and lied" Miko didn't like that at all.

"It's not your business Miko and I'm going to leave it at that"

"But I asked you" she said again.

"It's not your business"

"You made all those jokes about me and John," she added.

Lo laughed, "Ohh you think we on the same page, you thought we had something in common? Let me tell you something. You'll be the next Monica Lewinsky if you don't leave that man alone. Nasir ain't the President of the United States," she told her.

"But he has a woman, don't point the finger" Miko shot up from the couch.

She was nobody's punk and wouldn't allow Lo to treat her as such.

"Let me ask you this, what are you getting from fucking the President?"

"I have my own money," Miko told her quickly.

"It's not even about the money boo; you ain't even got the man heart. You just fucking to be fucking" Lo shook her head.

"And you and Nasir are what? Planning to run away and be together?" Miko asked sarcastically

Lo was delusional, it was obvious.

"You don't know what the fuck we have going on, you have no idea!" she spoke out of anger.

"But no seriously, tell me what are yall doing so different. Because I don't see you in a mansion" Miko spat.

Lo seethed, "Get the fuck out of my house bitch" she yelled

"My pleasure" Miko told her and snatched up her shit and walked right out.

Lo fell to the floor and held her heart, she hated the truth. It ate her up every single time and for that reason alone, no one knew about her and Nasir. It was the forbidden topic, the dirty secret. Speaking on Nasir King was like opening up Pandora's Box and she wasn't strong enough to deal with the naysayers opinions of him and her.

Miko walked out of Lo's building furious, with no other options she went to the airport and sat there until it was time for her to board.

∎∎∎

One more block
One more block

One more block

Nash repeated to himself, he just needed to make it to his cousin's car that he borrowed for the heist he was trying to pull off.

He heard the police officers behind him getting closer but he refused to slow, he was not going to jail.

Not only did he have a pocket full of stolen ID's but he had a warrant out for his arrest.

One more block.

Slap.

A Billy club slapped across his back sent him tumbling to the ground and before he knew it, handcuffs were clasped around his wrists.

Nash was so mad but there was no one to blame but himself.

He put himself into this predicament and when he was whisked away to prison and a month later was sentenced to a year in prison there was nothing he could do but do the time like a man.

Nash told himself that every day he was in jail it would be productive. Upon his release, he planned to launch his career as a solo artist

When he received the news that India Rose didn't waste any time replacing his position on the tour, he knew that it was time for him to remain loyal to himself.

India wasn't rich but she damn sure wasn't broke either, not once did she offer his mama any money to go towards a lawyer or to put his money on his books.

India and Nash had grown up together; she knew the struggle just as he.

Once she got a lil buzz around the city, Nash became a distant memory. Except when they were in the studio, that's when he would have all of her attention and that pussy on lock.

Nash was too blinded by what he thought was love to see that India wasn't stunting him at all. However, she was well aware that Nash was talented and he may have not had much of anything to offer a woman. But a girl like India, with a voice like hers along with a banging body, Nash had everything to give.

India used him for everything he had, including his brains for all of her marketing strategies to build her brand; she used his talent for beats and his creativity and passion for her songs.

Nash fucked up when he didn't make sure his name was on any of her paperwork. So as he sat in jail and she traveled the world slowly blowing up and climbing the Indy charts, making good money off the songs he put his blood, sweat and tears into.

Nash considered it all a lesson learned because once those songs became old, then what would she do.

The little money his mama and a few of his homies from the hood did muster up to send was spent on notebooks and pens. He filled notebooks up with all kinds of songs, love, rock, pop, R & B, and even a few gospel songs that he planned to sell one day.

Nash had a vision for his life and he was willing to do whatever it took to make sure it happened.

He dreamed of being famous and moving his mama out the hood, those were his two main goals.

This time in jail wasn't looked at as a setback but as time to prepare, because he knew that once he took off there was no looking back.

It would be on like popcorn and that little drummer boy that no one ever saw because India Rose was upfront, would soon be like the rose that grew from concrete.

He had a song that he had been working on for quite some time and it was about the struggle.

One day while he was outside on the yard, he asked one of the dudes, "Yo how this sound, I'm trying to get it like John Gotti, I got the money and the fame now all I need is a bitch to drive me"

"Aye that's dope youngin," one of the old heads told him

"You need to add that nigga Nasir to one of your lyrics," someone told him

Nash asked, "Who is that?" he was unfamiliar with the name

"This island nigga they say he got that work, he like the next big don to come out of New York" he told him.

"Ain't never heard of him, maybe he will make the album until then I'm using John Gotti" Nash joked.

"Yo son for real, that nigga the truth. He like a ghost or something you never see him nowhere but he out there" the lil dude told him.

"Well how you know him then" Nash questioned

"Man I used to run them streets I know everything," he said cockily

"I bet you do" Nash laughed and walked back to his cell.

He placed the notebook under his pillow, each time he would finish a notebook he would send them home to his mama for safekeeping.

He didn't need any of these jealous bums in here taking his shit and trying to get rich off his words.

Nash laid back and closed his eyes, envisioning billboards with his name on it and all kinds of celebrity shit.

The street life was behind him; no more pick pocketing and robbing folks

No more selling dime bags just to get a haircut and a Philly from the gas station. Nash wanted a nice a car and big crib.

The first step to achieving success was believing in yourself and that was one thing that he always lacked. He was never determined to win but that jail life would change your mind set.

Jail wasn't a place for a nigga like him, Nash had managed to dodge dodged jail his whole life and he was happy that they didn't find more shit on him.

He knew he deserved way more than a year in jail, which is why he was knocking those days out like a champion.

His cousin on his dad's side out in LA already promised to help him put a demo together but Nash wasn't leaving his lyrics in the hands of another person ever again.

He would be doing this shit all on his own, whatever free time he had was spent in the library reading up on copyright and entertainment law.

Nash refused to be one of those illiterate dumb broke niggas that eagerly signed on the dotted line because they were broke and hungry. He wanted the best deal but most importantly a fair deal and that's what the fuck he planned on getting.

"All I need in this life of sin" he rapped one of his favorite songs by one of his favorite rappers.

His mind traveled to Miko for a brief second. If the Lord were willing, he would run into her again, hopefully.

***

Miko closed her eyes as her fingers danced across the black and white keys on the old piano in her grandmother's living room.

It wasn't too often her family got together because everyone worked so much. They had just finished dinner on a Friday night when her grandmother asked her to play something for the family.

Everyone sat on the floor in the living room and watched Miko play.

Her grandmother smiled, she loved to hear Miko strum the keys especially since she rarely played anymore.

In high school, you couldn't keep Miko away from a piano.

"Okay I'm done" she said, her back was starting to hurt.

"Getting old," her mother teased.

Miko smiled, "Hardly"

Since turning the tender age of twenty-five, Miko had entered a different place mentally. She saw life differently; everything she did now took careful consideration.

She wasn't interested in wasting her time anymore; her spare time wasn't being spent in random hotel rooms waiting on the President to arrive. Meeting her brother was a breath of fresh air and she enjoyed bonding with her nieces and nephew.

Lo called her a few times claiming that she was hung over and wasn't thinking clearly, Miko told her there was no need for an apology since they both had crossed the line but she had kept her distance since the altercation.

She never had her hand in drama before or petty catfights and wouldn't start now. Miko was a grown ass woman with real life problems.

She was learning herself every day, it felt good to smile, and the smile wasn't covering up a frown.

Her grandmother motioned for her to come over and Miko went and sat near her.

"What's wrong?" she asked.

Her grandmother said, "Are you with child?"

Miko busted out laughing, "No maam, never" she had no plans of having any kids, her nieces and nephew were all she needed.

Her grandmother smiled and patted her thigh, "Yes you are"

Miko brushed her grandmother off, she wasn't pregnant and she knew that.

Kids weren't the last thing on her list but it damn sure wasn't the first, she had plans to travel more. There were some countries wanted to visit and now that she had the money, she planned on getting out and seeing the World through her own eyes.

Miko wanted to buy some land and build a few investment properties, her brother told her during their last conversation that his money made him money. She kept that with her and had been doing tons of research since then.

Her work phone rung loudly and Miko was surprised to hear it ring, she had just left work not too long ago.

She went to retrieve it from the mantel where she laid it along with her personal cell.

"Hello" she answered

"Report to the House stat" her supervisor told her.

"On the way" she said quickly and went to put her shoes back on.

"Is everything okay?" her cousin asked.

Miko nodded and said her goodbyes.

When she got in her car, she stopped and thought what could possibly be wrong.

None of the news applications that she had on her phone chimed to alert her of something going on so it couldn't have been anything too tragic.

She was still worried.

Oh my God what if I got caught.

She immediately called her brother, "Chi!" she said his name as soon as he answered.

"What up sis" he said coolly into the phone.

She pulled off her grandmother's block and onto the street so she could hit the highway and head towards the White House.

"I just got called into work for an emergency meeting," she told him.

"You're good," he told her.

"How do you know?" she asked, in panic mode.

"Because I do, call me as soon as you leave," he said.

Malachi wasn't one too talk much over the lines and Miko didn't know that.

"But Malachi-"the line clicked.

When she called him back, it went to voicemail.

Miko felt alone and deserted she had done their dirty work and now she was left to face the bullshit by herself.

She planned to leave a nasty voicemail on his phone until a text message came through from an unknown number but after she read it, she knew it was her brother, "YOU NEVER KNOW WHOSE LISTENING"

Miko calmed down and focused on the drive back to work. Once she checked in, she was told to go to the meeting room.

She could only recall one time when they had a meeting there and it was because the President's son was arrested for possession of marijuana.

Miko took a seat next to one of the press secretaries, "What's going on?" she whispered.

She shrugged her shoulders, "Who knows better be good though, I was sleep" she said.

Miko looked around but it looked as if everyone was clueless.

Minutes later, everyone stood when the President walked in, "Sit down" he barked.

She never seen him look so distraught, there was a purple bruise under his eye and his lip look busted.

He whispered into his Chief of Staff ear and he nodded his head then the President left the room.

Miko's heart stopped beating so fast; if this were about her, she would have been arrested.

It was obvious this situation had nothing to do with her and she was relieved.

The room was loud and phones were ringing off the hook, everyone sat in anticipation of the news.

Outside in the hallway, you could hear someone screaming and crying.

"No fuck you! John fuck you!" a woman wailed.

"Is that the first lady?" someone leaned ahead and asked Miko

She shook her head, "Doubt it"

The First Lady would never talk like that especially not in public; she was a woman of class and grace.

She was often linked to Eleanor Roosevelt in rankings and her beauty was comparable to Queen Diane.

But when the First Lady charged into the meeting room and scanned the area for someone in particular.

The woman who had been sleeping with her wife right under her nose.

"I don't know who she is personally but her name is Miko and she's sleeping with my husband," the First Lady said into the microphone.

Chapter 6

Staring at the television with her body plastered on the screen, she couldn't believe how fast everything went downward. Not only was she fired immediately but also it was as if she wore the Scarlet letter across her chest. People who she didn't even know were speaking on her as if they had been friends forever. She had watched interviews with her old roommate, even the woman that stayed across the hall from her had something to say. Miko had always been the quiet one; she stayed to herself and didn't bother anybody.

So why out of nowhere, she was a wild party girl who graduated college but her past followed her. They found all kinds of creepy pictures of her staring at college professors, innocent moments were now being twisted to make her look like the bad person here.

Not once did she see anyone ask the President did he like her or was it more than a fling, in fact, the President was being portrayed as the perfect person in the situation and that damn sure wasn't the case.

Hurt and embarrassed weren't even strong enough adjectives to describe how she was feeling at the time, Miko even contemplated suicide. Everywhere she went, even to the simplest places such as the grocery store and the gas station, people refused to service her.

She could understand if a sex video or something came to surface but a few sexy pictures had the world going crazy. Memes were being created in her name, all kinds of bullshit was occurring.

What hurt more than anything was that her mother hadn't answered the phone nor did she reach out to Miko to get her side of the story?

Her brother, Malachi called and suggested that she come to the city to getaway, apparently he had a house in the Hamptons that was fully furnished and move-in ready.

Miko wasn't even mad about the bullshit that was being displayed on every news outlet. The most devastating part about this whole ordeal was that she was now jobless. No, she wasn't broke or struggling but even with a perfect resume and being skilled the way she was in her job field no was one hiring a "Whore"

Even though she knew, she wasn't a hoe that's how they were portraying her.

She couldn't cry anymore, it had reached a point where she was having nosebleeds every other hour or so.

She just knew her blood pressure was out of the roof, she hadn't slept in days.

Five days ago, her world came tumbling down, Jade told her that this too would pass and sooner than later, something new would be being discussed on the news but Miko wanted to know when?

When would they stop showing her body on screens all across the United States?

Did anyone take in consideration that she had a family too? She assumed, since they thought she was happily fucking around with a married man she didn't have a reputation to uphold.

Miko shook her head and laid on her side on the couch, her condominium was freezing and she sat in darkness.

She couldn't believe this was happening to her, especially *AFTER* she had washed her hands with John.

A knock at the door took her out of her thoughts and she prayed that it wasn't reporter-asking questions.

As much money as she paid monthly to stay in the high-rise building, it shouldn't have been so easy for strangers to enter the building. On any other occasion, they would be arrested immediately, but her door had been knocked on more times these past few days than the year she had been staying there.

Questions asked such as, *"Is it true that your mother was a prostitute and your father a criminal?" Do you consider yourself*

an immigrant?" "Why would you come on to the President
knowing he was a married man, how foolish could you be?"
Miko wanted to tell those people to go ask the President
the same damn thing! He was a married man with vows.
She was a single woman technically free to do whatever
and whomever she chose, but apparently not the President
of the United States.

She made her way to the door and peeped through the hole
but was very surprised to see Mary Jane and Lo.

She opened the door and asked, "What are yall doing
here?"

Lo smiled and held up a bottle of Hennessy, "I bought the
strong shit wine wouldn't do" she teased since Miko swore
up and down she only drunk wine.

"And I bought some even stronger shit" Mary Jane added.
Miko moved from the doorway and allowed them access
into her home.

"Wow this is nice" Mary Jane praised the condominium
since that was her first time visiting.

"I thought you didn't leave your house?" Miko asked.

Lo busted out laughing because that shit was true.

Mary Jane said with sarcasm dripping from her voice, "Ha
ha that was solo funny"

Miko went to fill the ice bucket on the bar tray, in the
corner of her dining room, with ice.

"No pun intended, I appreciate you coming over," she told her honestly.

"And what about me?" Lo asked.

Miko ignored her; she still wasn't feeling Lo like that.

"Thank you for coming," Miko told her.

"I can only imagine how you feel right now," Mary Jane said sympathetically.

"They're painting me to be like this Marilyn Monroe chick," she said sadly.

Lo popped the bottle open and sat down on the couch, "Have you talked to him?"

Mary Jane wanted to know the answer to that question too; she looked at Miko for an answer.

"Of course not, he looked like a deer caught in headlights when she came in there and told his staff. I promise you I wasn't expecting her to say that," she said.

Miko hated thinking about how everything went down that day, she couldn't erase that moment of embarrassment no matter how hard she tried.

She was sitting there, running out of patience wondering what the fuck was going on, the only time they were summoned to The White House was in case of a real emergency. Emergency meaning terrorist attacks and shit like that.

Miko could have died a thousand deaths once she heard the whispering around her, her co-workers who she had grown to love all moved their seats, not wanting to be seen associated with the President's little slut bucket.

Miko stood to her feet and tried to explain the situation but a look in John's eyes silenced her.

What was crazy because she mistakenly took that look for sympathy and protection, she assumed that he was telling her that he would handle it but that's not what happened.

Miko wasn't even allowed to return to her office, she was escorted from the premises and her badges and tag were taken as well.

What put the icing on the cake was the First Lady coughed up the biggest glob of spit she could muster up and planted it right on Miko's left cheek.

Not only was it one of the biggest signs of disrespect but the fact that it came from the precious and perfect first lady spoke volumes.

The next day, headlines read, "First Lady spits on President's Mistress"

She was so disturbed by what had transpired along with the allegations against her name.

She was really going through it and every day it seemed as if it got worse.

"He's such a pussy," Lo said angrily.

Miko had called him so many names in the past thirty-six hours, she couldn't think of anything else mean or rude to say about him.

"I can't believe this happened to me," she mumbled.

Mary Jane sealed the blunt; "Well this will damn sure make you feel better love" she told her and lit it.

Mary Jane loved her weed; she didn't see how people made it through life and the bullshit that came along with it every day without being high.

She had been smoking since the tender age of twelve and would most likely smoke until she died.

"I don't smoke" Miko told her.

Lo said, "Hell me neither but today I do, I'm stressed"

"You stressed? No not you!" Miko said, she had never heard Lo complain before it was almost as if the girl woke up every day doing cartwheels.

"Yes, its pastor anniversary at my church and it's the one event my parents expect to see me at once a year" she said.

"What's the problem?" Mary Jane asked.

She wasn't big on girl talk but her heart went out to Miko and plus Lo was cool in her book.

"I'm like the black sheep of the family," she told them sadly.

Miko shook her head, "At least your family talks to you"

Mary Jane added, "*At least* yall got family"

She was in this cold world all by herself but was slowly coming around to The Underworld.

"I just don't feel like being asked a million questions" Lo laid back on the couch with the blunt in her mouth.

"I'll go with you I need church right now" Miko told her.

Lo sat up, "You will for real?' she was so happy and relieved.

Miko nodded her head, "I barely leave the house"

Lo said, "Girl my daddy gon' lay all kinds of holy oil on your head"

Mary Jane busted out laughing, "Chile hush"

Lo told them, "Honey I'm for real, growing up every time I told them something it was, go pray that's the devil"

"Do they know what you do?" Miko questioned.

"What do I do? I thought I planned events and ran a non-profit," she teased.

Mary Jane sighed, "Yeah and I'm living off of my grandmother's insurance policy"

Miko mumbled, "And I'm jobless"

Lo sat up and handed the blunt to Miko who hesitated before grabbing it.

"We are all blessed no matter the circumstances, its people in way worse situations than us," Lo said happily.

Miko asked Lo, "Do you think people recognize me?" once they made it to the Friday night revival.

"Girl of course they do," Lo responded.

Lo wouldn't pacify Miko at all, that's not the type of friend she was.

Once they walked into the church, Miko looked up and saw tall bulletins of a man and a wife, "Your dad is Pastor Dwayne Howard?" she asked surprisingly.

Lo nodded her head, "Who did you think he was?" She asked.

Miko thought to herself, *Not one of the biggest pastors in the world.*

Although, she was Korean and her mother was a Buddhist, the average American living in the United States and was born in the eighties knew whom Pastor Howard was. Not only did he create the term, mega-church, but also he was a very wealthy pastor at that. Pastor Howard was known for serving as the officiator of several weddings for celebrities and he offered counsel to the majority of the rich and famous. If you couldn't make it to the main church in Virginia, there were several other churches he owned spread across the states.

He had graced Essence, Jet, Ebony and even Forbes magazine covers, Oprah interviewed him a few times and he was the recipient of awards such as NAACP, Nobel Peace Prize and Humanitarian of the Year according to BET.

Pastor Howard had over millions of followers and Miko estimated at least a few thousand people in the church, which was also known as the dome.

They were escorted to the front row, Miko heard the whispers but she ignored them and so did Lo.

"Did you tell your family I was coming?" Miko asked, once they got closer.

Lo ignored her and slid down the row, bypassing her sisters and the stares, she kissed her mother's cheek and sat down with Miko doing the same.

The service was pleasant and Miko ended up being much more emotional than she predicted, for a second she felt like Lo's father was preaching to her.

He spoke on removing the mask and stepping into your destiny, those were two things that she struggled with and had struggled with since a child.

She wiped the falling tears from her face so was Lauren. When Pastor Howard said it was time for alter call she hesitated on going to the front, not wanting people to think she was begging God for forgiveness for her "sins"

Lo looked at her with eyeliner running down her face and asked, "You wanna go up there?"

Miko dropped her head in embarrassment, Lauren's older sister said, "Girl come get your breakthrough" and dragged Miko to the front of the altar, walking past other church members.

Miko was so nervous but once Lo's sister led her to the steps of the pulpit, it was as if the Spirit of God greeted her and she suddenly became overwhelmed with emotion and years of disappointing herself along with harboring her insecurities and her past came down on her and Miko cried for dear life.

She held her stomach as she wept and before she knew it, mothers of the church and even Lo's mother surrounded her and began to speak a language that she wasn't too familiar with, however whatever they were saying was working because Miko was feeling free by the second.

"Oh God, use her like never before" she heard someone shout behind her.

Miko wanted God to use her too; she just wanted the madness she found herself in to go away.

After church, the family had dinner at Lo's family estate, she was welcomed in as if she wasn't known as the "whore" of the century.

Dinner was pleasant and no one made her feel weird or disgusting, she was grateful for the love.

"So, Lauren how long will you be gracing with us with your presence?" her father asked.

Lo smiled and said, "Only for the weekend daddy"

"Busy with work sis?" her older brother asked.

Lauren nodded her head and placed a forkful of brussel sprouts in her mouth to keep from having to say anything else.

"So, Miko what are your plans now?" her father questioned.

She swallowed the air she was breathing, that was one thing she had yet to really think about. For now, money wasn't an issue but because she was such a pro-active person, she wanted to find something to do soon.

"I'm thinking about setting up a digital company and offer accounting and finance assistance from a private domain," she told him.

"Sounds good, technology is running the world right now," he said.

Lo mumbled, "Unfortunately"

"When are we meeting your significant other Lauren?" her mother asked.

Lo told her, "When I get one"

Miko wondered did Lo feel how she felt when it came to being with the President but she swore up and down that her and Nasir were different.

After dinner, the family went to the separate living quarters; tomorrow they were feeding the homeless before the workshop and second night of services.

Miko and Lo sat in her father's library, "I can't believe your dad is Pastor Howard" she beamed.

"Hell me neither" Lo mumbled.

"How was it growing up?" Miko asked.

"My life was under a magnifying glass, girl when graduation came I ran fast"

"Do you think you'll ever follow his footsteps?" Miko questioned.

Lo scrunched her face up, "No ma'am, my sisters and brothers got that covered enough for me"

Lo didn't desire the pastoral life nor did she knock it; she just had other plans in mind.

"They don't know about Nasir?" Miko asked.

Lo eyed her, she hated discussing her and Nas relationship and she could have swore she made that perfectly clear.

"Nobody does," she said in short.

Miko laughed, "You keep thinking that"

Lo eyes got big, "Who knows?"

Miko said, "Lauren! Have you seen the way he looks at you?"

Lo blushed, "I have but I didn't think other people noticed"

"Well I know for a fact my brother knows"

Lo shrugged her shoulders, "Girl what Malachi, Dr. Seuss ass don't know" she joked.

"What happened with yall?" Miko asked, really wanting to know what was up between the two.

"What do you mean?" Lo asked after taking a sip of her coffee.

Miko was more direct, "Why aren't yall together?"

Lo sighed, "Well I guess you haven't noticed Jordyn but he's with someone or whatever he wanna call it," she told Miko.

"Where does that leave you? Do you wanna talk to other people?" Miko asked.

Lo admitted, "It's complicated, like I'm okay with what we have because I'm not a clingy person, the days we go without seeing each other are okay with me and I've talked to dudes before…but it never works out its like Nasir always finds out"

Miko shook her head, "That's not fair to you though" she knew first-hand.

"Yeah I know but trust me once I get fed up with him I leave, I always do," she told Miko.

"You can do so much better I know I'm the wrong person to be giving advice but for real Lo," Miko told her.

Lo smiled and touched her hand, "Nasir is better you just don't know him like I do"

Miko decided to keep her comments to herself; women like Lo were what she called oblivious to reality and blind to what it really was.

Miko wouldn't waste her time preaching to a deaf and blind woman, which meant Lo didn't see Jordyn and she refused to hear the truth.

Miko had learned her lesson the hard and embarrassing way, which sadly resulted in a tarnished reputation and the loss of an amazing career, at the age of twenty-five. She would never in life settle again, in fact, a piece of meat dangling in between a man's legs was the last thing Miko wanted to see. Celibacy was about to become her lifestyle and all of the spare time she now had would be devoted to getting her shit together.

***

Miko held the door open as Malachi and Papa brought the last of her boxes in, "This is a nice ass crib, Demi need to come see this" Papa praised Miko's new home.

She told him thank you, movers were hired but there were a few things she didn't trust anyone other than herself and her brother to touch.

Moving to New York was not a hard decision to make, with her face still being fresh and pointed at around the D.C. area and her mother not having much to say to her, Miko packed her belongings up with the quickness.

She needed something new and fresh even if New York wasn't a drastic move to others, it was too her. D.C. was where she was born and raised and she truly loved her city but New York was much needed.

New York had tons of opportunities for her to take advantage of. Along with being closer to her family and conducting business with and for The Underworld would now be done in a quicker time frame.

She told her brother, "Thanks for everything Chi"

Malachi turned around and smiled at his sister, Miko was dressed comfortably in a jogging suit and tennis shoes, her hair was held high with a ponytail holder. She was a beautiful girl from what he saw; he just wished like most women…she saw what he saw when he looked at her.

The Underworld worried that business would decrease with Miko being fired or worse, they would trace her recent activity in a desperate attempt to press charges on her but nothing had happened….yet. Miko was smart enough to copy his schedule for the year to her email way before the scandal occurred.

She had a few connections still in the White House but told her brother that she wouldn't be reaching out to them on behalf of The Underworld, however she did pass their contact information along.

Malachi told her that Sasha was vetting the people on the list Miko gave them, and the goal was to find the perfect candidate to keep the ball rolling.

In the meantime, Miko had been "promoted" and she now worked for The Underworld full-time, handling pay roll and finances for distribution.

Miko was now directly involved in the everyday dealings of The Underworld. The good thing about her new job was that she would have no time to sit and ponder over her ruined career. The downside was the charges were now increased if they were to be caught. Miko was breaking so many damn laws it was ridiculous.

Her brother claimed that jail wasn't an option or in their view, he promised that this organization was run with class and discretion she just prayed that he was right.

She was upfront with her fear of prison and told him that "loyalty" wasn't something she struggled with especially when her freedom was involved. Malachi understood what she was saying and where she was coming from. Which wasn't the hood like the rest of them however, he told her to never repeat what she told him to anyone else.

Fear was like a drug habit in The Underworld, they needed people who had the heart and most importantly the hustle for this shit.

If little miss perfect preacher kid, Lauren could do this shit without no complaint then Miko should have been able to as well.

"You're welcome happy to have you closer," he told her truthfully.

Miko smiled at him and picked up a broom and began to sweep around the bar area in her new home.

The crib she copped was a big upgrade from the condo she had in D.C., it was the view and open kitchen space that captured her interest.

Lo had recommended a realtor to her and after a few days of looking, Miko signed a lease and had her keys the exact same day.

She knew that it would take her a few days to turn the house into a home, but with a candle lit and some good tunes, Miko would be done in no time.

The only thing she had to go buy was groceries and maybe a few toiletries. She also planned to purchase a baby grand piano similar to the one in her grandmother's house. Miko loved playing the piano and she planned on picking the hobby back up since she was now self-employed.

Once her brother and Papa left the home, she dug in the boxes labeled, Kitchen and pulled out a vintage bottle of wine.

She gave up on looking for her wine glasses and settled for a plastic red cup, after pouring her a drink she went to stand outside on the balcony.

The view was breath taking and she was looking forward to waking up early just to see the sunrise. Miko was trying to see the good in her current situation and moving to New York was the first step in getting her life together. The pieces of her puzzle were scattered but she had faith that things would find its way, things would somehow come together.

After the wind started to pick up, Miko went back into her condo and through the plastic up in the big bag of trash that sat by the door.

She took a deep breath and began unpacking the boxes, she told herself that if she sacrificed sleep for a few days, the house would be unpacked and settled in no time. Miko was one of those dedicated and determined type of individuals, she mentally accessed the house and placed rooms in order of importance and got to work.

A few days later, Miko was rushing home to get dressed. Her and Jade had plants to hit up an art gallery tonight but she had been out all day with Mary Jane.

Nasir insisted on Miko learning how certain things worked since she dealt with the money. He told her that she was now responsible for more and it was important that she learned how to eyeball the work and all kinds of other illegal hood shit that she really had no interest in. The bright side of her day was Mary Jane could cook her ass off and Miko had tasted all kinds of different foods for the first time.

When she parked in the lower level of the parking garage, a funny feeling entered the pit of her stomach but she told herself it was gas from all of the food she had indulged in today.

A truck came on the side of her and Miko stopped in her step wondering what the hell was going on, her heart beat increased and she knew that buying a gun would be on her to-do list for tomorrow if she made it out of whatever was about to happen dint kill her.

"Miko" a voice called her name.

Well, it wasn't just any voice; it was the voice, the devil's voice, the enemy's voice.

The reason for her destruction and semi-depression had said her name.

It didn't sound as pleasant as it used too.

Butterflies didn't fly, birds didn't chirp, she didn't blush or smile.

Her pussy didn't jump at the hearing of his voice.

In fact, she felt like she was about to throw up.

Her fingers balled into fists and the strap of her purse fell over her shoulder, Miko wasn't one of those always-angry women, nor was she a bitter person.

But for this selfish mother fucker to pull up on her as if it was nothing made her angry.

"What do you want?" she hissed.

"Let me talk to you honey" he insisted.

Miko shook her head, finally turning around to face the devil.

"You have some nerve," she told him, with tears of fire forming in her eyes.

John dropped his head she knew he wasn't too big of a dummy. The window was barely down so in case someone came off the elevator in the parking garage they wouldn't be able to notice who he was. The President of The United States of America of course.

"I need to talk to you, I've been calling you" he insisted.

"New number, new location new fucking life thanks to you" she snapped.

John told her, "She did that on purpose, she's trying to sabotage my legacy so she can run for senator when this is over"

Miko didn't give two flying fucks what the First Lady had up her sleeves, "Why are you telling me this?" she asked.

"I still want you, you're the one I want Miko," he told her.

Miko wondered why now? Never had he told her this sweet shit but now, oh now…he wanted to be her and she was the only he wanted.

She guessed that he was missing her pussy all of a sudden but she damn sure wasn't missing him.

"Oh well" she said nonchalantly

"Miko are you serious right now?" he was appalled.

"Are you serious? You can't even be seen with me, you ruined my life and not once did you stop your staff from dragging my name through the mud. Do you know what I've been through" she shouted.

He wanted to shush her but knowing Miko that would only make her talk louder.

John wasn't trying to bring too much attention to himself; he was already in the wrong place at the wrong time. In fact, he was ten minutes late to dinner with the governor of New York but when his favorite secret service agent spotted Miko he had to see her. John only needed a few minutes of her time, he was desperate to talk to her and possibly state his case and get her to see that they both were placed in a complicated situation.

His wife was on some spiteful shit and sadly, Miko was caught up in the cross fire.

"Miko forgive me," he begged.

But there was no sincerity in his voice and for that reason; she knew it was time for her to turn her back on him. She knew that she needed to leave his presence, walk into her home, and get dressed so that she could go spend time with the few family members that loved her. The family members that didn't judge her despite Miko telling them that the affair wasn't some made up scandal.

John didn't deserve her time or her attention so why was her feet still planted?

A small part of her enjoyed seeing him sweat and beg for her time, it was crazy how the tables had turned.

Miko questioned herself and what was she doing even considering taking him up to her home for just a few minutes.

John had lust in his eyes but no love in his voice.

She looked around the parking garage for anything out of the ordinary, cameras, reporters or any residents walking from their cars but it was empty.

Miko took a deep breath, shaking her head hoping that it would calm her hormones that were slowly rising.

She thought about the last time, she had some and it had been a minute, *What would a quickie do to hurt her?*

The worst had already been done, so now what?

Miko thought it was acceptable to climb her skinny ass in the back of the Escalade truck and lower her body onto the

President's penis. She didn't care that the secret service agents were in the front seat. The only thing on her mind was sex and getting her pussy fucked if only it was for a few minutes.

The president moaned loudly and so did Miko, the truck rocked and the smell of lust and infidelity lingered around the vehicle.

She climaxed and he did too, she grabbed her panties and looked at him once more before climbing out the truck and going into her home.

In the shower, she tried to beat herself up about what had just happened but the truth was she enjoyed it. Miko was actually looking forward to the President popping up on her again.

Chapter 7

"You got us fucked up! You're not the connect no more man what the fuck you think this is!" Papa roared across the table.

Spit flew from his mouth along with back-to-back insults and profane words, everyone was silent but in all truth, everything Papa said was the truth.

Miko took a deep breath she didn't expect her "simple request" of an increase on payment to cause all of this strife. But in her personal opinion, she really did feel like she was entitled to more than five hundred thousand dollars a month. She was risking her freedom on a daily basis and the charges were most likely piling up by the day if someone was watching them and building a case. The Underworld was an underground organization; this was a true statement indeed. But the people that they had employed were the ones really getting their hands dirty; people like Miko, Sasha and Mary Jane.

Lo was doing white-collar crime and if she was a little bit more smart, she would request more funds as well, what Lo failed to realize is that white-collar crimes were considered pre-meditated, which means that you were in your right mind while the crime was being committed.

There is no mercy whatsoever spared for crimes of this nature.

Lo had her hands in all kinds of illegal shit on behalf of The Underworld and in Miko's opinion she was risking her freedom for pointless shit, but again that wasn't her business. She was only here to look out for herself.

Malachi eyed his sister wondering why she didn't come to him first with her proposition. He was the one sticking his neck out for her. He was the one that requested her presence and membership into the Underworld. Now here she was looking greedy and very selfish.

Miko made more than anyone she ever knew, she made more than the president did too.

"Okay but you're not going to talk to me that way," Miko told Papa. She understood him not feeling what she was saying but to yell and curse at her.nah, she wasn't tolerating that at all.

"Man fuck that you really can leave!" Papa told her in a very heated tone.

He was so tired of people, new comers at that...laying low, watching, lurking, observing and in his opinion, plotting. He felt like now that Miko had been around the money, she did the books and handled payroll a few times so she felt compelled to want a bigger piece of the pie. But shit didn't work that way and over his dead mother fucking body would this fried rice-eating hoe get any more than she was already getting.

Sean cleared his throat; "I can see if you were still getting us the flash drive but you fucked that up for us" he spoke up.

Miko rolled her eyes; they had yet to let her affair with the President go.

Roderick suggested, "What exactly are you asking for? Maybe we can work something out"

Papa sat up in his chair, "My nigga that's not your call"

Miko snapped, "and it isn't yours either"

Papa eyes and cheeks turned red and Malachi now felt the need to step in, "Meek chill" he warned.

Miko looked at him with just as much frustration in her eyes as Papa had in his.

Sasha said, "I don't even get paid as much as you and I work harder than any of yall"

Mary Jane held her hand up, "Uh, speak for yourself cus I work all day every day" she let it be known.

Lo took a deep breath, she saw this conversation going in the wrong way really fast.

Malachi held his hands up to somewhat silence the room, "Let's all chill out, Miko you're not getting a raise Papa watch your mouth when you're talking to my sister" he said in one breath.

"Nah your sister need to watch her mother fucking mouth, coming in here demanding shit like we owe you something did you hear any of us ask for that five hundred back the month you got fired? Nah we ain't even do you like that. Cus that's not how we rock, we are family and when we say that shit we mean it," he told her straight up and everybody else nodded their head agreeing.

"I can understand where you're coming from…" Miko started to talk.

Nasir said, "Well then respect it and let's move on"

Miko knew not to say anything else, Nasir rarely talked so she knew to just sit back and shut the hell up at this point. The meeting continued but she was really ready to go at this point.

Once everything on the agenda was scratched off the list, Miko was the first out the door.

Malachi shook his head, he would make plans to go over to her crib later on in the week, his sister was on some other shit but being greedy wasn't cool.

She wasn't in a position to be asking for anything more than she was already getting and he prayed that the money wasn't getting to her.

"Watch your sister" Papa told him

Malachi said, "She alright I am going to holler at her though"

Sean said, "Hanging around Lo her ass gotta keep up"

Lo didn't appreciate his comment at all, "Mind your business" she stood to her feet and gathered her belongings.

She was going to a late dinner with her old college roommate who was in town tonight. Lo waved goodbye to everyone and left the meeting room.

Sasha and Mary Jane shortly followed, Papa said once it was just the men present.

"Sasha ass was about to come for your sister" he laughed.

Malachi said, "Stop instigating"

Sean laughed, "She was though for real, your sister started turning red"

Malachi didn't think anything they said was funny and plus his wife cooked his favorite so it was time for him to head out.

"I'll holler at y'all niggas later" he told them and dapped his brothers up before departing.

Nasir and Papa ended up being the last two to leave,

"What you about to get into?" Papa asked.

"Shit, a cigar and a drink" he told him, coolly.

"Cool cool" papa nodded his head.

"Aye" Nasir called out after Papa.

"You think she was wearing a wire?" Nasir questioned, it was just a mere thought nothing too major.

Papa shrugged his shoulders, "Doubted but I can have Sasha check on it"

Nasir held his chin, he didn't want to do anything behind Malachi's back especially since that was his sister but he wouldn't let anyone…not even Miko's lil' cute ass come in and tear down what took blood, sweat and tears to build.

"Yeah" Nasir told Papa, hopped in the back of the truck, and told his driver to take him home.

As he rode through the streets of New York City, he couldn't help but to feel disconnected. Nasir missed his home, his roots, and the island of St. Lucia. He missed the smell of salt water and taste of fish and coconut rice with fresh squeezed guava juice and most importantly, he missed his grandmother's soul and her wisdom and sound advice that only she could give him.

He missed the feeling of family but he wouldn't lie and say The Underworld hadn't become his sense of peace away from the island. That's why he would do anything to keep the demons away and the snitches too.

Once Lo made it home from her dinner, she dropped her keys into a small glass bowl that she had brought from Tiffany & Co. many years ago.

She went into her kitchen to grab a bottle of water and a fruit snack before going to room for the remainder of the night.

"You're home late," Nasir told her, once she entered her bedroom.

Lo stopped being surprised many years ago, Nasir would always find his way to her bed a few days out of the week and then sometimes he would go months without coming near. She had begun to play his game a long time ago.

"I told you earlier I was going to dinner," she told him, sitting the water on her nightstand and removing her heels followed by her clothing.

Nasir redirected his attention to Sports center. His chiseled chest and washboard abs were seen because he wore no shirt only silk boxers and white ankle socks.

The only piece of jewelry he wore was a gold chain around his neck, one that she had never seen him without.

"Come shower with me" she suggested but didn't wait for a response, assuming that he had an attitude about her coming in late.

Lo was a grown ass woman and although she didn't fuck around with other men, she still enjoyed life to the fullest because Nasir damn sure enjoyed his, with or without her at times.

A gust of cold air greeted her in the shower and she held her breath as Nasir entered the stall and held her body close to his chest.

"You looked nice tonight," he said, adding extra emphasis to the 't' in tonight.

"Hmm didn't think you noticed," she teased, knowing that he saw her.

"I always do even when you think I'm not watching I am" he enlightened her.

Lauren held her head back on his shoulder as he took the soap from her hands and ran it between her breast, down her stomach and against her thigh.

"Why are you here?" she questioned, not wanting to be too caught up in the moment.

It had a been a little while since they last shared intimacy and she told herself she wouldn't continue to give in to him so easy because Nasir was undeserving of her love, time, attention and loyalty too.

"Missed you" he admitted, biting into her shoulder blade.

"As you always do," she said sarcastically.

Nasir was tired of her snappy remarks. He pulled her around facing him and kissed her passionately. Leaving Lauren no other choice but to submit to his will and his way.

A small moan came from her throat and he told her, "What you moaning for?"

She winked and lowered herself to give him what she knew he loved. Head in the shower was her forte.

Before Lo could coat his dick with her lips, Nair pulled her back up and stared in her beautiful eyes.

"Do you think Miko is an informant?" he asked.

She now knew that was the reason he had joined her in the shower. Suddenly, her nipples went soft and her breathing decreased and pussy dried up.

She cocked her head to the side and ran her hands against his face.

"No I don't," she told him, truthfully.

Nasir couldn't be so sure.

"How do you know that?" he questioned.

"She loves us too much, me, her brother, I don't think she would do that. She wouldn't do that" Lo defended Miko.

"So why is she still seeing the President?" Nasir asked.

Lo stepped back in the shower, "She's not" she said.

Nasir smiled and went closer to her, "Oh yes she is"

"But why? After all of that stuff happened" Lo was now confused.

Nasir didn't want to talk about Miko anymore, "I don't know but just keep an eye on her for me babe" he asked and lifted her leg in the crook of her arm and slowly inserted his penis into Lo's vagina.

■ ■

Sasha, Mary Jane and Lo were sitting in Do, a pizza eatery in downtown Manhattan, their scheduled dinner date was at seven p.m. and here it was eight twenty and Miko had yet to arrive.

Lo took a peep at her Rolex watch once more before flagging a waitress down and ordering food for the table, they were already on their second round of drinks and would need food before they fucked the lining of their stomachs up.

"Is she coming?" Sasha asked.

It was Lo's idea for the women to start getting together and spending more time with each other and the one thing that Lo despised more than anything was tardiness. Years in the event planning business had her anxious. Lo was naturally a planner and she wanted things to always be done in decency and in order. More importantly, she respected a person's word. In her life, she learned that all you had was your word because it was bond.

Miko promised to ride with her to *Do* but cancelled on her ten minutes before she was supposed to be on the way to her house.

She then had yet to respond to a text message or answer the call.

"I can't believe I'm out on a Friday night" Mary Jane said, she wasn't too big on being out in public or even being around people but the chicks of the Underworld were cool as hell....so far.

"Hell me neither, my show came on tonight" Sasha agreed. Lo couldn't understand where either of them were coming from, she was in her twenties and was living life to the fullest. Lo loved the weekends in New York, she looked forward to going out and having her a good ole' time.

Miko greeted the group with a goofy look on her face. She took the seat across from Lo and Mary Jane and sat right next to Sasha.

'Sorry I'm late" she said nonchalantly.

Lo asked, "Are you really, sorry?"

Miko looked at her, "What's up with you?"

Sasha spoke up, "Bitch you almost two hours late"

"Yall could have ordered without me, I'm not even hungry" she spat.

Mary Jane said nothing but she did notice Miko's vibes and something was definitely off about her.

Lo said, "You have to be one of the dumbest bitches I know"

Sasha looked up from her wine glass and then looked at Miko because she knew good and damn well Lo wasn't talking to her.

Miko took a deep breath.

"You need to mind your business," she told Lo. She didn't know how Lo was able to put the pieces of the puzzle together and honestly, she didn't care. Miko was a grown ass woman and whatever she chose to do was her business. "No because your "business" affects everyone at this table and the ones that aren't. You are bringing heat to us and I'm not gon' let you fuck up my money," Lo snapped.

Miko wasn't about to let her do this to her, "What's your problem Lauren? Like seriously. Are you that mad because I was late to your little girls night in?"

Lo shook her head and laughed but shit wasn't funny, "No I'm not mad I pity you, I pity dumb bitches like you. You up here fucking this man after everything that he stood by a watched happen. He wasn't there to wipe your tears I was!" she told her.

"And whose wiping your tears when you see Nasir with Jordyn?" Miko threw the shade right back.

It was as if the entire restaurant went quiet when in fact, the night was still progressing around them.

Mary Jane dropped her head and Sasha's lips formed an "O", Miko had said the o*bvious* but damn…it was that one thing that no one discussed.

Lo closed her eyes and Mary Jane touched her thigh because it was shaking so fast but when Lo removed her hand, Mary Jane knew she was about to go the hell off. "Me and you are nothing alike," she told her.

Miko really thought something was wrong with Lo, in her eyes she believed that she was better than any other woman fucking around with another woman's man…when it fact her and Lo were just alike.

The president wasn't leaving his wife and Nasir damn sure wasn't leaving Jordyn.

"But we are Lauren, we really are" she said sarcastically and got up from the table and left.

Tears of anger rolled down Lo's cheeks, it wasn't even about the embarrassment or what she said about her and Nasir it was the fact that she had held her hand when she needed someone to be there for her. It felt like a slap in the face.

Miko was dancing with depression and struggling with suicide, updates on the scandal were still surfacing on the news, and every social media outlet there was.

As far as Lo knew, her family still wasn't talking to her and really, Miko had no one but Lauren. Yes, Malachi and Melissa were her siblings but they had their own lives to worry about. It was Lo who sat with her at night and made sure she ate and took a bath. It was Lo that prayed with her and kept her encouraged.

It was Lo that helped replace the girl's confidence and told her that the right man was coming for her. Lo felt like Miko had slapped her in the face.

Mary Jane said, "Sometimes we have to allow people to learn some lessons on their own"

Sasha then added, "You can bring a horse to water but you can't make them drink it, she gon' see boo"

Lo shook her head, she was done with Miko's ass and this time around.because paparazzi were watching. Reporters were on standby waiting on some shit to pop off, she wouldn't be there to help Miko and she meant that shit.

Miko straggled out of the pizza bar and caught a cab back to her home. She couldn't believe Lo tried to call her out like that.

She thought they were friends and on a few occasions, the word "best friend" had slipped from both of their lips.

In Miko's eyes, she felt like Lo was maybe jealous or envious but in reality, Lo pitied her.

Miko was settling and didn't even know it.

The president was making her all kinds of loose promises and giving her false hope, but the sad thing was Miko didn't even love him.

It didn't go farther than the physical for her, she enjoyed his sex nothing more or less. Miko wasn't looking for love or help, she was content with what they had and it was really okay with her.

It was John, the president, who whispered sweet nothings in her ear and Miko tried her hardest to tune them out.

The harder she tried to dodge him, the stronger his advances became.

The more she ignored his calls, the more he popped up unannounced.

In a weird way, it seemed as if the President was enjoying their cat and mouse game.

She warned him that things could get sticky all over again and maybe….they would be caught but he seemed to not care.

What Miko failed to realize was that he didn't care because in the public eye, he would be the good guy all over again. It would be Miko, who would be portrayed as the whore or mistress who couldn't leave the President alone.

Miko didn't stop to think about that, she was just caught up in…sex.

Her emotions got the best of her that night and four bottles of wine, a few shots of tequila and no food on her stomach had poor Miko running to the toilet the next morning throwing up her entire life.

As she laid over on the toilet bowl, she heaved and coughed

Her eyes caught a glimpse of the *Always* box of feminine pads, which caused her mind to ponder over her last period.

Damn it! Miko thought to herself.

When was the last time she even had a cycle? She couldn't remember.

After wiping her mouth and face from vomit, she struggled to stand which ended up bringing her back to her knees.

Miko gave up with wanting to get back in the bed and she crashed out on the cold floor in the middle of her bathroom.

Once she finally woke up the second time that Saturday afternoon, life seemed much easier to maneuver through. A hot shower and two Aleve pills did the trick of putting her body back together. Miko was out of the door and down to the local pharmacy, to pick up not one, or two…but three pregnancy tests.

She was still somewhat woozy from last night's turn up. She didn't notice the flashing camera lights of her purchasing ginger ale and pregnancy test.

The only thing on her mind was getting back home and under her covers.

Miko stared at the test not even surprised at what she saw; this was all of her fault.

She was being a hot ass in the pants, fucking Mr. President every chance she got, no condom, no pulling out or anything. Just getting dicked down in the heat of the moment.

There wasn't one emotion that she felt watching those two lines appear on the screen.

She went to call Lo but then remembered there stupid argument the night before. She knew that her mother wouldn't understand. She didn't want to call Malachi knowing he was probably with his wife and children.

Miko couldn't call John, she had to always wait until he called her, which was rare.

She then realized she was alone, on her own and with no one to hold her hand and get through this.

What was she getting through one might ask.

An ABORTION!

There was no way in living hell she would carry this child to full-term. She refused to wear the Scarlet letter and have her child be known as the bastard baby of the century. Nope, she wouldn't do it, she refused.

Without second thought, she decided to get an abortion first thing in the morning.

The next morning came and Miko was up and out the house.

She didn't allow her mind to ponder over child names, nursery ideas or any of that fairytale shit that most mothers thought about when they first found out they were carrying God's little blessing in their womb.

Miko was about to handle this little situation, as she called it through the night and find something productive to do with her life.

She was losing her momentum and needed to regain footing before she spiraled completely out of control.

Not really being in her mind because it was so much on her mental, she went to an abortion clinic outside of New York in a small and quaint town.

She assumed that since she wasn't in D.C. no one would recognize her but even with the hat, scarf and shades...she still stood out as the President's Mistress.

Miko had discussed over the phone before she disclosed her name and made the appointment to abort her child, the confidentiality of the clinic and she made it very clear that she didn't have a problem suing if something was to be leaked.

After the abortion procedure was complete and she had stayed the few hours at the clinic as she was instructed to do so, since she had no one there to assist her in getting up and going back home, Miko stayed at a hotel not too far from the clinic.

The next morning when she woke up and brushed her teeth, she turned the television on to drown at the sounds of lust and maybe love coming from the room next door. But when she saw face plastered on the screen for the second time in less than two months she quickly turned the television back off. she rather hear them moaning and fucking each other's brains out than to see the reporter say how Miko Sanderson, former White House employee and President's mistress was spotted buying pregnancy test and then the next day caught leaving an abortion clinic with a disgruntled face.

Miko laid back on the bed as tears filled her eyes and clouded her vision, what was she not getting from this? Did she not learn her lesson the first time?

She called down to the hotel front desk and requested an extra few nights. There was no way she was returning to her home, to only be bombarded with cameras and people all in her face asking her questions and disrespecting her. Miko's stomach was cramping and her panties were filled with blood from the abortion. She downed two Naproxen pills, laid down, and drifted off to sleep.

When she woke up, the sun was down and she was hungry.

She ordered pizza and went to take a bath, discarding the blood-filled bottoms and sheets. Her cell phone was lighting up to signify that she missed calls and texted messages.

Miko wasn't in the mood to talk and quite frankly too embarrassed to return anyone's calls. But one name tugged at her heart and without second-guessing her decision she clicked, call.

Three rings later, her mother's voice came over the line.

"Miko" her mother said in a very serious tone.

Miko wanted to cry, she hadn't heard her mother's voice in so long or her real name be called since she was a little girl.

"Yes mama" she said, happy to finally speak to her.

She knew her mother would come around, knowing that Miko needed her and needed their family's love and support at this time, it warmed her heart to know that God had answered her prayers the night before.

"You are embarrassing me please stop it Miko, stop messing with that man" her mother said in Korean and hung the phone up.

Miko gasped for air and held her stomach, not only was her body cramping but she felt her heart breaking as well. She was so hurt and felt like her mother had stabbed her back-to-back.

The tone she took with her was so icy and cold, she had no choice but to cry.

Miko was hurt and feeling abandoned, something had to give. She just didn't know what to do or who to turn too.

The only solution she now had was to run or die.

And Miko couldn't envision killing herself especially over something that she knew would one day pass.

She didn't want to take the sucker way out so she chose to run.

Miko had enough money to pay her rent up for a few months and take off, she needed to dip and get away.

It wasn't as if someone needed her at this time or wanted her around, she had no significant other, no real friends.

Her mother had basically just told her to fuck off, Miko got the wrong vibes from her father and her brother was too caught up in his own life.

Melissa was very open with her disappointment in Miko's actions and so was Lo. Miko didn't really have a relationship with Sasha or Mary Jane.

And of course, John was nowhere to be found.

She knew that one day she would laugh at how dumb and clueless she had been, but until then she cried for being so stupid and allowing this man to use her like a rag doll.

Miko was his personal sex slave and she now knew that he didn't care about her reputation or her well-being. She was nothing to the President, the rumors may have just been true, there were plenty before her and she was sure there would be more after her, but only she had been the dummy to allow him to degrade her by taking pictures and impregnating her.

Miko would consider this one of the greatest lessons learned. Love doesn't love anybody and sex isn't better than love.

She could fuck herself for all the bullshit she brought into her own life.

The will power to say no didn't exist.

She wasn't strong enough to fight the temptation or her raging hormones.

John wasn't there to promise her, "This too shall pass" as Lo had been.

Across the river, Lo and Nasir were cuddled up on the couch. They had just turned the television off because Lo couldn't stand to see them discuss Miko as if she was just this horrible person.

As mad as she was at Miko, her heart still went out to her and the fact that she most likely went through her abortion alone, saddened her. Unfortunately, this needed to happen so she could finally see what Lo was trying to her all along. The president didn't give a damn about her because if he did, none of this shit would have made the news. Now, look at her now…alone and embarrassed all over again.

"She just needs to go lay low in the Hamptons or something" Lo said.

Nasir shook his head, "The Hamptons ain't laying low' he told her.

"Well what do you suggest wise guy" she asked him.

Nasir pondered over the question and he thought deeply about where Miko could go for a few months to take the heat off her name and remove the strobe lights off her moves. Her decisions affected The Underworld, which in truth was the only thing he really cared about anyway. Bad press for her meant bad press for them and The Underworld needed to stay under the radar at all times, he had gave strict instructions for Miko to not go nowhere near Mary Jane's house and she wasn't to call or text any of them.

Nasir sat back on the couch and stretched his legs, "She needs to go to London for about six months"   .

"What's in London?" Lo asked.

Nasir said, "A new mindset and right about now that's what shorty need"

Chapter 8

Elizabeth Gilbert, author of the New York Times bestseller *Eat, Pray, Love*, "People think a soul mate is your perfect fit, and that's what everyone wants. But a true soul mate is a mirror, the person who shows you everything that is holding you back, the person who brings you to your own attention so you can change your life."

Miko had been reading that one passage daily in hopes that the words would somehow jump off the page and connect to her mental. The first few weeks on her hiatus were trying, she dealt with a plethora of emotions but after awhile she realized that the solitude was needed. Miko was able to learn herself and adapt to new surroundings. She was forced out of her comfort zone and with all the bullshit back in the states it was what she really needed at the time.

Her time in London had reached the thirty-day mark and in truth, she wasn't prepared to return home to the madness. Just when she had stopped crying and beating herself up for everything that happened, a month had gone by.

The suicide nights and depressing thoughts didn't go away over night but each day was better than the last, no one really knew her or they didn't care…she had yet to figure out which one it was.

Miko loved London, she ate well every day and put on an extra fifteen or twenty pounds but she loved every ounce of it. She was a tourist by day and artist at night. She had wrote so many songs during her free time in another country, if she had the courage she would have pursued a singing career but she really didn't have the vocal talent.

Miko reached out to her mother a few times but her cousins told her to respect her mother's request at that time, and that was to stay away.

Her brother called when his schedule allotted him too but for the most part, she was alone. It wasn't a bad thing anymore and Miko needed the time to herself.

When Nasir sent Lo over to her home with clear instructions to pack the things she couldn't live without and board the private plane. She didn't protest.

In fact, Miko didn't care where she was going she just knew she needed to escape and fast.

John had yet to reach out to her. She was unsure if it was because she changed her number or did her really cut her off.

Either way, Miko was moving forward in life.

Her brother promised her that her job was waiting on her when she got back but there would be decrease in her checks unless she could bring something else to the table when she sat down at it.

She knew that was all Papa's doing with his hateful self but she wouldn't argue or fuss, she was pretty sure no one else would be hiring her any time soon, so she had no choice but to accept whatever they were offering.

Miko still had tons of money saved up and a few million of it invested as well, she had never been a dummy when it came to her funds.

Growing up poor was now looked at as a good thing in her eyes because she valued a dollar and didn't believe in wasting money at all.

She woke up in the villa she had been staying in and opened the curtains.

One thing that she grown to love about London was the view. No matter what time it was or the weather, the view always astounded her.

Miko added traveling to her bucket list; she really wanted to see what else the world had to offer. She knew that if London was this beautiful, she could only imagine what other countries looked like.

After having a cup of coffee and eating a blueberry bagel, Miko grabbed her purse and headed out the house.

She walked up the street and around the corner and went to her favorite coffee shop. She spent her days walking around the small town where she was staying. Her closet was filled with linen pants, moccasins and cotton t-shirts. Everyone considered London to be a fashion place, which it was, but there were some people who dressed casual every day. Miko was one of those people.

Taking the seat she normally sat in and pulling out her newest obsession, a book written by Enitan Beroala. Lo suggested that she read it and so far, she hadn't been able to put it down.

Miko sat her glasses on her nose and got lost in the chapters.

An hour or so later, she felt her stomach grumbling again. *There is no way I'm hungry already,* she said to herself.

But after a few more minutes she couldn't ignore her tummy rumbling, Miko gathered her belongings and walked across the street to grab something to eat.

Before going into the Italian restaurant, her eyes landed on an emerald dress hanging on a mannequin.

"Oh my" she said. Miko stared at it for a little while longer before telling herself, "*What the hell*" and she walked into the boutique.

"Hi, can I try that blazer on in the window?" she asked the chick standing behind the counter.

"I don't work here sweetie but I'll let the girl know" the woman told her.

Miko went to apologize but the woman smiled and quickly told her, "Girl no it's okay, I shouldn't be behind here anyway, I was charging my phone"

She smiled back at the older woman and introduced herself something she had refrained from doing since the scandal, "I'm Miko" holding her hand out over the counter.

Miko had been in London for a month now and had barely spoken to anyone besides employees in stores wherever she was patronizing.

"I'm Farren, Farren Knight," the tall, bronze-blushed beauty told her.

Miko repeated the name, thinking to herself, *That name sounds so familiar.*

But little did Miko know she had just met the real definition of a WOMAN.

***

Women like Farren Knight weren't walking around every day. In fact, women such as Farren Knight weren't living in D.C. or shopping in New York. The type of woman that Farren Knight was…they were rare, cut from a different cloth. Built different, a unique breed, one of a kind, in her own league, above average…any slick and clever saying that you could possibly think of just add Farren Knight's picture next to it.

She was the product of her environment but never did she allow her upbringing or her past to dictate her future. Farren Knight always rose above her circumstances; she wasn't defined by what society said she was or who she was.

She didn't allow terms such as, widow, single mother, boss bitch, or even her all-time favorite, "The Connect's Wife" none of those titles made her who she was.

Miko was soaking it all in, she was taking everything she was learning and eating it up.

Farren was dropping wisdom on her like people who fed pigeons bread. With her heart and mind wide open, she was receiving it.

Miko sat in Farren's living room drinking tea with her feet crossed. Farren Knight sat across from her, this had become their *thing*.

She was so grateful for Farren Knight, talking to her was different from conversing with Lo and other girls that she had slowly grown to love.

Farren Knight kept it real but not in a rude way, it was in that motherly tone that you couldn't help but to nod your head and say okay.

She was allowed the opportunity to truly be herself and honest without feeling like she was being judged.

The one thing that they realized they had in common was the love-hate relationship with their mothers.

Farren helped Miko see that her mom was partially to blame for some of the wrong decisions she made as a teenager, in college and now in her adult life.

Farren was a firm believer that how you treated your children and how you loved on your kids would determine how others loved them. She was raising her kids to be strong and confident but most importantly brilliant.

Her children knew their worth and didn't allow anyone to treat them any kind of way.

Farren hated how she was raised, feeling alone and sometimes abandoned. She didn't grow up being tucked away at night, being told that she was beautiful, she didn't hear the words, I love you, nor was she told that the sky was the limit.

Farren got it out of the mud on her own and in return, she made some stupid decisions but it all made her the woman she was, and a phenomenal woman she was at that.

Miko never thought about how cold her mother was she chalked it up to her being how she was raised. No one in their family talked a lot, most meals were eaten in silence as well.

She didn't understand growing up what it meant to be told, "I love you," So as she got older without her really knowing what was going on, she began to seek validation. Miko didn't just seek it in men but she sought after it in other ways. In her career, she always wanted to be the top-notch member. In school when she would compete against other teams in sports. And in present day, she wanted to be the best in The Underworld. She saw how close everyone was to at least one person and she found herself latching on to Lo.

Miko didn't know how to be alone. Although she grew up damn near alone and had lived by herself for the most part after college. She still was seeking something.

Farren helped her to see that this was because she wasn't content.

She wasn't okay with who she was, so she found fulfillment in company.

Once Miko told Farren that she had no emotional attachment to The President, Farren knew then…that the girl didn't love herself.

Because anyone that did, wouldn't dare put up with a man treating them, the way The President had been treating her behind closed doors for so many years.

Miko had never told anyone how rough he was in bed but she told Farren.

Farren quickly told her that it's okay to turn it up every notch but when a man doesn't even look in your eyes as he's fucking you, you mean nothing to him.

If a man has to hide you then you're nothing to him.

Farren told Miko that God created women from the man's *rib*. A man should want to display you as his treasure, his gem, his gift from God.

"You should never be with someone who doesn't brag on you and a smile should grace their face when they see you," she told her over and over again.

Miko dropped her head down feeling ashamed and embarrassed.

Farren told her on that rainy day, "God made you in His image baby girl, don't ever let a man treat you as if you're anything less than gold itself"

Miko had adopted that mindset and in truth, she had been feeling herself ever since.

She was set to return to the states in a few days. So this would most likely be her and Farren's last time chatting.

"I don't wanna leave," she told her.

Farren sipped her tea, "Girl come visit anytime"

Miko heard something rumbling downstairs, instantly she became alarmed.

"Did you hear that?" she questioned.

Farren turned around and looked out of the bay window that was in open view from where they sat, "I think that's my daughter" she told Miko.

Miko waited on Farren to get up, but it looked as if she had no plans on moving from where she sat comfortably.

"Maaaaa" a voice rang out from downstairs.

Farren shook her head, "Chile I'm up here having tea, stop yelling in my house, we have intercoms," she told her daughter.

Seconds later, a tall light-skin replica of Farren Knight stood before them, the cut off shorts she wore and multi-colored dashiki she wore went well with the large afro above her head.

Miko's mind went to Miko, thinking that they would be the best of friends. Beaded bracelets and wooden jewelry filled Farren's daughter wrists.

"Noel this is Miko, Miko this is my baby girl Noel" she introduced the two.

Noel flashed her a smile, she couldn't tell if it was a genuine or not but she returned the smile either way.

"Nice to meet you" she told Noel.

"Same here" she said, sitting down beside her mom.

"How was the flight?" Farren asked her daughter, touching her daughter's exposed thigh.

Noel yawned, "I slept the whole time, where is Kool?" she asked.

"In Atlanta" Farren said in short.

Miko figured it was time for her to go. She knew that Noel didn't come around often so she didn't want to intrude on their mother/daughter time.

Plus, seeing them together had her feeling some type of way and she wanted to get alone so she ring her mother's phone. It was time for them to talk and Miko wasn't taking no for an answer. She was her mother's only child and she planned to refresh her mother's memory.

"Well, let me get out of here, I still have tons of packing to do" she told a white lie.

Miko saw a hint of sadness come across Farren's face, "You're leaving already?" Farren asked her.

She nodded her head, "Yeah I'll be in touch"

Farren stood to her feet but Miko told her quickly, "I know my way out, stay up here, nice meeting you Noel" Miko told Farren's daughter and gathered her purse and waved once more before going down the steps.

Noel waited until she heard the front door close, "Who is that?" she asked her mama.

"A friend of a friend" she said, picking up her teacup.

"She's pretty," Noel told her.

"And she reminds me so much of Carren" Farren said aloud.

"My sister?" Noel questioned.

"Yes, savvy and all just like Carren" Farren smiled. Thinking of her late daughter that passed before she was able to experience life.

Noel laid her head on her mother's shoulder, "I'm happy to be home," she told her.

Farren patted her hair. She didn't know when was the perfect time to tell Noel that she wouldn't be here for long. Farren had something in motion for Noel, since she couldn't get her life together on her own in California it was time for mommy dearest to step in and get Noel on the right path, even if it wasn't the ideal path she had in mind for her child, it will definitely be a profitable one.

The time winded down for Miko's flight to take off. She had been buckled up in her seat for more than thirty minutes. Growing antsy, she asked the flight attendant on the private jet that The Underworld chartered from time to time, "What's taking so long?"

The flight attendant told Miko, "We're waiting on one more passenger"

Miko was now confused, who else could possibly be boarding a private flight with her back to New York.

However, her mind didn't linger on the thought for too long, before she knew it the door was lifting up and in walked on the plane, Noel Knight, Farren Knight's daughter.

Miko removed her headphones, "You're going to New York?" she asked.

Noel nodded her head, she wasn't in the mood to talk, and she was really pissed the fuck off.

Even though Miko did nothing to her, Noel had a bad attitude and when she was in a bad mood, everyone could catch her evil wrath.

Miko caught the hint and put her headphones right back on, closed her eyes and minded her business.

Hours and hours later, they had landed in New York, common courtesy led Miko to ask Noel, "Do you need a ride to a hotel or something?"

Noel smirked, "I'm good boo, thank you"

Miko shook her head and walked towards her brother's car, she was surprised to see the pleasant look on his face.

"Somebody is happy to see me," she teased. It felt good to come home to some love.

"A lil bit, what's up sis?" Malachi asked, giving Miko a big ole' warm hug.

"Not much, hungry" she told him.

"Lo wanted to take you to dinner but I figured you would want to get up with her on your own time" he said.

Miko nodded her head, "Yeah for sure, thanks for looking out"

Once her bags were in the back seat and they pulled off and were on the highway, Malachi asked, "Who was that girl getting off the plane with you?"

Miko said, "Farren's daughter" she told him nonchalantly.

Malachi damn near slammed on the breaks, "Farren? Farren Knight" he asked, excitedly.

She laughed, "Yesss, why you acting like a groupie?

"Shit do you know who she is?" he asked.

Miko nodded her head, "Yeah I do"

She thought it was amusing to see people, mainly her brother turn up at the mentioning to someone as sweet as Farren. Yes, she had heard the stories of how infamous she was and how she came in and took over The Cartel.

Farren Knight had made them more money than they had ever seen in their life. But to Miko, Farren still didn't seem complete. She saw the false glimmer of love in her eyes when she looked at her lover. She wondered did her heart ever really heal from when she lost her husband, Christian. Miko would forever be indebted to Farren; she opened her eyes to see something in herself that she had never seen before.

Malachi took her from her thoughts and said, "I wonder do Nas know she here"

Miko said nothing, she wasn't sure how much her brother knew about him sending Farren to her as a mentor so she kept her mouth quiet and stifled a yawn.

"You sleepy?" he asked.

Miko shook her head, "I didn't think I was, but the way I can't stop-"she yawned again.

Malachi smiled, "Let's just grab you something to eat on the way to your house so you can get settled in, we have a meeting tomorrow"

Miko rolled her eyes and sighed under her breath, the last time she met with The Underworld it wasn't the best meeting and she knew Papa's rude, slick-mouthed ass would be there. Malachi had told her on several occasions to ignore him but for some reason he always got under her skin.

"I'll be there," she told him. She refused to complain; right now The Underworld was the only "company" willing to take her ass in. So she wouldn't dare part her lips to say anything crazy. She was as humble as ever these days.

"So you haven't spoken with dude?" he asked out of nowhere.

Miko looked at him with frustration on her face, "Really? What made you ask me that?"

He held one hand up in surrender, "Aye you said that last time sis, then next thing we know your ass on the news" he told her the truth.

Malachi would never sugar coat anything for her, that's not how he rocked.

"Well that was a slip-up, I'll admit that but it won't be happening again," she told him matter of fact.

He nodded his head, he wouldn't salute her for growing up just yet, it had only been a few hours since she was back in the city so he would wait and check on her in a few weeks. He knew from personal experience how easy it was to go back to a situation. Simply because you were comfortable.

Malachi went back and forth with Jade for years before she finally said, "Fuck it you're the one daddy"

He smiled just thinking about how much he loved and adored his wife, women like Jade weren't easy to come up on, he joked often that he had to hit the West Coast just to find a real one and that he did.

He loved and cherished the relationship and most importantly, the friendship he had with his wife. They were solid and growing in tuned with each other more and more every day.

The one thing that they both had to realize as time progressed is that a relationship is an on-going thing. It doesn't stop once you recite your vows; in fact, that's when the real work begins.

During the first year of them being married, Jade had been caught up with opening her art galleries, finishing her Master's degree and becoming a mother for the second time. She stopped going to counseling.

Well, at the time Jade wasn't mentally strong enough to not go to counseling and problems resurfaced in their marriage and it was only because Jade never really received the closure she needed on a certain situation.

So, years later Jade still went to counseling faithfully once a week, she was better now of course, but just to keep shit smooth, she didn't mess a session.

"I'm so happy to be back" Miko told her brother, Malachi had pulled up to a food truck and she hopped out and grabbed her two fish tacos and a beer.

"Ain't nothing like new York, it's the city that never sleeps for a reason," he said, proudly.

Malachi loved New York and he didn't plan on moving no time soon, whenever he needed to get away and duck off, him and jade would take the kids to Cali and chill out by the beach but for the most part he loved New York and over the years, Jade loved it too.

"Alright, I'll catch you tomorrow sis, lockup be safe" he told her after he had finished placing her bags in the bedroom and checking the house for anything out of the ordinary.

"Thank you, for everything. Even the little things, thank you," she told him.

Malachi eyed her suspiciously, she had changed. Miko seemed more vibrant and positive, which was a good thing.

"Anytime" he told her, kissing her forehead and leaving her alone.

Miko locked the door and went to plop down on the couch. She had a few swigs of beer left so she guzzled it down and then burped loudly.

Her house phone rang and she assumed it was Lo, so she went to answer, "Hey girl" she greeted her over the phone.

"So you're back now?" his voice came over the line.

Miko's heart began to beat rapidly and before she knew it, she hung the phone up.

WHAT THE FUCK DID HE WANT? She asked herself. Hell no, she refused to start the bullshit all over again with him, it wasn't happening. Where was he when she had to hold her own hand during her abortion? At The White House, with his WIFE.

The President was the last thing on her mind and he could really miss her with the bullshit.

Miko sat up and told herself, she needed a drink after that call. She walked downstairs and across the street and took a seat at the bar at The Pub.

"Let me get a Corona" she told the bartender.

"A pretty girl like you drinking beer?" the bartender joked, but Miko found nothing funny tonight, all she wanted was her damn beer.

"And a lime, thank you" she told him in a very dry tone. He handed her the Corona with a lime at the top and walked off.

She turned around and eyed the scene. People were walking around with their work clothes on and such. Miko took two big gulps of her beer before turning back around and snacking on some of the peanuts.

"Miko Sanderson? Is that you?" a voice came from behind her.

She prayed to God, it wasn't a reporter, today was not the day for her to be harassed.

She didn't even bother turning back around, "Girl I know that beautiful hair anywhere, how have you been?" the voice was now standing right next to her, she felt the person's eyes checking her profile out.

Miko turned her head slightly, it was one of her ex co-workers at The White House.

These people…people that she had worked late nights and early mornings with. No one reached out to her, called, emailed, hell she wondered did they pray? With one rumor, they treated her like the plague.

"What are you doing in New York?" she asked Adrian.

"I'm here doing press for the chief of staff" she said happily.

Miko didn't miss those days, doing everyone else's job except her own. Because they hired lazy fuckers who didn't believe in working after five pm.

"Oh" she said, uninterested.

"So girl how have you been?" Adrian asked her, as if everything was okay. Well, Miko was okay, in fact she was happy and replacing the pieces of her puzzle day by day.

"I'm well," she told Adrian.

"You know Miko, I used to have so much respect for you" Adrian openly disrespected her as if it was nothing.

Miko looked at her, eyes big and her lips curled, she tried to hide her shock.

"Sorry to disappoint you" she told her, and fished out a ten-dollar bill to cover her beer and left the bar before she went the fuck off.

Miko didn't understand how people felt entitled to give their opinion on another person's life.

She was never one to gossip or judge because she wasn't raised that way. And hell, she couldn't judge anyway her mother was a prostitute for Goodness's sake. Miko was never in the position to point the finger at anyone.

For Adrian to come at her like that was very rude and disrespectful, Miko had heard quite a few rumors about her, but she wouldn't dare stoop to her level and be petty. She had become better than that.

So instead, she left the situation before it escalated. She crossed the street and went back to the quiet and comforts of her own home.

After taking a hot shower, Miko curled up with a good book and read until her eyes couldn't keep themselves open anymore.

The next day, Miko busied herself with a trip to the salon and spa. She then had lunch alone at a sandwich shop before going back home to take a nap before the Underworld meeting.

Malachi told her the meeting was at six, which worked out perfectly. She and Lo had plans to get drinks, do dinner and then catch a live music set to close their night off. She sounded excited over the phone to have her friend back when Miko talked to her earlier she just prayed it stayed that way and that they didn't have any more stupid arguments. They were too grown to be in each other's business and Miko planned to make that clear tonight over dinner. Even though, she was done with the President. She wasn't putting the idea of dating down; it was Farren Knight who stressed the importance of love to her. She told Miko that she was worthy of love and that one day, she would meet a man, or a man would meet her….and love her despite her past.

Miko was waiting on that day, she wasn't tired of going to bed alone since she had been doing it her whole life but sooner than later, she wanted to experience something new.

Her nap came and went and before she knew it, Miko was up and changing out of her pajamas and into a pair of black True Religion jeans and a mesh black shirt with a black bra and black combat boots. She parted her down the middle and added a fresh coat of red lipstick.

After locking her front door, she hit the elevator to the parking garage, hopped in her whip, and headed to the Catholic Church. The unofficial headquarters of The Underworld.

Miko made sure she grabbed her bible before getting out of her car. She waved at Nasir's security guard before going up the steps, down the hallway and making a right into the boardroom.

Only a few people had arrived, Sasha and Mary Jane, Sean and Roderick.

"It's good to see you," Mary Jane told her warmly.

Sasha waved and smiled and Sean joked, "Girl you done gained some weight, I love it," he told her.

Miko looked down at her stomach, she knew she had went up two pants sizes but she didn't think it was noticeable

She took the seat next to Mary Jane, "Girl it's been so boring you ain't missed nothing," she told her after she asked what's been up.

She pulled out a notebook, "How are the numbers looking?" she asked.

Mary Jane told her, "I don't know from the top of my head, come over tomorrow"

She nodded her head, "Will do, can you make some of that autumn squash soup?"

Mary Jane smiled and said, "You're in luck, I just got some from the market today"

Miko clapped her hands, excitedly.

Slowly but surely, everyone began to fall in to the room.

Lo said, "Girl yes for these boobies, damn I need to go to London"

Everybody laughed and Miko shook her head and blew her a kiss.

She caught Nasir staring at her. She mouthed the words, "Thank You" to him once everybody got to talking.

He nodded his head, Nasir believed that Miko had the potential to become a bad and ruthless bitch in the Underworld, she just needed proper training and guidance, the guidance had somehow happened in London with the help of Farren Knight.

"So I got some news" Polo said.

It wasn't too often Miko seen him at a meeting so she knew it was important. She could bet her last dollar that she knew exactly what the announcement was.

She sat back in her chair and crossed her feet, one under the other. She eyed the Rolex her brother copped her for Christmas, her stomach growled. Lo had a few new favorite places to dine at and she had been bragging on them for the longest. So Miko was looking forward to eating good tonight.

A knock at the door caught everybody's attention and in walked Noel Knight.

No one knew who she was, so everyone grabbed their guns. Miko was the only that didn't carry one, she never had a reason too, or so she thought.

"Whoa yall niggas chill" Polo stood up and told them.

Papa was the last person to lower his gun, Polo eyed him and he said, "Man I got kids, I can't go out like a sucker" he spat.

Nasir shook his head and Miko rolled her eyes.

"This here is a legend in the making," Polo said happily.

Sasha was unfazed, "That's Christian Knight's daughter, and I wouldn't be so quick to call her a legend yet"

Lo laughed, Sasha was always chewing somebody out she never gave a fuck what came out of her mouth.

"Show some respect," Nasir snapped.

Malachi stood and kissed her cheek, he was such a gentlemen.

"You can have my chair, nice to meet you," he told her.

Papa didn't say anything but that's just how he was.

Everyone else spoke and Noel was dry and short. She had the same attitude she had yesterday on the airplane.

She didn't mutter one word to Miko and didn't even look in her direction. It was as if home girl had a permanent chip on her shoulder. But if you had been through what she been through, you would feel the same way.

People were always judging her and tagging her to her parents, Noel was her own damn woman.

"So Noel is about to take us into a different arena, we're shifting gears in the New Year" Polo said. He was referring to the New Year that would soon be upon them in a few months.

"International how? We already got a plug," Papa said.

Malachi said, "International is more risks" he wasn't feeling the cross over either.

Polo spoke up, "Are yall trying to get this money or not?

Roderick said, "No disrespect but we already getting money and tons of it'

Sasha raised her hand "Uh speak for yourself, I'm trying to make more too," she told him.

"How much more though do we need before we get caught?" Malachi said.

Nasir watched some of the members complain and some rejoice, Miko noticed he never really said anything in the meetings, he never did.

"Nas, what do you think?" Miko asked.

He removed his hand from his chin and sat up in his seat, "It's something to consider," he told the team.

Malachi wasn't fucking with it and his mind was made up, "What else do we need to discuss?" he asked.

Polo said, "Yall didn't hear me out?"

Roderick spoke, "We didn't even vote on this"

Noel let them all know, "I don't have to fucking be here"

Papa came right back on her ass, "Well bye bitch"

Nasir didn't like the disrespect, "Aye come on man watch it"

Papa shook his head, he wasn't kissing her ass just because of her last name.

"Let's talk about this later," Polo said.

Noel smacked her lips. Miko wasn't feeling her attitude at all and from the looks on Sasha, Mary Jane and Lo's face, she could tell they weren't feeling it either.

"Well I have plans, hit my celly if you need me" Sasha said and stood to her feet.

Mary Jane left too, Miko asked Lo, "You ready?"

Lo said, "I'll come get you from your crib, let me take care of something real quick"

Miko already knew what that meant, "Okay" was the only thing she told her before she stood to her feet.

She told everyone goodbye and left the room.

"Miko why don't you have a gun?" Malachi asked her, sticking his head out of the door.

She turned around and told her brother, "I don't need a gun," she told him.

"Yes you do, here" he came to her and handed her a small gun.

"Me and Lo only went to the gun range once," she said, shaking her head and handing it back to him.

"Trust me if somebody run up on you, you gon' know how to shoot that mother fucker" he said and gave it back to her.

Miko ensured him that she was good without one, "I promise I'm okay" she didn't want to carry a gun.

"Chi" Sean shouted his name.

Malachi didn't have enough time to preach to her about the importance of carrying a gun, Miko still didn't grasp how important and dangerous it was being a part of the underworld.

People who they didn't even know hated them just because of the position they were in.

"Be safe sis" he told her.

"Always" she reminded him and left the church.

Miko ended up falling asleep waiting on Lo, when she woke up the metallic gold clock on the wall of her bedroom told her it was a little past midnight. She rolled over and checked her cell phone. There were no missed calls or text messages from Lo so she figured that she was caught up with Nas. Her stomach wouldn't let her go back to sleep, everything that normally delivered to her building was probably closed at this time.

She got up and threw her shoes back on and made it to the parking garage so she could go grab some food, it was too late at night for her to be walking.

Unbeknownst to Miko, a tinted rented car had been parked right across from her car, waiting on her to return to the garage. she was so caught up in her cell phone, instead of her getting right in the car, locking the doors then resuming whatever she was doing, she stood there scrolling CNN.com, although Miko no longer worked at The White House she was still an avid lover of politics and anything government related.

Before she knew it, her face was being slammed into the cement and she could have sworn she heard her nose crack, a few kicks to her ribs and a major blow to the side of her face knocked her out.

She never saw it coming, seconds before she felt her eye closing in and her vision becoming blurry. A vivid memory of her handing the gun back to her brother replayed through her mental.

The last thing she heard was someone screaming for "HELP" before passing out.

Her eyes fluttered open and the first person she saw was Lo staring over her, "Move" Miko told her. She felt like she couldn't even breathe, Lo was so close.

"Yeah her mean ass is up" Lo told whoever was in the room.

Her head was banging and so was her heartbeat, she tried to sit up but the way the migraine was set up, she laid right back down.

"Ouch" she winced in pain.

Jade came over and said, "Sis you're going to have to take it very slow okay boo," she told her.

"What happened?" she whispered, closing her eyes because the bright light in the hospital room was bothering her.

"Well that hoe-"Sasha interjected but Malachi gave her the look of silence.

She shook her head and sat back down.

Miko knew something bad must have happened, "I don't even wanna know" she was starting to reconsider her decision to come back to the states. She was missing London like crazy right now.

"You're coming to my house and I'm going to make sure you recover" Lo told her.

Jade said, "No, she's coming to our house, with her family" Miko wanted to ask did anyone call her mother, but *hell*, her mother barely spoke English, she would have easily got frustrated and hung the phone up on whoever would have called her.

"I'm her family too what are you saying?" Lo raised her voice.

"Chill Lo, Jade is going to make sure she's straight, you're welcome to come over" Malachi told Lo.

She looked at Miko but her eyes were closed, "I'll be back tomorrow" she told Miko and left without offering a goodbye to anyone.

"Can't stand that hoe," Jade said aloud.

Malachi told her, "Don't do that"

Lo wouldn't even trip over Jade throwing the word, "family" in her face, she did that shit out of spite. She stopped and grabbed a bottle of wine and went home. She was the first person to make it to the hospital, not Jade or Malachi but whatever.

When Miko woke up again, hours later, her brother and Jade were the only ones still there.

"What happened?" she asked.

Jade got up and handed her a cup of what was iced water but it was now lukewarm, it was still soothing to her very dry throat.

"You were mugged boo," she told her.

"My body is aching" she said, touching her stomach, it was wrapped in heavy bandage.

"Yeah the doctor said they knocked your ass out" Malachi told her.

"So, did the police find out who did it?" she asked.

Jade looked at Malachi and she saw her do it too.

"Miko are you sure you and dude not talking no more?" he asked.

She took a deep breath, "You just don't take my word do you?" she snapped.

"I'm just asking," he told her.

"Yeah and you were just asking the other day as well, no I don't talk to him and I have no desire too" she was starting to feel like the girl who cried wolf.

"Alright alright get some rest" he shushed her.

"I'm hungry," Miko told him.

Jade laughed, "I'll go see what the cafeteria has, and they should have breakfast by now"

Once Jade had left the hospital room, she asked, "Was it him? Did he do this?" she asked.

Malachi sighed, "No but Sasha said strong leads led to his wife's cousin"

She shook her head, "This is pure bullshit," she said.

Malachi agreed with his sister, he knew one thing for sure, he didn't give a damn if she was the First Lady of the United States of America or not, she had one more time to fuck with his sister and he was going to have Sasha make her death look like an assassination.

Chapter 9

□ □□□□□ □□ □□□□□ □□□□□□□

□□□□□□□ □□□ □□□ □□□□□ □□□□

□□□□ □ □□□ □□□ - □□□□

"You are being so boring Miko, can you please change" Lo complained.

She rolled her eyes and went back into her walk-in closet, she spoke loud enough for Lo to hear her, "I don't even wanna go nowhere"

Lo wasn't in the mood for Miko's bipolar ass, she had been cooped up in the house since the mugging incident and that was almost two months ago, it was time for her to get back on the scene.

"Look girl, it's a Friday night we are both single and paid, let's go out and shake our money makers and get fucked up," Lo said happily.

She came over to Miko's crib thinking that she was already dressed and ready to jet out the house. But was in for a very rude awakening when a grumpy and smelly Miko came to the door, in an onesie and a dusty robe.

Two hours later, Lo had sent Miko back to her closet three times not satisfied with the grandmother get-up she was trying to wear tonight.

"Okay okay this is the last time I'm changing" she told Lo minutes later, emerging from her closet. Lo was lying against the foot of her bed, with a magazine in her hands. She sat up and got a good look at her good friend, "Girl hell yes you look like a million bucks!" Lo clapped her hands.

Lo was relieved to see that Miko was getting her mojo back. The mugging had her ass spooked. Her brother left her with a gun but Miko was too paranoid to take it out of the drawer. She rarely left the house and Lo told her over and over again, that was no way to live.

"You like it for real?" Miko looked in the mirror that was positioned over her dresser.

"Hell yeah look at them titties" Lo said. Miko shook her head, Lo's mouth could be so vulgar at times.

She admired her frame in the mirror, she did look cute tonight.

The cranberry long-sleeved dress she wore was slightly doing her body justice, the middle of the dress was corset-styled and the tall boots she wore completed the dress perfectly.

The only jewelry she wore was pearl earrings given to her by her grandmother many years ago. Miko never took them off. She missed her family so much but her mother was speaking for them all. So she respected her wish and stayed away.

"Let me do your makeup" Lo told her.

Miko shook her head, "No all I need is a lil mascara and eyeliner and some perfume then we can go," she told her.

Lo smacked her lips, "Let me hook you up, I'm not going to add that much I promise" she said.

They went to the bathroom and Miko plopped down on the toilet and let Lo work her magic.

"Hold your head back," she told her.

Before she closed her eyes, she noticed the ruby ring that Lo wore on the middle finger of her left hand.

"I love this ring, when did you get it" she asked.

"Early Christmas gift" Lo said nonchalantly.

"From Nas?" she questioned.

Lo ignored her, tilted her head back, and began applying concealer under her eyes.

"Do you think yall will ever be together?" she asked Lo.

Lo sighed, "What happened to us minding our own business?" she threw up the exact same line Miko told her months ago when they had their big talk.

"It was just a question," Miko said innocently.

"Well Meek I don't know, I think about it sometimes I would love that but then again I wouldn't" Lo said, sounding confused her damn self.

"But do you want him and only him?" she asked.

"Girl yeah I do" Lo said sadly.

"I want to feel that one day for someone, that no matter what type of love," Miko admitted.

"You didn't have that with the president?" Lo questioned.

Miko smacked her lips, "Not at all, it wasn't about that with him," she told her.

Lo said, "You're young and you got your whole life ahead of you. And I wish Nas didn't have this strong hold on me, I hate it sometimes"

Minutes later, Lo told her to look into the mirror.

"Wow" was the only word she could come up with.

"Do you like it?" Lo asked.

"Do I? I love it," she told her happily.

She brushed her hair down and sprayed it with some sheen, before grabbing a clutch and tossing her keys and phone in it.

"Okay I'm ready" she told Lo, finding her in the living room.

"Finally! Let's turn up!" Lo said, jumping to her feet and doing a little two-step.

They made it to their first stop, and when they yelled "cheers" before tossing back the first shot, Lo told Miko, "Girl I'm about to get so drunk"

Miko shook her head, knowing it was going to be a long night. But one thing she could say is that whenever she was with Lo, the night was always one to remember.

The duo barhopped all night before settling down at a lounge where Lo knew the owner. "Remember we came here when they first opened, my friend India had performed?" Lo asked Miko.

"Girl no I don't remember," she told her.

Lo laughed, although nothing was funny she was just *that fucked up*.

"What are yall ladies drinking?" Someone asked them.

Lo quickly said, "Vodka and orange juice, what you want Meek?" she asked, calling her by the nickname that Malachi used.

"Pineapple and patron please, thank you," she told the man.

They sat down in the private section that the owner hooked them up with, well Miko sat and Lo stood on the couch and danced, shaking her hair wildly and flagging her arms up and down.

"You always take drinks from strangers?" a voice asked her.

The lounge was dark and smoky but the voice was so close, Miko turned to her right. She closed her eyes and opened them again.

"I think I know you but I'm a little tipsy," she admitted. The guy flashed her a beautiful smile. The two gold teeth he had at the top and the two he had at the bottom were cute on him and something different to look at for Miko. "You should remember me, I definitely didn't forget your face or voice," he told her.

Miko blushed but she came back with, "Well how many Korean girls do you meet on a daily basis?" she joked.

He laughed, "You got me there, but none of them are like you," he said confidently.

Miko couldn't help but to smile, he was laying the game on thick.

"I'm Nash, in case you forgot my name," he told her holding his hand out.

She didn't give him her name in fear that it would toss up a red flag on the play. Apparently, Mr. Nash didn't know she was the "mistress" of the President or better yet, he didn't care. Either way it went, Miko wouldn't be the one to remind him, at least not tonight.

"Is your friend good?" he asked, referring to a very excited Lo.

Miko looked back at Lo, "Yeah she good, this is her life every weekend"

Nash raised an eyebrow, "You dance like that?" he asked.

She told him, "I have no rhythm at all"

He smiled, "I beg to differ"

She wondered did he know something about her she didn't because last Miko checked she had no rhythm at all, at least not the type of booty shaking and hip gyrating rhythm people such as Lo did.

"How have you been? Are you still playing the drums?" she asked.

He took a sip of his drink and said, "So, you do remember me?"

She was now guilty, "Okay maybe a little bit, but I told you I was tipsy not drunk"

He nodded his head, "I'm doing a lil something *something* right now, not really focusing on the drums," he told her.

Miko felt the same way with her career when classmates from college commented on her Face book status being nosey.

"Trust me I know how that is," she told him.

Nash stared into her eyes, feeling the same connection he did the last time he was this close to her.

She didn't age, the only thing that had changed about her was she gained weight, it was obvious but he had always loved a woman with some meat on her bones.

He was raised by black Queens with big breasts and thick thighs, although Miko clearly didn't resemble his mother and grandmother, she was still a sight to stop and admire.

An hour or so had passed; Nash asked her how were they getting home.

"A cab" she told him.

"Well come on" he said, standing up and holding his hand out.

A drunken Lo was sitting on the couch with her head being held up by the wall.

"Come on boo" Miko bent down and helped Lo.

"Call Nas tell him to come get me" she whined.

Miko knew that Nas was out of town because Malachi and Jade went on the trip as well but she wouldn't tell her friend that.

"I will just come on" she told her.

With Nash's help, Miko was able to put Lo in the front seat of the cab, while she and Nash occupied the back seat. She and Lo had quite a few drinks and since the mugging, Miko had been so fucking paranoid, so she welcomed Nash's presence.

On the way to her home, Nash's fingers somehow made it to her thigh and Miko was so sleepy she ended up laying her head down on his shoulder, feeling comfortable enough to do so. Nash didn't protest, she still smelled sweet even after being in a hot and musty lounge.

"Right here" she told Nash, once they made it to her floor. He was carrying a passed out Lauren.

Miko got the door open and guided Nash towards the guest bedroom near the kitchen of her condo. He put Lo in the bed and then stepped back turning his head out of respect for Lo. Miko undressed her and laid her under the covers and they both walked out of the room.

"Thank you so much, do you want some water? I feel parched" she told Nash, walking to the refrigerator to get a bottle of water out.

"Yeah I am too," he told her.

Nash admired her home. He was from the hood and had only seen cribs on the top-floor similar to hers on television shows and in music videos. In less than a year, hopefully he planned to have a home just like this and probably even bigger.

"Here you go," she told him, handing him the water bottle. Nash told her thank you and gulped the entire bottle down.

Miko felt her body getting hot watching his brown juicy lips suckle the water down, his Adam's apple throbbing the whole time.

"Shit I was thirsty," he said.

Miko smiled, "Yeah that much was obvious"

Nash smiled too, "Oh you got jokes.damn look at this view" he exclaimed.

"Please go enjoy it, its breath taking," she told him.

Nash walked over towards the window and before he knew it, the window was sliding over. He looked back at Miko who had a remote in her hand.

"In just a few minutes, you'll probably see the sun start to peek," she told him.

"Come watch it with me then" Nash told her.

Miko took his hand and walked onto her balcony, she pulled him a seat out from the corner of her balcony.

"Do you mind if I smoke?" he asked.

"As long as it's not cigarettes," she told him.

"Hell nah" he said, and pulled a sack of weed and a blunt wrapper.

Miko took a deep breath, it was chilly but not as cold as she expected it to be for it to be the last month of the year.

"This lil heater player, where you get this?" Nash asked.

"Target I think" she told him, referring to the circular heater she had near their feet.

She sat outside so much, especially during the morning time. One thing Farren Knight had stressed to her during their talks was the importance of meditation. She told her that the first hour when she woke up and opened her eyes belonged to two people, her and God.

Miko had adopted that habit and kept it ever since returning to London. She started her days with one hour of complete silence.

"What's on your mind?" Nash asked.

She wasn't one to be all open about her personal feelings, especially with a stranger, but hell he was in her house and smoking on her balcony, she had already crossed all lines.

"The new year, I'm so ready for it," she admitted.

Nash lit the blunt using a lighter from his back pocket, "You have a few goals you want to accomplish?" he asked.

She loved how he spoke; his voice was light and raspy.

"A few is an understatement," she told him.

Nash pulled on the blunt and exhaled before saying, "Yeah me too next year is mines" he told her.

She smiled, Miko loved how determined he sounded to do whatever he had his mindset on.

"And it's mines too" she added.

Nash nodded his head, "For sure"

She wrapped the blanket around her body a little tighter, "So what you do in your spare time, Miko," Nash asked.

Miko looked at him with shock all over her face, "What you thought I ain't know your name?" Nash asked with a big smirk on his face.

She was still silent, he added, "I know you ain't think I was gon' come in ya crib without knowing your name what if you tried to kill me?

She laughed, "In your dreams, just surprised, the first time we met was a very long time ago," she said.

"I felt like my heart just started beating for the first time when I saw you tonight," he openly admitted.

Miko was now speechless for real. Never in life had she heard something like that before.

He smiled, "You good?" he asked.

She closed her open mouth and nodded her head, "Umm yeah…let me go get some more…umm….water. I will, be right…back" it was hard for her to put her words together but she managed.

Nash blushed, he thought it was cute that she was a lil nervous.

He sat back and puffed on his blunt.

Miko ran to Lo's room and woke her up, "Lo! Lo! Wake up" she said.

Lo mumbled, "Go away"

"The dude from the club is here," she whispered.

"Bye meek I'm sleep" she told her, before rolling over and snoring loudly.

Miko didn't know what to do, she returned back to the front area to see Nash sitting at her piano.

"You play the piano?" she asked him

He shook his head, "Not really, I'm assuming you do?" he asked.

She told him, "Yes"

"I would love to hear you play" Nash told her. His eyes were so low and she could barely see them. She figured her was high.

Nash was a handsome black man, not just a handsome black man but he was sexy period.

He was taller than she was, and Miko was thankful for that.

His arms were covered in tattoos from what she could see now that he no longer had a jacket on.

His hair was dreaded and the tips were honey blonde, something else that was new for her.

"Come here" he told her with his raspy voice.

"We can't play this late," she warned, as she took a seat next to her.

"I know" he told her, taking her hand over his and gracing the piano keys.

His skin was cold from being outside, hers warm.

His complexion was dark brown, hers resembling milk, his knuckles covered in tattoos, her fingertips painted red his fingers were a little dirty.

"How long have you been playing?" he asked her.

"Since I was a little girl," she told him, he got up and came behind her.

"I know a little something" he told her, bringing his head near the crook of her shoulder.

Miko's breathing sped up, she hadn't been this close to a man in so damn long, her hormones were acting up.

"It's something so special about the piano many people can't master the keys," he whispered in her ear.

Miko took a deep breath, wondering why did that one brass touch of his tongue send octave waves through her soul and down in between her legs. Why?

"I can agree," she whispered.

Nash kept his hands atop hers, Miko stroked the keys but not adding enough pressure to make a noise.

"I wonder does music connect us?" he asked.

Miko wondered too, "Who knows?" she said.

"I do," he told her, confidently.

The sun was coming up and she was surprised that she wasn't sleepy.

Miko turned around and faced him, standing up and meeting his intense stare.

"Why are you staring at me like that?" she asked him.

"I been waiting to see you again, do you believe me?" he asked her.

Miko didn't believe much of nothing these days but she did believe in love, Farren Knight had made her promise that she would never stop believing in love and being in love.

"That could be possible" she gave him an answer, even if it wasn't the one he was looking for.

Nash said fuck it and went in and kissed her, the worst that could happen was that she could slap him and put him out and if that happened, then cool.

But when Miko moaned and kissed him back, he knew that they were on the same page.

The heat ignited in the room although the balcony was open and it was cold outside, the chill didn't bother him. They stood together, wrapped in each other, kissing for seconds that turned into minutes.

When they finally separated for air, Nash's dick was rock hard and Miko's dress was hiked up because somehow his hands had made their way towards her ass.

"What are you doing?" she moaned in his ear.

He didn't bother answering her question because he planned to show her exactly what he was *about* to do to her, in just a matter of a few seconds.

She stared in his eyes, he went from palming her butt to massaging her shoulders then playing her hair. It was as if everything he did felt good to her. Miko couldn't grasp control over anything that was going down. She just knew that she didn't want him to remove his hands from her body.

"Lay back" he told her.

Miko looked at him for further instructions, "Lay back where?" she asked. Knowing good and well he wasn't telling to her laying her body down on the grand piano. Nash ignored her for the second time tonight. He figured the alcohol she had consumed was wearing off so he took control of the situation. He whipped her dress off her and picked her up, she instantly wrapped her legs around his waist not wanting him to drop her.

"I got you ma," he promised before putting her down on top of the piano.

Nash took a seat on the bench that was at the piano and pulled her closer to his face.

Miko was so damn nervous it was ridiculous.

He pulled her thong to the side and dived in head first, something that he didn't normally do but she was so beautiful, her voice so melodic, her personality so inviting. He knew she was the one.

Nash was a freak, a certified one at that. He didn't need her to do anything but lay back and take him all in, starting with the stroke of his tongue.

"Ohhh" she muttered, once his lips met hers for the first time.

He smiled, she even sounded sexy grunting.

Nash took his time becoming acquainted with her most intimate parts. Time was the one thing they had. Just from being with her tonight, he knew that she had been through some shit, just as he had. But tonight, well in the wee hours of the morning, none of that mattered.

He wanted to allow her to experience heaven on earth for the first time. He planned to make her climax over and over again.

He envisioned her Cumming in his mouth and him licking the excess up before kissing her and making her taste her the juices that she created by being a nasty girl for him.

"Shit" she said, once they got comfortable into a rhythm, she rocked her hips slowly against his mouth and lips and he stroked his tongue in and out of her, real slow and wet.

Not too long after, he got her to the perfect temperature.

A stirring noise was heard as he stuck two fingers inside of her and pulled them in and out of her, causing her to hop off the piano just a little.

He loved the sight before him, the sun was coming up, and her hair laid over the piano.

Miko held on to her breasts, pinching her nipples and fumbling with her belly button every other minute.

She was truly on cloud nine.

Never had she felt this way before.

Nash pulled himself closer to her pussy and buckled her down. He didn't have time to play with her anymore. He planned to give this pussy the business and that's what he did.

He took a deep breath then exhaled on her lips, causing her little clit to jump and twitch.

She clenched her eyes shut not being able to handle the intense pressure.

Nash bit her clit just a little before sucking on it harder than he did before and at the same time, finger fucking her.

Miko was struggling to maintain her composure and remain a woman. She didn't know a piano could also be used as a serving platter.

"Fuckkkkkkkk" she moaned.

"Hell yeah get that shit out of ya" he told her, playing and toying with her clit. He watched her juices pour out of her like a ticking time bomb.

"Aah aah aah" Miko panted as she came off an orgasmic high. One that she had never experienced before.

"How are you feeling?" he asked.

Miko covered her face and shook her head, she was so embarrassed.

"I'm drunk" she lied.

Nash threw his head back in laughter, "Girl please, come here" he told her, pulling her legs towards him and plopping her down on his dick without thinking twice about getting protection.

However, Miko had learned her lesson.

"Condom" she said, hopping up.

Nash didn't stop her and he wasn't in any position to become a daddy right now anyway.

"You got some?" he asked, cursing himself mentally for not being better prepared.

"In my room" she told him, not making eye contact.

Nash caught on to that, "Look at me" he commanded.

Miko took a deep breath and eyed him.

He stared in her chinky eyes, "You're beautiful" he told her.

She didn't grow up hearing such nice compliments. The few men she did allow to date her didn't shower her with praises and compliments either.

She looked down and he quickly picked her chin up, and kissed her lips.

"Stop that" he told her.

Miko loved how he took control of everything, in and out of the bedroom.

He stood up with her wrapped around his waist, his pants were sagging but he didn't care, they were about to come off anyway.

"Where am I going?" he asked as he walked around her condo.

"To the back, straight back" she told him, pointing in the opposite direction of where he was going.

Nash kissed her lips and Miko even turned up a little and added some tongue.

"Nasty" he joked.

Once they made it to her bedroom, Nash didn't waste any time undressing and lying down with his arms behind his head.

She went to retrieve the condoms from the second drawer in her nightstand and tossed them to him.

"Nah come put it on" he told her, not even bothering to touch the gold package.

Miko was a grown ass woman so she didn't argue with him, she locked her bedroom door and closed the curtains and climbed on top of his body with the gold package in her mouth.

"Oh, what you about to do with that?" he asked with a sly smirk on his face.

She shushed him, by putting her index finger in his mouth, which he hungrily sucked.

Miko lowered herself down to his waist, applying the condom in one swift motion only using her mouth.

She would curse herself in the morning for being such a fast ass with a complete stranger. But what the hell she only lived once.

Coming back up, to make eye contact with him once more, just to make sure they were still on the same page.

Nash sat up and ran his hands down the sides of her arms, and pulling her in for a hard kiss, she loved the way he kissed…..so magical.

He pushed her down on his dick and she winced in pain. It had been a little minute since the last time she had sex and it had been an even longer time since she shared a bed with a man whose title wasn't the leader of the United States of America.

But hell, after two strokes and a loud slap on the ass, Miko had forgotten all about John and the White House. By the second round, she was scratching his back up and calling his name.

It was safe to say that Miko got her rocks off, back broken, body stretched, pussy licked and ate….from the back too. She was covered in passionate markings, but didn't dare complain. When they finally both agreed to call it a night, it was nine the next morning and she was begging him to stay.

Nash was so tired and his body was sore, he pulled her closer and they drifted off to sleep.

Hours and hours later, the morning had come and gone and the afternoon did too.

Lauren finally woke up from the dead and was banging on Miko's door to tell her she that she was about to leave.

Miko was so sore she couldn't even get up and see her friend out and plus she was exhausted.

"Girl I will call you tomorrow," she told her from under a satin pillow.

She heard Lo smack her lips, "Bye slut bucket" Lo teased.

Miko smirked, she could be called whatever because it was worth it.

She rolled over and kissed his shoulder before going back to sleep.

Once they finally woke up for good, Nash had showered and so did Miko.

"Do you need a ride home?" she asked him, once he had put his clothes back on.

He smiled and told her, "Nah I'm good"

Miko really didn't want him to leave but she wouldn't dare look clingy or needy already, she was sure that Nash thought it was a good night and nothing more.

"I want to hear you play," he told her.

Her face lit up and he saw it too.

"The piano?" she asked to be sure.

"Yeah I think we had enough of each other to last us for the rest of the year" he joked, since the year was coming to an end.

Miko smiled and got up from the couch and went to the piano, after tuning the keys. She stretched her arms and fingers and sat up straight, closed her eyes and zoned out. Before she knew it, she had started singing a song and Miko knew her ass couldn't sing.

"What did you just say?" he asked, jolting up and looking around the room for something to write on.

She opened her eyes, "Huh?" she stopped playing the piano to watch his tall and lanky ass wander around her living room.

"Don't stop playing, point me into the direction of a pen and some paper," he commanded.

Miko laughed and kept playing, she told him to grab the to-do list off the fridge.

Nash came back into the living room and bobbed his head at the melody she played and began writing lyrics.

"Love you down, oh let me love you down" Miko crooned.

"My mama used to love that song when I was growing up" Nash said.

She told him, "Me too"

"I need to remix that," he told her.

"You should," she said.

"How old are you?" Miko asked, of course it was a little too late because she had already given up the cookies. "Twenty three" he said. They were only two years apart. Miko wasn't tripping on the age difference at all, it was clear to see that Nash was wise beyond his years.

"I really enjoyed myself," she told him, after they ate Chinese food that she ordered.

Nash smiled and wiped some sesame sauce from the chicken they shared from the corner of her mouth, "I enjoyed myself too love" he told her.

Miko blushed, he was just too much for her right now. She had a lot going on; apparently, after the New Year there would be major changes in The Underworld. Since she was responsible for the finances of the organization, she knew she would be busy as hell.

"Leave your number so we can stay in contact" she told him, once he got up and put his coat on, he told her that he had a gig tonight.

"Already did," he told her pointing to the digits scrambled on a sticky note on the refrigerator.

Miko hopped off the bar stool and walked him to the door. "Be safe," she told him.

Nash kissed her forehead, nose and then her lips passionately, "You too, don't be a stranger," he told her.

He had made all of the moves last night and the ball was now in her court.

"We shall see," she said before closing the door.

She placed her back on the door and exhaled.

Nash, Nash, Nash, what a man, what a man, what a mighty fine ass man.

***

Nash sat in the basement studio at his cousin's house. He had spent his last few hundred dollars to get to California. The few people that knew he was catching the bus to California thought he was crazy but apparently, they never had a dollar and a dream.

He even borrowed two hundred dollars from his auntie just so he could have some money in his pocket. He promised her that this time next year she would be pushing a new whip. His aunt believed him too, and she even gave him an extra twenty-dollar bill and kissed his cheek.

Nash was now in his cousin's studio, grinding like never before. He hadn't slept in days and he stopped this morning just to wash his ass and eat the sandwich that his cousin's wife made for him.

"How is it looking?" he asked him.

Nash blew a breath of frustration, "I got the verse but the hook. I don't know like I'm not really feeling it," he told him.

"Take your time," his cousin suggested.

"I don't have time!" he stressed. Nash picked up the ragged notebook and stared at the lyrics that he had written and he rewrote them over and over again until he was satisfied. He sat back in the office desk chair and closed his eyes, somehow thoughts of Miko and traces of her red lipstick ran through his mind. He smiled a little thinking about how nervous and timid she was before they made it to her bedroom.

Man, once the curtains closed and the door was locked she turned into an equestrian and rode his dick for hours.

He would come back for her one day, the timing wasn't right. He was trying to get on his feet and get his own shit.

From the looks of her crib, Miko was well off and he had nothing to offer her.

He wouldn't even feel comfortable being around her and laying up in her shit, as of right now there was nothing he could bring to the table.

Nash knew he was a real nigga but he wanted to be a rich nigga too.

Memories from that night replayed in his head which led him to remembering that dope ass melody she came up with.

"I got it," he said loudly.

He rolled the chair towards the computer in the studio and pulled up a song on YouTube. The same song that him and her were singing.

He bobbed his head and held his hand in the air, his fingers danced to the beat.

His cousin rolled a blunt, "Damn that used to be my shit back in the day" he told Nash.

"Hell yeah mines too," he said, moving his head to the beat.

"I'm about to rip this mother fucker apart" he said, tearing the sheet of lyrics that he had been working on for the past few days and allowed it to fall on the floor.

With Miko's sexy ass on his mental, he wrote a ballad for the ladies then added a hot verse at the end of him rapping to connect with all the hood niggas that desired love.

Two hours later, Nash was ready to hit the booth. He was high and his cousin had passed him a double cup of ice, sprite, Jolly Ranchers, and a eighth of Promethazine cough syrup. This was something new to Nash, he had always been a weed smoker but his cousin had him on that "drank" as he called it.

"This ya' boy Nash, one hunnid" he said into the microphone.

Nash looked over the paper one more time, before closing his eyes and picturing himself in a nice ass studio instead of the small space he was in.

He knew that if he stayed down and most importantly remained humble things would be sure to change for him. Determination and hard work were the two things that he had so to the top he went.

"Aye that shit sound good" his cousin told him after they had listened to it a few times.

Nash thought the song was dope but he wasn't really impressed, something was missing.

"How much does it cost to get it mastered and all of that?" he asked.

His cousin told him, "About three hundred to have it done right"

Nash knew he didn't have three hundred dollars. He did have a pinky ring his daddy gave him before he died. His mother would kill him if he pawned it but he knew his daddy believed in him.

"Alright let's get that done," he told his cousin.

He planned to sacrifice any and everything to make his dream come true.

"I love it here," Miko said, as she lay back on the beach chair. The Chanel sunnies she wore were too big for her face and she blamed it on Lo.

"You stretched my shades," she complained for the hundredth time that day.

"Girl okay, I will buy you some more tomorrow" Lo fussed.

Mary Jane laughed, "You can't get mad cus your head big" Everyone chimed in laughter and Lo flicked Mary Jane a middle finger. The girls of The Underworld all decided at the last minute to shoot to Belize to bring in the New Year. Lo put the trip together and on the last day, they were soaking in the sun and no one was eager to leave.

"I might get me a spot here next year," Lo said, enjoying the view.

"Good, me and my man can come out here and relax in yo shit" Sasha said.

'Girl what man?" Lo asked, nosily.

"Mind your business" Sasha told her quickly.

Miko laughed, "We should definitely come back soon"

Mary Jane passed the blunt to Sasha, "When? I feel like this year is about to be crazy"

Sasha shook her head, "I already told Chi they not about to have me all over the place I got to spend more time with my kids"

Sasha was the only one in the bunch with children. Lo didn't plan to have any, ever. Miko preferred to be married first and Mary Jane claimed the idea never crossed her mind but Miko didn't believe that.

"Well I don't know about yall but I'm ready to get this moneyyyyyy" Lo said, she was tipsy.

"I'm just ready to travel more," Miko said, speaking on her upcoming trip with Noel to Cambodia to meet a potential connect out there.

"That girl crazy, watch her ass" Lo pointed her finger at Miko.

Mary Jane nodded her head, "Something isn't right I will agree"

Sasha told them "I know her people, she ain't crazy. Just been through a lot but who hasn't"

Miko nodded her head agreeing. After spending personal time with Farren, she knew that Noel was raised right. Because Farren Knight didn't play no games.

"Let's make our new year's resolution," Lo said, changing the subject.

She didn't give a damn about Noel, as long as she stayed away from Nasir, they would have no problems.

"Okay you start" Sasha told her, taking a sip of champagne.

Lo thought for a second, "I want to talk to my parents this year" she said.

Everyone laughed except Miko. She knew that Lauren was dead ass serious about repairing the broken relationship with her parents.

Mary Jane said, "I want to learn how to drive"

Sasha said, "You don't know how to drive?"

Mary Jane told her, "Come on you're from new York too don't act like everybody knows how to drive"

She knew that MJ had a point, "Okay you right well damn bitch I'll teach you"

Lo asked Sasha what was her new year's resolution, Sasha said, "To get out the game and be a better mama" she spoke from the heart.

Sasha didn't do a lot of shit right but one thing for sure was that she loved her kids with everything in her and everything she did was for them. The smiles on their faces when she walked in the house bearing gifts gave her life. Sooner rather than later, Sasha would realize that material items didn't buy love and her kids rather have her company than a new phone or pair of shoes.

Mary Jane told Miko, "You're up next Meek"

Miko sat up on the lawn chair, Lo smiled at her, she loved her best friend. Miko was looking real grown and sexy in the one piece she wore with sheer cut out sides and Chanel flip-flops.

"I want to fall in love for the first time," she told her girls. Sasha smiled, that love shit wasn't for them, not in the line of work they were in but she wouldn't crush Miko's dreams.

"To love and getting this fucking money" a drunken Lo yelled.

"And to the UNDERWORLD!" Sasha shouted and popped open another bottle of champagne spraying it over all of the ladies.

They ran into the warm waters right when the sun was setting, "I love yall," Sasha said.

Her kind words took everyone by surprise, Sasha was the cold-hearted and ruthless one.

Lo said, "Group hug! Group hug!"

Miko was just thankful for them entering her life. She never understood the importance of sisterhood and friendship until now.

The next morning when they checked out of their villa, everybody went separate ways. Sasha was headed to California to meet Malachi to handle something. Mary Jane and Lo went back to the city and Miko was hopping on a flight to Atlanta to meet Noel. From there they were taking a twenty-four hour flight with two layovers to Siem Reap, Cambodia.

She was looking forward to kicking the New Year off in a different country. Nasir didn't give her an estimated time of returning. He just gave her clear instructions to keep shit in order because Noel's mouth was lil' off the chain and she had the green light to wire funds once a deal was agreed upon between her and the suppliers in Cambodia.

Miko smiled at Noel once she took a seat in the chair that could turn into a bed if Noel got sleepy, for ten thousand dollars a seat, she felt like it should have came with way more than that but she was traveling on The Underworld dime so she didn't complain.

"How was your New Year?" she asked Noel, making pleasant conversation. She refused to be out of town with this girl for the next two weeks or however long they were scheduled to be gone and not talk to her.

Miko wasn't the friendliest but she wasn't a bitch either.

"Pleasant" Noel told her.

Miko shook her head, it was obvious that the girl didn't want to talk and she gave up that quick on trying to befriend her.

After two layovers and a horrible meal, they had finally made it to the hotel they were staying in and all Miko wanted to do was lay down and get some rest.

"Let's link in the morning over coffee," Miko suggested. Noel told her, "Don't drink coffee"

Miko took a deep breath, "Look little girl I'm not here to kiss your ass but you won't keep talking to me like I'm getting on your nerves. I will see you in the morning, whatever you drink and eat that's what we will have tomorrow, goodnight" she told her and went into the hotel room she was occupying leaving Noel in the living room of the suite.

She took a hot shower and laid down with thoughts of Nash on her mind, she hadn't called him…and didn't know why.

Before going to Belize, she had spent every morning and night staring at his phone number wondering why the hesitation.

She didn't understand what was so hard about picking up her cell phone and calling the man and telling him what was on her mind.

She missed him dearly even after only spending one night with him, but that night was everything.

She promised herself that she would call him when she returned. Before closing her eyes and going to bed.

The next morning, she walked into the living room to see Noel sitting on her head, "What are you doing?" she asked.

Noel didn't bother responding. Miko shook her head and went towards the tray of food and pitchers. She assumed Noel ordered breakfast.

Miko took a seat at the small table in the corner of the room with a bagel in her hand and a cup of coffee.

Minutes later, Noel unfolded her body like a pretzel and took a few deep breaths before telling Miko, "Good morning" she sounded like she was in a better mood.

"Morning" she told her back.

"So before we go meet with Dahl, let's go over some brief information," Noel told her, coming to the table with a notebook and pen.

Her body was covered in sweat, she wore a yellow sports bra and black compression shorts.

"Okay I'm listening" Miko told her.

Noel took a seat and opened her notebook, "Quick background on Cambodia, for many years it's been known as the drug trade Mecca. People from the states come here to get three things, cannabis, methamphetamine, and high-grade heroin and shake it down to make more of a profit"

"I thought we were coming here for a coke plug?" Miko asked.

Noel smiled, "It's time to step it up" she told her.

She thought the young girl was a rookie but apparently not. Miko was stunned as she listened to Noel run it down. "We can offer heroine for the same price as we sell the coke but I promise we will make more off the H." Noel told her.

"Hey I just pay for it, I don't know what's better or not, that's not my area," she said.

Noel then stated, "The drug trade in Cambodia utilizes outside sources for the majority of their income, they tend to sell to people who buy wholesale before anyone else. The golden triangle in southeast Asia is our first stop"

Miko nodded her head, "I'm ready when you are," she told her.

"Let me shower and get dressed" she said and went into her room.

Miko read a book as she patiently waited on Noel to emerge from her room.

"Okay let's ride," she said an hour later.

"You look just like your mom," Miko told her.

Noel smiled for the first time ever, "Thank you"

"You are very welcome," she said.

Noel and Miko walked out of the hotel building side-by-side, they both had designer shades on and bags on their back.

After catching a cab to a rental car place, Noel told her, "Stay in the cab"

Before she could protest, Noel had hopped out and went to handle business without her.

She came back smiling and dangling keys to a truck and told her to come on.

This girl was full of energy, once they had plugged the directions into the GPS Miko asked Noel, "How are you not sleepy from the flight?"

Noel shrugged her shoulders, "Used to traveling, been traveling my whole life I guess"

Miko wished she could say the same but by the end of the New Year, she would be able too. This was definitely the year of the passport. Miko planned on overstepping boundaries, tackling all her fears, getting her family back and most importantly accomplishing every goal she set for herself.

"You got your gun?" Noel asked before she knocked on the door of the house of Dahl.

Miko shook her head, "no I don't have one"

Noel looked at her with surprise in her eyes, "What the hell?" she couldn't even fuss, the door had opened and they were being summoned in.

Minutes later, they were escorted into a private room where a housekeeper served them food.

Miko picked up a cookie before Noel slapped her hand and made her drop it.

She was about to go off on her ass before Noel whispered, "We don't know these people don't eat nothing," she hissed as if she was a bad child with no home training. When the Great Dahl entered, they both stood and bowed. Noel started speaking to him in his language, another thing that surprised her. Miko hated to admit that she had really underestimated the daughter of Christian and Farren Knight.

The meeting was pleasant until he brought out the heroin for them to "taste"'

Miko politely declined, and Noel told him that they would take a sample.

They left with plans to return in the morning with a decision. Miko would call Nasir tonight with the numbers and results from the sample. Noel told her it wouldn't be hard to find a junkie to try it out.

The two stopped at a small hole in the wall to grab lunch, they both settled on soup and bottled water.

She was too scared to eat the local meat and get food poisoning.

"We have the whole day to do nothing, what you wanna do?" Miko asked her.

"You need to be going to buy a gun, matter of fact that's our next stop," she said, slurping the soup up.

With the help of Google, they found some ransacked gun shop. Noel told her not to worry and whatever she picked out would be for practice.

"My mama always told me once you learn how to shoot, it don't matter what you got in your hand you gon' shoot that mother fucker" she told Miko seriously.

Miko busted out laughing, imagining Farren saying just that exact same statement.

She bought a .44 caliber then asked the man who sold them the guns where could they go shoot around, he pointed out the back door telling her it was an open passage.

She turned around and smiled at Miko, excited.

"I love guns," Noel told her, as they walked through the wild grass.

Miko was too busy making sure there weren't any snakes or creatures biting around her legs.

"Is that a good or bad thing?" she mumbled.

Noel turned around and walked backwards, "In your case it's a good thing I can't believe you came here with no protection" she shook her head.

Miko couldn't believe it, now that she actually processed the thought. A gun wasn't just something that was on her don't forget to pack list. She was more concerned with grabbing enough tampons and pantie liners.

"Okay so show me what you got" Noel told her, standing back and crossing her arms.

"I've only been to the gun range once," she explained before taking the gun off safety. At least Miko knew how to do that.

"I'm not judging" Noel said.

Miko took a deep breath, closed her eyes, and held her arm up.

"Whoa whoa how are you going to kill your target if your eyes are closed?" Noel told her, coming towards her and pushing her legs apart and moving her arms in a better position.

"You see that middle tree right there," she pointed straight ahead.

Miko nodded her head.

Noel told her, "Shoot"

She shot and missed.

Noel took a deep breath, "Okay watch me"

Miko stood back and watched her get in position and shoot, marking her target every time.

She studied her closely, looking at Noel with intent. She was pretty and graceful. The tall and round afro gave off a centric and neo-soul vibe.

"You see how I just did that? Okay try to do that," she told Miko.

Two hours later, Miko was better than she was when they first got there, but with extensive practice. She would be a pro in no time.

"I'm hungry again," Noel said.

Miko agreed, "Let's try to find some rice and vegetables"

"Sounds good to me," she told her.

Over dinner, the two ended up talking about way more shit than Miko would have imagined. Noel seemed distant and cold but once you got to know her, one would easily fall in love with her soul.

"Soooo" Noel started.

Miko took a bite of her broccoli, "I'm listening," she told her.

"The issue with the President how does that make you feel?" Noel questioned.

Miko started choking on her food, Noel was now alarmed, she handed her a glass of water that was for her but she quickly gave it to her.

After two big gulps of water and a few deep breaths, Miko had finally stopped choking.

"Are you okay?" Noel asked.

Miko pounded her chest "Yeah...uh yeah I'm good"

She still looked as if she was waiting on an answer to her question.

"I'm not sure how you want me to answer that"

Noel told her sarcastically, "Oh the truth will do"

She rolled her eyes, "I don't know how it makes me feel, it was a part of my life that's not in the past," she said.

Noel told her, "Fair enough"

She was happy that didn't she press the subject, if that was Lo was sitting before her, she would have asked a million more questions until Miko had no choice but to spill her guts.

She was such an open diary when it came to talking to Lo.

"I'm tired now" Noel sat back in her chair and rubbed her belly.

"Me too" Miko yawned.

They made it back to the hotel and left the car with valet.

"Tomorrow after we handle the price with Dahl we can leave," she told her.

Miko said, "Nasir told me we were going to be here for about two weeks"

She smiled and said, "Tell him that we met with Dahl and will be on a plane tomorrow night" before going to her bedroom and closing the door.

Miko decided to take a shower before calling Nas.

After they spoke, he sounded very surprised that she was able to handle everything in less than twelve hours, he said if it all checked out then they were set to come on home.

Miko was happy to hear that and it made sleeping in a hotel bed easier knowing that tonight would be her last night in the foreign country.

The next day, Dahl wrote his account and routing number on a piece of paper and even offered them a ride to the private airstrip but Noel declined for them both.

"Before we leave I want to take you somewhere," she told her. Once they were back in the rented car and driving from Dahl's estate.

"Where?" Miko asked out of curiosity.

"One of my favorite places in Cambodia" she told her.

"You've been here before?" Miko asked surprised.

Noel said, "A few times"

She was soon realizing that Noel was full of life and all kinds of hidden mysteries.

The drive was long wherever they were going but once they made it, Miko told Noel, "Definitely worth the drive" she told her, staring at the mountains.

"We used to come here when we were little and just lay out and talk about our future," she said, walking around and taking deep breaths of the fresh air.

Miko wiped the sweat beads that were forming on her forehead, it was a little humid but it was worth it.

"I feel the peace here," Miko admitted.

Noel nodded her head, "It's like the energy is just all over this place right?" she loved when people understood what she was saying, it wasn't too often that happened.

It seemed like forever before the pilot told them they would be cleared for landing in less than ten minutes. Miko exhaled loudly, she was more than ready to get home to her bed. Tomorrow she planned on doing nothing but pampering herself, then going to the bar to drink beer and eat hot dogs with Lo.

"Well one trip down a few more lined up" Noel told her, once they had gathered their luggage.

"I know right, I'm ready" she told her.

"Cool, see you around" Noel told Miko, before hopping in the back seat of a truck that had pulled up to get her.

Miko was still a city girl and she caught a cab to her condo. She kept Lo on the phone the entire cab ride and even while she walked towards her front door.

"I think I'm going to call him tomorrow," she told Lo, after she asked about Nash.

"Uh, you should he is fine as hell" Lo told her.

"What are you eating?" she asked because Lo had been smacking in her ear since they got on the phone.

"Girl some pork skins, I ain't had these things in years" Lo told her.

Miko unlocked her door and turned the alarm off. She turned the hallway light on and dropped her belongings in the foyer. She had to pee badly.

Ouch. She exclaimed loudly.

"What happened?" Lo told her.

Miko had tripped over something in the floor. She normally kept her house pretty clean so she wondered what was possibly in the middle of the hallway. Once she made it to her feet, she turned another light and turned around noticing that her home had been completely trashed.

Paintings were taken from the walls, Persian rugs shredded and her clothes were tossed all over the place. Tears immediately sprang from her eyes.

Lo's voice was heard yelling across the line.

"Miko!" she kept saying.

"Call my brother," she told Lo, crying.

Miko knew she had to get a gun. Too much shit was happening to her. It was as if these were all signs for her to move but she loved her home.

An hour later, Malachi had went off on the security guards and told Miko she needed to call the cable company that her alarm was serviced through and curse their asses out.

Miko sat in shock, wondering when would the madness stop.

Living right seemed to be the hard part. It was like when she was being a fuck-up and sleeping with a married man, she didn't have any problems.

Lo had been cleaning non-stop since she arrived, she stopped and made Miko a cup of tea, "My daddy used to tell me all the time, don't be weary in well doing"

Miko asked, "What does that mean?"

Lo sat beside her and took her hand in hers "It means don't question why it's happening, God is probably testing your faith. Stay on the right path" she told her.

Miko nodded her head and took a sip of the coffee.

"I really think you should move" Malachi told her.

Miko agreed, "I'll look at some places tomorrow"

He nodded his head, "and you still haven't talked to him?" he asked.

Miko rolled her eyes her brother would never let that shit go.

"Thanks for checking on me, kiss the kids for me" she dismissed him.

Malachi sighed; he wasn't trying to upset his sister.

He knew she was probably tired, after a twenty-four hour flight with two layovers and he assumed that traveling with Miss. Noel Knight wasn't the easiest task to do.

"Call me tomorrow," he told her.

He told Lo goodbye and left her crib.

"He means well you know that" Lo told her, sweeping the kitchen of glass.

"Yeah but he doesn't have to keep accusing me of sleeping with John and then he does it with this look in his eye…I just hate it" she said, flopping over and closing her eyes.

The next day was a very busy one, Miko and Lo started the day off looking at other places for her to live, none of them captured her eye like the house she lived in and Miko was getting irritated.

"Maybe you should get a brownstone in Harlem, like Mary Jane has" Lo suggested.

"Or maybe you can get one" Miko told her.

Lo rolled her eyes, "Okay, we need drinks, it's been a long day" she did an illegal U-turn in the street and headed to one of her favorite bars.

A song on the radio caught her attention, "Turn that up, turn that up," she said, loudly.

Lo was convinced that Miko ass was bipolar, she was just snapping on her and the realtor back at the last building they looked at ,but now had the goofiest smile on her face because of some song playing on the radio.

Lo turned the song up using a button on her steering wheel, "Girl this better be your song" she told her.

Nash's raspy voice came through the speakers and Miko was only able to catch the last few seconds. It was the exact same melody she came up with in her home that day along with the sample of the old school tune he told her he was going to use. She wished she had his number but whatever fucker messed her house up made sure to tear the number up as well, however she knew that if they were meant their paths would cross again. Miko now believed in faith and she had faith in their union, they would be together again.

"You like that song?" Lo asked her.

"I love it" Miko blushed.

***

"So, Miko how was Belize?" Jade asked.

She had a mouthful of baked ziti so she wasn't able to answer right away, she wiped her mouth and said, "Oh my Jade it was beautiful! The food was so good," she told her.

Malachi said, "Yeah that's on our list for this year"

Miko told them, "Me and Noel went to Cambodia. It was nice I didn't get to see as much as I wanted too, I told Lo me and her got to go back"

She saw Jade roll her eyes so she asked, "Did Lo do something to you?"

The kids looked at their auntie and back at their mommy.

Malachi knew this was conversation was about to go all the way left, his wife had never been one to bite her tongue and lately Miko hadn't been either.

"It's not that, I just think that you should choose your friend wisely," she told her.

Miko was caught off guard, she chuckled, "Oh, last time I checked I was an adult"

Malachi sent the kids to their rooms, MJ asked, "But mama baked cookies"

He told them to grab the damn cookies and go to bed.

Jade put her fork down, "Yeah but just because you pay bills don't make you grown boo"'

Miko was confused as to where this was coming from and why, "I don't understand," she told Jade.

Jade said, "It's a lot you don't understand but when you're hanging with someone who brags on sleeping with a married man it's a direct reflection of your character"

Malachi put his head in his hands. It was obvious to Miko now that her brother had been pillow talking.

"What she does is her business I can't put a gun to her hand and make her stop sleeping with him"

"But with everything that you had going on last year, why even hang around someone like that?" Jade asked her.

Miko didn't understand why they were discussing Lauren and she wasn't here to defend herself, that wasn't her style.

"Listen Jade, no disrespect because I look up to you as a mother and a wife but Lauren is my friend and I love her and she doesn't judge me so I don't judge her" she told her.

Malachi spoke up finally, "Okay can we get back to enjoying our dinner now?"

Jade bit her tongue, she saw it happening but she didn't care. Lauren was her friend, her best friend, ace boon coon and ride or die at that.

Miko made a mental note not to tell Malachi anything else. She didn't know that he and Jade were *that* close but she definitely knew now.

After dinner, instead of her spending the night as she normally did, Miko caught a cab home.

Her boxes were packed and she would be moving at the end of the month and she could not wait.

Miko had learned more than one valuable lesson last year and she now carried her gun, which she had a license for.

Once she was out of the tub, she sipped from a mug that her niece bought her for Christmas and stared at the nightlife happening below her.

 She was in the mood to dance but not in the mood to dress up, so she stayed in for the night. Every time she looked at her piano, nasty thoughts ran through her mind and her pussy tingled just a little.

If she never saw him again, she would be okay because the night they spent together was so overwhelming and magical.

Nash couldn't tell her that they didn't make love because she would tell him to stop lying to himself. His touch was so gentle, his strokes were light yet they held so much power. He took his time as he made his way in and out of her. His kisses were sweet and pleasant. Hell, even his sweat tasted good as she licked his collarbone and bit into his shoulder to keep from screaming out and waking a sleeping Lauren.

Sex had been taken to all new heights after being up under him.

She ran her hand across the piano keys before retreating to her bedroom. The kimono she wore over her naked body graced the hardwood floors. She walked barefoot against the grain.

Miko lay down, said her prayers and pulled the comforter over her head.

She knew it was the wine talking, when she bent over, kissed her pillow and said "Goodnight Nash"

Three days later, The Underworld had gathered for dinner at the restaurant that Papa was scheduled to open next month. He and his wife, Demi was always opening up something.

Miko loved how they worked together and raised their kids and every time she ran into Demi, she was full of life. One would never think she was dancing, being a wife, a mom, in school obtaining a degree and running about four successful businesses. She was like the modern day wonder woman.

"This calamari is good," she told Sasha.

"Bitch calamari taste like rubber, pass me some more of that free wine," she told Miko.

Miko shook her head because Sasha was crazy as hell.

"Meek you look cute!" Lo told her friend, when she made it to the table.

She was the last to arrive, which was new because Lauren hated when other people arrived late.

"Thanks love" Miko told her, she thought she looked cute too but she wouldn't sound cocky in front of the others. Miko had recently treated herself to a much-needed shopping trip. She rarely spent her money but since the New Year, she had been working tirelessly.

Today she wore denim jeans and a white button down with a knee-length blush pink fur vest. The high-top bun she wore was neat with only a few loose strands hanging around the crown of her head.

She had on the gold Rolex watch her brother copped her for Christmas a year ago, along with two Cartier bracelets that Lo got her randomly one day. That's just how Lo was, always giving endlessly to others.

Miko wore a gold cross necklace that she bought from H & M, the other day when she took her nieces shopping.

"Lo you don't see anybody else but Miko" Malachi joked.

Lo ignored him and spoke to everyone else, that's when Miko knew that she was feeling some type of way about what she told her the other day over lunch. Lo swore up and down that she was unbothered by Jade's comments but apparently, that was not the case.

Miko caught Lo's attention but Lo flashed her a fake smile. "Oh God" she mumbled under her breath.

Papa said, "Lo I know you gon keep it real with me, tell me how the calamari taste"

Sasha fake coughed and said, "Don't eat it" causing everybody to laugh.

Lo smiled, "Yeah you know I gotta keep it real with FAMILY," she said eyeing Malachi.

Miko saw the hurt in her eyes.

"Why you staring at my nigga like that?" Roderick asked her.

She shook her head and poured herself a glass of wine until it overflowed.

Mary Jane asked her was she okay and Lauren said, "I'm real good, as good as my hoe ass gon' get" she snapped. Mary Jane and everyone else were confused all except for Miko and Malachi.

He looked at his sister with disappointment in his eyes. She dropped her head, a beautiful afternoon was about to be ruined.

Nasir remained cool as always.

"Speak your mind it's obvious you came here on the bullshit" Malachi spat.

"Okay first and foremost, stop pillow talking with your wife and you tell that bitch to keep my name out of her mouth," she snapped.

Papa said, "Whoa! That's disrespect right there" he wasn't feeling the name calling about anybodies wives, even if it wasn't Demi Westbrook-Huffington.

"Lauren!" Miko shouted her name because she couldn't believe she said that.

Nasir continued eating his food.

"Lauren you crossing the line" Malachi warned, he was a very cool man until you spoke on his family.

"Oh am I? Well let me slide across it, what I do is my business, I don't make Meek do anything she don't want to do. I can't believe you allowed her to come at me like that.

I've been nothing but nice to her, it was me that helped plan your wedding, me that helped with the nursery-"

Nasir stopped her with one word, "Chill"

Lo looked at him, she was really just getting started. Lauren had a mouthful for Malachi's ass, her feelings were hurt.

"Okay y'all let's all take a deep breath" Roderick suggested.

Lauren shook her head, "Fuck all of yall" she told them and got up and left just as quickly as she had come.

The table was silent for quite some time, Malachi told his sister, "Yo let me talk to you"

Sasha smirked, "Big daddy gon get you" bringing the laughter back to the table.

Miko pushed her chair back and followed Malachi out of the private room and into the hallway.

"Wasup with you? That was a conversation you just had to repeat?" he went in on her immediately.

"It wasn't that way and she told me she wasn't tripping on it and then she come in here acting an ass" Miko told him.

"Let me tell you something about Lauren, I know you think you know her oh so well but you really don't. When it comes to Nas, she'll do anything, kill, steal or /and, it makes the sentence more exaggerated destroy. When someone speaks on him, she's offended automatically. You

see how nobody ever brings it up, huh? You saw how
Nasir acted like the like that shit didn't even happen. What
does that tell you" he made her think.

Miko shook her head, she begged to differ.

"That should have never went down" Malachi preached.
She apologized but he wasn't buying it, "Wise up sis" he
told her and left her alone with her thoughts.

Miko planned on texting Lauren once the dinner was over
to make sure she wasn't too into her feelings but she
already knew that Lauren was probably at the nearest L
store buying her a bottle or two.

On the other side of town, once the sun fell and the moon
had peeked back out, Lauren was staring at the television
screen.

She loved Lifetime, especially the horror movies. She wore
one of her collegiate t-shits from her alma mater and her
hair was wrapped in a silk scarf with a bonnet atop.

 She had been digging into a pint of ice cream and
drinking a bottle of water, in a weird way Lauren felt like
she was still on her diet just because she was drinking
water as well.

Lo heard a key being inserted into the hole of the front
door of her apartment. The gun that she kept under the
cushion of her couch was nearby but she knew it was *him*.

She didn't even bother to get up, crack a smile or snatch the wrap from her head. His presence had done nothing for her on this rainy night.

"Why you looking like my grama over there?" he joked, as he removed his coat, scarf and gloves.

Nasir came closer to her, taking the ice cream from her hands and sitting it on the coffee table before them.

He placed Lo on his lap, facing him and asked her, "You know I love you right?"

Lo had been questioning that word for a few months now. Things weren't progressing in her favor and she was now wanting more from herself and less from him.

"I wonder," she told him.

Nasir kissed her lips, not really in the mood to talk. He had been kicking it with the fellas all night and was scheduled to head back to Atlanta to be with Jordyn, and wanted to see Lo before he left.

She turned her head, rejecting his affection.

"What's up?" he pressed.

"Why didn't you say anything earlier?" she finally asked him.

Nasir sat back on the couch, resting his hands on the sides of her thick brown thighs.

"Babe what did you expect me to say?" he asked.

"I EXPECTED you to defend me Nas" she exclaimed loudly.

He shot her a look that brought her voice down a few levels, she continued, "You made me look stupid"

"You be wanting me to do what? Go off on Chi for talking to his wife, that's not my place" he argued.

"But it's okay for her to talk about me?" she asked.

Nasir took a deep breath, "People gon always talk, let them talk you good and I'm good, that's all that matters" he told her.

She rolled her eyes at the game he was trying to run on her, "Please leave" she asked. Lauren rather be alone tonight than listen to him feed her bullshit.

"Tell me what made you so mad?" he asked, really wanting to gain a better understanding.

"If you don't see it, I can't make you," she told him, shaking her head and attempting to get up off his lap.

He wouldn't let her go, "I don't know what Jade's issue is," he told her.

Lo's feelings were hurt, "I've never done anything to her," she said.

"Yeah I know," he agreed.

"Are her and Jordyn friends?" she questioned.

He shrugged his shoulders, "Not sure about the word, friend. But we've took a few trips together. Jordyn is to herself and Jade doesn't know anything," he said.

Lo cringed at the thought of him and his long time girlfriend all in Aspen on the slopes and shit.

"So why did she tell Miko that?" she asked.

Nasir didn't care what she told Miko and he wished Lauren didn't care either, but she did.

"Who knows love" he rubbed her back.

"Can't believe Malachi," she said sadly.

"Yeah but to be calling his wife a bitch where did that come from? Not lady like at all Lauren" he told her, his accent was so heavy especially when he said her name. The L in Lauren never sounded so sexy.

"I was mad," she told him. Lauren wanted to call her more than that but she refrained.

He reached up and took her bonnet off, "I hate that thing," he confessed.

Lauren laughed, "I don't care, you ain't about to come in here and fuck my hair up" she told him.

He kissed her lips and pulled her closer to his chest, "Oh yeah? I'm not," he said, slowly moving his hips against her private areas.

Lo let out a little moan, "Hmmmm no cus I'm mad at you" she told him.

He moved his mouth behind her ear, knowing that was one of her hot spots. His long, wet, juicy tongue planted kisses around that area.

"What I gotta do baby?" he whispered in her ear.

She closed her eyes and moaned a little louder this go round, "Say my name," she begged.

"Lauren" he repeated her name.

Nasir knew she loved to hear her name being called, especially when she was riding his dick, just like he liked it and that's exactly what he was about to have her doing, as he moved the granny panties she wore to the side....

Miko woke up from a very peaceful sleep to her phone ringing. Whoever was calling her must have clearly been in need of something. She had tossed and turned for a few minutes before crawling out of bed and fumbling through her purse to find her cell phone.

She was irritated and tipsy, in her opinion the best sleep came after sex and after a few drinks.

Once Lo had stormed out of the restaurant, surprisingly everything went back to normal. She thanked the man above because not less than twenty minutes after she had left, Jade and Demi had arrived to the restaurant, claiming that they were in the area.

It was like an unspoken tension between the wives of The Underworld and the women who were employed by The Underworld, she had never seen it before today.

Sasha barely spoke to them and Mary Jane was naturally quiet anyway. Miko didn't let any of that stop her from eating all of the good food and drinking some of the best wine she had ever tasted in her life.

She even bought a bottle back home to pack in a box for when she moved into her new home.

She finally found her phone buried all kinds of shit in her purse; it was time for her to clean the bag out anyway.

She dropped the phone on her big toe, "Ouch!" She said loudly.

After pulling the notification bar down and seeing the familiar number fill the screen, she instantly became enraged.

Before she could redial the number to go off, the phone had rang and vibrated again.

Miko couldn't answer the damn phone fast enough, she was so mad.

She answered and waited on him to speak, just to make sure it was his dumb ass.

"Miko" he said her name in that tone...oh, she used to love his voice so much.

Miko used to watch his speeches online in her spare time or when she was missing him.

Those days were long gone and now his voice sounded like Lucifer's.

He said, "I MISS YOU" after he heard her breathing loudly over the line.

She told him in one quick and short breath, "Stop fucking calling me before I report you to the National Enquirer" she threatened and hung the phone up.

This time she made sure to turn her cell phone on silent. She pulled the trap phone she had for The Underworld from a pocket in her purse and sat it on the nightstand before getting back in the bed and going to sleep.

For the first time in a while, it felt damn good to not go to bed with worry on her mind.

Life was finally looking up for her and she was happy about it.

Chapter 10

Miko ran around her dining room, making sure everything was together. Since dawn, she had been up preparing for tonight's housewarming/girls night in. She was excited for the girls to get together, between working for The Underworld and moving into her dream home at the tender age of twenty-six, Miko had been a very busy girl.

It was Lo's idea for her to buy a house on the outskirts of the city, in a small subdivision in Newark, New Jersey. The five bedroom ranch-styled home was perfect for her. She turned one of the rooms into an office and the others besides the Master served as guest rooms.

She dodged the idea of an interior decorator and decided on putting her creativity skills to use. The color scheme of the home were several shades of brown, Miko was on her grown and sexy.

Tonight's menu consisted of all of her favorite foods, her dining room paid homage to her Korean roots, the wooden brown table that she had refurbished sat low and the large pillows that she had sewn herself were placed around the table. Large vases in the corner along with a long bright orange rug completed the look for the room. She had a dresser table on the back wall that would serve as a dining station whenever she entertained.

Miko lit a candle near the foyer before going to take a bath and get dressed. She encouraged all of the girls to dress comfortable since they were sitting on the floor.

After bathing and sliding on a Nike jogging suit, she went into the kitchen and took the bottles of wine out of the refrigerator so they could chill.

The doorbell rang and she knew it was Lo because she told her she was on the way almost an hour ago.

"Girl who did your yard? It looks good," She praised.

Lo had been to the home a few times but not since it was, complete.

"Me and Chi" she said nonchalantly.

"You planted those trees and pretty flowers, even the lil brown stuff in the front?" she asked.

Miko laughed, "Girl yes it wasn't hard at all" she told her.

Lo said, "Ok Miko Stewart, ooh I love what you did with this room" she told her, walking into the sitting room.

Miko liked it too, she had a large white chaise in the middle of the floor and her piano in the corner, the cushion to the piano bench was covered in cheetah, another do-it-yourself project done by Miko.

She had a large gold mirror leaned against the opposite wall and two small chairs with an end table in the middle.

"Girl I might move in" Lo joked.

Miko went into the kitchen to start bringing the dishes into the dining room, the doorbell chimed again and Lo hollered, "I'll get it"

Mary Jane came into the kitchen, "I love your home Meek," she told her.

Miko smiled and gave her a hug, "You didn't have to get me a gift" she told her, after Mary Jane handed her a small gift bag.

"It's sage to burn after we leave, keep the energy in your house positive," she said.

Only Mary Jane would think to get her a gift like that, but she was grateful for it and planned to burn it.

"Thank you" she told her and sat the bag by the bar in her kitchen.

"I'll give the tour, Sasha just arrived" Lo said.

"Okay we waiting on one more person then we can start" Miko told them.

"I know you didn't invite Jade?" Lo asked.

Miko shook her head, "No Lauren I didn't but that is my sister in law"

Sasha asked, "Well who is the extra guest?"

By then, the doorbell had ringed again.

"There she is" Miko told the group of women.

She walked into her foyer and opened the door to see Noel standing there with a gift in her hand, "I'm so happy you made it," she told her.

"I was in the area visiting my grandmother at the nursing home" she said and stepped in.

Noel couldn't act as if she was happy to be there but Miko wouldn't say anything, she gave her a hug and escorted her into the kitchen where the rest of the crew was.

"Yall know Noel, Noel here is everybody again" she said.

Lo stared, Mary Jane said, "hello" and Sasha asked where the stronger alcohol was.

"My mom got you a gift," Noel told Miko.

She stopped washing her hands and smiled, "I'll be sure to call her and say thank you, can you open it for me," she asked Noel.

Noel pulled it out of the brown wrapping, "Wow that is beautiful" Lo praised.

It was a large canvas, hand-painted with the words, "God bless this home"

Miko loved it and she knew exactly where was going to put it.

Everyone washed their hands after Lo gave a tour, as if it was her home.

They all sat down on the floor and crossed their legs.

"I shouldn't have worn these tight ass pants," Sasha complained.

Plates were passed back and forth across the table.

"Miko what is that smell burning, it smells so good?" Mary Jane asked.

"It's a lavender candle I got from Bath and Body Works, that's my new favorite store," she told her.

"Girl I love it in there," Sasha said.

Even Noel chimed in, "I love the mahogany teakwood candle," she said.

"Hmm that sound like it smells good," Lo laughed.

Over dinner, the women discussed just about everything, no topic was off limits.

Somehow, they migrated from the dining room to the living room, with dessert and coffee, everybody was in a place of their own in the room.

Lo said, "Shit I done gained a few pounds"

Miko shook her head, "Stop it Lo" she laughed. Lo was always saying she was gaining weight but in truth, her figure was breath taking.

"I really enjoyed myself," Mary Jane told everyone.

"Girl I used to think you were a gypsy, the only person you would talk to was Papa," Sasha said.

"That's like my brother, we're here, you feel me," she said, pointing to her heart.

"So yall never talked?" Lo pressed.

Mary Jane quickly said, "Hell no, he not even my type"

"Mines neither" Noel mumbled.

"You got a type girl?" Miko asked her.

"Foreign rich men" she teased, the wine had Noel feeling good and dandy.

"Hell me too!" Lo raised her wine glass.

"Well I like thug niggas, I'm talking about gun toting, pants sagging, gold teeth, big and sexy, black mother fucker!" Sasha said.

Everyone busted out laughing, Sasha's ass was crazy.

"I like black men" Miko told them.

"Correction you like Nash" Lo teased.

Miko blushed him, she had been thinking about him so much lately, hoping she saw him again really soon.

"I don't know what I like, I'm so to myself" Mary Jane shook her head.

"Let me hook you up with my cousin" Sasha suggested.

Lo spoke for her, "Girl hell no she good, we don't want none of your fresh out the pin cousins. Them niggas be having too much stamina for me"

Everyone laughed again, "Lo you are crazy!" Noel said.

Lo danced in her seat, "Hey I'm real" she told them.

The night was merry and it was safe to say that all of the women in The Underworld had more in common than making money.

***

Miko stood on the curb waiting for Lo to pull up. She held her body not feeling comfortable with the stares she was getting. Right when she pulled her cell phone out to call her for the second time, Lo was coming up the sidewalk,

"I couldn't find a parking spot," she told her.

Miko shook her head, "You used to get on me about being on time what happened?"

Lo laughed, "I'm sorry I had to get some dick real quick, geesh"

"I knew it!" Miko looped her arm in hers and they bypassed the growing line and walked into the club heading straight for the bar.

"Girl I been working all week, I need a strong drink" Lo told her after she heard Miko order a wine.

"I'm taking it light, I think I'm coming on my cycle soon," she said.

Lo nodded her head, she had been on birth control for years so her period was very irregular.

"It's popping in here tonight" Lo did a little two-step.

Miko bobbed her head to the beat. She was definitely feeling the vibe in Aroma tonight.

She was comfortable, casual and cute.

"I'm staying at your house tonight," she told Lo.

"Girl you know I don't care" Lo shrugged her shoulders.

Miko knew she would be too tired to drive back to Jersey after a long night out with her best girl.

They migrated from the bar to the VIP section of someone that Lo knew from college, as always the girl knew everybody in the damn place.

A tall and very handsome man approached them and Miko could have sworn she saw Lo blush. What took her by surprise is that she had never seen her smile at any other man besides Nasir.

Miko watched them interact and she had a million and one questions.

The man bent down and whispered in her ear causing her to giggle.

"Meek I'll be right back," Lo told her.

She raised an eyebrow and Lo winked her eye and stood up, walking away with the man.

Miko watched her to see where the stranger was taking her friend but when they stopped at the bar, she went back to enjoying herself.

"I know my eyes are playing tricks on me," she said aloud. Looking up at the DJ booth and seeing *him*. Miko thought her eyes were playing tricks on her. But when he opened his mouth and she saw the gold in his mouth, she knew it was him. Miko was staring at Nash in the flesh and she wanted him at the moment.

She contemplated on her next move, would she sit there hoping that he just happened to walk past and see her but in a crowded club such as Aroma, was it possible?

Then she thought about bossing up and walking up on him, demanding his attention and a little bit of his time. Miko looked back up and watched him laugh with the DJ and he looked like a natural up there.

She wondered if he thought about her just as much as he crossed her mind. She often thought if he kissed another woman the way he kissed her.

She wanted him to herself, did she sound crazy?

Was love in first sight real? Because if it was Miko was thinking about dropping to one knee and proposing to his fine ass.

She tossed Lo's shot back and said "to hell" with the glass of red wine that she ordered. Miko knew that the vodka would give her the confidence she needed to go forth with her second move of approaching him.

She stood to her feet and used her hands to smooth the fitted plum colored knee-length skirt that she wore and began to walk near the steps towards the DJ booth.

Once she got closer and saw the husky security guards she cursed herself, *What the fuck was she thinking?* She was in a club for goodness sake of course the DJ booth was off limits.

She smacked her lips, feeling defeated and turned on her designer pumps and went back to the section full of people that Lo knew and she didn't.

Nash would remember that lil ass anywhere, he told his cousin, Maine to hold the fort down. They were trying to get the DJ to play his track. When he saw Miko, he knew that he needed to holler at her now. Nash was unaware if he would ever see her again the city of New York was huge.

"Miko!" he called her name but the club was booming and bunking.

He made his way in between the security guards and followed her into the crowd, "Miko!" he said her name again but she was on a mission to get to wherever she was going.

Nash tried his hardest to get through the multitudes of people, finally when he was close enough he lunged forward and grabbed her arm.

She turned around with a menacing look on her face but when she recognized his face, she relaxed and the frown she wore was replaced with a warm and inviting smile. He got closer to her and pulled her, resting his hands around her waist.

"I'm mad at you," he told her.

She shook her head, "My house was broken into" she informed him.

"And they stole my number?" he questioned.

Miko laughed, "Yes they did"

Nash would let her off the hook for now, "How have you been?"

It was as if they weren't in a club, the way he was attempting to hold a conversation as if they were alone in a restaurant on a dinner date. She didn't care that she could barely hear him and that her eyes were beginning to water because she was near several smokers. Nothing mattered now that she was standing before him, the man of her dreams. As cliché as it sounded, it was true. Miko instantly felt a connection to him.

People pushed each other around them trying to get to a comfortable place in the crowded club, Miko ended up being way closer to him than she would want to so soon, "It's so crowded" she complained.

"I know, I got to get my record played, you wasn't about to leave were you?" he asked, hoping that the answer was no.

His prayers were answered when she shook her head.

"Don't leave without me," he told her.

She promised that she wouldn't by pledging girl scout's honor, he held on to her waist for a lil longer before pulling away and disappearing back into the crowd and going to the DJ booth.

Miko found her way to the section and Lo told her, "Girl I been calling your phone, where you been?" she asked.

"I ran into Nash," she told her.

Lo smiled, she knew how much her friend was feeling him on the low.

"Is he still sexy?" she asked.

Miko laughed, "Yes" and covered her face to conceal her happiness.

"Girl so let me tell you who that was, the dude who pulled me away" she started.

Miko moved closer so she could hear Lo well enough so that she wouldn't have to repeat herself.

"That was my boyfriend from high school, girl my parents love him," she told Miko.

"Did you love him?" Miko asked.

She moved her hands to say, *so-so*, "He was sweet anyway girl, so he's divorced and getting back on the scene. We're going to brunch in the morning," she said.

Miko gave her the eye but remained silent, "Why you looking at me like that?" Lo asked.

"What about Nas?" she questioned.

She waved her hand, "I'm doing me this year," she told her.

Miko didn't believe her but she hoped that she did, her friend was beautiful and not only did her external shine but so did her spirit. Miko wanted more for Lo, so she was hoping that she didn't cancel the brunch tomorrow.

Apparently, this guy was important if she even gave him the green light to whisk her away in a well-known club in the city.

Miko and Lo enjoyed their night, they wasn't too turnt up though they mainly danced in their seats and took cute pictures the whole night.

Somehow, Nash made his way to her and Lo motioned for him to come to their section. He asked if his cousin could come too and she told him that was cool.

"Hey brother in law" she said.

Miko quickly spoke for her, "Lauren is tipsy ignore her"

"No I'm not," she said.

Miko kicked her under the bar table and Nash saw it,

"Don't do my sister in law like that"

Lo smiled, "That' right!"

She thought they both were out of their damn mind, already discussing marriage and such.

Nash stood and rolled a blunt, then lit it and passed it to his cousin.

Soon after the DJ announced, "New track from Brooklyn's finest, NASHHHHHHHHHHH! Yall show the kid some love," he said.

Miko bobbed her head to the beat and Lo stood up and hit the blunt with Nash and his cousin, she must have really been feeling the song because she normally only smoked with The Underworld.

Nash silently observed the crowd and they seemed to be fucking with the song that was a good thing.

His cousin reached over, draped his arm over Nash's shoulder, "You know who that girl is?"

He asked, "What girl?"

Before Maine, Nash's cousin could give him the 411 on Miko, gun shots went off in the club.

Lo and Miko both pulled their gun, in the life they lived they could never be sure.

Miko had been spending all her spare time at the damn gun range, if she wasn't going with her big brother then her and Noel would meet her there. Noel had told her one day, "Love your gun because one day it's going to be the one thing to save your life"

Ever since then Miko had been carrying it everywhere she went.

Nash turned around to make sure his girl... *Yeah, his girl.*.Was straight but when he saw her with a .40 caliber in her hand he knew his little Korean cutie could hold her own down? But still the man in him pulled her up and told her to stay behind him.

Miko had Lo's hand tight in hers, "Girl I gotta call Nas," she whispered.

She ignored her. The only goal on her mind was getting the fuck out of the club in the midst of people running around crazy.

They took a side door and dipped into an alley, "Meek I gotta call Nasir!" she said it again.

"For what! We are trying to make sure we get the fuck out of here alive and you keep screaming his damn name!" she was frustrated and sick of Lo screaming his name every other second.

She loved her friend but in the case of them trying to save their life, Nasir couldn't do shit.

Lo screamed, "Shut the fuck up! You don't even know what's really going on"

Miko looked at her and saw it in her eyes...what her brother had tried to warn her about.

"You riding with me?" she turned around and asked Nash, as if Lo wasn't even staring there with tears in her eyes.

Nash nodded his head, his cousin was a grown ass man and he could handle his own.

She walked off and he followed, but his cousin did too.

"Yall can drop me off near the subway," he told them.

"You sure cuz?" Nash asked.

Miko never mumbled a word, her six-inch heels clicked across the pavement. The wind was chilly so she walked with her arms across her chest.

"Why you got that big ole gun?" his cousin asked her. She told him, "My safety"

They made it to public parking lot where she parked her car and Nash was impressed to see the newest Mercedes Benz jeep.

His cousin whistled at the black on black beauty.

Miko bought the truck one day when she was bored, she still had her Lexus but she barely drove it anymore. The jeep was so smooth and it was good on gas.

She hopped in her truck and turned the truck on, Nash got into the passenger and his cousin in the back seat.

He silently thanked God for growth because a year or two ago, he would have robbed her ass and split the funds with his cousin. But he was feeling shorty and wouldn't even do her like that.

Nash believed that his time was coming any day now so there was no need to bring karma into his life, he didn't need anything fucking up the blessings he was waiting on. He pushed the seat back, stretching his long legs, "Take him to the subway" he told her.

Miko was so fucking irritated she couldn't even concentrate on what was going on around her.

Her fingers were wrapped so tight around the steering wheel, her knuckles became ashy.

"You good ma?" he asked.

She told him, "Yeah" then pulled out of the parking lot. Instead of making a right, she went into the direction of the club to see if saw Lo. She knew it was wrong for leaving her ass in that alley by herself but the comment she made rubbed her the wrong way.

Miko spotted her car at the red light and she felt better knowing her girl was okay.

She did an illegal U-turn in the middle of the street, "Yo, its cops out here and you doing an Illegal U-turn," Nash said.

She ignored him, the entire NYPD was on The Underworld payroll so she wasn't worried at all. Miko knew them on first name basis mainly because she was the one that paid them monthly.

After dropping Nash's cousin at the subway, she hopped on the highway and headed to her home.

"Where we going?" Nash asked her after he slowly saw the city he loved become further and further away. He was seeing highway signs and exits he wasn't familiar with. The fact that she hadn't said anything since the club had him worried.

He was hoping that his past wasn't coming back to fuck with him and this wasn't no damn set up.

"I have a lot on mind, just relax" she told him and turned the radio up.

Lauryn Hill filled the truck as her sultry voice oozed out of the speakers.

Nash shook his head and sparked up a blunt. He didn't even bother asking her was it okay but out of respect, he cracked the window.

Miko's phone rang and she answered it because it was her trap phone and not the personal one, "Yeah" she said in short.

"You good?" Lo asked.

That's just how their relationship had grown to become since linking up, even if they were mad at each other they still talked before bed, like lovers.

"Yeah are you?" Miko questioned.

Lo sighed, "Yeah we will talk tomorrow when your company leaves, be safe," she said.

"Okay night" she told her.

Lo called her name, "Meek?"

"Yes" she answered, Miko was really feeling some type of way and she couldn't wait to talk to her brother.

"I love you," Lauren told her.

"Love you too" Miko told her and hung the phone up.

"That was your friend?" Nash asked.

Miko said, "You're nosey"

Nash puffed his chest out and sat up, coughing from pulling on the blunt too hard, "Aye ma let me tell you something I was looking forward to seeing you again, don't be catching no attitude with me let that shit go" he let her ass know.

She swallowed air and said nothing, never had she been put in her place before, but hell she liked it.

He went back to smoking his blunt, knowing that he wouldn't have any more problems out of Miss Miko tonight.

They finally made it to Jersey and to her subdivision. When she clicked the button on the gate clicker to grant them access into the gated subdivision she lived in. Nash was in awe but he played it cool.

The truck pulled into the opened garage and Miko turned the truck off and took a deep breath.

She ran her hands through her hair. She knew that Lauren was going to give her the scoop tomorrow she just hoped that she could get some sleep until then.

"Whatever it is, put it on the back burner for now," Nash told her, damn near reading her thoughts.

She turned to him and said, "You're right, come on, are you hungry?"

They got out of the truck and she opened the door that led them into the house.

"This is nice," he told her.

"Thank you, I just moved not too long ago," she said, walking into the kitchen to see what she can whip up.

"I'm high as a mother fucker," he said, sitting on a bar stool chair facing her.

Miko slid out of her feels and kicked them to the side and opening the refrigerator, "What about fried bologna sandwiches? Do you eat that?" she asked.

Nash was super shocked to hear her suggest that, "Yo you eat fried bologna?"

Miko turned around, "Uh yeah? Are you being racist right now!" she asked.

Nash quickly told her, "Nah took me by surprise that's all, it's a hood meal"

Miko pulled out a skillet and grabbed the pack of Bar-S bologna out of the produce drawer in her fridge.

"I'm from the hood, in D.C." she let him know.

"Word?" he asked.

She nodded her head and made them a few sandwiches. Miko didn't know how he *got* her, but it was as if Nash was picking up on her spirits. She wasn't in the mood to do much talking, she had a lot of shit on her mind and the raging hormones she had prior in the club were now stowed away.

However, she was happy that he was here. Her nights weren't lonely because she had begun to live a life pleasing to herself. She was quite fulfilled in every aspect of her life but she knew that she wanted love.

After they ate, he asked for a tour, she was happy to finally give one since the time her girls came over, and Lo took over.

"I love this piano" he stared at in admiration.

"The song you did is dope" she finally was able to tell him how much she enjoyed it.

"'Preciate it" Nash was such a modest man.

Miko left him there and went to get a bottle of water, when she came back to the room he was laying on the chaise with headphones over his ear.

"I hope you don't mind, I saw these and wanted to hear a song on my phone" he told her, pausing the song once he saw her.

"No, do you" she told him, giving him the green light.

He stared at her, "You look good too" he licked his lips.

Nash was delighted to be in her presence yet another time, when his career wasn't on his mind, his future was and hopefully that would include Miko.

Miko blushed, "Thank you"

"Come here, stop acting shy" he held his arm out, wanting her close to him.

She laid on the chaise beside him, lifting one leg and laying it over his.

The beat of her heart somehow put her to peace and before she knew it, she was sleeping.

Nash tapped her but lightly, "Let's go get in the bed," he suggested.

Miko lifted her head and wiped the slob from the side of her mouth, "Oh my I'm so sorry I didn't mean to fall asleep" she told him.

"You good love, I'm tired too" he admitted.

Miko got off him and went to her bedroom with Nash in tow, "I don't mind sleeping in the guest bed if you're not comfortable," he told her.

Miko yawned, "I want you here.. I mean its okay like we can sleep in the bed together" she switched it around.

Nash smiled and stripped down to his boxers and socks. Miko went into her closet and undressed, she came to bed with blue flannel shorts and a white t-shirt and no bra.

He was already in bed on his back looking up to the sky, counting down the days until he had a nice ass crib such as the one he was in right now.

"Goodnight" Miko told him, turning the lamp off on her nightstand

"Come here" he commanded.

"You come here, I like my side of the bed," she told him, not moving from where she was.

Nash rolled over with no hesitation and got closer to her. He kissed her lips once and held her.

"Dream about me" he teased.

"Won't be the first night I do that," she told him, under her breath.

***

"Is everything okay?" Miko asked him nervously, they had just finished having mind-blowing sex and she was feeling damn good about herself. She was able to keep up with his young energetic ass without complaining or cramping. Nash had the stamina of a stallion but so did she, when he went hard she went harder.

"You don't get tired of coming to get me and being cooped up in the house?" he spat.

She covered her body with the thin sheet that was barely holding on to the bed.

"Excuse me?" before she answered his question she wanted to make sure she heard him correctly.

Nash shook his head and crawled out of bed, his tall frame leaned against the dresser, even though his dick was now limp it still hung long and caused her mouth to water just looking at it.

"Miko!" he called her name for the second time, she didn't even know she had clocked out.

"Huh? Oh yes I heard you. What made you say that?" she asked.

Nash took a deep breath, "Look I gotta tell you something" he told her.

She waited patiently for him to continue, sensing that whatever he was about to say would sadly bring whatever they were working on, building, or doing these past two months to an end.

If it was one thing Miko was familiar with it was rejection. She automatically assumed that what they had was no more than a good night and he no longer wanted her. The pussy wasn't enough to keep this fine specimen and he was now preparing to end things with her.

Before the words could fall from his lips, she decided that she didn't even want to hear it, at least not now. She preferred him to leave while she slept; it made it easier to deal with.

She went over to him and stroked his cheek, Nash turned his head, and Miko was making this difficult for him.

"Meek we need to talk," he told her.

She shook her head and reached in and kissed his lips, she wasn't even tripping that he didn't necessarily kiss her back.

She lowered her body onto the floor, getting on her knees and pulling his soft penis into her mouth.

Slowly savoring the salty taste of pre-cum that she had grown to love. Since they had began to spend tons of time together.

She closed her eyes and got into character, a dirty stripper is what she imagined herself to be.

In the back of a Cadillac with no panties on, Miko stuck one of her hands in between her legs and stroked herself back to life as well.

She felt her clit hardening and it caused her to suck his dick just a little bit faster than she was before.

Nash relaxed and leaned his head back using his neck for support, Miko and that little tongue. She knew just what to do with it.

He moaned under his breath but she heard him, her head bobbed up and down, using her tongue to stroke his shaft at the same time. Miko loved when he nutted in her mouth, she encouraged him to do so even when he laid atop her.

He was no longer allowed to release himself anywhere else but in her mouth and down her throat, she would hungrily suck every last morsel of cum out of him.

"Yes daddy yes" she mumbled.

Nash only used one hand to slow her down and there was no need for her to rush. They had all day, it was a Sunday afternoon and they had been locked in the house all weekend having sex, fucking, and even on Friday night in the wee hours of the morning, he considered that one session between two and five thirty…love.

The intensity that built up throughout the week because they both were busy had finally come out once she picked him up from the hood.

Nash had been trying his hardest to stay out of trouble but he was a broke as a motherfucker, that one song didn't make a big enough buzz as he was expecting it to.

He was saddened that he wouldn't become a superstar overnight, like most rappers these days. All they needed was one hit to take them to the top. But in his case, it wasn't happening that way.

Nash had to put in double the dedication but with no money for studio time, he was stuck at his mama's house and forced to sit on the stoop and write songs with no beats or studio.

The only time he felt complete or not miserable was when Miko came and scooped him.

It bothered him that she didn't want more for herself, and when he thought of the word, 'more'. He was referring to trips and shopping sprees. Nash couldn't even afford a dinner date now.

In his eyes, he wasn't shit and Miko deserved much better.

"Fuck!" before he knew it he was cumming.

They had been fucking non-stop and he wasn't able to hold out as long as he used too...but this was only the case when Miko had her mouth on his balls.

She swallowed him and even cleaned his dick with her tongue and lips before getting back up, she tried to bypass him quickly and go to the bathroom to shower but he grabbed her up quick.

"Stop running from this conversation" he told her.

She looked away, "Why are you trying to leave me? What am I doing wrong?" she asked.

He pulled her chin closer to his, "It's not you it's me Miko," he told her

Staring at him with disappointment in her eyes, she liked to think that the time they had spent together whether ninety-nine percent of it was spent in the bed or not. She had hoped that Nash had learned a little more about her. But the sorry ass line he just hit her with had told her that their time spent together had been in vain.

She smacked her lips and stormed off, Nash shook his head, knowing she was doing that shit on purpose.

He followed her into the bathroom after hitting the blunt a few times, joining her in the shower.

"I don't have shit and you know that," he finally said it aloud.

She turned around, body filled with soapsuds, "What have I asked you for?"

He shook his head, "Miko as a man I can't keep coming over here and not offering you anything, I can't even take you out to eat"

"I love to cook and you know that," she said quickly.

"Don't make excuses for me," he told her with finality in his voice.

"What's the real problem?" she asked.

He pulled her closer and kissed her wet face, "Let me get on my shit and come back and treat you proper" he told her.

"Nash don't leave me," she said.

No, he hadn't whisked her away to a villa on a private island, and yes, she had to pick him up from his mama's house but so what? She liked him a lot and she enjoyed her time with him.

It wasn't about being bored or lonely because she had crossed those barriers with the help of Farren Knight. Miko couldn't just come out and explain how her heart skipped a beat when she rolled over in the middle of the night and saw him sleeping with a smile on his face.

She knew that she had become his calm in the midst of a storm and that was okay with her.

"If you fuck with me like you say you do, you'll respect my decision baby," he said.

She took a deep breath and nodded her head, "I guess"

Nash smiled, "You know I'm rocking with you" he told her, grabbing the loofah that had slowly become his and started washing his body.

Miko watched him out of the corner of her eye, hoping that what he had told her was the God honest truth.

She couldn't stand to be hurt again, she refused.

The way her trips to the gun range had been set up lately, she would have to have to run up on Nash ass and show him what's really good.

"What you thinking about?" Nash caught her staring.

"Us" she told him, to a certain extent her answer was the truth.

She knew that there were a few things they needed to discuss, such as the scandal and even how she got her bread. Nash never asked what she did for a living nor did he ask about the men she had been with before coming into constant contact with him. Miko was curious to know if he already knew what was up with the President. She assumed that he was choosing to not ask because he didn't care or he was unaware.

However, until they crossed the bridge she was enjoying every minute spent with him. The time they spent together was delicate. Of course, they were having sex like horny teenagers but besides the physical, she really enjoyed her time with him. She was pretty confident that he felt the same way. Miko had been waking him up to breakfast and head in bed what man wouldn't be pleased?

"Oh yeah? What about us?" he asked, coming closer, backing her up against the wall in the shower.

"How much I enjoy your company" she kissed his lips. Nash kissed her back, "You enjoy me or this dick?" he teased.

Miko smirked, "Can I say both?"

He opened her legs and told her, "Nope" as he slowly inserted two of his fingers into her pussy.

She watched him get comfortable in between her legs. Even with the shower water cascading over them, the exotic sounds that her pussy was churning out could still be heard.

Little moans here and there escaped her lips. Nash stared at her with lust in her eyes. Her lips would form a circle and as he went further into her, she would gasp then close her mouth.

"Nah let it out" he told her, bending down and picking her up. He had enough of the foreplay and it was time for him to tear that pussy up.

"Shit!" she said loudly as they switched positions, Nash sat on the bench in the shower and sat Miko on his dick, putting her back towards his chest.

"Ride it," he commanded, bending her over and smacking her on the ass roughly.

"Nash" she whined.

"Take it," he ordered.

Putting one hand on the wall and the other on his thigh, as she rode his dick with expertise. She arched her back and placed all of her weight on one foot, Nash pushed her back lower, wanting her in a certain angel so he could gain full access into his pussy.

"Yes baby yes" she encouraged him to continue to be the captain of the ship.

He pulled her up and pulled her back down, then rocked her forward, moving her hips to a beat that he had been working on in his head for the past three days.

"What you doing?" she turned her head and asked.

"Does it feel good?" he asked her, with his eyes closed and his toes curled.

"Yesss" she moaned in pure satisfaction.

"Alright then" he said and began to move her faster on his dick.

She held on for dear life, Nash had her coming up and off his dick then sliding her back on.

The sight was so pleasant if they would have an audience. Miko bent over and took control of the situation, holding her ankles and riding him as fast as her hips would allow her too.

"Damnnnnnnnnnn" Nash roared.

She wouldn't stop though, she wouldn't give in or let up, she dared him to mumble the words, "She deserved better" Hell, she had been with the most powerful man in the United States of America for years, who was to tell her what she deserved? Power, money, status, account balances….those things no longer mattered to Miko. She wanted substance and quality, the heart of a man was now more important than his acquired wealth.

Miko would gladly take a long passionate kiss than bite marks and spankings. She would choose a long and honest conversation over a quickie in a closet.

See, for Miko things had changed. She wanted value, she wanted love.

She hoped and prayed that things would move in a better direction for Nash, the hunger in his eyes was so evident. She wanted more for him because he wanted more for himself.

"I'm cumming babe" he told her.

Miko got up and turned around, doing what she felt like she did best, swallowing him whole and that's exactly what the fuck she did.

***

Mary's Jane house was like a peace retreat. Her home was filled with incense, candles and love.

She lived in solitude except for the occasional visitor, the only two people that came to her house was Papa and Miko. Mary Jane would admit that since linking up with The Underworld her life had changed tremendously. She was never broke or had to struggle but with the extra cushion of funds. She wouldn't deny that she slept better at night. For the first time in her life, she hopped on a plane and went to Belize for the New Year and she really enjoyed herself.

In the New Year, she planned on traveling and getting out the house more. Miko always invited her out when she and Lo hung but Mary Jane didn't do crowds or clubs. She did promise Papa that she was going to the strip club with him for his birthday and he made her put a thousand dollars on her word so she knew she had to go.

Today she wore a brown dress and pink house shoes, not in the mood to get dressed. Her head had been hurting for two days and it wasn't the first time she had an intense migraine. Papa told her to carry her ass to the doctor but she was refusing to do so, she wasn't sure if it was from being around the drugs even though she wore a mask or was it stress and the overwhelming amount of work she did on a daily basis.

She stuck the tea bags in the carafe before sitting it on the tray and bringing it into the living room. Miko put her phone back into her purse and told MJ, "Thank you, you know I love your tea"

She smiled and sat down, "How much did you come to get?" she asked her.

Miko questioned, "Nothing, Nasir said I had to pick something up?"

Miko prayed Nasir didn't ask to her pick up any drugs. She didn't touch the product and refused to start.

Counting money and distributing funds was one thing, she wasn't fucking with no drugs.

"Oh I guess I heard you wrong when you called, my head has been hurting really bad," she told her.

"Are you okay?" Miko asked, genuinely concerned.

Mary Jane fanned her worrisome ass off, "Girl I will be okay trust me, it's the potency of the product," she told her.

"Well take a few days off" Miko suggested.

Mary Jane nodded her head, "Papa said the same thing"

Miko picked up the carafe and poured her a cup of warm tea, "Hmm it even smells good" she told her.

"Girl you are hilarious, I've been drinking tea for years I don't know what you be smelling" Miko said.

"I'm telling you, whenever I come over here I feel like I'm healed instantly," she said, sitting back and crossing her legs.

Mary Jane was starting to believe her and Papa when they told her, she did pray daily so maybe they were right. Ever since her brother died, Mary Jane had changed her life around and it was one of the best decisions she had ever made in life.

"So what's wrong?" she asked Miko, noticing the worry and stress lines across her forehead.

Miko sighed, "I need some advice"

Mary Jane waited on her to continue, one thing that she had mastered over the years was listening.

Mary Jane realized that most times when people came to you saying they needed advice, they typically already have their minds made up. They just needed one more person to either touch and agree or justify their wrongs.

She had grown to love Miko like a sister and she looked up to her in many ways, the strength that she exemplified was inspiring. Mary had watched Miko deal with blow to blow because of her dealings with a fuck nigga. But she bounced back every time.

Mary Jane admired that about her.

"I'm seeing someone" she started.

Mary Jane saw the glimmer in her eyes, "The guy that Lo was telling us about?" she asked to be sure.

"Yes, Nash…we've been together like super together for the past three months and it's been amazing. From the talks, to us going to the grocery store. Mary it's been perfect," she told her.

She didn't see the problem, "Okay and?"

Miko took a deep breath and sat the teacup on the table, "He's broke" she told her seriously.

Mary Jane busted out laughing, loud.

"Girl, are you for real right now?" she asked, before laughing again.

Miko knew that she came to the right person. Because had she had this conversation with her best friend, Lauren....it would have ended in an argument. The first thing that Lauren would have said was, "Girl that broke ass nigga" and probably would have hurt Miko's feelings because she really did like Nash.

"Meek you acting like he got ten kids, wait does he have children?" she questioned.

Miko shook her head, "No kids at all"

"Well, what's his reason for not getting a job?" Mary Jane asked.

That was a good ass question, Miko never thought to ask him that, "He wants to be a rapper"

She said, "Oh he's one of those?"

Miko was offended, "What does that mean?"

Mary Jane took a deep breath, "Look in New York, you'll sometimes meet that fine ass dude, with no job because he's chasing super star dreams. Is he good?"

Miko really believed that he had the potential to be great. His sound and delivery was different from other rappers in the game right now. Nash was mixing that street shit with a rock mix and Metallica feel it was dope.

"So why won't you invest in his dreams then?" Mary Jane asked.

Miko's face scrunched up, "I'm not a sugar mama," she told her.

"Investing in the man that you think you want to be with and from the looks on your face, there is a possibility you love him so what's the problem?" Mary Jane asked her a good ass question that caused her to think.

"I don't want anybody thinking I'm taking care of him," Miko told her.

Mary Jane shook her head, "And if you do then that's your business, you work as hell for your money. Girl do you" Miko knew that she was right.

Mary Jane lit a blunt, "Let me tell you something that my grandmother told me all the time as I was growing up, your business is your business. Another woman can't tell you what she wouldn't do because she isn't in your shoes and no one knows how he treats you. So Meek, if you're happy then be happy girl"

Miko nodded her head, Mary Jane was absolutely right. She probably wouldn't leave her house and head to the bank just yet. But she did plan on talking to Nash in depth, the next time they kicked it.

She had a few questions on her own, she wanted to know how much longer did he plan on pursuing his rap career in hopes that it takes off and if it didn't take off what was his back-up plan.

"Thank you" Miko told her.

Mary Jane went to nod her head but the throbbing pain on the right side of her face felt like it was taking over.

"You okay?" she asked her.

Mary Jane put the blunt out, "Yes, is that all you wanted to talk about? I think I need a nap," she told her not trying to be rude but her vision was becoming blurry and she needed to lie down.

Miko told her yes and stood quickly, "I'm going to call and check on you later on," she told her.

Mary Jane said, "Yes and if I don't answer call Papa, he's closer to me" she said.

Miko detected panic and worry in her, it was loud and clear.

She hugged Mary Jane, left her crib, and went to the Fresh Market to grab two lobster tails and a pound of scallops. For dinner, she planned to cook seafood. Nash's favorite.

Miko and Nash sat at the table in the kitchen peeling shrimp, dipping lobster in butter and smacking on scallops, in a large bowl in the center of the table was boiled red potatoes cut in halves and corn on the cob.

"I'm full as hell" Nash leaned back in the chair and rubbed his stomach.

Miko smiled and got up and began to clear the table.

"Thanks bae, it was good," he told her.

"You're welcome," she said quietly.

All day and even the night before, her and Mary Jane's conversation replayed in her head and she was battling with trying to find the perfect time to talk to him.

After she had loaded the dishwater and put a bowl of vinegar on her countertop to rid the room of the fishy smell, the two went to her bedroom to prepare for bed.

"What do you want to watch tonight?" she asked him, turning the television on.

Nash sat at the edge of the bed, breaking weed down so he can roll a blunt.

She rolled her eyes wondering how he claimed to be "broke" but always came to her house with Ziploc bags of weed.

"How much did that cost?" she questioned.

Nash looked at her, "Thinking about becoming a trapper?" he teased.

She bit her tongue Nash had no clue the life she really lived.

"No seriously how much was it?" she asked, with her arms crossed.

Nash stuffed the blunt with the weed and concealed with the licking of his tongue, "What's up with you?" he asked not really feeling her tone.

"I just don't understand how you complain about being broke and not being able to afford me but you always have money to buy weed," she told him.

Nash lit the blunt and scooted back towards *his side of the bed.*

"My brother sells weed Miko," he said.

She shook her head and went into the bathroom, slamming the door and turning the shower on.

She took a seat on the toilet and wondered what the fuck was she doing. She was either going to like him for who he was or she was going to let him go because of what he lacked.

It didn't matter to her before he came out and stated the obvious, now it was all she thought about

Miko was a millionaire and counting, her money was piling up and her accounts, all three of them were well over six figures.

She could afford just about anything she wanted and her credit was A-1, so why did what Nash *didn't* have bother her so much?

She prayed that she wasn't becoming one of those, "My man gotta be a baller" type of women just because of the money she now had.

Miko prided herself on remaining on who she had always been. Of course in a few areas she had grown but the growth was in areas that she really needed to get her shit together.

She made herself get into the shower and she washed her hair and her body. She was feeling naked as a baby, since her and Lo went to get their monthly waxes earlier in the day.

Miko washed off in one of her favorite body washes, Gucci Guilty before rinsing for the last time and stepping out. She took a deep breath as she brushed her teeth and towel dried her hair.

Nash was a man and she refused to treat him as if he wasn't. Plus the way he acted, he wouldn't even stick around and allow her to belittle him.

She threw on a pink silk gown and opened the door. Nash's tall and tattooed frame was looking good enough to lick from his ears to his toes; it was obvious that he was stoned.

 His eyes were low and even though he was watching something on television, it looked as if he was sleeping. Miko walked around the room, setting the alarm and turning the lights off.

"Come here Meek" he told her, once he saw her going to her side of the bed with a book in her hand.

Nash wasn't about to have her on the bullshit tonight, they had a good dinner and she was trying to start something with nothing.

She took a deep breath and went to stand before him. In one swift motion, he pulled her onto him and she now lay on top of his body.

"You smell good," he told her.

"Nash" she said his name.

"What's the problem boo?" he questioned.

Time had progressed, memories were slowly being created and he cared for her, he liked her more than he had ever liked any woman before and that was deep. Unlike Miko, Nash had experienced love before, a few times he would say.

He had been the boyfriend of the year. He did the magical Valentine's Day dates and all that other artificial shit that girls used to measure a man's love for them.

When Nash was out in the trenches robbing, he was doing well for himself. But that life was behind him now and unfortunately for Miko, they met at the wrong time but to him it was the right time.

Nash had the upmost faith in his career, in his dreams, his vision and his future.

He knew he was going places, he knew that God was about to turn his life around. The question was Miko down to ride? Could she really hold him down while he made shit happen? Could she be the supportive chick he needed her to be while he figured some things out?

"Can I tell you a secret?" Miko whispered.

Nash traced her jaw line and then ran his finger across her bottom lip, "yes" he said.

"I don't want to be without you, when you're not here I'm missing you" she admitted.

"I already knew that" he smiled.

Miko looked down, she was being serious and he was playing.

But, what she didn't know is that he felt the exact same way.

"Meek, we are here" he used his fingers to motion between the two of them.

He touched her heart, "'I'm here" he told her.

He continued, "But I need you stop letting this fuck us up" he said, pointing to her mind.

Miko closed her eyes and kissed him, "Open your eyes" he commanded.

She opened them and he saw doubt.

Nash didn't want her to doubt their love.

"Do you believe in me?" his voice croaked when he asked her, fearful of her answer.

Without a second passing, she said, "Yes I do"

Nash heart beat returned to normal, "Good, don't stop, even if I give up on myself don't you give up on me babe" he told her and hugged her.

Miko stayed on top of him the remainder of the night, no more words were exchanged but they didn't have to be. Everything that needed to be said…had been said.

They were now on the same page and their faith had been rooted in each other.

Relationships weren't easy but Miko was willing to put her all into this one, especially since it was considered her first real one.

She loved him, but wouldn't tell him that so soon.

Nash felt the same way though.

The next morning, Miko woke up with her man's head in between her legs.

"Baby what you doing?" she moaned.

Nash had his hands up her dress, massaging her breast and feasting on her kitty.

Miko closed her eyes again and enjoyed the special treat.

"Fuck" she hissed, once he went lower and licked her ass hole, twirling her tongue around it.

She moved up in the bed not really knowing how to take that feeling.

Nash sat up, wiped his face, "Stop moving" he told her and she nodded her head. Loving the way he just looked at her with that, *Daddy gon get you* face.

She relaxed and allowed him to have his way with her. Oh, boy did he and before she knew it, Miko was holding the sheets and screaming at the top of her lungs begging for him to let up but he didn't.

Nash was getting her ass back for all the times she stayed on her knees long after he had finished cumming.

Once he was full of his favorite dessert, he came up and kissed her face, smothering her body with his.

"Are you mine?" he asked in between kisses.

She kissed his lips and held his tongue, never answering the question.

Nash rolled her over and got her into doggy-style position.

"I guess you didn't hear me?" he asked.

Miko was too busy, preparing her mind and pussy for the strokes and spanking.

"Huh?" she asked.

"You didn't hear my question?" he slapped her booty cheek.

SLAP!

"Nash!" Miko winced in pain.

"Nah don't call my name just yet" he told her, arching her back lower and sliding his rock-hard penis into her soaking hot pussy.

Miko's eyes rolled to the back of her head, she couldn't find the words to say anymore but the moans fell from her lips like a demon or something had possessed her.

"I said are you mine?" he asked, slapping her butt again. Nash was balls deep in her pussy giving her the mother fucking business. She couldn't take it all at one time but on this sweet Sunday morning, he left her no choice.

"Yes you know that Nash, you already know!" she whimpered.

Nash wasn't satisfied with her answer. He flipped her over in one motion and stroked her slowly while looking into her eyes.

"I want you to tell me what I want to hear," he said, in between strokes.

Miko knew he wanted to scream and holler but he never did, unless they were in the shower.

She bit her bottom lip and held it, knowing he loved that shit.

"Say it" Nash began to toy with her clit while he fucked her, since Miko was trying to be a bad girl

"Shit, okay baby okay!" she told him. Miko wasn't able to deal with all of that pressure. It was too much, dick and fingers, stroking her pussy and playing with her hardened clit. Their sex was consuming her, physically.

Nash was still waiting on her to submit.

"I am yours Nash," she told him, as she felt herself climaxing.

Nash felt the nut rushing to the tip of his dick, "Say it again" he begged, as he pulled out and stroked his love muscle.

"I'M YOURS DADDDYYYYYYYYYY," she moaned as her pussy began to squirt.

Those magic words sent Nash's release all over her stomach.

"I'm yours," she panted, as she came off the sexual high.

Nash fell beside her and draped his arm around her neck, pulling her in for a kiss.

"I know," he said cockily.

Miko stared into his eyes, praying that this was *it* for her. She didn't want another. Nash had to be hers forever.

Chapter 11

Miko was sitting on the top of the island in one of the trap houses that The Underworld had purchased. Ever since Noel was brought on board, the money had been coming in via dump trucks. They were making so much fucking money it was ridiculous, life was good and Miko was living even better than she was two years ago. Overall, she was one happy woman. Miko was traveling the world with Noel, making good money with the family, and slowly falling in love with her beau. There was nothing to complain, worry or stress about. The only pressing issue in her life was the distant relationship with her mother, Miko had reached out to her a few more times and it was as if her mother forgot that she was her child.

She had no words for Miko and when she told her months ago to stop calling, she really meant it.

Miko cracked her neck and went back to counting the money. She had been up since five o'clock in the morning and made it to the trap house around eight. It was the only thing on her agenda for today.

She loved and hated the first of the month for various reasons, the love came in because her cycle came and she rather it come while she was busy at work and not thinking about her man. She also loved the first because that half a mill would be deposited in her account before she woke up the next morning. She loved the first because she and Lo's favorite bar had an open wine tasting on the first Fridays of the month. And on the other hand, Miko despised the first few days of the month. She would spend hours, and hours is an understatement. She would spend days making sure everyone was paid, and The Underworld was paid as well. The payroll for the organization was over twenty pages long. Nasir made sure everyone was taken care of from the big mama's on the blocks where the trap houses were located, pilots who flew them back and forth. From coast to coast, police officers, judges, district attorneys and even the hoes were paid. Miko was responsible for making sure the workers, runners, mules, and dope boys were paid. She had to handle it all.

So here she was, the first of the month, counting money then running it through a money machine before writing the amount down, checking it off her list and putting two rubber bands around it and dropping it labeled duffel bags, another idea of hers.

She was hungry but didn't trust anyone to bring her food, not even the local delivery drivers.

No one knew where she was but Malachi and Nasir. Whenever she would be at the trap, she wouldn't answer the phone or text back. The quicker she handled her business, the easier she got out of there.

The alarm started going off causing Miko to quickly grab her gun and hop off the counter.

She moved one of the brown boxes of money out of her way and walked out of the kitchen.

She was about to shoot whoever the fuck thought they was about to rob her but when she heard her brother's voice she relaxed.

"Sis where you at?" Malachi's voice was heard as he walked down the hallway.

"Kitchen" she shouted.

Her heartbeat was still thumping erratically, when Malachi came in he asked, "You was about to shoot me?"

She asked a question of her own, "Why didn't you call before you came?"

"I did call you, I'm surprised Lo ain't called," he told her, taking a seat at the rickety table in the kitchen.

This house was furnished but only in case someone thought to run up in here, the money was stored in the locked basement.

"Call me for what?" she asked him.

Malachi took a deep breath, "When was the last time you seen ole boy?" he asked her.

Miko stopped fumbling with the crumpled dollar bills, "Who is ole boy, I don't know who that is," she told him.

"The President Miko" he said in an irritated tone.

She looked at her brother and rolled her eyes, "You still on this really?" she wasn't in the mood for her brother's bullshit.

"Nah the question is are you still on him?" he snapped right back.

"Malachi I'm seeing someone" she finally told him.

"Well does he know the President was at your house?" he asked her, pulling out his phone to show her the screenshots from CNN.

Miko came closer and snatched the phone from his hand. She stared at the headline, "President is caught banging on mistress door in drunken act, and neighbors say he comes over all the time"

She shook her head, "I don't even be there no more" she told him.

It was true that she kept her condo but someone was renting it out. She planned on calling the tenant she had staying there to ask why he hadn't called to tell her John had been stopping by.

She fell back on the counter, holding her heart.

"Why does this keep happening to me?" she mumbled.

"You need to get a restraining order," he suggested.

"He doesn't bother me though, I haven't heard from him or saw him, he was calling me for a while but then I told him to stop and he hasn't called since then" she told her brother.

"So why the fuck is he stalking you?" Malachi asked.

Miko couldn't answer his question because she had no idea what the fuck John had going on.

"My mom is never going to talk to me again," she said, holding back tears.

This shit would never stop, right when she thought everything was going right, more bullshit fell at her feet. She wished she could kill John because he was causing her so much misery. Their relationship wasn't even all that for him to be acting so sprung. But unbeknownst to her, John missed her for various reasons aside from the mind-blowing sex. It was Miko that helped him make some of the most important decisions in his career.

It was Miko that went over his speeches and kept him in the loop about what was going around in the work place without her he felt lost, seriously.

Even if she never dropped her panties and bent over for him again, he missed his friend.

John didn't give a fuck about his wife or the press, he needed to see Miko, and he needed his Miko back.

"Well you better be calling your nigga and make sure yall good and when will I meet him?" Malachi asked.

He was surprised to hear that she was seeing someone since this was his first time hearing about it.

Miko took a deep breath and called his cell phone but when it rang twice before going to voicemail, she knew that she had been sent to voicemail.

"He's mad" she panicked.

Malachi said, "He will be okay just tell him that shit is screwed up and you wasn't even there"

"It's more to it," she mumbled.

Miko had four more bags of money to count before she could leave, "Thank you for giving me the heads up but I got work to do," she told him.

Malachi smiled, he had turned her into a hustler and he loved it.

"I'll help so you can get out of here faster," he suggested.

"I got a system" she shook her head, really wanting to be alone right now.

"You sure?" he asked.

Miko told him, "Yeah" and turned her back not wanting her brother to see her distraught and worried over a man. She wasn't stunting the scandal on the news. She knew who she was and that's all that mattered to her.

Malachi left and Miko zoned out and got back to work.

She wasn't done counting the money until two in the morning but she didn't care how late it was she locked the house up and headed straight for where she often picked Nash up.

She needed to see him now.

Miko called his phone again but he didn't answer, she texted him a few times in between breaks of counting the money but Nash never responded.

She ignored the other calls and messages from "concerned" friends and family members. She even told Lo that she would have to call her tomorrow before hanging up in her face.

The only thing on her mind right now was talking to Nash face-to-face, she couldn't have her baby mad at her, she refused to let the one good and constant thing in her life right now go astray.

A brand-new Mercedes Benz truck with rims and tinted windows stuck out like a sore-thumb on the dead end street that Nash and his mama lived on.

It was late and dark outside but it seemed as if the hood he lived in had just come alive, it didn't take long for the word to spread that a truck was creeping up and down the block.

Nash called her phone, "Yo what you doing over here?" he snapped.

"Babe I've been calling you," she told him quickly.

"Why you sound like that?" he asked, as mad as he was at her right now, he knew Miko and she didn't sound like herself.

"I'm cramping and tired I've been at work all day," she told him. Nash assumed that she worked at a corporate office considering her background at The White House and she never corrected him.

"Turn around and take your ass home then" he spat. Miko took a deep breath because she didn't feel like arguing with him.

"Are you mad at me?" she asked.

"No mad for what, I know you were with me the night they said that shit," he told her nonchalantly. She heard the flicker of a light and she figured he was getting high.

"So why do you have an attitude?" she asked. Miko was relieved to hear that he believed her, when her brother handed her his phone to read the new article she barely read it.

"Because Meek that's something you tell a nigga in the beginning. I'm bragging on you to my mama and shit and then the news came on, not a good feeling babe," he told her straight up.

"Does your mom hate me now?" she asked.

Never in life had she cared about what a man's mother thought of her. She was usually all about getting her rocks off but with Nash, it was much more than that.

"Nah" he told her.

She prayed that he was telling the truth, Nash spoke highly of his mother and she couldn't wait until she met her and the rest of his family one day.

"Are you going to come give me a hug?" she asked in a whining tone

"Go home, I'll holler at you tomorrow" he told her. Nash wasn't fucking with her tonight. After the news went off, he did his research on the entire scandal situation. And even though he personally knew Miko, it still pained him to read some of that shit.

"Nash don't do this," she begged

"Do what? I've kept it one hundred with you from the jump," he told her.

Miko hesitated before she said, "You wouldn't understand"

"How would I not bae? I'm with you, you got it all and I ain't got shit. I'm not in a position to judge you so don't even play with me like that," he snapped.

Miko was too tired to argue with him, she just wanted him to drive her truck home. Nash could sleep in the guest bedroom for all she cared.

"I'm too sleepy to drive all the way to Jersey," she said.

Nash knew that she was probably telling the truth about that and he would be fucked up if something happened to her.

"Here I come," he told her a minute later.

"Okay" she told him.

They hung up and she slid over in the passenger seat before calling Lo back.

"Girl oh my God!" she screamed into the phone.

"I know I know" Miko said sadly.

"My dad called me I said damn you must really liked Miko," Lo laughed.

That made her smile; she had enjoyed her time with Lo's family.

"What did he say?"

"Just told me to tell you they're praying for you and they know that the enemy is trying to distract you girl all of that" she said.

"We should go visit soon," Miko suggested.

Lo yawned into the phone, Miko knew she wasn't feeling that shit.

"Hmm girl, what you doing?" she changed the subject.

"I had to talk to Nash," she told her best friend.

Lo asked, "Was he mad?"

"Kind of, he said I should have told him"

"True" Lo agreed and she had been telling Miko that for quite some time.

"Where you?" Miko asked her.

"Girl ducked the hell off, I'm glad you called me back. Hit me next week let's go shopping" she suggested.

Miko shook her head all Lo did was spend money, "Okay cool" she told her

"Love you" Lo told her best friend.

Miko was saying I love you too when Nash tapped on the window for her to unlock the door.

"My mama said the next time you come over here and not come in she gon cuss you out," he told her.

Miko panicked, "Oh my God are you for real?"

Nash laughed, "Yeah she was in the bed this time though"

She reached over and kissed his cheek then ran her hands over his dreads, "Time for a retwist" she told him.

"Yeah I know, I'm going to have one of these chicken heads do something to it," he said in a nonchalant tone.

Miko rolled her eyes and buckled her seat belt.

"You ate?" he asked.

"I been working all day, I forgot I was hungry" she shook her head.

"You work too hard but I love that shit about you" he gripped her thigh as he used his other hand to maneuver the truck through the hood and towards the highway.

"So you not mad?" she asked him, minutes later after they had been riding in silence.

Nash shook his head, "I know for a fact I got you on lock anything before me is irrelevant"

Miko blushed, she was thankful for her heaven sent blessing.

Farren Knight had told her that the one for her would come and not give a damn about her past and lo and behold, Nash entered her life.

A few states over at 1600 Pennsylvania Avenue NW Washington, DC 20500, First Lady Laura Ann Wilburn had a little too much to drink and popped one too many pain pills. She was on one hundred and ten, and the recent news that she had been delivered was the last fucking straw.

Laura Ann was fed the hell up with John and was two seconds from demanding a divorce. The White House had ruined a good man, the stress of being the best and staying afloat when so many great men had come from him…John wasn't the same.

She would gladly hand these days back if she could get her loving and doting husband back.

She stared at him with mascara and eyeliner streaked face he sat in the corner with one leg draped over the other looking at the window.

"John are you ignoring me?" she yelled.

He was counting to ten, praying that when he made it to the end of his countdown she got mad, walked out and left him alone or passed out from being too intoxicated.

"John don't make me throw this damn bottle at your head!" she shouted.

He knew that the Secret Service agents outside of their bedroom door was growing tired of hearing her high-pitched voice because he knew for a fact he was sick of it.

"Laura Ann please lower your voice, you're giving me a headache," he told her holding the side of his head.

If he could be anywhere right now, it wouldn't be in this room. It wouldn't be here with her. In fact, it wouldn't even be at The White House. He couldn't wait until his term was over; he planned on divorcing his wife, writing a few books then retiring down in Ft. Lauderdale, Florida. Secretly, John had been counting down until the day came when he packed his things up and left.

He wanted Miko to go with him but she was refusing to talk to him.

John was missing her more and more as the days passed, he didn't treat her right when he had her and he wished he would have. Miko was his peace, his therapy, his favorite hobby but now she was a memory

"John, you mother fucker answer me!" his wife, Laura Ann yelled from the top of her lungs.

He faced her, "Miko will you-"and before he could realize what he had just said, his wife through the wine bottle in the direction of his head and she was successful.

He felt the glass cut into his skin as blood trickled down the side of his face.

"Miko my ass" she said bitterly and walked out of the room.

Laura Ann had something up her sleeve for her husband's mistress, since Miko didn't know how to leave him alone Laura Ann was going to have to teach her a lesson.

***

Nash hopped out of the shower and brushed his teeth while his body dried off, he dropped his toothbrush in the sink.

"Damn" he was nervous as hell and he couldn't even act like he wasn't. But tonight was the night and he needed to pull it together.

The day before, he went and got his dreads tightened and styled into two fish tails and a fresh line-up so he was looking very crispy like the future superstar he was.

After he brushed his teeth, he opened the bathroom door and went into Miko's room, well she called it their room but his name wasn't on the house deed so he still called it her room.

When he saw a few bags on the bed, he got closer to see what else new had she bought. Miko swore up and down she didn't have a shopping problem but he begged to differ.

Gucci, Prada, Burberry and gray bags with the label Saks Fifth Avenue were on the bed.

He wrapped the towel around his waist before going to find her in the kitchen.

Tonight, she was having a girl's night in with her nieces.

"Damn it smells good in here," he told her.

She turned around from stirring something on the stove, "Look at you" she said sexily.

"Nah look at you, with these lil ass shorts on" he came over and tugged at her waist.

"I'm changing before the girls get here," she told him.

"What you cooking?" he asked.

"Pizza and nachos and some wings" she said.

Miko eyed the clock on the stove, "You're going to be late," she reminded him of the time.

"It wasn't a specific time" he told her, kissing the back of her neck.

"You must didn't see the stuff on the bed?" Miko
questioned.

"Yeah you and Lo went shopping and you finally bringing
it in the house?" he asked.

She shook her head and turned the stove down before
turning around and kissing his lips, "Noooo that's for you,
I wanted you to look and feel your best tonight, I know
how important this is to you" she told him.

He eyed her before smiling and correcting her, "for us"
Miko blushed, she loved how he always included her in his
plans.

"Go get dressed," she told him.

"Come with me" he pulled her closer to the bed.

She shook her head, 'I'm cooking I'll come in there when I
finish"

Nash left her alone so she could handle her domestic
duties and he went back into the bedroom.

He closed the door not wanting her to see him to act like a
kid on Christmas but it had been so long since he bought
new clothes.

His girl went the fuck in for him. He popped the tag on
brand-new Burberry boxers before putting them on. The
Balmain distressed jeans she bought him were the perfect
fit. Instead of putting on the shirt she bought to go with

the jeans. He threw on a white t-shirt fresh out the pack that he copped from the corner store.

Miko even bought him a pair of Givenchy sneakers and a pair of shades. In one of the bags was tons of cologne, he chose the Prada silver bottle with a red stripe on the front. Nash looked in the mirror and he had to admit that he was feeling himself.

He went into the kitchen and cleared his throat, Miko turned around and her smile was just as wide as he is.

He laughed as she started clapping and screaming, "That's my man, come model for me baby!"

After she stopped clowning, he kissed her passionately, "You didn't have to do this but thank you" he told her.

Nash was extremely grateful for having a real woman holding him down.

"You let that producer know that you the hottest thing out" she said.

He loved the way she talked with her lil cute Korean ass.

He kissed her once more, "Can you call me a cab while I roll this blunt," he asked.

"You can take my truck or car, whichever you want to drive," she told him.

Nash eyed her, "You for real?"

She laughed, "Yeah babe you going to pull up to the studio in a cab?"

He shrugged his shoulders, "Shit I'm from the hood hell yeah"

She shook her head, "No take my car," she told him.

Nash rolled a few blunts before he told her Miko he was headed out.

"House key is on there, I'll probably be sleep when you get in" she told him.

He pulled her in for a hug "You not going to stay up till I get back?"

She told him, "I'll try my hardest"

Nash kissed her forehead before dipping out.

When he pulled off and hit the freeway, "It's some cash in the compartment. In case you have an emergency or they want to go out" she texted him.

Nash responded, "Business only tonight then I'm coming back to you"

It wasn't shit going down in the strip club for him.

Nash had been invited to the studio tonight, DJ Monday, a Hip-Hop legend and producer was in town for a few nights and had got in touch with Nash through a few OG's in the hood.

His hopes weren't up however he was thankful for the opportunity.

The only thing he could pray was that when he talked to him, he didn't seem disappointed once Nash told him he only had one recorded song.

He did have his book bag full of notebooks in the back seat, Nash had so many songs written and composed in his head that he could record about ten albums in one weekend if he was given the opportunity.

Once he made it to the studio, he sent a prayer up to the man above before getting out the truck.

Little did Nash know, this meeting was about to change his life.

***

Power is defined as the ability to do or act; capability of doing or accomplishing something. Political or national strength, great or marked ability to do or act; strength; might; force. The possession of control or command over others; authority; ascendency. To inspire, spur or sustain. Since coming into contact with her brother against her will at first, Miko had no idea how important power was. Having the power to change something and make a difference in someone's lives was real and touching. Although, The Underworld was built on the foundation of supplying top-grade product around the United States and now, the World they still were people with hearts.

It was nothing for Papa to pay for all the kids to get haircuts and new shoes before school start, in the hood where he grew up. Malachi and Jade donated millions of dollars under an alias to schools in inner-city neighborhoods; she was a lover of the arts and fought vicariously for those programs to be reinstated in the public school system. Roderick and his wife, Julia was advocates for autistic kids since one of their children was autistic. Sean would just drop money off to Lo to do whatever she wanted to with it, Lo was a member of so many different non-profit organizations and she sat on the board for several government-funded projects and private charities. Her heart was truly made of gold.

Miko hadn't found the one thing that tugged her heart but she did donate to all of the organizations that The Underworld supported. In a weird way, she thanked God for blessing her with a job in The Underworld. She didn't focus on the "bad" things they did but the good deeds they were planting.

On tonight, the gang was together, dressed in the finest threads in full-support of Lauren's first auction. The goal was to raise ten million dollars to be donated to a woman she met who wanted to open group homes in the hood, after being rejected several times when she applied for grants from the government the lady turned around and reached out to the gangsters in the hood, she was a good friend of Papa's Uncle.

Miko and Jade was at the bar ordering drinks, "Oh Lord" Miko mumbled

Jade turned and asked her, "What happened?

Miko tossed her drink back and scanned the room for Lo. "Nothing, I'll be right back sis" she told her sister in law. The person that Lo had been secretly dating had just walked in the mother fucking building! Miko knew that wherever Mary Jane was that's where Lo was since she didn't see her or Sasha.

Demi stopped her, "You look so good girl, where did you get your dress?" she asked.

Miko hated to cut her off but she had to find her best friend, "It's Gucci, thank you. I'll be right back. Jade is at the bar" she told her and walked off.

Demi wasn't lying at all, Miko looked amazing, and the black long-sleeved dress with a small train did her body wonders. She could barely get dressed, Nash was all over her. He loved the weight she was slowly gaining and kept joking that she was pregnant but she knew that wasn't the case. Miko had been popping her birth control like they were Percocets.

She was happy that Nash wasn't one of those men that always wanted to be joined at the hip; they gave each other their space. When she told him she had a company dinner tonight, he made him a frozen pizza, rolled a few blunts, got comfortable in the living room, and told her he would be playing the game until she got back.

One day, Miko prayed that when she told him about her life and her "career" he would understand her reasoning for her keeping it to herself for so long.

Malachi had warned her that no one was to be trusted. Not even the nigga she sucked and fucked on the regular. She took the steps knowing that's where they probably were, and lo and behold, Sasha, Noel, Mary Jane and Lo's ass were all up there smoking a blunt.

"Lauren this is your event what are you doing up here?" Miko asked.

"Girl it ain't even started yet" she fanned her off.

Everyone looked good as hell, "Yall look cute" she told them.

Sasha passed the blunt to Mary Jane and blew smoke through her nose, "Bitch you do too" she told Miko.

"Lo did you invite Ben?" she asked.

Lauren eyes got big, "He's here?" she panicked.

Miko nodded her head, "Yes he looks nice and he has roses," she told her.

"Give me the blunt!" she shouted.

She took a deep pull before walking off with Miko in tow.

"Why would you invite him if you knew Nasir was coming" Miko asked.

"I didn't think he was going to come for real because he told me had business to handle in Virginia"

She said, holding on to the rail as she walked down the steps in her heels.

"Well I guess he surprised you," Miko told her.

Lauren shook her head, "This is all bad"

Miko spoke up finally, "Well I don't see how it's bad, Nasir just walked in with Jordyn, teach his ass a lesson"

Lo rolled her eyes and walked off, she hated to hear the truth.

Miko went and took her seat at the table that was reserved for The Underworld, for ten thousand dollar a plate, she told Jade, "This food better be good"

Jade laughed, "Girl I'm telling you I told Chi the same thing"

Jordyn just happened to take the seat right next to Miko.

Jade smiled, "Girl I didn't know you was in town" she told her.

Miko didn't know much about Jordyn, she had only met her once and that was at her 25th birthday dinner. She turned in her seat, to get a better look at her. Lo swore up and down the girl as ugly as hell but from Miko's view she was actually beautiful.

It was obvious that life was good with Nasir, the ice on her finger, wrist, neck and ears were blinding them all.

Jordyn told Jade, "I'm going to the Prada fashion show tomorrow night. I leave back out the next day"

Miko remembered that Lo told her Jordyn lived in Atlanta for safety reasons, but she didn't see how Jordyn thought that was okay, she couldn't do the long-distance thing Miko loved sex too much.

Before they could get into a conversation, the mistress of ceremony approached the podium and the night had started.

Miko scanned the room for Lo but she caught her staring a damn hole into Jordyn, she scrunched her face up at Lauren and she removed her eyes from their table all together. She prayed that her friend wasn't being petty because she was sitting next to Jordyn. For goodness sake what was she supposed to say, *"Hey I don't know you but my best friend is fucking your man so you can't sit here"*

The night was pleasant and although they didn't reach the ten million dollar mark they came close enough, the woman who the night was in honor of came to the microphone and thanked Lo over and over again.

Miko thought her friend looked adorable tonight and from the looks of Nasir staring at the stage, he thought so too.

Once the auction was over, everyone stood around having dessert and coffee.

She watched Ben approach Lo, Mary Jane whispered, "Girl look at Nas"

Miko saw his attention go from whatever Demi was yapping about to Lo and Ben.

She yawned, "I'm about to go, I don't even wanna be here when this shit pop off" she told them.

After kissing everyone goodbye, she went to get her car from valet.

When she walked outside to hand her ticket to the valet, Jordyn was standing outside.

"I could have sworn I just saw you," she told her.

Miko smiled, "Yeah I can't hang as long as I used too"

"You should come to with me and the girls tomorrow," Jordyn suggested.

Miko raised an eyebrow, "The girls?" she asked.

"Julia, Demi and I, we're going to lunch," she told her.

Miko would be out of place but she didn't want to be rude and decline, Jordyn added, "It will be fun I promise"

"Is Jade going?" Miko asked.

Jordyn nodded her head, "I invited her tonight, I really want to start coming around more I keep telling Nas that"

Miko swallowed loudly, things would definitely get ugly if that was to happen.

Unbeknownst to Miko and Jordyn, Lo and Ben had walked upstairs because she was tired of Nas staring at her as if she had done something wrong. Lauren stood over the balcony watching those two talk as if they were long lost best friends.

"Okay well I'll get the details from Jade," she told her. Jordyn gave her the location and time, "Carmines at 4" Miko's truck had pulled up to the rear, "That's me," she told Jordyn.

When she pulled off, she shook her head, there was no telling what the hell Jordyn was up too but at the end of the day her loyalty was too Lauren.

Once Miko made it back home, her man was knocked out in bed. She removed the ashtray from the bed, along with empty bags of chips and all kinds of other shit.

She turned the alarm on and shut the house down, by locking doors and turning lights off.

After showering and removing the pins from her hair, Miko climbed into bed and fell asleep right beside her babe. Tomorrow would be crazy; she already had a feeling about it.

Lauren rolled over in her sleep and when she sat up to flip her pillow on the other side she caught a glimpse of someone standing over her but she *just* knew she was tripping.

"Who was that man all on you tonight?" Nasir's heavy accent was low but she knew his voice anywhere.

Lauren sat up in the bed and turned the light on, she yawned. It was nothing new for him to pop up at her house, she hated the day she gave him a key.

"Isn't Jordyn in town? Let me guess she thinks you went out?" she asked sarcastically.

"Lauren I'm not here to argue with you" he told her.

"Well why are you here at all?" she snapped.

He took a deep breath, "Why didn't you tell me you were seeing someone?" he asked.

She looked at him with a crazed look on her face, *this motherfucker was delusional.*

"Those days are over Nas," she told him straight up.

"What days? What are you talking about?" he questioned.

"I am moving on" she told him, not even believing her damn self when the words came from her mouth.

"Moving on to what?" Nasir asked, acting clueless.

"To better fucking things, to a real man. To a man who won't treat me like a secret?" she roared.

He had heard this so many times it was starting to sound like a broken record, "Why?" he asked.

She laughed, "Why? Because Nasir before I know it I'll be thirty and I want children, I want a husband I want a wedding, I want a ring and a house" she told him.

Nasir folded his arms, he had took the tuxedo jacket off right after the event had ended, after putting Jordyn to sleep he slipped out of the house and came to Lauren's house.

Now he stood before her wondering what was it about her that kept him so attached. For one, she was fucking crazy, she drank like an old man who didn't care about his liquor and her mouth was filthy. But then again, when he was in her presence, he felt something that he never felt before in life…

"Lo, let me run this down for you that ring on your finger cost more than my car, I asked you did you want a house and you opted out and got this raggedy ass apartment. There is nothing you don't have that you wanted. I spend more time with you than I do J-"she stopped him.

"Don't say that bitch name in my house!" she shouted.

He knew it was time for him to go, "Yo watch your mouth," he hissed.

"Stop checking me in my house" she yelled.

"Goodnight Lauren get some sleep and get rid of that nigga" he told her, before picking up his phone and gun.

"That's it?" she asked once she realized he wasn't kissing her ass tonight.

"I can't talk to you when you in your feelings, we get nowhere" Nasir informed her.

She relaxed and laughed, "I'm in my feelings, you drove across the city but I'm in my feelings? Oh okay" she said.

He told her, "No I came over to make sure that nigga wasn't in *our* bed"

"He had a flight to catch that's the only reason," she mumbled.

Before she knew it, he had dragged her ass to the edge of the bed and pulled her up, so that they were face to face.

"I'm starting to think you're not taking me serious, LAUREN," he stated, using emphasis on her name.

"And I'm starting to think that you don't want to see me happy because if you did you wouldn't keep playing with my fucking feelings" she shot back.

Nasir mushed her head, "Go to bed, I'm out" he wasn't trying to hear shit she was saying.

"Hmm that's what I thought. You won't believe me until you get an invite to my wedding and baby shower, Uncle Nas. Can my kids call you that?" Lauren taunted.

Nasir yanked her hand and in one swift motion, he snatched the ring off her middle finger, "Goodnight and take care love," he told her in a very serious tone.

Tears slowly fell down her face, "Give me my ring back," she whispered.

"Nah, tell that lame ass nigga to cop you one" Nasir told her and left the room.

She fell off the bed trying to get to him as quickly as she could, "Give me my fucking ring back," she asked again.

"Take your ass to bed," he told her, jerking away.

"I'm not playing with you," she shouted.

"And I'm not playing with you either Lo, you talked all that shit now I'm going to show you" he told her straight up.

She cried, "Show me what? You always try to flip this shit around on me, it's not fair"

"I love you but you want to move on so fuck it," he said nonchalantly.

"Nas" she said his name.

He put his key on the counter and headed for the front door.

She asked him again, "Why are you doing this?"

But Nasir had nothing else to say, Lo had pissed him off for good this time.

She knew better than to act an ass in the hallway so instead of begging him to stay so they could hash it out. She watched him walk out of her apartment and her life as well.

Lauren was unsure of why it didn't hurt as much as it used too, maybe God was telling her that better was on the way and there was no need to fret.

She picked her heart off the floor and went back to bed, crying silently until her energy drained and she fell back asleep.

Nasir hopped in the back seat of the truck that he was escorted around the city in. He put the ring in his pocket and leaned his head against the headrest. Sometimes, you had to let the closest ones to you free so they can experience life elsewhere.

Nasir knew he was a real nigga, and yeah, he was in a complicated situation but a little part of his heart belonged to Lauren and she knew that if she knew nothing else, he hoped that when she laid down tonight she believed that he loved her more than his mouth would ever allow him to tell her.

The next day, Miko was up and making breakfast for Nash and herself.

He wasn't an early bird but she couldn't sleep past eight in the morning, sometimes seven, depending on how late she went to bed the night before.

She put the omelette on a plate before placing it in the warmer.

She got a head start on laundry and cleaning the house.

"Morning" Nash told her, as he wandered into her sitting room.

"Hi baby how did you sleep?"She asked.

Nash came over and kissed her on the lips before taking a seat, he still looked sleepy.

"Good, what time you got in?" he questioned.

"Around eleven why?" she asked.

He shrugged his shoulders, "I was horny as hell waiting on you to get home"

Miko chuckled, "I bet"

"I made breakfast, are you hungry?'" she asked.

He told her that he wanted to shower before he ate and left her in the sitting room by herself.

Miko was really contemplating joining the "wives" for brunch, she wondered why didn't Jordyn invite anyone else, like what was the case with her extending an invite to her and her only?

After handling her domestic duties around the house, she went to take a bubble bath.

Nash came in and asked, "You busy today?"

She told him, "I'm going to brunch with my sister in law then after that I'm coming back home"

"Well I want to take you out tonight," he told her, proudly.

Miko was surprised to hear that, "You do? Where are we going?" she asked.

"I don't know yet but we gon' slide around eight" he told her.

She nodded her head, "I'll be dressed"

Nash bent down and gave her a kiss, "I'll call you later"

"You're about to go?" she questioned.

"Yeah my cousin outside, we gotta go handle something" he told her quickly.

"Handle what?" she asked, worried.

Nash had shared his past with her and she prayed that he hadn't resorted to his old ways.

"Come on babe don't do that" he wasn't feeling Miko questioning him.

"I'm just saying like you leaving out of nowhere and then you can't tell me what you going to do?" she got out of the tub.

"Enjoy your bath, ma why you getting out" he asked.

"'I'm just trying to make sure your cousin really coming to get you, why didn't you ask to use the truck" she questioned.

"Because that's' not my car and I don't wanna keep asking you that. Plus I don't want shit in the hood" he told her.

Miko walked her soapy naked ass to the window to see if Nash cousin was really parked outside.

"Man get your tail from the window" he snatched her back.

"Tell me where you going?" she insisted.

"You must don't trust me?" he shot back.

She shook her head, "Of course I do I don't want you in any trouble"

He smiled, "Come here" he commanded. But Miko still wanted answers, "No tell me first"

"My cousin daddy got a lil gig for us couple hundred dollars, damn meek I didn't want to tell that shit," he finally told her.

She smiled at the fact that he was going to do hard labor just so he could take her out, "You're so cute to me when you mad at me" she told him.

He blushed, "You won't even let me surprise you though"

"I'll be dressed at eight babes" she kissed his lips.

"You getting me wet," he told her but he really didn't care.

"You getting me wet too" she teased.

Nash felt his dick jumping, he knew that if he didn't leave now he would miss the money opportunity and he needed them lil' five hundred dollars in his empty pockets.

Once he left, Miko made the bed and went to get dressed for the brunch. She planned to run a few errands in the city to kill time before the brunch.

She put on a tangerine fitted dress with fringes on the side. The Minnetonka boots she wore came up her leg and they too had fringes. Miko made sure she grabbed her favorite pair of Chanel shades before she left the house.

At Carmine's in a table towards the back of the restaurant were Jade Morgan, Julia Christ, Demi Huffington and Jordyn.

Of course, Miko was the last to arrive but she did that shit on purpose. She didn't want to arrive on time and then was forced to make conversation with one of the wives. The only one she knew well enough not to feel nervous around was Jade and that's because she was family.

They all waved her over, everyone smile seemed genuine so that made her relax once she sat at the table.

"Sorry I'm late" she lied, Miko had been at Mary Jane's house watching television.

"It's okay, we just ordered a bottle of champagne," Demi told her.

Miko smiled and sat her purse on the back of the chair. They resumed their conversation on college and the importance of attending an HBCU.

Jade spoke up and said, "Well I didn't attend an HBCU but I'm from the country so hell it didn't matter to me"

Demi said, "I don't think it matters either"

Whereas, Jordyn didn't agree with them at all, she asked Miko, "You went to Howard right?"

She wanted to ask how did she know that but instead she told her, "Yeah I did"

"And how was that?" Demi asked.

"It was great I went on a scholarship for orchestra," she said.

"What do you play?" Julia asked.

"I played the piano," she told them.

"Wow my baby wants to learn how to play the piano," Julia told her.

"It's an amazing skill to learn," she told them

Miko didn't want kids any time soon. She could barely keep up with her nieces and nephew.

"So how is it working with our men?" Julia questioned.

They all waited on her to answer the question and that's when she concluded, she was invited to get the scoop.

They must have assumed because she wasn't as edgy as Sasha was, or as quiet as Mary Jane or aggressive as Lauren and Noel was still considered a newcomer. They could play on her intelligence but she had trick for these hoes.

"I mainly work with Malachi," she told them and that was the truth.

"Ohh okay" Julia said.

She smiled and ordered French toast with extra bacon.

"So have you thought about doing any interviews to clear your name?" Demi questioned.

Jade spoke, "Hell no she ain't doing that, Miko you haven't thought about that have you?"

Miko said, "Of course not"

"I would have done it probably," Demi added.

Miko wanted to tell her, *Until you're in my shoes don't say what you would have done.*

But she said nothing.

Jordyn was very reserved and quiet throughout the brunch, the complete opposite of Lo.

Luckily, she made it to the end of the brunch and surprisingly it went well. Every now and then, they all tried to slide a question in on the low but Jade had her back.

"We're about to hit the malls, you want to go?" Julia asked.

Miko told them, "No I have a date tonight I need to prepare for" she told them, holding up her chipped fingernail.

"I know how that is, girl get to the nail shop, see you next time" Demi hugged her.

"Dinner next week don't forget and bring that man with you" Jade reminded her and kissed her cheek.

"I will be there, I don't know about him coming yet" she told her.

Jordyn held her hand out, "Thank you for coming" she didn't offer a hug like the others but Miko expected that.

"Thank you for inviting me, have a safe trip back" Miko said and told them goodbye before walking down the street to her truck.

Julia said once they all walked out of the restaurant, "She's cool"

"Different from the others" Demi added.

"That's my man's sister of course she's cool" Jade laughed.

Jordyn said nothing as she watched Miko hop into her truck, with her cell phone glued to her ear.

She answered her ringing phone while trying to put an address in her GPS at the same time.

"Miko please don't hang up" John begged.

She took a deep breath not in the mood for any bullshit today, not at all!

"You got one minute and I'm counting," she told him.

"Can I come see you? Where are you?" he pressed for information.

"No, you cannot" she said.

John was desperate, he missed her so much. "I owe you an apology face to face"

"We both were grown and made a conscious decision, no apology needed" Miko let him know an apology wasn't needed.

"Miko I want to be with you, I'm going to leave her as soon as my term is over"

She eyed her watch, "Time is up, don't call me no more" she said and hung the phone up.

Pulling her truck into traffic, she had to go get her nails done and her face painted. Her man was taking her to dinner tonight and Miko planned to look like a million bucks for Mr. Daddy.

Once she made it home, the sun had settled. She didn't have much time to play around, she showered quickly, careful not to mess her pressed hair up.

After her shower, Miko slid into a black jumpsuit with her back completely exposed, the bedazzled red bottom winged-toe pumps made the outfit sparkle. She added a silver bracelet and a pink diamond pendant necklace.

She dabbed one of her favorite perfumes, Tory by Tory Burch behind her ears and wrist and switched from purse to clutch.

Nash came through the garage, hollering her name.

"Damn you look good" he told her, eying her hungrily.

"Oh no I'm not giving you any until we get back to the house," she told him. It took her too long to get the jumpsuit zipped up since he wasn't home to help her.

"I missed you today why you ain't call me?" he asked, turning the shower on.

"You said you were going to check in with me," she reminded him.

"Aye babe can you iron me something to wear" he changed the subject.

Miko removed her feet from her heels and walked out of the bathroom to complete his request.

Not less than an hour later, they were out the door. Miko drove so Nash could roll and smoke his blunt before they made it to the restaurant of her choice.

He didn't know much about where she liked to dine at, so he told her to pull up to whichever restaurant she had a taste for.

Not in the mood to drive to the city, she chose something in Jersey.

"This place is nice" he told her, once they were seated.

"It's my first time here, Lo brags on their shrimp Alfredo," she told him.

He nodded his head, "that's what I'm going to get then" he said.

"You look good baby," she cooed.

Nash blushed, they were always showering each other with praises, "You think it's going to always be like this?" he asked.

"I hope so" she automatically knew what he was talking about.

"Long as we stay on the same page I think it will" he reached his hand across the table wanting to hold hers.

"This bracelet is nice," he told her, holding her hand up.

Miko lied, "My brother bought it" that was slowly becoming her favorite line.

"Let me find out your brother the plug" he joked.

Miko damn near choked on the ice water she had just sipped.

"You okay?" he asked.

She nodded her head and patted her chest.

"Ye-yeah, yes let's order" she said, holding the menu in front of her face, in an attempt to save face and regain composure.

She was well aware that these were all signs for her to tell him what was really up with her before it was too late.

The next day, Miko didn't want to leave the house, last night's dinner date was amazing and so was the sex that they partook in once they made it back home.

Her pussy was aching and so was her back and legs, Nash took her body to higher heights last night and she was paying for it today.

He left out early in the morning, saying that his uncle had more work for him. She wished that they could have hung around the house until it was time for her to head to the city. But he was happy to be making money again so she wouldn't stand in the way of that.

After her body was well rested and she couldn't lie in the bed and be a lazy bum any longer. She heated up the remainder of her food from last night before showering. Miko then headed out the door, to the last minute meeting that Sean called.

It wasn't often Sean wanted to meet with everybody and after talking to Sasha earlier, no one knew what he wanted.

Miko walked into Papa's restaurant and headed straight to the back, "Hey yall" she told the few people that were on time.

"Hey chick" Noel told her.

Miko went and took a seat by her, "I wish I would have known it would be food," she said, looking at the trays of food.

"Yeah we should meet here all the time," Rod said.

Slowly but surely, every one fell through.

"What are we meeting for?" Mary Jane asked.

"I got a proposition and wanted to know if yall wanted in" Sean said happily.

"Nigga this couldn't be discussed through text message" Papa complained.

Everyone knew that he hated Sunday meetings because Papa was a family man.

"Shut up I told yall we wasn't going to be here long," he told them.

After he informed them of the business venture, he was investing in. A few people were interested and others said they would pass.

Miko told him she would think about it.

"So is that all?" Sasha asked.

"Well since we are all here," Malachi said.

Everyone smacked their lips and started complaining.

"Hey hey give my brother the floor" Papa told them, banging on the table.

"Jade is expecting again," Malachi said happily.

"She is? I was just at lunch with her yesterday I couldn't tell," she said aloud.

Roderick then said, "Yeah my wife loved you she thought you were cool as hell"

"J said the same thing," Nasir added.

Miko looked at him and she knew he did that shit on purpose.

Lo spoke up it was the first thing she said during the whole meeting, "You went to lunch with Jordyn?"

She took a deep breath, "It wasn't like that" she was prepared to present her case.

Lo shook her head, got up, and left the room.

"Why would you do that?" Miko snapped on Nasir.

He ignored her and told Malachi, "Congrats bro"

Miko grabbed her purse and ran after Lauren. She asked the server what direction her friend went into.

She knew she didn't leave without her cell phone and purse.

Miko hesitated before opening the door to the bathroom, Lo was staring in the mirror.

She turned when the door opened and Miko saw the tears in her eyes.

"Why didn't you tell me Miko?" she questioned.

"I planned on it," she told her best friend.

"I saw yall talking after the auction, she wants to take you from me," Lo told her.

Miko shook her head, this shit sounded so high school and she wanted no parts of it.

"She didn't bring you up not once," Miko said.

Lo laughed, "She didn't have too, she studied you"

Miko got silent, that much was true.

"The next time she sees you it will be different trust me" Lo said.

"And how do you know this?" Miko asked.

"Because it's HIM! It's the mind games he plays. I know because the same shit he taught her he taught me. I saw you way before we started hanging. I watched you for months, damn near a year. I know what the fuck is he doing" she fussed.

"What do you mean mind games? You watched me for months, why?" Miko wasn't feeling this conversation.

"Not like that" she cried.

Miko noticed for the first time, how distraught Lauren appeared to be, "Are you okay?" she questioned.

"No, I'm fucking not" she sighed and ran her hands over her face.

"Let's get out of here," Miko told her friend.

Tears ran down Lo's face, "I think that's best"

Miko gave her the keys to the truck and she went to get Lo's stuff.

Mary Jane asked was she okay, "No, we're going to go get some drinks" she told her.

Immediately, all of the other women hopped up and prepared to leave as well.

When one of them was going through, they all went through. Noel wasn't really linked with them just yet but she came along as well.

Papa peeped how close Mary Jane was getting to them and he was happy, she needed that.

Miko told her brother she would call him later before rolling her eyes at Nasir, who did nothing but hit her with a smirk in return.

"What happened?" Noel asked.

"Niggas... Honey, one word sums it all up," Sasha, said shaking her head.

***

"Okay come to the left, to the left babe," Miko told Nash. She had him blind folded but he was making it hard for her to guide him.

"Can I take this off now?" he asked her for the fortieth time, since she came and got him from the hood.

"Two more seconds" she promised.

She pulled a set of keys out of her pocket and opened the door and pulled him in, "Man where we at?" he asked, growing impatient.

"Okay take it off" she told him, after turning all of the lights on.

Nash quickly snatched the blindfold out.

She held her heart, praying that he loved the surprise she had been working on for quite a few weeks now.

He stared in awe; tears slowly fell down his face. Nash wasn't a sensitive ass nigga but never in life had someone went out of their way to do something like this for him.

When he turned around and she saw the tears, she smiled and went towards him.

"You the shit" he told her

Miko laughed, "Well thanks babe"

Nash asked, "How did you know what to get?" he said referring to all of the studio equipment, soundboards, microphone and speakers.

"I know a few people," she told him.

Miko had ran a errand for Sean one day since he was out of town and the place she had to meet the dude was a studio and they were selling everything because the nigga was about to go to jail.

Without a second thought, she paid cash for everything and told her tenant he had one month to move. She even paid his ass to leave early and she turned her condo into a studio for Nash.

She had someone come and make the walls soundproof. She stocked the fridge and even had him a lil stash of weed that she copped from Mary Jane.

"I'm going to make you proud bae, just watch" he told her, picking her up and twirling her around.

"Make yourself proud first, I'll be happy with that," she told him, straight up.

Chapter 12

"I had so much fun," Miko told her boyfriend, happily.
He looked over at her as they prepared for bed.

"Yes, I didn't expect them to be so..Cool. And your
mother's cooking I need to get the recipe, those orange
potatoes with the marshmallows. I loved those," she said,
referring to sweet candied yams.

He laughed, forgetting that his beau wasn't too familiar
with soul food. Miko loved anything with rice and grilled
vegetables. His homies cracked on him when he pulled up
to the hood with a tray of California King Rolls and
packets of soy sauce. All he needed was a few pieces of
ginger and he was good.

"I'll get it for you" he told her, pulling the decorative
pillows off the bed.

She was on cloud nine and was praying that her good
mood stayed with her for the rest of the week. Their time
together had been scarce and tonight was needed and
refreshing. In between doing payroll and traveling almost
three to four days out of the week, setting up shops around
the states for stash houses and trap houses and Nash
recording his demo to send to DJ Monday they both had
been grinding.

She had him under the impression that her client had her flying to wherever he was. So when she asked him to drop him off at the private strip to hop on the private jet that she bought for The Underworld, Nash never asked any questions. He just got her things out of the trunk and kissed her goodbye.

Miko knew that one day she would have to come clean and tell her man what was really going on but until then they were doing perfect and her money was piling up.

"I wish you could meet my family" somehow her mind drifted to the distance between her and her mother and she hated it but what could be done when her mother ignored her calls.

Miko hadn't been to DC in so long due to the scandal, she felt like her face was a fresh target for bullshit. In New York, she blended in with the rest of the Koreans, or so she thought.

"I will babe, the time is coming" he reassured her.

She nodded her head, "You're right love," she agreed before going in to the bathroom to rid her face of the mascara, eyeliner and the light foundation that she applied to her face.

"What you gotta do tomorrow?" he asked from the comforts of his side of the bed.

"Hmmm, after work? Nothing that I know besides come home and cook dinner," she told him.

Nash asked, "You think you can slide to the stu when you get some free time?"

She stuck her head out of the bathroom, covered in facial cleanser, "I would love too, and you got something for me to hear?"

He nodded his head, "Lil something something, dude told me to prepare a demo good enough to be turned into album instantly if a record company wanted to sign me" Nash replayed the conversation he had with DJ Monday. Miko went to rinse her face then came to bed, "So a demo is about twelve songs?" she asked.

"Yeah I'll probably do twenty though," he told her. Nash had so many songs written out and he had been in the studio day in and out getting his shit together.

"Did he give you a time limit?" Miko asked him.

"Nah, but I know time is of the essence, I rather get it to him while I'm still on his mind," he said.

She definitely agreed with him there, "You'll get it done" she told him, getting closer to him and laying her head on his chest.

They had a long weekend, well she did. She flew out to Texas Friday morning and didn't return until early this morning. After a shower and an hour nap, her and Nash was en route to his mother's house for Sunday dinner. His mother, grandmother, sister, brothers, cousins, everyone hugged and kissed her like she and Nash had been married twenty years, she fell right in with the family.

When Nash went to the basement to smoke with the other men, she wasn't even tripping that he left her alone with the females. She was happy that they accepted her despite the constant rumors surrounding her name and the President.

Her mother told her before they left, "Thank you for being by my boy's side, he talk about you every time he come by here"

Miko hugged her and told her good night. If she had a few drinks she would have confided in his mother, Nash had changed her life, saved her life, made her better. She needed him more than he needed her, even if Miko was the one with the "money and nice house"

Nash had his happiness and his peace; those were two things that no matter how hard you worked, how much money you had in the bank; they could never be bought.

"Goodnight" she mumbled, feeling her eyes getting heavy.

"Night boo" Nash said, he was all into the recap of the game from earlier.

He reached over her, feeling for the remote control to turn the television down. At night, Nash didn't need the commentary. Half of him watched the reels while the rest of his mind was deep in thought.

Nash had a lot to do this week, the most important being locking himself away in the studio and getting his demo done. Every time he went to record, he realized something was missing. He had the songs, the melody was perfect, verses were tight and the hook was very catchy. He had songs that the hood could vibe too and some that the ladies could rock with as well. Tomorrow, he would see if Miko's energy in the building would help focus and get at least two songs recorded. Looking over at his princess, he moved her wild hair out of her face and kissed her forehead. To trade those late wild nights out for being laid up with his woman, best mother fucking decision of all time. Miko had been a true blessing to his life and he couldn't wait to repay her in a million different ways, besides moving his mama out of the hood, Miko was also his motivation. The world was hers as soon as he signed a deal.

The next morning, Miko was out of the house before Nash could get up for his morning pee. She had a scheduled spa date with Lauren, and as much traveling as she had been doing these past few weeks, the hot stone massage and tea-tree facial was needed.

When she walked into the spa, her best friend was sitting pretty with her shades on, khakis and cardigans and a caramel macchiato from Starbuck's.

She waved to Miko and pointed to a coffee on the small glass table before her. She kissed Lo on the cheek and stuck a straw into the coffee. Lauren was wrapping up a business call, so she scanned her email while she talked.

"Ooh girl, okay remember that lady we donated the money too?" she asked Miko.

She nodded her head, "Yeah with the group homes"

"Why has she turned into a bitch? Complaining about the size of the televisions I gave her, key word, gave her," Lo said, shaking her head.

"That's crazy," she agreed, taking a sip of the coffee.

"I feel like I haven't seen you in forever, how did meeting your in-loves go?" she questioned.

Miko's smile grew big, "Lo, it was so fun and the food was good, they're all really close" she told her.

"So his mom liked you? That's good girl you win the mama over and you'll have that ring before you know it," Lo said with happiness. She had been planning Miko's wedding ever since she saw that her and Nash were growing closer and closer.

"Ring? No, not yet. I'm not ready" she brainwashed herself to think.

"Girl please, you cooking, cleaning and making him cum back to back, his ass better marry you!" Lo said.

"I like us how we are, I've seen marriages ruin people" she told her, shaking her head.

She and Nash never discussed shit like that; he was still trying to get on his feet unbeknownst to Lo.

"Don't count your happily ever after out" she wagged her finger.

"My happily ever after isn't the same as yours" Miko told her, getting irritated with the conversation.

She hated being pressured into doing something she didn't want to do.

Lauren stuck her finger in the whipped cream at the top of her cup and licked her finger.

"What's wrong friend?" Lo asked, sensing her irritation.

"Nothing, what time is our appointment?" she asked changing the subject.

"They'll come get us when it's time Meek," Lo told her.

Miko sat her coffee down and picked up a magazine, talking about weddings and long-term shit made her head hurt.

Whereas, Lauren already had her wedding mapped out, baby shower, and even her ten-year anniversary dinner menu together as well. She lived for shit like that; Lauren was a planner and a hopeless romantic.

Miko wasn't, one day at a time was her mindset.

Soon, two sexy men came towards them with sky blue scrubs on, "Hmm eye candy in the morning" Miko broke out of her funk.

Lo winked at her, "Perfect way to start the morning off" Miko definitely agreed, although she loved the hunk of a man she had back home in Jersey. She wasn't a blind woman and the man who told her he was her masseuse was sexy as hell.

After their massage and facial, they agreed on grabbing lunch in the same building where the spa was located.

"I'm not like starving but I want something to fill me up because I have a long day" Lo scanned the menu.

Miko already knew what she was getting; she had been to this place a few times with Jade.

"What you getting?" Lo asked her.

"Umm, last time I came I had the lobster bisque and it was tasty" she told her.

"You've been here before, with you?" Lo questioned Miko.

"With Jade and Demi" Miko said nonchalantly.

Lo rolled her eyes, "Oh let me find out you been hanging with the wives lately, has Jordyn been back up here?" she asked.

Miko looked up and stared at her, Lo was a mess.

"I hang with Jade because she's family and I'm not sure I don't keep up with Jordyn," she told her.

"I'm your family too, I hate the way you say that shit sometimes," she told her sadly

Miko knew how sensitive Lauren could be at times, so she changed the subject.

"I gotta go to Paris next week, I'm thinking about inviting Nash to go with me," she told her.

Lo blushed, "I think that will be cool, awl I love yall" she told her.

Miko blushed as well, every time she thought of him her face lit up and so did her heart.

"I have to tell you something," Lo told her, after they had ordered and were waiting on their food.

"You're pregnant?" she asked.

Lo damn near choked, "Girl the devil is a lie" she held her hands up in prayer.

"What is it then?" Miko was curious!

"I'm seeing Ben, like for real" she told her trying to contain her happiness.

Miko smirked, "No bullshit Lo? No Nasir?" she questioned.

Lauren was good for going on a few dates, even take a out of town trip but as soon as Nasir confessed his love for her as if he really had plans on leaving Jordyn, she would drop the man quicker than her grandmother use to drop chicken wings in hot grease.

"No Nasir. I haven't talked to him since the night of the auction and that was a long time ago," she informed her.

"How do you feel?" Miko asked.

"Good, I'm happy. I told him upfront about my relationship with Nas and he said we're going to take things slow but so far girl, he's the perfect gentlemen and it works out because my dad adores him" she rambled.

Miko was happy for her friend, for real. She reached over and grabbed her hand, "I know how hard it was for you to leave him so I'm proud of you and I'm happy that you're happy" she kept it gully with her.

Lo didn't expect to get so emotional but Miko only knew the half of her dealings with Nasir, the hardest thing she did in life was to watch him walk out of her house and never hear from him again.

What she didn't tell her best friend was that he left her on some, "I'm going to teach you lesson bullshit"

Either way, it went that was the best thing he could have ever done for her, Lo was slowly realizing her worth. She didn't have to be ducked off when she was with Ben; he loved on her in public and in private.

"Is it too early for a toast?" Miko asked.

"Girl now you know it's never too early for a drink, waitress!" she said, calling their server over.

Minutes later, they had two champagne flutes in the air, "To happiness" Miko said.

Lo added, "And to love" with a big ass smile on her face.

***

Miko stood in the kitchen, trying to keep herself busy with anything she could put her hands on. "Meek what you in there doing?" Chi asked, from the dining room.

"Coming, I was getting a paper napkin" she lied.

She felt cornered and wanted to leave but she knew her brother would be so hurt if she walked out of his house without saying goodbye.

However, being invited to dinner at the last minute is one thing. She wasn't tripping on that because for one she was hungry and two, she was in the area running errands for Papa.

But when she walked in the house and saw Malachi's mother, Miko had been uncomfortable ever since.

Jade told her she was a sweetheart and the kids wanted her to spend the night with them for the rest of the week. Apparently, she had no idea of who Miko was and Malachi had to calm her down and restrain her from damn near taking Miko's head off.

She ran out of the foyer, into the room that they basically turned into hers when she visited, Melissa, her half-sister promised her that everything was okay, and it was safe for her to return.

Throughout dinner, their mom stared at her with hell and hate in her eyes and she found it difficult to enjoy Jade's cooking in peace.

Malachi came into the kitchen, "Sis you good?" he asked, coming up behind her.

Miko turned around, "No I am not," she told him.

"You know my mom is not mentally stable, you do know that right?" he said in a chastising tone.

She took a deep breath, hating how he was about to turn this around on her.

"Malachi I am not comfortable" she tried to take the best approach in order to leave without upsetting him.

"She flipped out, big deal" he laughed.

Apparently, they were used to her frantic behavior but she wasn't, "It is a big deal, it's a very big deal. My heart is beating like crazy," she told him, in a stressed tone.

She felt like their mother was staring at her wanting to slice a damn knife through her heart.

Miko couldn't figure out her next move and she felt like it was best to remove herself from a very tense situation.

"You trust me right?" Malachi asked.

She sighed, he didn't understand.

"Nah for real, you trust me? Come on, I know you do. I'm your big brother. I got your back," he told her with that big ass goofy smile that was always plastered on his face.

She smiled, "Let me go home, I miss my boyfriend" she told the truth.

She and Nash hadn't talked all day and she wanted to be up under him right now.

"Oh Mr. Imaginary, how is he by the way?" Malachi teased.

Miko shook her head and laughed, "In due time, we're all going to get together" she promised.

"As long as you're safe and sound I'm good, anybody is better than that ole sorry mother-"

Jade entered the kitchen, interrupting their conversation, "Babe, what yall in here doing?" she asked.

Malachi's face lit up whenever Jade was near and in past times, Miko used to be filled with envy but no longer was that the case. Because her man looked at her the same way.

Miko could have on over-sized pajamas and no makeup, and he was kissing all over on her.

When she was dressed up in designer from head to toe and even when all she wore was her favorite hat and a pair of old jeans, he still blushed in her presence.

In confidence, she knew that their love for each other becoming unconditional.

Even when she was out of town and he was in her house, driving her cars, she trusted and didn't question his whereabouts.

Miko never had that sense of security, stability and most importantly, confidence in a relationship and it was so refreshing not to worry.

"Talking about her imaginary boyfriend, what's his name? Venus?" he asked.

She giggled, "It's Nash, why you trying to be funny" she told him.

"I knew it was one of them space names" he laughed.

Jade told them to come back in the family room, since dinner was now finished and they had migrated through the house.

"Five minutes please sis," he begged.

She took a deep breath, "You're the only person that gets their way with me," she told him.

Malachi draped his arm over her shoulder, "I feel special" he said and he meant it whole-heartedly.

Miko knew that she would never make it home, her nieces didn't want her to leave, she ended up painting their nails, braiding their hair in a halo style, they wanted their hair

like their aunt's and then she stayed behind and filled
Malachi in on the past few trips she had took with Noel.
Miko was saddened to see that her Lexus wasn't in the
driveway when she made it in, which meant that her man
was still out.

 Before going to run herself a hot bath, she turned the
alarm on. Thankfully, she had nothing to do tomorrow
and she prayed that Nash's schedule reflected hers. All she
wanted was a few rounds of sex and hot pizza delivered to
their front door.

A few minutes into her relaxing shower, the alarm chimed
which signified that her beau was home.

Nash made his way to the back of the house, assuming that
she was already sleeping. He planned on bathing in the
guest bathroom so that he wouldn't wake her.

Once he never came in and spoke to her, she sped up her
time in the bath before stepping out and sliding her arms
into her kimono and walking barefoot around the house to
find him

Before she made it to the kitchen, she heard water running
and Nash singing in the guest bathroom.

She decided to let him bathe in peace and she went to
make a pot of tea.

"What you doing up?" he asked.

She turned around, "You scared me" he was now dressed in a pair of boxers and white socks.

"I came in the house I thought you were sleep, did I wake you?" he asked coming closer.

"No I was in the tub when you got here and I stopped by my brother's house for dinner. I called you but your phone was dead I suppose" she said, staring into his eyes.

Nash ignored her line of questioning. His phone was dead but because he knew that, she trusted him it was no need in him acknowledging what she said. He pulled her kimono down, "How was your day?" he asked, touching her collarbone.

"Productive" she told him.

He nodded his head and wrapped his arms around her now, naked frame.

"I love you, have I ever told you that before?" he asked.

She stared at him with love in her eyes, "I know you do," she told him in confidence.

"And how do you know that Ms. Sanderson?" Nash questioned, as he rubbed her but.

"I just do," she said, kissing him.

"Hmmmm what kind of kiss was that?" he moaned, savoring the taste of green tea that was on her tongue.

"It's an I love you more kiss" she said, above a whisper.

Nash didn't waste any more time, picking her ass up and sitting her on the kitchen island.

It had been a long day for him and the best way for him to end his night was with his head in between Miko's legs and then her on top of his dick.

He had been thinking of her sweet pussy the whole way home, the only reason he didn't come straight to bed because he helped one of his partners moved today and was smelling a little musty.

"I've missed you," he confessed.

Sweet nothings that came from his lips would never grow old. Even as time progressed and their journey continued. The butterflies still existed. Her cheeks still turned rosy red and most importantly, they still craved each other's existence.

Miko was sure that as the days passed, he would grow tired of waking up to her and going to sleep with her all on his side of the bed. She thought that the complaints would come of her Korean cooking and the old habits that she refused to break, but he never said anything. In fact, his love for sushi, grilled fish and vegetables increased. Their time spent together was always full of bliss and affection and even when he wasn't touching her soul, they were cuddled up watching movies.

Over time, she had grown to love *Paid In Full* and *Baby Boy*. Whenever she was tired and had a long day, Nash would make her soup and put a good movie on and they would kick back with her head in his lap as he stroked her scalp.

"Show me then" she told him in a bossy tone.

Every now and then, she would discard the good and submissive act that he adored.

Nash loved when she took control but tonight he was calling the shots.

On his knees, in the middle of the kitchen, he licked her for dear life.

She thought about her and Lo's conversation the other day discussing children and marriage and she wondered would her sex life stay as spicy as it was now if they had little rug rats running around the world.

 Children weren't something she desired right now, not to say that maybe in a few years her opinion wouldn't change. But right now? Eh, Miko wasn't feeling the idea of swollen feet and a widened nose.

"Open up" he commanded, once he felt her legs getting closer and closer to his ears.

The pressure that was building up behind her walls was causing tears to form and as they cascaded down their face so did her love, erupting in his mouth.

"Oh, babyyyyy" she moaned and grunted, panting due to the pleasure and satisfaction she felt from climaxing.

In between her legs, Nash could never get Miko to hold out for long, as soon as his tongue came into contact with that little tiny hole that only opened up only when he was near, she would release immediately.

Miko was like a leaking sink, always leaking and pouring and he loved it.

Hungrily licking up every single drop as if he would be punished if the kitchen wasn't clean.

"Baby come close" she begged of him.

He pulled her off the island and onto her feet. Running his hands through her wild hair as he deep kissed her with his tongue. He put all of his energy into making sure that Miko knew she was his.

Every single piece of her belonged to him, he had so much in store for her, for them.

Like magnets, they clung towards to one another.

Not only was her pussy his, but her soul was too, her heart was rightfully his.

His Miko, she wasn't broken anymore, she didn't turn her head when he looked at her, she didn't cry during sex anymore either. The butterfly had blossomed from the cocoon. Nash took full credit for transforming her; he was honored to be the one who got Miss Miko together.

"I love you, I love you, I just fucking love you," she told him and with each word, she felt it more and more. Everything about him made her cringe but in a good way, no one had ever had her the way he did.

Her ego was the way it is because of him. Nash constantly told her how bad she was and with all due respect, he would say. She was the baddest bitch.

He loved her she loved him, with nothing, with everything, none of that shit mattered.

Miko took his hand and led him to bed.

Locking the door as if someone may come and interrupt their precious time together.

Tonight, felt different. Although she had long lost track of their sex sessions, tonight was intense.

Before he entered her, she knew that it would be mind-blowing.

It was the way he watched her naked body move around the room, turning the lights off in the bathroom, making sure the closet door was pushed up all the way.

She went to light a few candles, wanting to set the mood. "Fuck them candles, bring your ass here," he told her. His voice hoarse and sounding raspier than it did on a normal basis.

She looked at him, with a face of anticipation and a coy smile on her face.

Strutting closer to him, Miko was ready for whatever he had in store.

"I'm here now," she sassed.

Nash took a seat on the bed, his feet planted firmly on the floor, Miko made her way in between his legs, he slipped her nipple in his mouth, savoring the taste of the pink berries.

"Hmm" she moaned, running her hands through his dreads.

"Babeeee" she warned him not to get anything started. But what was she thinking. The night had yet to begin.

He smacked her but motioning for her to hop on his dick, as he pulled his mouth from her nipple and laying back. The sight before him was breath taking, her face bare and shoulders relaxed, she was an angel.

Miko took her time getting comfortable on his dick as if she didn't just ride him that morning, right before they started their day.

She held her breath, as she slid down onto his penis and slowly rocked herself on it.

"How does it feel?" Nash asked, wanting his ego stroked.

His hands behind his head, Miko no longer needed his help riding him the way he liked for her too.

"Good baby real good" she told him, never taking her eyes off him.

They loved to watch each other, fight against the good feeling that she brought him and he brought her.

"I love you" he mouthed the words, not being able to say anything else once she sped up her pace and instead of rocking she was damn near slamming her cheeks into his lap.

Her moans turned into shrieks and all-out screaming. Nash loved when she got this way. His little beau turned into Miko the porn star. He used his hand to increase the experience by playing with her clit.

"Baby I'm about to cum" she forewarned.

"Cum then, shit cum on this dick," he begged of her.

Miko went faster, riding his dick like tonight was the last night of them being together and tomorrow he was going away for some time.

Putting her all into giving him the best mother fucking pussy of his life, she held her muscles together, trying to control the jumping of her clit but she couldn't.

It had a life of its own and honestly, Nash was its master. She screamed and came only to hop off and suck him until he did the same.

He held her head close to the tip of his dick. She knew that he liked her to lick the tip like a lollipop until he nutted.

"Shit bae" he moaned, as Miko swallowed all of it.

Nash laid back, feeling like he was having a stroke but he knew it was just the after effects of fellatio from Miko. She kissed his stomach before going to wash up and coming back to the bathroom with a soapy rag for him as well.

"I want to hold you," he told her, as she got into bed with her back to him.

Sometimes she forgot that they lived together. She was so used to watching the President leave right after sex. Miko was tired but she wouldn't tell Nash that, hell, she was happy that he wanted to cuddle after sex.

She rolled over and laid her head on his chest.

"I love you," he told her again, meaning it more and more every time he said it.

Nash would tell her again in the middle of the night when he woke her up for more, then he would say it once more in the morning as he sucked on her pussy.

"I love you too Nash" she said after stifling a yawn.

He closed his eyes, thanking God for the millionth time for his personal blessing, his Miko.

***

Nash sat in the back of the church, he hated funerals and from the looks of it Lauren and her brother, Malachi did too. But they all came together to support Miko.

The Tom Ford suit he wore, courtesy of his beau was clean as a ma'fucka though. Even the Prada shades she went and got him yesterday for the "sun". Which is what she told him when he told her he couldn't accept the gifts.

Nash couldn't really read her emotions, she sat at the piano with her eyes closed, stroking the keys as if she was paid to be there instead of playing her grandmother's favorite song which was her dying request. It was custom tradition to be cremated after death but the family still insisted on having a memorial.

Lo was in awe of Miko, she had never seen her play the piano and apparently her brother didn't either.

He wondered how "well" they knew her, because Miko was a beast on the keys.

"Does she play at home?" Lo leaned over and asked him.

Nash nodded his head and smiled in admiration of his girl.

After the funeral, he waited on Miko to finish the family thing while he stood off to the side with Lo and Malachi.

Her brother looked familiar but he couldn't place his face, Nash knew so many niggas it was ridiculous.

"It's hot and my feet hurt" Lo complained.

Nash told her, "Miko has some flats in here" he handed Lo Miko's purse

"You're so sweet, holding her purse," she told him with a warm smile.

He didn't look at it like that, he was just holding the damn purse what was the big deal.

"Yo, tell Meek I had to slide" Malachi finished a call.

Lo asked with worry lines across her forehead, "Everything is okay right?"

She had been praying that God kept Nasir safe, while they were together or whatever they called it, Lo prayed with him constantly.

Nasir moved in silence but Lauren told him that devil was always lurking.

Her biggest fear was something happening to him while they were being distant.

Malachi told her, "Yeah"

He held his hand out towards Nash, "Nice meeting you my man, keep my sis safe" he said coolly.

Nash nodded his head and dapped him up instead, Lo smirked but Chi paid it no mind.

He had bigger shit going on at the moment.

Miko finally found her way to them, "I'm ready to go," she said in an irritated tone.

"What's wrong? Did you talk to your mom" Lo asked her.

They couldn't see her eyes because they were covered in shades. She shook her head, "I'm just ready to go," she said.

Miko and Nash had been in DC all week, and would be there until tomorrow.

"Meek you good?" Lo questioned.

Nash knew how she was when she was in a bad mood, so he left her alone and headed towards the car knowing that they would soon make their way.

"She looked dead at me like she didn't even know me and turned her head," Miko cried, once they were back at the hotel room.

Nash sighed, "That shit fucked up, but that tells you that she's hurt babe"

She didn't want to hear that bullshit and her mother had a past so filthy. She wasn't in a position to judge at all.

If anything, she should have been comforting her child and apologizing for allowing her past to linger and affect Miko's life. But no, her mother was blaming her for being embarrassed.

Miko wiped the tears from her eyes as she undressed out of her black dress.

It still hadn't hit her that her grandmother had passed away, the matriarch of their family.

She was feeling some type of way, none of her aunts, cousins, uncles...no one thought to call Miko and tell her that grandmother was sick and didn't have much time left on earth.

Miko wasn't allowed to spend time with her, tell her how much she looked up to her and loved her.

The phone call that she received in the middle of the night, around this same time last week had hit her like a bag of bricks.

The little love and respect Miko had left for her mother had dwindled, she was well aware of much Miko loved her grandmother and for her own selfish reasons she didn't call and tell Miko that her grandmother was sick.

Miko tossed and turned the entire night, not being able to sleep because her mind was on her mother. She felt betrayed and wanted answers.

The clock in the hotel room read two thirty in the morning, when she decided that enough was enough and she was going to talk to her mom.

"Babe you don't want to call first?" Nash asked, sleepily.

Miko told him to go back to bed, as she opened her suitcase and slid on a pair of jogging pants she brought along for her daily mile run.

"It's too late for you to be driving" he told her, getting out of the bed as well.

Miko didn't bother to refute what he was saying because she knew his mind was made up.

Whenever Nash was near, he protected her and treated her like a Queen. She was grateful for his love and support and also, putting up with her distant and cold family.

All of her cousins were nice and pleasant but her mother ignored her when she introduced them. Nash told Miko he really didn't give a fuck, however, she was still embarrassed.

With her man in the passenger seat, as she drove the rental car through the neighborhood in which she was raised, she took it all in.

Miko lived a life that she wouldn't dare repeat, but she made it through.

She loved her mother despite her flaws and she expected the same in return.

Leaving the car running, she promised Nash she was going to clear her heart and mind then turn around on her heels and leave.

Even if her mama didn't mumble a word, she planned to get it all off her chest. Miko couldn't go another day harboring the pain. She missed her mother but tonight would be the last time she kissed her ass and begged for forgiveness.

Knocking on the door three times then ringing the doorbell, she had amped herself to speak her mind and she hoped that she kept that same courage once she came face to face with her mama.

"What do you want? Being loud and waking neighbors up Miko" her mother fussed in Korean, once she opened the door.

"LET ME TELL YOU SOMETHING!" Miko went right back at her, in Korean as well.

Nash had never heard her speak her language, he was a lil' turned on.

"Come in the house!" she told Miko and left her alone in the doorway.

Miko turned around and smiled at Nash before disappearing in the home.

Her mother stood in the kitchen, with her sleeping mask around her neck.

"I need to talk to you," Miko said.

"Me don't care what you have to say," she told her.

"I never judged you, even when you slept with half of the block ma...I never ever *ever* judged you. I made one mistake and you disown me" she went in automatically. Miko could have tip toed around the subject but she said fuck it and told her mama how she really felt.

Her mother looked at her with tears in her eyes, "It was for you," she pointed to Miko.

She rolled her eyes, "Ma I don't care who it was for I was still a child"

Miko's mother turned her back, but she wasn't done.

"You kept me away from grandmother why would you hurt me like that?"

"You kept yourself away, you on your own Miko!" her mother fussed.

"Get your new brother and piss poor dad and forget about us," her mama cried

She took a deep breath; this is what all of this was about, *aha.*

Miko never knew her mother felt some type of way, because she appeared not to have feelings, it had been that way since she was a little girl

"Ma no it's not like that and you know it"

"No Sunday dinner, no movie with me, you don't care" her mother spoke sadly.

Miko felt horrible, "It's still time to do all of those things"

Her mother took a deep breath and turned around facing her daughter with tears in her eyes.

"My mama is dead and I have no one" she released her pain, finally.

Throughout the funeral, she remained frozen, counting down the time until it was over.

"Oh ma" she went to her mom and took her tiny self into her arms, and held her until she got it all out.

"Love you Miko," she told her.

With tears in her eyes, Miko told her mother, "Love you more mama" she felt like the world was now lifted from her shoulders.

"Stay here with me" she asked.

Miko told her that Nash was in the car and they had to go back to the hotel.

"He can sleep on couch," she told her.

Wanting to stay on her mother's good side, she went and got her man and made him as comfortable as possible on the brown couch.

Kissing his forehead and promising him they could leave first thing in the morning, Nash silenced her and told her, "I'm good boo, get some rest"

Miko smiled at him before making sure the house was locked up and going to get in bed with her mom like old times.

She was relieved that all it took was one conversation and things were repaired.

Miko made a mental note and a personal promise to herself that no matter how busy she was or amount of trips she had scheduled in a month, she was still going to fly to DC once a month and spend some quality time with her mother.

The next morning, she woke up to hearing laughter coming from the kitchen, Miko walked lazily into the room to see Nash and her mom chatting it up like lost friends.

"Hey sleepy head" he said.

"Morning" she yawned.

"Morning? Miko it's two in the afternoon" her mother fussed.

"It is?" she couldn't believe she slept that long.

"When was the last time you got good rest, you look tired," her mother questioned in Korean.

Miko eyed Nash; he had no idea what she said.

She answered her mother, "Been a long time" and winked at Nash.

Sleeping through the night without being awaken with a kiss, a slap on the butt or her favorite, head, was rare. Her young man had a healthy appetite, he was always craving one thing in particular, and that was Miko.

After her mother served them lunch, she bid them farewell.

Nash had already called the hotel and added another day since they weren't back by the checkout time, "We can stay an extra day I'm cool with that," he suggested.

Miko would have loved to stay one more day in the city she was born and raised but tomorrow was the first of the month.

"I have to get back to work," she told him sadly.

Even though nothing was sad about the first of the month, she had to put on a façade.

The first of the month made her richer every month and she was looking forward to transferring the half a million dollars to her account since she handled the finances for The Underworld.

"Money to be made huh?" he teased, not having a clue just how serious his comment was in her book.

She nodded her head and kept things kosher, "Yep babe money to be made" she agreed /agreeing with her lover.

***

The Underworld didn't fuck the clubs up unless they were out of town and laying low where no one knew them. New York was where the foundation was laid so it wasn't too often they all stepped out together, catching dinner was different because *hey...* it was just dinner with family.

But, when ten millionaires linked up it was guaranteed to be a lituation. Sean invested into a casino in Vegas and invited the team down for the grand opening.

Miko was sad that Nash was busy working on putting together the perfect demo because she really wanted him to come. Of course, whenever The Underworld would make plans to turn up, she would just tell him she had to work to do but throughout the day, she had plans of being with him.

The good thing about going out of town with The Underworld was not only did she work with them but the people that were going were also her friends. So for the past few days, they all had been shopping like crazy, eating good and gaining weight they would worry about once they got back in the city. Tonight, they had plans on tearing the clubs down, popping bottles, smoking on nothing but the best and enjoying themselves. So far, the year had been treating them well, everything was going smooth. No one was locked up or dead, in The Underworld those two things alone deserved a celebration.

Although, they were still pushing every drug known to man, individually everyone had begun to launch businesses, invest into different businesses and slowly but surely settle down...well, not really but the time was coming.

Sean was the only bachelor in the crew and he had no plans on dropping down on one knee any time soon, or so they thought. He was a very private man; he had always been that way.

Tonight they planned to make a movie; Miko knew that she would be turnt. She and Mary Jane had been grinding day in and out for months straight. When Sean told them to stop what they were they doing and hop on the plane with the rest of the gang. They both didn't hesitate.

Mary Jane needed a vacation more than anyone did, she had the hardest job and being around those fumes all day was slowly taking a toll on her body.

"I hope the wives don't come" Lo complained.

Noel was sitting at the table in Miko's hotel suite, where the girls had gathered to walk down to the lobby of the hotel together.

"Why don't you like them?" she asked, as she rolled enough blunts to last them for the night.

"Because they think they all that" Lo said, not knowing how childish she sounded.

"Ignore her Noel" Miko said, from the bathroom where she was fixing her makeup.

Sasha spoke up, "I don't think it's like that, they just be getting on my fucking nerves"

Mary Jane didn't say anything because she stayed in her own lane and minded her business and that's the same way Miko felt.

"Meek you wearing these red bottoms?" Lo asked, eyeing a pair of fuck me pumps.

"Yeah I am," she told her.

"These cute girl" Lo said, picking up one of them.

"Your man bought you those?" Sasha asked.

Mary Jane looked at Sasha wondering what made her ask Miko that, they never discussed Nash, ever.

Miko said, "No I bought them" not thinking much of the conversation.

But Lo did and she asked, "Why does it matter?"

Sasha eyed Lo, "Miko's cheerleader I wasn't talking to you"

Lo put the shoe down, "Okay bitch but I'm talking to you"

Noel shook her head, she hated when those two got into it but most of the time it was because Sasha was picking and everyone knew how Lo was when it came to Miko. Plus, Lo was drunk and usually went the hell off whenever she had an ounce of alcohol in her system.

"I just asked a question, did her nigga buy the shoes, that are it," Sasha said but it was obvious she really had something else she wanted to say.

Miko finished applying her eyeliner before she came out of the bathroom, "Why are y'all arguing?" she asked.

Lo said, "Talk to her, cus I'm good"

Mary Jane sat on the bed, crocheting a blanket, she was so weird but Miko loved her just how she was.

"Sasha is everything okay?" Miko asked her.

"Yeah, I heard you were a sugar mama that's all" Sasha blurted.

Miko was taken back by her comment, "What does that have to do with you?" she asked.

Everyone in the fucking room was surprised to hear quiet lil' Meek clapping back.

Noel stopped rolling the blunt and waited on Sasha to respond.

Mary Jane never stopped crocheting her blanket.

And Lo was ready for whatever, although that was her first time hearing that, she didn't care. What Miko did with her money was her business and from what she saw, the nigga clearly was feeling her so who cared if she was tricking off.

"Nothing do you, I just know how those niggas from Brooklyn are" Sasha said nonchalantly.

"Yeah but you don't know him and you really don't know me" she told her, and went back into the bathroom.

Miko wasn't even going to trip on that shit; the turn up was still in effect.

Once they made it to the car, Lo passed a bottle around, "Let's turn up, we work hard as hell" she said drunkenly.

Noel asked her was she okay and Miko told her that she was.

Because of her confidence and most importantly the faith that she planted in her relationship, Miko wouldn't trip on the rumors.

At Club Flavor, The Underworld rented out the entire VIP section, not only was it filled with bottles and good food but the realest niggas was in the building.

Mary Jane and Papa shared a blunt, he couldn't believe she came out but that was his best friend so he made sure to show her a good time.

Lo and Noel went to the dance floor even though Nasir would want her closer to keep an eye on her, Lo was no longer his business.

Demi, Jade and Julia sat on the couch dancing in their seat; they all were missing their kids.

Miko sat alone toying with her phone, wanting to duck off and call Nash but the time difference is what kept her from doing so.

Sugar Mama

Who was around him saying that and then how did it get back to Sasha? No one knew Miko she kept a low profile.

Was it because Nash often drove her truck or Lexus to the hood?

Gosh, she had so many questions right now.

Lo came back upstairs and when a Jamaican song blazed through the speakers, she winded her hips around the VIP section, with her eyes closed and a bottle of champagne in her hand.

She took her time going down to the ground and slowly gyrating her hips, her ass cheeks moved one at a time as she came back up.

Her girls cheered her on as she danced and snapped her fingers, Miko looked over at her, laughing.

Lo loved to go out, she was in her atmosphere when she heard music and was drinking.

"Get it boo" Demi cheered her on.

She went over and grabbed Demi, knowing that she loved to dance just as much as she did.

Another song came on and they both turnt up together.

Papa went over the balcony, bouncing his shoulders and blew a stack of one hundred ones; he was high as a mu'fucka.

Malachi and Roderick had a few strippers giving them lap dances, Jade kept her head turned not even watching him because she knew that she was going home with him, it didn't even matter to her what the fuck he was doing.

"You good?" Nasir asked Miko, as he took the seat next to her.

She nodded her head, Miko admired Nasir when it came to business but that was about it. She didn't appreciate how he treated Lauren and for that reason, she normally kept her distance from him.

Lo was still dancing and even had spooky Mary Jane to dance with her, "How is she?" Nasir asked.

Miko sipped her champagne, "Perfect" she told him.

Nasir nodded his head and said, "Cool" before getting back up and going to chop it up with Malachi and Roderick.

Sean was so high, him and Noel was in the corner sharing a blunt.

The night was fun and it felt good to get together with her team, not only did they grind together but they celebrated together as well.

"I am drunk" Noel said, she wasn't big on drinking.

"Make sure you eat some toast before you go to bed," Mary Jane suggested.

"I miss my man" Lo whined, as they walked back to their hotel suite.

Sasha teased, "Which one?"

Lo flicked her the middle finger.

"Damn" Mary Jane said after she removed her phone from her ear.

Miko turned around thinking her head had started hurting, lately Mary Jane's migraines had been getting worse, "DJ Monday in the hospital" she said sadly.

"Oh my God, I grew up listening to him," Sasha said.

"He not dead, why you saying it like that?" Lo's drunk ass asked.

'How do you know?" Miko asked, before she jumped to conclusions.

"His grandmother lives on my street, my neighbor just left me a voicemail," she told them.

"That syrup probably" Sasha said.

Mary Jane nodded her head, "That's why I don't fuck with that shit," she said.

"Meek you good" Noel asked her, noticing that she had spaced out.

DJ Monday? No. Couldn't be. She prayed everything was okay.

Nash needed him, his demo…..his career…he had been working on his demo to give to him.

What the hell?

She knew there was nothing she could do to heal him; all she could do was pray for the best *but damn*!

After calling Nash's phone a few times but not being able to get him on the line, she lay down and closed her eyes.

Miko sat up seconds later, after hearing the front door close.

She eyed the clock, 5:41 am. Who in the hell was leaving the suite this late?

It didn't take her long to derive a conclusion. Lo knocked on the door once before it opened, she walked in and closed the door behind her, locking it.

She stared in his eyes and he stared back, she saw the hurt but couldn't connect. Lo had moved on, and yes, she was happy with Ben. He was perfect, kind, sweet, loving, attentive and most importantly SINGLE.

Ben didn't come with baggage, Lo didn't feel like she was in competition, she didn't feel like she wasn't enough or worthy of his time. He didn't leave her with questions unanswered.

So why…why…why was Lauren in Suite 1034 staring into the eyes of the man who had broken her heart more times, than she could count.

She would be lying to herself if she said it was the sex that she craved, although he was the best she ever had, but sex didn't make her get out of bed when he called her phone requesting her presence.

Their history…..the past, the memories they created, the promises he made to her, she wanted to know if they were still intact.

"You looked nice tonight," Nasir, told her.

She hated and loved his accent at the same time, not sure, whether she wanted to roll her eyes and smack his ass in the back of the head or drop her panties and give him what she knew he had been missing.

"So did you" she told him.

Nasir walked further into the suite that he rented for the weekend.

"Nice" she complimented.

"Lauren come here," he commanded.

She took a deep breath and went towards him, standing before him.

He touched her face and held her hands in his.

"Please tell me you're still not seeing that sucker," he asked.

She told him, "Yes I am"

Nasir dropped her hands and went back to bed.

"Goodnight" he dismissed her.

"Are you serious right now?" she couldn't believe this shit.

"I'm not kissing or touching you," he told her, sounding disgusted.

He had not changed, always having to have his cake, the pan, icing and even the damn kitchen.

"And you're still with Jordyn, correct?" she asked.

"Lo get out" he told her, regretting even calling her up.

"No you don't tell me what the fuck to do" she went over to him.

"What you gon sit here and do? Watch me sleep, because I'm going to bed," he told her.

She crossed her arms and eyed him angrily.

"You don't get to do me like this," she told him.

"You're right that's why I'm not doing you at all" he laughed and rolled over, not wanting to look at her sexy ass any longer.

She wasn't his anymore.

"Do you miss me?" she asked.

He yawned, "You already know the answer to that"

She knew he missed her, in The Underworld meetings and even when they got together in support of one another, he looked at her with so much intent.

"Okay so give me a hug or something Nas," she told him. She hated how quickly she forgot that she was supposed to hate him

He sighed but did as she asked, Nasir got out of bed and wrapped his arms around her waist and she brought her arms around his head.

"I love you," she told him.

"I know," he said cockily.

Lo kissed his neck and Nasir moved out of her way, "Chill" he warned.

"Stop it," she begged, kissing him again in the exact same area.

"Not doing that with you Lauren, I mean that shit," he said firmly.

Lauren knew how important his health was to him and because she was fucking someone else meant that he couldn't hit her raw like he preferred to.

She decided to leave with her pride, "Goodnight" she told him.

He kissed her forehead, "Night"

Nasir watched her as she left his hotel room. He thought to himself, *She will be back…one day.*

***

Miko had just finished running errands and dropping her nieces and nephew off to their parents, Nash hadn't been home in days due to trying to finish his demo.

DJ Monday was in a coma but everyone had faith that he would pull through and when he did, Nash wanted to be right there with his demo, mixed and mastered and hopefully ready to shop for a deal.

Miko entered her own home and his new safe haven, the place was filthy. It had been a while since she visited.

The trash overflowed and the smell could have killed her if the marijuana fragrance wasn't so heavy.

There were empty pizza boxes and Sprite bottles all over the counters, her once beautiful million-dollar condo now looked like a trap house.

Not only was it dirty, but it was filled with niggas and even a few bitches.

Miko counted to ten as she walked through the condo looking for her boyfriend

She heard his raspy voice it sounded like he was recording, "I'ma real nigga, I fuck with foreign bitches, ya hear me. Foreign bitches!" he said over and over again.

"Aye run that track back" Nash said, he was high as hell and was gone off that syrup.

The clothing he wore was the same shit he had on when he left the house three days ago; Miko just prayed that he had washed his ass.

"Babe what it do" Nash said, lazily.

Miko didn't return his joyous greeting, she was pissed off "Can y'all give us a second" she asked his cousin, and another dude who she didn't know but assumed was the engineer that she was paying by the hour.

Nash never even came into the room, so she went into the recording closet.

"Why haven't you been answering the phone?" she asked him, her arms were crossed and her jaws were tight.

"Been grinding, gottta get you that new crib and a mink. You want a mink?" he asked.

Miko shook her head, "I don't need anything from you," she snapped.

After taking a deep breath she continued, "What I need for you to do is, come home and when I call answer the phone"

Nash laughed and ran his hands over his face, "Yes master"

Miko looked at him, "That's how you feel?"

"I mean that's how you came in here" he shot back.

Miko wasn't in the mood for this shit; she was tired and needed rest.

"Nash the least you can do is answer the phone, it takes three seconds to tell me that you're not coming home"

He yelled, "I ain't got three minutes, I'm trying to mother fucking get it! I can't live off you forever"

Her heart broke, "Live off me?"

Nash dropped his head; his statement came out the wrong way.

"That's not what I meant Meek," he told her.

She walked backwards, "I guess the rumors are true, I am your sugar mama" she shook her head.

"Miko" he said her name.

"Give me my keys" she yelled.

Nash looked at her, "I'm fucked up, and I'm high. I didn't mean it like that"

"Give me my fucking keys, to my house, my car everything" she shouted.

He by passed her and went to the bedroom that used to be hers, and fished the keys out of the MCM book bag that she copped him.

Coming back into the studio room, he tossed her the keys.

"What you gon take the studio back too?" he asked.

She ignored him, "I'll have your clothes sent to your mom's," she said.

"Miko what about us?" he asked.

"Ain't no us, you got what you wanted from me" she told him, her words laced with anger and hurt.

Nash tried to touch her, "Don't fucking touch me" she spat.

He backed up and she walked past him and left the condo before she broke out in tears.

As soon as she made it to the elevator, tears sprang from her eyes as she felt her heart break into a million pieces.

Nash had become a part of her and to hurt him would kill her but damn, if she wasn't contemplating going back into the condo and wetting his ass up.

Chapter 13

The side effects of Promethazine/ Codeine cough syrup
that rappers have penned the term, "DRANK",
promethazine causes severe and fatal breathing problems
when consumed excessively. You're not supposed to take
more than one prescribed dosage at a time, but people
have begun to drop a "four" which is considered a large

amount being deposited inside a bottle of Sprite, it becomes "drinkable" by adding a few pieces of sweet candy, which cuts the sharp taste.

Promethazine causes dizziness, lightheadedness, and fainting, blurred vision, tightness in the chest, unusual hoarseness, abnormal thoughts, mood or mental change, hallucinations and in DJ Monday's case loss of coordination.

The life that we live, and the media is affecting how we think, how we operate, how interact with each other.

Grown men are mimicking the famous monkey see, monkey do. It's not too often we see people living their own lives, and doing what *they* want to do.

The funeral for DJ Monday was a memorable occasion, of course, fans weren't allowed to attend but that didn't stop them from surrounding the church with candles, booze and speakers playing some of his greatest hits.

DJ Monday started off as a rapper, which is what gave him the accreditation of being considered a Hip-Hop legend, he then became a producer and to date he's responsible for being the mastermind of some of the greatest hits that this generation has ever listened too.

Nash was one of the many who decided to stay home and mourn his death, he was in his mother's living room in a daze, a blunt sat in the ashtray, and he had yet to light it, although it had been rolled for almost an hour now.

What he had been doing the past few days was drinking that *drank*, he had consumed so much, and Nash was beginning to feel like he was losing his mind.

He was in a fucked up position right now. His career would never go anywhere now that the person who he felt like held the key to his riches was no longer here. He was placed on life support once the doctors said there was no reported brain activity. His wife made the decision to pull the plug. Nash cried for days, yeah, DJ Monday was a legend. Nut he was more hurt because the demo he had worked his ass to complete, his blood, sweat and tears now meant nothing. Not only did he fail at making his dreams coming true but also he lost his girl in the process. Miko had nothing to say to him and he could only respect her wishes.

It was true that you never realized how much you loved a person until they left your ass. It was the little things that Nash remembered, how she would try to cook his favorite even though it didn't taste like his mama's cooking, the effort was still appreciated.

Miko made breakfast, lunch and dinner on the weekends when she wasn't busy working. Nash would wake up to some of the best weed, he never asked her where she got the weed from but it was the best he had ever smoked in life.

It was nothing for Miko to send a masseuse to the house when he complained about his back hurting from being in the studio all night.

The way she loved and catered to him, made him feel so special and now…he was alone.

Nash wanted his girl back but the detached look on her face that she left him with before she walked out of the studio that day would forever be etched in his memory. He wished he had the courage to call Lo, knowing that was the closest person to Miko and plus, she had told him on several occasions how much Lo adored him and was happy that they were together. Lo took full credit for being the reason they had hooked up the first place, saying that if she wasn't drunk Nash would have never got the goodies that night. It was a light joke between the two of them that Miko never found funny.

He missed hanging out with his girl, not only was she a beast in bed but she was his number one cheerleader, his supporter, and most importantly Miko was his best friend, He could only imagine how stressed she had been since she no longer had him to come home too and unwind her body and relax her mind after a long day.

If it wasn't for Nash being her constant peace, she would have probably quit her stressful job, he assumed.

He was now back at his mother's house and broke as a hoe that couldn't make any money because she was on her period.

"Nash get your ass up and go take a bath or something" his mother fussed.

He couldn't believe he ended up back here, he loved his mama but the constant nagging was something he had forgotten about.

"I gotta go get me some money," he told himself, before picking up the blunt and lighting it.

His lil' cousin had a play to make and he planned on going with him tonight, even if he only got a few hundred out of the niggas they planned on robbing, he would still be happy.

Nash didn't have a dollar to his name and he was miserable.

Miko sipped her wine and watched the people close to her laugh, smile and be merry. She had nothing to laugh or smile about and she damn sure wasn't merry. Mary Jane touched her thigh, "We can leave when you're ready," she told her.

She looked at her friend, so thankful for her, "Ten more minutes?" she asked.

Mary Jane winked her eye, "Sounds good to me, I'm ready to get in the bed, smoke my weed and watch my shows," she whispered.

Lo reached over and took a forkful of Sean's steak, Lo looked cute tonight unlike Miko who wore gym clothes to a five star restaurant. Even though Miko was depressed right now she found joy in seeing her friend smile, it was obvious that Ben was the reason for that smile.

"Ooh Meek taste this" she cut a piece of Sean's steak and handed her the fork.

Miko shook her head, "I'm fasting with MJ," she told her.

Sasha asked, "What y'all fasting from?"

Mary Jane said, "Dick and beef"

Papa laughed, "What the hell"

Sean noticed that neither Mary Jane nor Miko laughed, they were dead ass serious.

"Y'all for real?" Noel questioned.

Miko didn't say anything; she just drank more....and more.

Mary Jane smiled at Noel "Yes, wanna join?" she asked.

Noel told her, "Yeah I'm damn near celibate anyway and I don't eat meat"

Lo hated how distant her friend appeared to be, it had been a few weeks since her and Nash broke up and she was worried that Miko would never bounce back.

They had to beg her to come out tonight, "I'm ready" Lo watched Miko tell Mary Jane.

Those two had grown closer this year, she knew that both of their jobs went hand in hand but still Miko was *her* best friend.

"You're leaving?" Lo asked.

Miko told her, "Yes I told you I wasn't going to stay long; me and Noel have a flight tomorrow"

Her brother asked, "Why are you leaving?"

Miko took a deep breath, now all eyes were on her, she was getting agitated.

"Because me and Noel are going to London in the morning," she said for the second time, she hated repeating herself.

"You act like y'all got a plane to catch; it's a private plane leave when you ready" Malachi told her.

Miko rolled her eyes, "I haven't packed and I have to drive back to Jersey"

"Are you good to drive, I been watching you drink all night" Sean said worriedly.

"Fuck you Sean!" she snapped.

The table grew quiet; no one had expected her to flip out like that.

Lo stood along with Miko and Mary Jane.

She took a deep breath, "I apologize, I just have a lot going on and y'all keep coming at me," she explained

Papa eyed her suspiciously; something was going on with her.

But what they probably assumed it to be it wasn't, she was just experiencing heartbreak and heartache for the first time and it was damn near killing her.

Getting out of bed was a struggle and she wanted her man back, but his words stung and she couldn't forget that shit.

"It's okay boo, we understand" Sasha told her in comfort.

She smiled weakly at her and grabbed her purse and left.

Nasir looked at Sean and he shrugged his shoulders,

"Women and they attitudes, that's why 'm I'm single" he said.

"Oh shut up nigga, you can't tell me you don't have a bitch down there," Papa told him.

"I got plenty of bitches, but not a woman it's a difference," he told them straight up.

Nasir nodded his head, "Agreed"

"Well I got a woman who's my wife and I love her dirty draws," Malachi said happily.

Lo came back after seeing Miko and Mary Jane out, Papa said, "That's how I feel about Demi"

Sasha loved to see grown men be open about love, it was as if the conversation was forbidden these days.

Hearing them talk about love had Noel in her feelings. She knew that she needed to soften her exterior and allow someone in but it was easier said than done.

Miko dropped Mary Jane off at home since she didn't drive and had yet to learn.

She asked her, "Can I sleep here for like an hour? I need to sober up"

Mary Jane said, "Lo said the same thing, come on girl"

She made sure her truck was as close to the sidewalk as possible, they walked through her back yard and used the side door to enter the home.

She immediately crashed on the couch, her jacket and shoes weren't even pulled off, she was tired and tipsy the perfect combination for a good nap.

Her phone ringing woke her up, Miko fumbled in her pocket for the cell phone.

Not recognizing the number she still answered in case it was an emergency, "Hello" she said groggily.

"You have a collect call from...pick up ma it's me" She sat up once she heard Nash's voice over the line.

"Hello" he said.

"What happened?" she asked immediately.

"Jammed up, are you in town?" he questioned, his time on the phone was limited.

"Yeah where are you?" she asked, standing up and stretching.

"Brooklyn" he told her quickly.

"I'm on the way" she said and hung the phone up.

Yes, he hurt her and damn near broke her heart but Miko knew that she was all he really had.

He was so full of pride that he would rather sit in jail over the weekend before he called his mom and have her spend money that he knew she didn't have.

His mama made just enough to pay her bills, putting money aside for rainy days didn't really happen in the hood. They stayed prayed up that nothing happened, because if it did they couldn't afford to get anyone out of a bind.

It was the life Nash lived and one he was desperately trying to escape.

Miko had to show proof of income and then Nash was processed out, she sat in her truck across the street from the jail while she waited on him to come out.

When he made it to the truck, she unlocked the door and he slid in.

"I appreciate it Meek," he told her.

She nodded her head, "You going to your mom's house?" she asked, ready to get him out of her presence.

"I can't come home with you?" he questioned.

Nash missed her so much.

"Why? Because you're broke?" she snapped.

He knew that this would happen, he took a deep breath.

"So you telling me that you won't forgive me until I become a millionaire, my love for you will still be the same whether I had ten dollars in my pocket or ten million Miko" he explained.

She wasn't hearing shit he was saying, "I bet" she mumbled.

"That's fucked up" he told her.

"Trust me I feel the exact same way" she let him know real quick that he wasn't the only one feeling some type of way about how things ended.

"You don't miss me?" he asked.

"Nash please stop talking to me" she turned the radio up but he turned it right back down.

"I don't want you with nobody else" he let her know.

"And I don't want to be with anybody-"she stopped mid-sentence. Miko refused to do this with him.

"Can we please ride in silence, please," she asked.

"No man you treating me like some nigga off of the street" he was frustrated.

"I don't trust you. I can't have you around me and I got to question your intention that's not fair to me," she cried.

Nash took a deep breath, her words hurt

"I got you second guessing me?" he hated to ask but he needed to confirm her accusations.

"You did this not me Nash," she told him.

"Say no more" he was done talking to her ass then.

Once she pulled up on his block, "Hold on, let me go get your stuff" he said, she missed his raspy voice.

"What stuff?" she asked.

"The shit you bought, I don't need any handouts," he said angrily.

Miko sighed, "You can keep that stuff I bought it for you and you know that"

"Nah because if you did if it came from the heart you wouldn't have said the shit you did" he said and walked off.

Miko thought about pulling off while he went into his mama's house but he left his phone on her console so she knew she couldn't leave. Nash was smart.

He lugged two large trash bags and banged on the hood of her truck, "open the trunk" he yelled.

Miko winded her window down, "Don't bang on my car," she yelled.

"Open the fucking trunk man," he shouted.

She turned her truck off and got out, ready to go the fuck off on his ass, "Stop pulling on my handle" she shouted.

"Man get your ass back in the car"

"No don't handle my truck like that" she pushed him out of the way and opened it using her fingerprint.

Nash pushed her back roughly, "Move" he said.

She mushed him in the back of the head, he turned around so fast and that's when she saw the hurt in his eyes but she couldn't care, she refused to give in.

He came closer to her and she shook her head and moved backwards, "No" she whispered.

"Meek" he said her name in that cute ass way that only he could.

She wasn't allowing him any closer to her, she couldn't. Miko wasn't strong enough to deal with him in her personal space; Nash walked forward and pulled her to him.

She tried to wiggle away but not hard enough because in truth, if she really wanted him not to touch her she would have opened her mouth and said so.

"I love you," he said.

The block was popping in the midnight hour but he didn't care, he loved Miko and wanted her back.

Hoes that he had fucked with back in the day, stared at him with malice in their eyes.

They hated Miko and didn't even know her.

"I can't do this with you," she told him, shaking her head.

"We can Meek we can do this baby I love you I'm sorry" he pleaded.

"How I don't know you not just saying that because you don't want to be at your mom's?" she asked.

"This been my life since I was born, I'm used to this. You gotta know that you here" he pointed to his heart.

So desperately did she wanna believe him, she wanted him to move back in, she wanted to be back in the studio with him watching him work hard and put songs together. She missed cooking dinner, she missed the breakfast and head combo in bed on Saturday mornings, and she missed confiding in him about her past.

"How do I know though?" she asked him.

"I can't answer that for you" he kept it one hundred with her.

"Follow your heart baby and stop thinking with your mind," he preached.

Miko rolled her eyes, she felt like a sucker giving in so easily but the truth was he was the first man that she had ever submitted too. The first man that she loved. The first man that she allowed to give her constructive criticism and make her right.

Nash touched her cheek, "I ain't even been able to sleep with you," he confessed.

"Me neither" she admitted.

He came closer and planted a kiss on her forehead, "Miko let's go home babe" he said.

She closed her eyes wishing God would give her a sign but one didn't come.

Contemplating her decision…

Nash bent down and leaned in her ear and whispered, "I know she missing me" he grabbed her pussy not caring who was watching.

Miko's insides tingled and instead of thinking clearly, lust consumed her thoughts. She handed him the keys and walked around to the passenger door waiting on him to hop in and drive them home.

Lo smiled at Ben, "This is one my favorite places to eat" she told him.

"I know that's why I suggested it," he told her.

She took a sip of the most expensive wines in the restaurant; her hair was pulled up in an elegant bun. The burgundy velvet dress she wore fit her body like a glove and the yellow heels that strapped around the ankle made the dull dress POP.

Ben traveled often with work but whenever his schedule cleared up his first stop had been Lauren lately.

"Daddy asked about you," she told him. Now that she and Ben had rekindled their flame, she had something to call home about.

Her parents had always adored Ben and everyone just knew that he was the one she would marry right out of high school and give him a flock of babies. But somehow their plans changed and they ended up on two different paths.

"We should head that way next weekend," he told her.

"Are you free?" she asked, with a raised eyebrow.

"The question is are you free, Ms. event planner?" he returned the question.

Lo scanned her schedule mentally and if no one called a last minute meeting then she was free to go home and spend time with her family.

"I'll know for sure by tomorrow," she told him.

"Sounds good to me" he said and picked up one of the shrimp that they ordered as an appetizer.

Lauren was about to eat one as well but the two people that had walked in the restaurant stopped her from doing so.

They didn't see her but she saw them, Lo was now uncomfortable and it showed on her face.

"What's wrong?" Ben followed her eyes over his shoulder and he turned around to see what caught her attention. Lauren took a deep breath, "Nothing I know them that's all, this shrimp smells so fresh" she changed the subject, and plopped the colossal shrimp in her mouth.

Ben wouldn't press the issue, Lo quickly returned to her jolly self but on the inside, she was steaming. Across the restaurant, Nasir and Jordyn were being escorted to a private level that only the "regulars" knew about.

Nasir thought it was cute that Lo brought her little boy toy to their favorite restaurant but she too found it funny, as well unnecessary, that Jordyn was on his arm.

Before the popular seafood restaurant became a five star, it had been their favorite place to dine for lunch.

"What do you recommend?" Jordyn asked, once they were seated and menus were handed to them.

He lit a cigar, "Whatever the chef brings," he said

"Well what if I don't want that?" she asked.

He puffed and exhaled, "Then order something on the menu," he told her.

Jordyn rolled her eyes; she didn't even know why she bothered sometimes.

"I saw your friend, why didn't you speak?" she asked her man.

Nasir ignored her and poured him a glass of Remy; prior to them arriving, he had requested a bottle of Remy and a hand-rolled cigar.

The owner had a cigar shop up top and Nasir was a frequent visitor whenever he wanted to get away from the bullshit that life came with.

"I think you should order the Mahi served with capers and asparagus, its good," he told her.

"It sounds good," she told him, happily.

Nasir smiled at her "you look beautiful tonight, did I tell you /that already?" he asked.

Jordyn blushed, Nasir was smooth as hell when it came to word play.

"No you didn't but thank you," she told him.

He held his glass up and said, "To you, my Queen" offering her a toast

Jordyn held the wine glass up and said, "To MY king" with heavy emphasis on *my*.

Dinner was pleasant and to each couple's luck, they both ended up at the valet corner stand at the exact same time.

Lo had her head on Ben's chest and his hands wrapped around her waist, while Jordyn and Nasir held hands.

"Aren't you going to speak?" Jordyn asked.

Nasir said, "Nah I'll see her around"

Lo told her date, "I'm so ready to get home"

When Ben's BMW pulled up to the curb, Nasir couldn't hold back his amusement in seeing Lauren hop in.

He told her, "Be safe getting home"

She didn't bother with a response, knowing that he was being funny.

As soon as Ben got in, one out of the five special edition Porsche trucks pulled up and Nasir's driver got out, helped Jordyn into the car before stepping back and letting Nas hop in, and closed the door.

"That girl look like she had an attitude" Jordyn noticed and spoke on it.

"She always got an attitude" he lied.

Lo was one of the most happiest woman he had ever met in his life, her smile was contagious and she was full of good vibes but he couldn't praise her like he wanted too.

He wouldn't be disrespectful, Jordyn did nothing to deserve the way he treated her sometimes.

Well not the way he treated her because he damn near worshipped the ground she walked on, add something

It was the conscious decisions that he made, those were wrong.

Nasir had been walking the straight and narrow lately, spending all his time in Atlanta and being with Jordyn day in and out.

The only reason she was in New York with him was to attend Jade's baby shower this weekend.

Other than that, he would have wifey tucked low in the suburbs, she was his prized possession.

Jordyn was untouchable and a topic that was never up for discussion.

For her safety, it would always remain that way.

He used to treat Lo with the same respect but she gave her body away. Nasir was possessive and she refused to submit and be exclusively his, any longer.

She desired more from a man and while Nasir drove back to their condo with his precious Lauren on his mind, unfortunately, he wasn't on hers.

The Next Morning...

Miko stared at Nash, she didn't have much time to lie in bed...her and Noel had to get to London.

"Good morning" he said, his eyes still closed.

"I thought you were still sleeping," she told him.

He shook his head, "You stopped snoring that's when I woke up"

She pinched his arm, knowing he was trying to be funny.

"I haven't been getting much sleep," she admitted.

"Working harder and not smarter? I keep preaching that to you for a reason" he got on to her.

Nash hated how she worked at her "corporate job" her clients were too demanding, she treated them like Gods but the money he "assumed" she was bringing in monthly wasn't enough for how much she had to travel and be away from home…from him.

"I'll slow down one day" she said just to keep from starting an argument. Miko forced herself to sit up, last night's remnants were all over the room.

She knew what would happen once they made it to her house, and she didn't protest not once.

Craving him just as much as he craved her, desiring the taste of his brown skin as much as he lusted after hers. They both were like cats in the street fighting to get each other's clothes off, wanting the other to cum first. Built up pressure brought them to their knees, literally. Miko's needs were met all night, last night and as the sun came up.

She was pleased and made it a personal goal to make sure Nash was drained completely before she closed her eyes to get some sleep.

He made her whole so why was she contemplating on making him leave before she got up to throw clothes in a bag for her trip?

Why was her mind in constant battle between loving him and leaving him?

How was it that all of the good memories they made now meant nothing because of the one hurtful thing he said? She couldn't shake his ass from her thoughts if she wanted too, but she needed too. She wanted too...or she did? Miko wanted love so bad and now that she had it, beside her, staring at her with admiration, grazing her spine...why was she trying so hard to push him away? Why?

"Do you want kids and stuff?" she asked him, randomly.

"Kids and stuff? Like kids and a dog?" he asked, not understanding her question.

She turned her naked body towards his way and nodded her head, *Come on Nash answer this question the way I want you too*, she thought to herself.

"Yeah but not now" he said.

She was with that, Miko wasn't anxious to be barefoot and pregnant. Not with the way her and Noel had been traveling, she was enjoying seeing different places and learning about other cultures.

And Noel had become her very own personal travel agent; there wasn't a country the chick hadn't been too.

"What about marriage?" she asked her next question.

Nash sat up in bed and pulled her over, she stopped him, "I got a plane to catch" there wasn't even five minutes to spare for a morning quickie.

He ignored her and dragged her to his lap, "I want to marry you when the time comes, and we will both know it. But it ain't right now babe" he told her.

"I know that, I'm not ready right now either. It's important to me that our long-term goals mirror each other's, it's no point in wasting time if we not on the same page" she told him.

He nodded his head, "That's respect but your ass ain't going anywhere, we forever," he said cockily.

She looked at him with a suspicious smirk on her face, "Oh yeah?"

He nuzzled his face in her bosom, "Yep you all mines," he told her, kissing in between her small breasts.

"Well you better start act liking it," she told him.

"What I gotta do boo?" Nash asked happily

Getting off his lap and going to pack, she ignored his question.

Miko wanted him to get it together without her being on his ass.

"Tell me" he shouted, once she left her closet and went into the bathroom to bathe.

"You already know," she said and closed the door.

After she was dressed and had her bags in the trunk, Nash asked, "So you want to drop me off first then catch your flight?"

She eyed her watch, "no time, just drop me off" she told him.

"You sure? Cus last time the first thing you did was snatch your keys back and I didn't like that shit" he told her straight up.

She shook her head, "Won't happen again"

He kissed her forehead, "Good baby good"

They left her home and headed for the city, of course Noel was late, what was new. The girl was always late.

"Who is that?" Nash asked, once her lil' light-skinned ass got out and headed towards the steps of the plane.

"My assistant, okay babe I'll call when I land" she told him, reached over, and kissed his lips.

"Be safe," he said.

Miko winked at him and got out.

She put her shades on as Nasir always suggested in case someone was lurking on top of a building.

Once she made it on the plane, "Girl I been here for twenty minutes waiting on you" Noel lied.

She looked at her and shook her head, "You're a little liar, I BEEN here" she said.

"I didn't see your truck," Noel told her.

"I'm in my Lexus" she said and took the seat across from her.

"Well whatever I had to stop and get some star fruit"
shrugging her shoulders.

"I bet" Miko got comfortable.

"Somebody is in a better mood today, good, because I
didn't want to be on the plane with the Grinch" Noel
teased.

"Me? The Grinch? You clearly have me mistaken with
you," Miko laughed.

Noel held her head, as if her feelings were hurt.

"Hey I didn't know, I never been the friendly type" she
said in her defense.

Miko nodded her head, "Well that's good to know"

"How long are we scheduled to be here?" noel asked.

"No time limit, why? You want to stay a few extra days?"
Miko questioned.

She sat back in her seat and buckled her seatbelt, "Nah I
was just asking, I do love London though so if you don't
have to get back we can stay and do some shopping" she
said.

Miko looked at the window but Nash was long gone, her
mind traveled back to their conversation from this
morning and then to the mind-blowing sex last night.

In that moment, she made the decision to put her all into
their relationship...for the second time in hopes that this
would be the last time.

She wanted him and it was obvious he felt the exact same way.

"I'm going to have come on back," Miko told Noel.

"Cool with me" she told her.

Hours later, the pilot announced they would be landing soon. Miko stretched, she was grateful for that nap, it was needed.

1600 Pennsylvania Avenue NW

Washington, DC 20500

Oval Office

"So tomorrow we can announce the passing of the healthcare bill, if no one proceeds to filibuster" President Wilburn told his staff.

"Mr. President would you like to make a statement to the press?" his press secretary asked.

He shook his head, "Let's hold off on that until after everything is official," he said.

"What about to CNN they would appreciate first dibs?" the Vice President of the United States asked.

John thought about leaking something to the press, but before he could comment, First Lady Laura Ann barges into the Oval Office like a maniac with a stack of papers in her hand.

She appeared to be distraught to the others, hair not combed and she didn't look as polished and reserved as they're using to seeing her.

Laura Ann reeked of alcohol and she needed a touch-up of makeup to make her look alive.

"A divorce? You're asking for a divorce John?"

His assistant stood in the door, praying that she wasn't fired.

The President had given his staff firm instructions not to allow the First Lady, his wife into his office whether he was there or not.

She no longer had the "open door" privileges that he openly granted to everyone who worked for him.

"Do you not see me in a meeting?" he asked her in a very relaxed tone.

One thing that the President took very serious and kept dear to his heart was his Presidency.

It was true that some days he questioned his purpose but for the most part, he loved politics. Even with the scandal still somehow lingering in the air, the citizens of the United States of America still loved and respected him dearly.

Every decision he made was with the United States in mind, and that's why long he would be known as one of the greatest Presidents the country has ever had. It was because of his compassion that he held his position in the office as long as he did.

"I DON'T CARE, ANSWER ME!" she shouted at the top of her lungs.

"First Lady" John's secret service agent approached her. John told him, "Don't touch her, she's looking for an excuse to act an ass."

"I apologize can you all give us a moment, just one moment" he turned his direction to his staff.

They all stood and left the room quickly.

John took a deep breath before walking to Laura Ann and grabbing her face forcefully before slamming her body down onto his oak desk.

The same oak desk that many great Presidents sat at and made good and bad decisions for the country.

The same oak desk that he had fucked Miko on after a few late nights in the office.

The same oak desk where he sat and called an attorney to draw up divorce papers.

He couldn't do this any longer; marriage was no longer something he had an interest in.

If John couldn't have Miko he rather be alone and be single, date when he wanted too and fuck if and when he was in the mood.

Laura Ann wasn't the one and she hadn't been the one for quite some time.

The President refused to compromise his happiness any longer for likes or for votes, he refused and he prayed that the people of this great nation understood that.

Holding his estranged wife neck, "Sign the damn papers" he hissed.

She could barely breathe but Laura Ann found strength anyhow and she mustered up two words for his ass,

"FUCK YOU!" she tried to spit in his face but was unsuccessful.

He removed his hands from her neck to pull a handkerchief out of his suit jacket and wiped the collar of his shirt where her saliva landed.

"What is wrong with you? Why would you come in here knowing I'm working?" he asked her.

"Well if you came to bed then I wouldn't have to come act a fool John," she cried.

The sound of her voice caused his head to hurt instantly,

"Sign the papers, I've made everything fair" he told her, not in the mood to have this conversation with her.

She stared into his eyes, those pupils that she used to love so much.

He changed.

And she knew the reason why.

Over her dead body would she be the First Lady to receive a divorce because her husband was too busy chasing another woman's skirt.

Laura Ann came from a long line of highly esteemed woman; she wouldn't dare ruin her family's legacy.

Miko and Farren finally found some spare time in each other's schedule to do lunch and catch up.

Noel was busy at a warehouse overseeing a smooth transaction between The Underworld and their client. She insisted on going alone claiming that she had a crush on the person who was buying the product.

Miko ordered a sidecar, Farren asked, "What's in it? I don't drink anything but wine these days"

She told her what all went into her favorite drink, "Hennessy, Grand Marnier and orange liqueur, it's good, some people call it a French Connection"

Farren nodded her head, "My husband used to love Hennessy, I stayed at the L store getting it for him"

"Do you miss him?" she asked.

Farren smiled, "Every day, I see Noel in him these days"

Miko shared with her, "She's to herself but every now and then she'll let me in then when I see her again it's a whole different person"

"She's been through a lot and hasn't received closure for her sister's death, and then her dad and her step dad died. Noel is harboring a lot, bare with her," she asked.

She told her, "Trust me I am, she's my tour guide. I'm like Noel how many languages do you speak"

Farren thought that was so funny, "We traveled with them their whole lives, Noel was ordering filet mignon at five," she laughed.

She said, "I can believe you, she's quick to send her food back if she don't like it"

Farren shook her head, "Just like her mama"

Miko received a text message from Nash, **- missing u**

She would respond later, not wanting anything to distract her from the conversation she was having with Farren Knight.

"So, it's been a while since you called, sorry about the loss of your grandmother" she told her with much sincerity

"That's the last time we talked?" she asked.

She told her yes.

"Well me and Nash had taken a break, I dumped him but we made up last night....so he's anticipating my return and I don't know. I just don't know," she admitted.

Farren bit into her salmon with lemon dill sauce and capers.

"Why did y'all stop talking?" she questioned.

Miko sat her fork down and told her the story, giving her the short version of what happened that night at the studio and then she told her what Sasha said in Vegas. Farren cleared her throat, Miko watched her every move. Never in life had she admired someone the way she looked up too Farren Knight. She was so graceful and dainty. Always listening never, shouting or speaking over you, when Miko talked to her, her voice was always so calm and sweet. She respected her so much.

"Let me tell you a story, did I ever tell you about Jonte? Well *hell*, Kool too, but I'll tell you about Jonte" she told her.

Miko asked, "Yes, your youngest daughter's father right?"

"Hmm hmm girl, my lil' tenderoni" she smiled thinking about the good ole days with her man.

Farren Knight really loved her some Jonte, the good always died too soon and Jonte was a real nigga, if not the realest.

"When I met Jonte, girl I thought he was so fine. I knew him from around the way but he was always in and out jail"

Miko mumbled, "Sound like my boyfriend"

She continued, "So Jonte was known in the hood where I grew up, Hardy"

"You're from Hardy?" Miko asked she was surprised to hear that.

Although she was Korean and was born and raised in D.C. She had heard the horror stories about Hardy projects; the neighborhood was so notorious that they made the news in her city.

"Yep" she told her.

"Jonte was from there too, in the beginning we was just kicking it because things with me and Chrissy were very rocky and he was sweating me for a divorce but I wasn't taking him serious"

"Somehow Jonte eased up on me and blew my mind, before I knew it, I was pregnant and he had moved in my house girl" she told her.

Farren knew Miko was wondering what was the connection between Nash and Jonte, so she continued.

"Jonte wasn't even making a fourth of the money I was, he was what they call a petty hustler. Making pennies in my eyes, but he had his own. Enough to take care of him. I had wealth, real wealth. Land, investments, businesses and all of that. It was rumored around the way that I was Jonte's sugar mama and I would tell them hell yeah I'm his sugar mama cus' he was one of the realest men I had ever met in my life. Girl for Christmas I bought him TWO cars. I didn't care, I loved him so much because he loved me at my worst," she told her.

Miko felt everything she said because that's how she treated Nash, unwillingly and without much thought, she spoiled him but she wasn't looking for anything in return. Never had she been a tick for tack person.

"So what are you telling me?" Miko asked to be sure that Farren was basically telling her, *Fuck the haters and the rumors.*

"I'm not telling you nothing that you don't already know sweet heart," she told her with a warm smile.

Miko nodded her head because she was right, she had to make her own decisions and in the pit of her stomach, she knew that Nash was the one. However, when she returned to the states they needed to have a serious talk. Baby boy needed a backup plan, she didn't want him to give up on his dreams, but as time passed nothing else was popping off and Miko needed him to start considering other options for income.

She loved and supported him wholeheartedly but Nash had to be more realistic.

When their plane touched back down in the city, Nash was there to pick her up.

After he grabbed her luggage from the pilot and stashed it in the trunk. He hopped in and told her, "I hope you're hungry because I cooked," he said.

"You did?" she asked him.

He smiled at her, happy that she was back home.

"Yep it's good too, well it's good to me," Nash said proudly.

"What did you make honey" Miko questioned, she had never known Nash to be a cook, all he did was boil noodles and put frozen pizza in the oven.

"Fried chicken, broccoli casserole and yams your favorite" he said.

Her stomach rumbled just thinking about the yams, "I hope it taste like your mom's," she teased.

"Oh baby it taste better, it's her recipe though," he admitted.

Miko laughed, "I figured that much"

He kept one hand on the steering wheel and used the other to massage the back of her neck, "You tired? How you feel? How was the trip?" he was always concerned about her well-being.

"Business was business, boring. What you been up too?" she asked, never feeling comfortable lying to him about what she really did to her money.

Sometimes, Miko felt like she was living a double life.

"Grinding babe, trying to get it," he said. She noticed the doubt in his voice and decided that tonight wasn't the right time to come down on him about getting a job.

"Everything will work out" she told him, giving him hope. Miko didn't want to keep pacifying him and she refused too.

"Yeah I'm going to send the demo out but if I don't hear anything back in a few weeks then fuck it" he shrugged his shoulders.

Did God hear her thoughts?

She closed her eyes and thanked God for coming through then opened them and reached over and squeezed his thigh, reassuring him that she was with him no matter what.

"I need to stop and get some swishers," he said.

Miko thought she saw that same car behind them on the highway but she told herself she was tripping.

"Meek" Nash called her name for the third time.

"Huh? Sorry" she apologized

He looked at her, "You good?" he asked.

"Yeah I'm good baby," she told him. Looking out the rearview mirror but the car was no longer in sight.

"I'm going to stop at this Shell, cus the gas stations by your house be having them stale ass blunts" he said, making a right into the Shell gas station parking lot.

"You want something out of here?" he asked, once they pulled up to pump two.

"No I'm okay," she told him.

Miko waited until he was out of the truck before she reached behind her and stuck her hand in the overnight bag that she tossed in the back seat, fumbling around in search of her trap phone.

She needed to call Sasha to see if anything went down while she was gone, but knowing that if anything did Lo's ass would have been blowing her up.

Before she could unlock the phone…………

Rat.

Rat.

Rat.

Pow.

Pow.

Nash had run in the bathroom to take a quick piss and while he washed his hands, he stopped to admire his appearance in the mirror.

"I'm a sexy ass nigga," he said to himself.

When he heard the familiar sound of gunshots, he ran out of the bathroom, not even bothering to zip his jeans back up.

Running through the aisles of the large gas station and outside the door, where the few patrons that were getting gas or finishing up from getting gas stood around.

A car was seen speeding out of the parking lot and the sight before him, caused all of the food that he had cooked earlier for his Queen out of his mouth and down his shirt.

Miko's precious body slumped over the dashboard.

He looked around to see two people dead on the ground, the sounds of a crying baby took him out the daze.

"Meek" he mumbled.

Nash was a street nigga, he had seen blood before, he had witnessed death plenty of times, and in fact, he watched his mama kill her abusive ex-boyfriend not too many years ago.

Death? He could only pray that his Miko was good.

He ran to her truck and opened the door, the front window was scattered but the passenger window was cracked down the middle.

"Baby" he leaned her back and saw the large deep gash on the side of her head, blood covered her face and it leaked from her nose.

"Say something," he begged but she was unresponsive.

A squeeze or the mumbling of a word would have given him hope but she did nothing.

Nash pushed her head back, it too was streaked with blood.

Luckily, someone had called the ambulance. He couldn't find the strength or energy to pull himself away from her to get his phone or hers out of the cup holder.

Even when the medical staff approached the vehicle and asked him to step aside he gave them hell, until the gas station owner talked him into moving so they could do all they can to save Miko.

The last thing he remembered hearing was, "I found a pulse, weak but it's a pulse, let's get her up in the truck"

Nash went back to the truck and called his cousin to call his mama then he phoned Lo.

He hated to deliver the news to her but he didn't have Miko's mother or brother number.

The only reason he had Lo's number was because she threatened him one night saying that she needed his number in case of an emergency and now he was thankful he had it.

He couldn't deal with Lo's million and one questions because he didn't have the answers, he went into the gas station to pee and when he came out her truck was shot up.

He followed his first mind by having his cousin meet him up at the hospital in case her brother was on some bullshit.

Nash loved him some Miko and right now, the only thing that mattered was that she pulled through.

Seven Hours Later
St. Paul A.M.E. Church

Sasha held a crying Lo, no one had taken the news well of Miko being shot up, especially Lauren.

Malachi and Jade didn't leave her side but when Sasha called with news, everyone else left the hospital and promised to come right back.

Nasir was pissed too. He never wanted anyone that he considered family to be fucked with.

Mary Jane wasn't an emotional person all she could do was pray that her girl pulled through, Miko was a strong one.

"Fuck the First Lady bruh straight up" Papa spoke out of anger. He wasn't really close to Miko but that was his best friend's sister.

Sean and Nasir was the only two thinking straight, Sean said, "Are you fucking crazy? Ain't no fuck the first lady. We all going to jail. No disrespect ladies, but this is the one thing you gotta let ride. We got too much to lose"

Nasir agreed but he didn't say anything, he couldn't take his eyes off Lo, she looked like she was going through it.

Nasir knew how attached Lo had gotten to Miko, she wasn't even that close to her family and Lauren had tons of sisters but she considered Miko her real sister.

He wanted to hold her and tell her that she still had him, no matter what. But now was not the time.

"I can't believe this, like she wasn't even talking to him," she cried.

Noel kept her head down on the table the entire time, she hated death. It made her sick to her stomach literally.

"Who was that nigga in there with the dreads?" Roderick questioned.

"Jack boy from the hood" Papa knew exactly who the fuck he was.

"That's her boyfriend" Sasha spoke up.

Papa raised an eyebrow, "Miko lil' bourgeois ass is fucking Nash?" he was shocked to hear that.

Mary Jane clenched her teeth, she hated when people passed judgement.

"They're more than that," she mumbled.

"They is? Fuck she meet him at?" Papa asked, being nosey.

Mary Jane shook her head, Miko was in the hospital fighting for her life and they were in the basement of a church gossiping, she had enough.

"Noel can you give me a ride back to the hospital please?" she asked.

Noel was ready to go too, "Yeah can we smoke on the way there?"

Mary Jane was thinking the same damn thing, she nodded her head and just like that, they were gone.

"Let's all head back there," Nasir suggested.

Everyone agreed and stood while Lo sat back in her chair and wiped her runny nose. Her cheeks were puffy and bags had formed under her eyes, her nose started peeling because she had blown it so much in the past few hours.

"Lo ride with me," Nasir said.

Sasha patted her on the shoulder before she left, pushing the door up behind her.

Nasir got up and locked the door before taking a seat beside her, she was holding her head.

He pulled her on to his lap, "It's going to be okay" he told her in hopes of comforting her.

She took one deep breath and then released her pain once more on his shoulder.

He rubbed her back and brushed her wild hair down, "It's okay babe, I promise it is, where is your faith" he told her.

She cried, cried and cried.

Lo wasn't raised to question God but she wondered why? Why Miko? She wasn't even stunting the old ass President? Miko was excited about her new house and she had been doing research on finding a charity or non-profit organization to give her time back too.

Everything was going good for her, like what the hell? Why did this happen?

"I need my sister," she cried to Nasir.

"And you still have her Lo" he told her. No one knew the outcome for Miko, the doctors weren't saying much because she was in surgery.

Her mother didn't speak English well so it was hard for them to communicate with her, the only person who understood anything she was saying was Noel and even she had a hard time keeping up with Miko's mom because she said she spoke so fast and low.

"I can't believe this shit," she told him, after she slowly pulled it together and got her emotions under control.

"Me neither" he agreed.

"What happened to you?" she noticed a bruise on his neck. Nas turned his head but it was too late Lo had already noticed it.

"Oh a hickie? Cute" she said sarcastically and got off his lap.

Nasir pulled her right back down, "Where you going?" he asked.

"Take me to the hospital," Lo snapped.

"What you tripping for?" he questioned.

She shook her head, Thank God for growth because nothing about him had changed.

"You all on me but you got a fresh passion mark on your neck," she told him.

"I'm all on you? Comforting you in a time of need is all on you?" he asked.

"You know what I mean" she shook her head.

"Actually I don't , God forbid if I was in your shoes I would expect you to put your pride to the side and be here for me as well" Nasir kept it gully with her.

She knew without a doubt, that if something happened to anyone Nasir considered close she would be there for him. She told him, "Thank you" because he was right.

"No worries Lo," he told her, coolly.

"Can we go now?" she asked, really wanting to get to the hospital.

He stood and texted his driver to pull the truck around.

"You been good though?" he questioned.

"I'm sure you already know the answer to your question" Lo wasn't playing games with his ass. She knew he wanted some of her sweet pussy but until she received some kind of news on the status of her best friend's life everything was put on pause.

1700 West Washington St.

Phoenix, Arizona 85007

Governor's Mansion

It wasn't too often the President of the United States of
America traveled to other states when he was invited to
certain state functions. The only events he considered
mandatory to attend was when he was trying to get a bill
passed and needed more support.

John wasn't a social butterfly and any spare time he had
was spent with his children or on the golf court.

But Governor Ducey wasn't just "another" governor; he
was John's college roommate and teammate on the soccer
team in high school. They had been friends since the
sandbox so whenever his pal phoned and requested his
presence, John stopped and went, if time permitted.

Tonight, he was the Keynote Speaker for a charity event
that Governor's Ducey wife had been desperately trying to
raise more awareness on and raise funds at the same time.

Unfortunately, the press had caught wind to Miko's
shooting and the investigation team was full of the best
detectives in the state of New York, it was as if people
were just waiting to see if the First Lady had her hands in
on it.

On behalf of The White House, a statement had been
released saying that the First Lady was with her children

and husband during the time of the shooting and that the couple has been working on their marriage ever since the scandal surfaced.

Behind closed doors, John had damn near beat the skin off Laura Ann but she stuck to her story, promising him she had nothing to do with the shooting.

In the back of his mind, he knew she was lying, Laura Ann had been keeping her distance ever since and coming to bed later and later.

John wanted to reach out but he was under a magnifying glass right now and he had to play it safe, it would be just his luck if all of this turned around and was blamed on him.

John started his speech with an anecdote then a joke about the Governor. Before putting on the million-dollar smile that could swoon the room and hopefully get them to write six figure donation checks. Before the speech ended, he asked everyone to clap for his "lovely, beautiful" wife and Laura Ann stood and played the role of the doting First Lady to perfection, she waved her hand around the room as if she was a Queen and even topped the act off by blowing a kiss to the President.

When she sat back down, a note was on her dessert plate.

The First Lady looked around to see where did the note come from, she opened it and the message read, *"Tick tock, the gun is cocked"*

Not being able to scream in fear of embarrassing her and her husband, she pissed her panties immediately.

Who sent the note, Laura Ann was very discreet when she ordered the hit.

But little did she know THE UNDERWORLD's connections ran much deeper than those of the government did.

It took Sasha ten minutes to locate the people she hired and they were amateurs. With the green light from Malachi, the men were killed. For the time being the First Lady was being spared, but as the note read, *Tick tock, the gun is cocked.*

***

Nash held Miko's hand in his; he bent down and kissed it before sitting back in his chair and staring at her.

His eyes began to fill with tears but he sucked them back, his mama came up to the hospital earlier and brought him a change of clothes and a plate.

She told him to stop all that fucking crying because it did nothing. He wasn't big on praying but him and the Lord had been chopping it up a lot lately.

Whenever her "family", niggas that he had never seen before would visit, Nash would leave to clear his head and get some fresh air.

No one introduced himself or herself and even when Lauren came to visit Miko with them in tow, she acted differently towards him.

The warm gesture didn't exist and she barely made eye contact with him.

Nash didn't care, he loved Miko and Miko loved him.

When visiting hours were over, it was him sitting up here in the cold by her side.

Nash had learned every doctor and nurse assigned to her case. He watched carefully when they came and checked her vitals.

Miko was going to pull through, as soon as they eased her out of the medical induced coma then he was praying she would wake up and hopefully be her crazy, sexy cool self again.

The doctor had warned them that she may have suffered memory loss and could possibly have to learn how to walk and talk again but he was fine with that.

One thing Nash had tons of was patience and for his girl, he would do whatever it took to get her back to herself.

He stared at her, thinking of that day, wondering if he didn't stop at the gas station would they be in the hospital right now.

Nash had been questioning himself so much lately. He knew he wasn't necessarily the one to blame but still he still blamed himself for failing to protect her.

Miko looked so peaceful, almost as if she was dead...and that's what scared the fuck out of him.

He needed his baby girl to wake up because good news had finally come.

Nash hadn't shared it with anyone yet because he wanted Miko to be the first one.

His hard work paid off, the sacrifices were worth it, his blood, sweat and tears...it was for good reason.

Two days ago, BET called his cousin, who had took the position of being his manager asking if Nash was free to perform at the taping of the memorial concert for DJ Monday. Apparently old videos had been found of him saying that Nash was the hottest unsigned artist out right now, which was nowhere near true but the fact that he said that and it was recorded sparked the interest of the major network.

His cousin believed that this opportunity would give him the light he needed to shine.

Nash whispered, "Wake up babe, please"

He couldn't start his career without Miko by his side.

Chapter 14

Lauren sat in her car, her head rested on the seat. She had been outside, across the street for quite some time. Watching *him* in the window. She knew his schedule better than he knew his own. It was a Tuesday night and his favorite team had just won according to the updates on her phone. He had probably just ordered take-out from the steak house around the corner. He always tipped the hostess to drop his food off once she got off.

Nasir let the girl know his name and gave her instructions to leave his food at the front desk. The receptionist in the building where he lived would tip her on behalf of him. No one knew where he laid his head at and everyone assumed he stayed in a big mansion where he invited guests whenever Jordyn was in town with him. Lauren had found the condo for him, suggesting that he get a "duck off" spot to lay his head in peace.

Nasir shook his head at the idea many years ago, but now she could drive by at any time and find the light on his bedroom. The bedroom that she decorated, the comforter that she picked out, the bed that she ordered from a top of the line Italian manufacturer.

He was most likely sitting on his couch, the brown leather sectional, bare chest with a pair of Nike basketball shorts and ankle socks. Knowing him, he turned off all of his phones on silent or off and zoned out.

No one understood the life he lived but Lauren did, she *got* him better than anyone.

Lo picked up her cell phone for the third time in the last hour, wanting to call so he can buzz her up. She wanted to lay her head in his lap, while he ran his hands through her hair.

She needed him right now and she was relieved that her best friend had made it out of all her surgeries successfully.

The doctors were calling her a miracle; Lauren's parents even flew in to pray with her, Miko was grateful she loved Lo's parents so much.

Nash had been at her side day in and out, the love that he had for her was obvious, to the blind and to the ones who wanted to be ignorant about, like Malachi.

Nash was a stand up dude and he didn't let Malachi punk him out either, he made it clear that he loved Miko and wasn't leaving her side.

But what about Lauren? Yes, she was attempting to build something with Ben but in truth, they had tangoed before. Something was missing between the two and she couldn't figure it out.

Oh yeah…Miko told her today when she went to visit her, Ben wasn't Nas. Point. Blank. Period.

She took a deep breath and told herself, *Fuck it* and dialed him up.

After two rings he answered, "What do you want stalker?"

Lo couldn't help but to laugh, he knew her too well.

"Excuse me?" she played it off.

He paused the television, "You know my people spotted you out there soon as you pulled up" he told her in a matter of fact tone.

Lo looked around and she didn't see anything out the ordinary, but that's how Nas lived, low-key and in silence.

"How are you?" she asked.

"I'm well Lo, how are you?" he questioned.

"Miko is up and talking"

"That's not what I asked you though" he knew how she was. Lauren was always seeing about everyone else and not herself.

Even though Nasir was technically with Jordyn, he still made sure Lauren was taken care of and seen about. She didn't feel like she was a priority but if she *really* knew how much he had going on, she would be grateful for the time she did get to spend with him.

"I'm fine" she lied.

"What's wrong?" he asked.

"How is Jordyn?" she ignored his question and asked one of her own.

She could see him now, getting irritated with her turning the tables around on him.

"Jordyn is Jordyn," he said.

"What does that mean?" lo asked him.

He took a deep breath, "She's good, she's always good, no need for you to ask about her" he was so sensitive when it came to talking about his precious Jordyn.

Lo hated to be on the phone with him right now and she regretted dialing him up.

"Goodnight" she said and hung the phone up.

He called back immediately, "Let me tell you something Lauren" oh she missed the way he would say her name, the way his tongue pronounced the L in Lauren caused her pussy to scream.

"Don't come by my crib, don't call and question me about my girl, you got you a new nigga so be happy with him" he said and hung the phone up.

Lo was so unbothered by the conversation, she knew he was in his feelings and wanted to have the last word.

Those were the type of mind games Nas thought he could play with her, if she wanted to go up there and ride his dick for the rest of the night he would let her.

As much as he had her wrapped around his finger, she felt like she had him around hers too… especially when she was being stingy with the sex.

Oh well, she was sticking to her guns…and her coming here was a waste of her time but in a weird wicked way, she loved to see him in New York alone and not in Atlanta with Jordyn.

***

"La la, I love you, I love you baby, you got me saying la la la" Nash sung with his eyes closed and his hand on his heart.

True enough he was a thug at heart but God had blessed him with a voice so melodic, the boy could sing and then come with a hot sixteen in a matter of twenty-two seconds.

Nash had mastered both and that's what would eventually set him apart in the music industry.

"I love that, okay but right here. When you say, it was you from the beginning and you know that babyyyyy, that's when I think you should put the bridge at," Miko suggested, using a red pen to mark out some of the lines on the notebook.

Time had passed and she was slowly getting back to herself. The road to recovery wasn't as difficult as she predicted it to be but it was still quite a challenge. When she woke up for the first time, not everything came back to her remembrance off top but when it did, she was filled with anger.

Miko wanted to march her narrow ass into The White House and sling the First Lady across the damn room, but she played it smart.

Miko knew that one day, she just may need the President and when that time came, she would hold what his dumb ass lunatic wife did over his head.

Miko was adamant about her decision and ordered The Underworld to leave Laura Ann alone, karma never played fair and what she failed to realize is that Miko wasn't the first or the only, and she damn sure wouldn't be the last.

Her mother had been at her house every day making sure Miko was gaining her weight back and taking her medicine, but Miko wanted her home to herself.

She missed spending time with Nash, and with her doorbell steadily ringing and people stopping by and calling, she quickly become overwhelmed.

So in the middle of the night, Miko woke a sleeping Nash up and they got dressed in and went to the studio to lay low.

The couple had been up since yesterday, a song had come into his spirit and he was desperate to get it out.

With Miko on the keys and him in the booth, magic was happening.

She sat in a black swivel chair, with not much on but one of his t-shirts, her hair sloppily braided to the back of her hand, courtesy of Mary Jane and her favorite red Fendi reading glasses on her nose.

They were putting a hit song together and didn't plan to sleep until it was perfect.

"Babe nah that's too soon" Nash told her, taking the headphones off and leaving the booth.

"Trust me, it's going to be perfect," she told him, looking over the notebook.

Nash looked at his girl, all into his career and smiled.

"You love this shit don't you?" he asked her.

She put the notebook down and stood up, but too soon…because the stitches in her stomach had yet to heal properly.

"Ooh" she winced in pain.

Nash hurriedly made his way closer, "You moving too fast" he told her, helping her sit back down in the chair.

"I know I'm sorry" she apologized.

"Don't be saying sorry to me, it's your body" he got on to her ass, Miko was trying to get back to work the day she was discharged but between Nash, her mom and Malachi everyone had strict orders for her to stay in the bed.

"Just go try the song for me" she fanned him away.

He swore he was her daddy at times and in many ways, she let him reign supreme.

She wasn't complaining about being stuck in the house all day and night because she needed the rest and with Nash's big performance around the corner, something told her that now was the time for them to spend as much quality time together as possible.

"For you I will, its gon be wack though boo" he said and went back into the booth.

Nash had taught her how to work the machines, but all she did was press a button when he motioned for her to do so, and then she pressed another one to bring the beat in and then one more button to stop it.

Pretty simple for a girl that survived multiple gunshots.

Minutes later, Miko watched him with intent as he played what he had just recorded over and over again

He nodded his head and then pulled his cell phone out so his cousin could hear the song, "Hell yeah that shit sound good as hell don't it?" he asked his cousin.

Apparently, his cousin agreed because Nash played it two more times.

When he ended the conversation, Nash told his girl, "I guess you know what you are talking about"

Miko stuck her tongue out at him, "Trust me trust me" she said

"I do more than you know," he said.

Miko felt it was more to that, "Everything okay?" she asked him.

Nash folded his arms and leaned back on the soundboard, "You not hustling are you?" he asked.

Because she had become so good with masking her feelings, and hell her identity too over the last two years, she kept her game face no.

"No, why would you ask me that?" she asked him.

"Because one day I went into the laundry room to wash clothes while you were in the hospital and I never understood why you had two washer and dryer sets and when I opened one it was full if money" he said.

Miko forgot all about that money in there, "Some money I need to put in the bank that's all" she told him.

"Yeah but that much money and then its dirty and everything" he said.

She knew that he was a man in the streets, or had been the streets prior to being arrested so she wouldn't play on his intelligence.

"I've handled some things for some people that know my brother"

"Who?" he questioned.

Damn, he was not letting this shit go.

"I don't know their names," she told him.

"You risking your life for people you don't even know what they had you doing?" he asked.

See, Nash considered Miko to be a simple Korean chick that was smart and didn't know any better.

He didn't know that the woman he laid beside was a criminal in her own right, he was unaware that she worked for a drug cartel, and really soon they would be the biggest drug organization in the world if Noel continued to sew her oats the right way.

Nash didn't know that Miko was so close to becoming a multi-millionaire, he had no idea.

When she would tell him she was going out of town to business, he was unaware that she was jet setting across the world, the only trip he knew of for sure was London, but Miko had damn near circled the globe in the past few months.

Miko has had dinner with Kings and Queens, Princes and Princesses, royal priests and Presidents, everyone wanted a piece of the money pie and Miko was the one who finalized the deals and broke the bread amongst the two.

Money makin' Miko, as Nas liked to call her.

She kept the organization afloat, she made the budget for the month, she told Mary Jane how much to cook up and whip.

Miko was that bitch, behind the scenes she played a very important role in The Underworld.

And no, they were not suffering in her absence while she recovered, but no one could lie and say that things had been the same since she left.

Before Miko, everything was unorganized and was ran by niggas who really had to much going on to handle business the right way, it was Miko that got everyone on one accord.

And many years from now it would be Miko to save their asses once the product run low and the streets become dry.

See, she had always had it in her, but it took the right motherfuckers to bring it out, her brother introduced her to the game, Noel taught her how to shoot, Farren Knight instilled in her the important of trusting her gut and using her discernment.

And then there was Nash, her sweet and yet thugged out boyfriend.

He made an honest woman out of her, prior to meeting him; her loyalty could have been questioned. She was sneaky, slimy, and even vindictive. She didn't care about others, she wasn't sensitive or caring.

She was just Miko, out for herself, always.

Nash softened her, he smuggled his way into her heart and her soul.

"Miko be safe man, really just don't do that shit no more" he said frustrated with the entire conversation.

She exhaled loudly, full of relief that he was letting it go, she hated lying to him.

"Okay babe" she told him, quickly.

"See when I get my money right, you ain't gottta be doing that grimy shit," he said. She loved how eager he was to start grinding but even when the time came, she had no plans on leaving The Underworld, knowing they needed her. They was her family and if she didn't learn anything else in the last two years. She learned that you don't turn you back on your family.

"Come on let's go eat" she told him, standing up.

"You not going nowhere but to the bed, I'll go get us something," he told her firmly.

Miko rolled her eyes and kept walking but she made sure to walk her ass right into the bedroom in the back of the condo, as he demanded.

About half an hour later, Nash was carrying a tray into the room. He sat on the edge of the bed, opening the plastic bags and handing her the things he ordered for her.

"Thank you" she told him.

"You welcome greedy," he said.

She shook her head, "No, thank you for everything. Thank you for you being you" she told him, holding back tears.

Nash blushed, "Thank you for loving me despite…you know. Just thank you Meek, that's real" he said, feeling himself getting emotional too.

Never had a woman make him feel the way she did and that's why he had to keep her close because Miko drove him crazy and without her, he was worse.

The vibrations of Miko's cell phone buzzing on the nightstand woke Nash up, he was a light sleeper, and robbing niggas growing up always kept him on his toes. Miko was knocked out due to the pain medicine that the doctors had her on. The heavy dosages caused her to fall asleep minutes after taking it. He only let her take the medicine at night, not wanting his girl to become dependent on painkillers.

"Babe your phone ringing" he shook her lightly; the only reason he woke her up was that there were several missed calls from Lo and her sister in law, Jade.

The phone rang again and he decided to answer it, in case it was an emergency…and oh boy, was it an urgent emergency…

The Next Day

Miko sat on the couch in the house that Malachi grew up in; she had her niece in her lap sleeping. In truth, she didn't know what to say or how to react, so she stayed out the way.

After Nash woke her up and told her that, her sister had been killed by her mother on accident. The first thing she did was correct him by saying, "Half-sister, she was my half-sister"

She got out of the bed; of course, it was a struggle considering she was drowsy from the pills she popped only a few hours prior to the call.

Miko went onto the balcony trying to gather her thoughts; she took a deep breath and closed her eyes. Her mind traveled to Malachi.

She could only imagine the pain he was experiencing right now. For quite some time, they were the only two women in his life, before Aaliyah, his oldest child's mother came around. He shared with her, one day during an intimate conversation that they were the primary reason why he joined The Underworld. The little money he was making hustling was enough to afford his lifestyle, but since a child it had never been about him, he was responsible for tons of people.

Malachi held his entire family on his back, playing the role of father, uncle, cousin, big brother and son to several people.

She held her body tight with her arms wrapped around her midsection, she was numb. There were no tears, her heart wasn't crushed, and she felt bad for not feeling anything but she just didn't.

She and Melissa weren't as close as they could have been. She came around when she wanted something and Miko spoiled her because Malachi did. But she seemed spiteful and when Jade confirmed it after their first "family dinner", Miko kept her distance for the most part.

She didn't remember Melissa coming to the hospital to check on her and she made a mental note to ask Lo, but what did it matter now, the poor girl was dead.

Nash gave her some time to herself before going to check on her, "You ready? We got to get there," he reminded her.

She didn't bother turning around, "Few more minutes" she said.

He left her alone.

Snapping out of her thoughts, Lo sat beside her and whispered, "This shit is sad"

She nodded her head agreeing with her best friend.

Malachi had been sitting in his mother's room by himself since he left the coroner. Nash dropped her off and went to his mom's house to kick it with them.

Miko had been in a daze since the news came, Jade was flying back from California but a thunderstorm kept her flight delayed.

Nasir came down the steps and his eyes fell on Lo but he kept walking towards the kitchen, where the rest of The Underworld was.

Mary Jane had rolled blunts and made tea, in her opinion it was the perfect combination to make everything better.

Demi left the kitchen and came into the living room with Miko and Lo, "Have you checked on your brother?" she asked once she sat down.

She shook her head; she was too scared to go up there.

Lo looked at her, "Y'all haven't talked?" she too was surprised.

"I don't know what to say," she mumbled

"Meek get your ass up, his wife not here you all he got," she told her.

Miko looked around at all of his other family members here and she didn't feel like he was alone but technically she was the only sister he had.

She removed her niece from her lap and laid her on the couch, with her head in Lo's lap, "I will be right back," she said

Lo gave her a weak smile, she knew that Miko didn't deal with situations like these well, but it wasn't less than a month or two ago where her brother was at her side so she needed to pull it together and be there for him.

Miko took the steps one at time, she had never been here before but the house was decorated nice, even though it was obvious Malachi had upgraded somethings, the house still had that 80s touch to it

She stopped and looked at the photos on the wall, smiling at a young Malachi.

She saw a few pictures of her daddy and tried her hardest not to roll her eyes.

Continuing up the steps, she searched around the hallway wondering what room her brother was in.

She picked one door and opened it but that was the bathroom, she turned around and tried another, apparently, that was Melissa's room.

She closed the door immediately.

"What are you doing?" she heard her brother's voice.

She jumped and faced him, "You scared me," she said.

Taking a good look at him and he looked horrible.

His clothes were wrinkled and thrown on, he had a scratch on his face, and that she found out came from his mom when the police came to arrest her.

His lawyer was handling that situation because his mother was mentally ill and had an episode when she shot Melissa by accident. Malachi eyes held so much sadness in them.

She went to him and hugged his body, he took a deep breath before holding her back, when she went to let go, he didn't. So she continued to rub his back, when she felt his tears fall on her, her demeanor softened.

"It's going to be okay, we are going to get through this" Miko reassured him.

Lo stood at the bottom of the steps, getting one good look at them before going back into the kitchen for the wake and bake session.

"I been begging her to put my mom in a house for years" he cried.

She nodded her head, Jade had told her that too one day while they were talking.

"That was her mom, I wouldn't put my mom in a house either," she told him.

He moved away and wiped his face, "I can't believe this shit," he said, sadly.

Miko couldn't either, but it had happened and now they had to grow through this situation.

Over the next few days, Miko had no idea that his sister's death would bring them closer together. She was the only person besides Jade that he was communicating with; Miko could only imagine how hard this was for him. The Underworld understood what he was going through; they were keeping him in prayer and handling business on his behalf.

Malachi told Jade and his aunts to handle the funeral arrangements. As soon as she landed in the city, she got straight to work. Jade didn't take death well and she had planned on seeing her therapist as soon as the funeral was over, oh how quickly could she slide into a depression and she didn't want that to happen. Lo took over the planning of the repast because Jade couldn't do it all.

Miko decided to stay with them and help out with the kids until everything passed over.

Getting his mom released wasn't as easy as his attorney told him it would be, so Malachi had been in a funk for the past few days.

Everything still seemed so unreal to him, he had literally just finished chopping it up with his sister about taking a trip to London for her birthday and he told her, "The world is yours baby girl"

Not less than an hour after, their neighbor had called saying she heard a gunshot, one gunshot.

Malachi asked her, "Why do you think it came from my mama house?"

The woman told him, "Because your mom is right here with the gun"

Instantly, Malachi got up and headed there.

The vision of his sister kept replaying over and over and at night when he tried to sleep, he couldn't understand why this happened.

If he wasn't somewhere hiding out, crying and getting high. He was bent over the toilet throwing up and coughing up blood.

Jade warned him that stress could kill him but he wasn't listening to her.

He had lost his sister by his mother's hand and now they were trying to charge his mentally ill mother with murder.

Shit was crazy right now and after the funeral he was planning to take a trip, he needed to clear his mind.

On top of dealing with his mother's case, his father had been blowing his phone up but he had yet to answer. He knew eventually his daddy was going to send a letter or worse, have someone pull up with him on the phone.

His daddy, Maxwell was good for getting him on the phone no matter what. One thing he hated was hearing rumors or getting news about his family from people on the inside before his family told him.

He had told his son on several occasions that it made him feel like he wasn't involved in the family or worse, forgotten about.

Looking down at the phone he said, "I'm going to come see you pops, I promise"

The next morning, he pepped himself up to go visit his father.

But he didn't plan to go alone, he went and woke his sister up, "Nash stop" she moaned in her sleep.

Malachi looked down at her before flicking the lamp on, "Man I ain't your nigga get up," he said.

Miko eyes popped open and she flung the comforter over the satin gown she wore, for a second she forgot where she was.

"What's wrong?" she asked.

"Ride with me somewhere" he told her and headed for the door.

Miko knew not to ask him any questions especially with the way he been acting lately.

She got up, showered and dressed quickly, she met him in the kitchen but as soon he saw her, he picked up his cell phone and gun and headed for the elevator, which somewhat served as their front door to the penthouse that him and his family lived in.

Once they were in the back of the truck and the driver had pulled out of the parking garage, "Where are we going?" she asked while yawning.

He slid his designer frames over his face, he looked horrible and he knew it.

"To go see my daddy," he told her.

She said, "Oh no! Take me back home" she wasn't going to see him...over her dead body!

Miko didn't consider him her daddy and she was sticking to that.

Melissa and Malachi were granted the opportunity to be raised in the same house with both parents. While her mother struggled to keep lights on and after her day job, she turned tricks at night. Miko wasn't fucking with her daddy at all.

"Come on its too early right now" he told her, not in the mood to go back and forth or even speak at all.

"Exactly Chi it is too early and I don't want to go," she told him.

Malachi said, "Look I don't ask you for shit, can you please do this with me. We won't be there long" playing the victim card.

Miko smacked her lips and crossed her arms, she was mad as hell but that was her brother and right now he needed her. So for this one visit, and this visit only, she would put her feelings to the side and be supportive.

Since the drive wasn't a quick one, she pulled her phone out and saw a missed call from Nash and a message saying that he missed her.

He was in California getting ready for the memorial concert, and would be back any day now.

"What you smiling at?" her brother asked her.

The way he asked the question made her feel bad for smiling, but she was happy and she really missed her beau.

"Nash texted me" she told him

"He doesn't know who I am do he?" Chi asked.

Miko eyed him, "Of course not, he doesn't even know who I am," she told him.

"Good keep it that way, you don't even know him," he said.

She decided to let his comment pass, in an attempt to understand that he had a lot going on. But if he said it again Miko planned to check him.

Her relationship with Nash was nobody's business but his and hers and because she kept her business and personal private, Malachi had no reason to worry.

They made it there faster than she expected them to do, but the quicker they got there meant the sooner she made it back to the house and to the bed. She was sleepy and Malachi's kids were so active. Once she picked them up from school, they drove her crazy until it was bedtime. Miko knew she wouldn't be having kids any time she didn't have enough patience.

"Jesus" she heard her brother mumble once Maxwell made it to the table.

"I wanna fuck you up right now" was the first thing he said once he sat down.

Literally, he sat down, banged his fist on the table causing Miko to jump back, and watched him tell his son with hatred in his eyes, "I WANNA FUCK YOU UP RIGHT NOW"

She didn't know what to say especially since it seemed like he wasn't even interested in her being present at the table, which was cool with her.

Malachi rubbed his beard, "Pops" he started to explain.

But Miko wanted to ask him why was he explaining himself. It was a mistake that no one could predict was going to happen.

"Shut the fuck up, let me talk" he told him.

Malachi gave him the floor.

"I can't believe you let this go down, you so busy on that lil' wife of yours that you didn't see this coming? Your mama been missing you around the house, how often do you go visit? Then you never gave Melissa a break? She was losing her mind over there. How selfish can you be? You dumb ass bitch," Maxwell roared disrespectfully.

Miko looked down and saw how fast Malachi's leg was moving under the table, she knew he was barely holding it together.

On top of him probably already blaming himself for what happened here was his daddy rubbing it in.

"You ought to' be ashamed of yourself, you're a fuck up" he spat.

Miko said, "Okay, that's enough"

Maxwell laughed, "And who told you to talk? You little slut I'm glad no one knows I'm your daddy" he said

Before she could respond, Malachi had come across the table and knocked his daddy out.

Miko held her mouth in shock.

He stood and shook his hand before saying, "Let's go"

Maxwell had came to his senses and had started yelling obscenities, the guards came over trying to question Miko and Malachi, threatening to lock them up but Miko kept telling them they were leaving and that's what they did. The car ride was a very silent one, Malachi's knuckles were bleeding but he seemed not to care.

She removed the Versace scarf from around her hairline and took his hand in hers, "I couldn't see that blood drip any longer," she told him.

"I'll never let anyone disrespect you in front of me and I can't control those damn reporters but anybody in my presence…"

She shook her head, "It doesn't even bother me anymore," she told him the truth.

"Good don't let it, but it bothers me. Pops was dead wrong," he said angrily.

She asked him, "Your feelings aren't hurt?"

"You got to know him to understand him" he brushed the situation off, but she saw the pain in his eyes.

He was hurt by his father's words and Miko was in pain for him.

"Everything is going to be okay" she didn't know what else to say so she just repeated what Lo always told her. No matter the situation, Lo always told her, "Everything is going to be okay" and Miko had started to believe it.

She called it faith, so Miko had faith too.

***

"And who is this hoe supposed to be?" Sasha asked ready for whatever.

Miko shrugged her shoulders, just when it looked like things were finally looking up for her of course some bullshit had to occur.

When Nash returned home, things were distant and she had started to question her appearance. After the scars from the multiple surgeries she had to undergo, she wasn't feeling sexy at all and had become very insecure.

Nash wasn't kissing her or making love to her at all, he stayed out all night…in her car of course and when he did come to bed, he turned his back on her and went straight to sleep.

She just knew that it was all her fault but when she went to ask him last night what was going on and did she do something wrong.

He couldn't even look at her he was so disappointed in himself.

"I have a baby on the way, Meek. A baby" he told her. She had so many questions but all he did was drop the bomb on her and stormed out of the house as if she did something wrong. When clearly it was the other way around.

Miko spent the whole night crying and calling his phone but he never answered.

She wanted to know was the baby conceived while she was in a coma. Did he fuck this chick in one of her cars or worse, her house?

Miko had so many questions and the more he ignored her the more her mind raced with all kinds of different scenarios and accusations. Miko called his mama but she didn't answer the phone, she just wanted him to come home so they could talk about it.

The fact that he was ignoring her made her angrier and it was forcing Miko to think that he felt like he was guilty.

"Well if it's his what are you going to do?" Lo asked.

Miko told her, "I don't know I just don't know anything right now"

Mary Jane rubbed her back, in her head she was thinking, *These women had more problems than a lil' bit.*

Every other week it was something, if Lo wasn't in her feelings about Nasir and Sasha wasn't arguing with her baby daddy then Miko was sad about something. The only two normal people were she and Noel.

Mary Jane concluded that Noel was sneaky, she was always dipping out of town and whispering on the phone but she told Papa, "I have my eye on her" and she meant that shit.

"It's probably some old hoe trying to make herself relevant cus they know he about to blow up, I swear I hate bitches" Sasha spat.

Miko said, "I hope she gets an abortion, hell I'll pay for it" Everyone got silent and stared at her.

Sasha wasn't feeling her comment, "A child? Who had nothing to do with this? I love all three of my kids I wish my baby daddy would have asked me to get an abortion, I would have cut that mother fucker dick off," she told them.

Lo kept her comments to herself because abortion was a sticky subject to her, she would always say no one knows what they would do until they were in the situation.

"I'm not against them but what if the girl is an ex and they were in love, why are we assuming she's a whore," Noel asked.

Mary Jane didn't say anything; she would talk to Miko in private. She felt like every time they got together to deal with a crisis it was always too many opinions and, "If it was me," comments.

"I've seen y'all together Meek and I don't think he did this while you were together," she said.

"Do you know how long we have been talking?" Miko reminded her.

"And y'all did break up" Lo said.

"I didn't have sex when we broke up" Miko shook her head.

"That doesn't mean he didn't" noel said.

Miko was tired of talking about this shit, the only person she wanted to discuss this with was Nash and like a coward, he was hiding out.

An hour or so later after the wine was gone, everyone left Lo's apartment.

"I knew things were too good to be true," Miko added.

Lo cringed, "Well how perfect is it? He's broke"

Miko rolled her eyes, "Ugh let me go I will call you tomorrow" she wasn't tipsy like the others; she couldn't drink until she finished her medicine.

Lo chuckled, "Hey Lo-Lo gotta keep it real with you sis"

Miko said, "Yeah yeah whatever bye"

"Text me when you make it in" she told her.

When she got to the highway, she couldn't see herself going home and her man wasn't there.

After checking the time and seeing that it wasn't too late at night, she made her way to Nash's mom house.

She didn't know any of his other hang out spots so she was hoping he was there.

When she pulled up on the block and didn't see her Lexus, she knew he wasn't at the house but her gut, told her to go knock on the door and check just in case.

"Miko what you doing here girl?' his mama asked when she answered the door

"I was trying to see if Nash was here," she told her.

"I told you he wasn't when you called, come on in" she said and moved out of the way so Miko could walk in.

Once they sat at the table, she went on and asked, "Did you know about the baby?"

His mama lit a cigarette and puffed on it before saying "I didn't and he didn't either, this lil' heffa done came out of nowhere"

Miko exhaled, Ms. Nadine was honest and one of the realest woman that Miko had ever met, even though Nash was her son she had always kept it one hundred with her.

"Well why isn't he talking to me?" she asked.

"He don't want no damn kids I'm sure you know that by now," Ms. Nadine laughed.

Miko thought to herself, *Hell me neither.*

"Let me tell you something chile'" Ms. Nadine started.

"This is only the beginning for y'all, do you know what I mean when I say that" she questioned.

Miko already knew where she was going with this conversation.

"I'm not insecure at all," she told her quickly.

"Didn't say you were, but you need to trust your man cus' folks gon come out the wood works with stories," she said.

Miko wouldn't even do him like that; it wasn't in her plans to go to him with speculations.

The only time she did go to him with what she had heard was when Sasha called her a sugar mama.

In a relationship, trust was so important and that was one thing she felt like they had up until last night.

Miko believed that Nash knew about the chick prior to him going out of town and he had been looking for the right time to tell her.

"My baby loves you and I love how he loves you because I know he didn't see that growing up" Ms. Nadine told her.

Miko smiled, even though she was mad as hell at him right now, she definitely agreed with her.

Nash was kind, patient, tender hearted, caring, concerned and he had to be the world's best listener and lover. He watched her closely wherever they were and catered to her every need, she was confident that when the time came and children entered the picture she would probably have the smoothest pregnancy ever just because of how she observed the way he tended to her every need after her surgeries.

"If the baby is his we are going to get through this, after a DNA test of course," she said.

Ms. Nadine laughed and held her hand out for a high-five, "Hey I know that's right"

Miko laughed and hung out with her for a little while longer, before deciding to begin her journey home.

On the way to the house, she thought long and hard about her life. Miko was learning to trust where she was and most importantly, where she wanted to be.

Children and marriage were considered her long-term goals, and long-term meaning five to ten years from now. Her only focus right now was traveling and stacking her checks, she wanted to move her mother into another house and she could afford to do so but her mom didn't want to move.

Miko wanted to become more involved with the charities and non-profits that Lauren busied herself with; she desired to become a pillar in the community.

She wasn't taking living live for granted, God spared her that day at the gas station and she really believed He did it because he had a greater purpose in mind.

She yawned as she entered her subdivision and pulled into the garage, she planned on sleeping well into the morning before heading back to the city for lunch with Jade, if anyone knew about dealing with baby mamas it was Jade.

When she walked into the house, the piano was being played and she figured Nash was there.

She was so sleepy she didn't even notice the car parked beside hers.

She stuck her head into the room, at the sight of him, instantly all frustration and anger left her.

She no longer wanted to tear his head off and kick him out; she simply wanted the truth and nothing more than that.

"Hey you" she said.

He stopped playing and said, "Come here"

Miko went and sat by his side.

"You know my mama called me" he had a smirk on his face.

"Yes I am becoming the crazy girlfriend who goes to your mom house I don't care," she said proudly.

Nash laughed and kissed her cheek, "I love it though, I want you and moms to be close" he told her.

"What's going on, I've been calling and calling you left me here alone and I don't know---"she rambled.

Nash shushed her with a kiss, one kiss. That was all it took.

"Do you trust me?" he asked.

She told him, "You know I do"

Nash took her hand, "I haven't fucked that girl in so long and that's on my mama"

"Why did you even tell me?" she questioned.

"Because she on some rah rah shit in the hood and it seems like whomever you are with always know my damn business," he told her, Nash had a few things to get off his chest just as she did.

Nash definitely had a point there, Sasha found out everything.

"So are you going to get a DNA test when the baby comes," she asked.

"Hell nah" he told her, knowing the baby wasn't his.

Miko laughed, "We shall see"

Nash rubbed her thigh, "My bad for leaving I was feeling stressed the show coming up and then that hoe came out nowhere" he explained himself.

"Understood" she said, she didn't want to talk any more, all she wanted was for him to make love to her.

She stroked the keys of the piano, "Remember the first time we did it, you ate me out on the piano?" she asked.

He shook his head "I was drunk as hell" he defended himself.

Miko didn't care if he was drunk, high or gone off mushrooms and she wanted to replay that same scene.

"You made me feel so good that night," she told him.

"Oh for real?" Nash asked, finally getting the hint.

She looked at him and nodded her head, as she slowly removed her jacket.

"Right here, you want it right here," he asked, teasing her, moving his notebook off the piano.

"Yes baby" she said, removing her clothes faster and letting her hair down.

Nash picked her up and helped her out of her panties and bra, "What If I want to bend you over first?" he asked, turning her around.

"Do whatever you want" she gave him the green light.

Nash slid his shorts down and inserted himself into her, "Whatever?" he asked.

Arching her back and looking back at him with lust and love pouring out of her eyes, "Whatever baby"

He loved when he was granted full access to her body, it was about to be a long night for the young couple, make-up sex was the best sex.

***

"How are you?" Miko asked her brother.

Everyone was gathered at her home to watch the memorial concert for DJ Monday, Nash was opening the concert up and Miko was so excited to have her loved ones and his at her home, while he was in California performing.

She had walked to the kitchen to get a platter of wings since everyone had demolished all of the ones she laid out prior to the guests arriving.

When she walked in the kitchen, Malachi was sitting at the bar nursing a drink. She knew that his sister's death was taking a toll on him. His mother was released but immediately after he had no choice but to put her in a home. Jade wasn't comfortable with her living with them and the kids and he couldn't blame his wife.

"I'm making it," he told her.

She patted his shoulder, "I'm here if you need me you know that" she reassured him before picking up the tray and leaving him to his thoughts.

When she made it back to the living room, Ms. Nadine, Nash's mom was hushing everyone because they had just announced Nash.

"Oh my God look at my baby," she cried.

Miko whispered to Lo, "Look at daddy"

She laughed and told her, "He do look cute girl, you picked his outfit out?"

"Stop throwing shade" Sasha chuckled.

Miko flashed them both the middle finger, her boo did look good and they all knew it.

She was so proud of him and filled with joy, the time had finally come for him to shut it down

He kept the song he was doing a surprise and no one knew but the crew who handled the sounds and stage lights.

Of course, no one stood to their feet when he came out but Nash didn't care he knew that soon enough everyone would be clapping and screaming at the sound of his voice.

When the beat dropped, Miko wasn't familiar with the song but it was still jamming.

She snapped her finger and bobbed her head, Papa said, "Damn I keep forgetting you're Korean"

Everyone laughed, she spoke up and said, "Look y'all not gon' keep talking about me"

Lo kissed her cheek, "You know we love you Meek"

She rolled her eyes and put her attention back on the television screen.

She turned the sound up and tuned in, "Wait what did he just say?" Mary Jane asked.

Miko knew she didn't hear what she thought she heard but when Nash repeated it for the second time. She could have died.

On live television he rapped, "I'm livin' low key high life getting paper/ all I really want is the cash fuck a hater/ these niggas faking and they flodging, I heard they undercover/ this The Underworld nigga, can't trust ya' own brother"

And after he repeated it for the second time, fire blew up behind him and he disappeared.

His family went crazy because Nash killed his performance.

Whereas, The Underworld all turned around and stared at Miko wondering what the fuck just happened.

Never had the organization been mentioned on live television or on a song at all for that matter.

This is how the BMF went down and now they were all in jail.

She shook her head, "He doesn't know," she whispered.

Lo said, "Nasir is probably going to lose it when he hears this shit"

Sasha said, "Y'all worried about Nas but look at Chi"

She looked up and saw her brother glaring at her...

Miko got up and pulled him out of the room, "I promise to God he doesn't know"

"Or do you think he don't know?" he asked.

"He doesn't. I cover my tracks" she needed him to believe her because she was telling the truth, she really was.

"This shit better not come back and bite us Miko I swear to you" he pointed his finger in her face and walked off.

She finally exhaled but the thing was Malachi wasn't the only one worried because she was too.

How much longer was she going to be able to hold her dirty little secret?

It seemed as if anything she did came to the light, but The Underworld was that one subject she wouldn't dare discuss.

Miko prayed that it never came out and if and when that time came, she could only hope that he loved her unconditionally. She needed him to love him to the point where nothing mattered. Not even her being a criminal or a member of the infamous drug cartel, THE UNDERWORLD.

Epilogue

Miko sat Indian-style on the bed, watching her man pack his bags.

"I don't know if I'm sad or happy that you're going to be gone for six weeks," she pouted.

Nash stopped throwing socks into a duffle bag and came over to his girlfriend, "You can come with me, I keep telling you that baby," he told her for the tenth time in the past hour.

She shook her head, "You need to stay focused and I have work to do anyway" she refused to crowd his personal space.

Miko trusted Nash whole-heartedly, however, her and Lo already made plans to be popping up on his ass whenever she was in the mood to be around her man.

She had seen him on stage a few times since the BET concert, true enough as everyone predicted the concert definitely jump started his career. Radio hosts and bloggers had already proclaimed that Nash had all the fixings of becoming one of the greats. Miko loved seeing her babe perform; each time brought her a different euphoric feeling. Nash gave his all on the stage, he wasn't a millionaire yet but his songs were on the charts, videos had been filmed and he was now preparing for his first tour where he would be opening up for a popular rap group.

It hadn't him hit yet that he was finally seeing the prayers of the righteousness manifest. The first thing he did when he got his first check was hand half to his mama and the other half to Miko.

He owed those two women everything and every time he hit the booth or the stage, they were on his mind.

His mother ended up spending the money he gave her, whereas Miko invested it into stocks for him.

She knew he would appreciate her for doing that on his behalf.

"You look sad as hell that I'm leaving" he stuck his bottom lip out and pretended to pout.

Miko nodded her head, "I am babe, and I really am. But I'm so proud of you and we knew this day was coming" she told him.

He looked at her and smiled, "We did, didn't we?" he asked.

Nash could never find the right words to express his gratitude and appreciation for his girl. Miko definitely deserved the award for "ride or die"

She held him down when he didn't have five dollars in his pocket, she loved him when he only had two pair of jeans and was wearing the same tired Polo white t-shirt.

Nash didn't give a fuck what anybody had to say about her and her past, because that's exactly what it was to him, the past.

He knew she belonged to him, he was confident that their love was here to stay.

In his opinion, it was fuck the President. He didn't vote for his ass no way.

Nash locked Miko down two years ago and he threw away the key.

"We gon get married one day" he told her.

She rolled her eyes, Miko loved them just how they were she wasn't rushing anything.

If it were up to her, the couple would have matching Cartier bands and simply be life partners until God called them home.

A white wedding dress and vows wouldn't make her love him more or less.

"We are good how we are," she told him quickly.

Nash knew she hated talking about their future but that's how all he thought about when he laid in bed at night.

He wanted to give her the world but Miko wasn't stunting the world, she just wanted her money, love and his loyalty.

Those three things kept a smile on her face.

He smothered her body and kissed her face all over, "Love you," he said.

After the shooting, his level of love increased tremendously.

After seeing Miko damn near push herself to a full-recovery, he realized he never wanted to be without her again.

Miko was a soldier, his soldier at that.

"I love you more," she told him.

He stopped kissing her and looked into her eyes.

Miko asked, "What's on your mind?"

He said, "I was about to ask you the same thing"

She took a deep breath, "You never asked me about the shooting we never talked about the scandal," she said.

Nash rolled over and faced her, "Is there something you wanna tell me?"

Quickly, she said, "No, I told you what it was, well I tried to tell you when we first started dating but you said you didn't care"

He nodded his head, "And I still don't, I don't wanna hear about another man degrading you Meek" he hated the direction of his conversation.

His plans included packing for the concert, taking his woman to dinner then coming home and watching her soak in a bubble bath while he smoked on some loud before making sweet love to her body until the sun came up.

"I know, I know but still like it was nothing you wanted to know, absolutely nothing," she pressed for him to open up to her.

He sighed, "Miko I didn't care because it was before me. You didn't judge me so I didn't judge you and you're my rib babe it is what it is," he told her.

She sat up and propped her weight on her elbow, "What you mean?" he asked.

"From my rib, you were created for me. So anything you did before I came into your life is irrelevant" he spoke to her soul.

"From here?" she pointed to his rib cage that was covered in red and black ink.

He nodded his head and reached in and kissed her lips, "Yeah babe from me, from my rib"

Miko had never heard the saying before but wherever it came from it sounded good.

In that moment, she decided to rid her mind of her past. She had a beautiful life, her career in The Underworld was blossoming, her loved ones were content and finally, she was complete.

The End

Sneak Peek into Book 4 on the next page!

Please Leave A Review

xoxoNAKO

To stay updated with NAKO'S RELEASES

Text **NAKOEXPO** to 22828

Connect with NAKO

Instagram: nakoexpo

Facebook: www.facebook.com/NAKO

Twitter:nakoexpo

Join Join Join

Nako's Reading Group on Facebook, we have so much fun

on a daily basis and we would love to have you!

www.nakoexpo.com for more information on NAKO and

booking info for speaking engagements.

The Passport is the personal blog of Nako, check her

website out today to read.

From His Rib was such an amazing experience to write. Midway throughout the story, my mind changed and I went into a completely different direction so I trust and hope that you enjoyed it just as much as I enjoyed writing it.

It has never taken me this long to complete a story, but I really enjoyed myself.

Miko was more than a character to me; I lived and learned her as if she was a long-lost sister.

I prayed for this story and if you're reading this and you have a dream such as Nash did, I am here to tell you those obstacles come; you won't always win the first time.

But never give up, ever.

It's a blessing with your name on it

With love, NAKO

The Underworld is a twelve-book street-crime series collection.

The first story was Please Catch My Soul

The second story was Pointe of No Return

You just finished reading the third, From His Rib now here is a sneak peek into the 4th story coming next month:

Book Four

"I stayed" I whispered, I knew he could barely hear me but I didn't care, I heard my own voice loud and clear and that's what mattered to me. I finally heard MY voice.

"What?" Rod turned around and faced me, he stopped in mid-stride, he was headed out to do God knows what and with God knows who.

"I stayed...I stayed with you, through it all. I left my happy home for you and this is what I get" I shook my head and wiped the tears that so desperately wanted to fall from my face. Mascara along with eyeliner ran down the side of my cheek. I knew I was looking deranged but that's what love did to you sometimes.

Right after our lovemaking, he attempted to leave me, making up some bullshit ass lie about having to go check on something.

Bosses didn't get out of bed for foolishness; Rod was never one of those dudes to stop what he had going on to tend to the affairs of the street. His attitude was fuck them, they can wait.

It had always been that way, but I knew my husband. I knew him better than he knew himself.

"What happy home? Jules look around baby this isn't happiness to you?" he smirked.

That fucking smirk, what was there to smile about?

"Rod you know damn well what I'm talking about don't fucking play with me" I threw the remote to the television in his direction.

He ducked, ""Aye now watch it" Rod threatened.

"Fuck you!" I shouted as loud as my lungs would allow me too.

"What is the fucking problem now damn woman you're never satisfied?" he complained.

A woman scorned once is a woman that you can possibly lie too, but a woman...a woman like me..See I've been around the block one too many times to be played.

"You are my problem," I told him, with my arms crossed.

This had to come to an end, I deserved better, my vows meant nothing, my children cared about their mama and would want to see me happy and where I was...this present place. This million-dollar home..Nothing in here made me smile or laugh. Not even the nine-inch dick that dangled between my husband's legs. I wanted out, I wanted more...but not before, I got my half.

I, Julia Martinez was getting my half.